Unfinished Business

CAROL SMITH

Unfinished Business

LITTLE, BROWN AND COMPANY

A *Little, Brown* Book

First published in Great Britain in 2000
by Little, Brown and Company

Copyright © Carol Smith 2000

The moral right of the author has been asserted.

A CIP catalogue record for this book
is available from the British Library.

HARDBACK ISBN 0 316 64564 8
C FORMAT ISBN 0 316 64679 2

Typeset in Berkeley by
Palimpsest Book Production Limited,
Polmont, Stirlingshire
Printed and bound in Great Britain by
Clays Ltd, St Ives plc

Little, Brown and Company (UK)
Brettenham House
Lancaster Place
London WC2E 7EN

For Sarah Harrison

every night at six

Acknowledgements

Many thanks to my agents, Sarah Molloy and Sara Fisher of A. M. Heath Ltd. And also, as always, to my inspired editor, Imogen Taylor. And to the quite outstanding Rebecca Kerby for her relentless editorial eye, picking up details that have eluded me and for getting this book into chronological shape.

I also remain grateful to Little, Brown's Sales and Marketing teams who continue to do such great work in the field.

Part One

1

Rough hands woke her, scrabbling at her breasts. At first she thought it was one of those shameful dreams, but the accompanying grunts and muttered curses were anything but erotic. Also it hurt, in a very real way. She rolled instinctively to try to evade them but the hands pursued her relentlessly. 'Ow!' she complained, as her nipple was savagely twisted and searching fingers were thrust between her unwilling thighs.

'Silence, bitch!' He hit her, then the fingers continued to probe.

She had folded down the sheet because of the unseasonable warmth, and was now aware that her T-shirt had been pushed up and partly obscured her face. Everything she had was on display, though veiled by the protecting darkness. He had one knee on the bed by now and was manoeuvring to straddle her, the better to pin her down. She made a valiant effort to hurl him off, but he cracked her round the face again then moved a pillow to stifle her squeals and held it down firmly while he continued his ruthless exploration.

It was worse than anything she'd encountered even at the clinic, rough, inept, spiteful fingers jabbing into her most intimate places, all the while punctuated by those terrible words.

'Fucking cunt! Filthy whore! Slut!'

She could smell his sweat and sense his growing excitement. She continued to struggle but her assailant was that much stronger and the lack of air was beginning to make her weak. She could feel him now fumbling with his zip but was far too frantic to focus on that. All she needed, and urgently, was air. Unless he released her she was surely going to suffocate. And that had to be worse than anything else he might have in mind.

She made an extra effort to throw him off and succeeded in unseating him long enough to grab some great gulps of air. With a renewed bout of cursing he clipped her again, then threw aside the pillow and flipped her instead on to her face.

'Bitch! Whore!'

The voice was dimly familiar but how on earth could that be? Whoever was violating her in this terrible way had to be sub-human and viewing her solely as his prey. Perhaps if she lay still enough he would finish and go away. She ceased her struggling for an instant and he grabbed her wrists and pinned them in one hand, searching wildly in the dense darkness for something with which to tie them. His hand located the bedside phone. She heard its clatter as it tumbled from the table and that impersonal operator's voice repeating over and over until he jerked the wire from the wall. Cold plastic cord was wrapped around both wrists and he knotted it tightly before he let her go. She was trussed face down as firmly as a chicken, powerless to stop him as she heard him unzip his fly.

It hurt far more than she ever might have imagined, had she been in the habit of thinking about such things – a fierce, tearing spasm of unendurable agony as he pulled apart her buttocks and drove himself inside her with the force of molten steel.

He left her for a while, bleeding and deeply in shock, and

through her muted sobbing she heard descending feet on the stairs. A tiny flicker of hope rallied then in her numbed brain; he was going, he had finished. She might yet come out of this alive.

The house was so still and the street outside so empty that her ears could track him as he moved stealthily about. He was in the kitchen and looking in the fridge. All that exertion must have given him a powerful thirst he was needing now to slake. She remembered, with a jolt, the half-finished bottle of Australian sauternes. He had found it and was glugging it down, she could imagine that from his silence. Would that make him wilder? She really didn't know, but had heard how men could get on drink. There was a sudden sharp crack as if of glass shattering, then he began to move again. Slowly, carefully, he was remounting the stairs. Her reprieve was over; he was coming back after all to finish the job.

The pain of the jagged glass, as the bottle entered her vagina, was worse, far worse, than anything that had preceded it, and when she moaned and feebly fought him off, he hit her again and then savagely slashed her face.

'Bitch,' he kept muttering, and 'filthy, sodding cunt,' as she waited in terror for the next excruciating assault. There was no way she was going to survive this, she realised now for certain, so that when the heavy, repeated blows began to hammer down and pulverise her brain it was almost a relief as her consciousness flickered away. She was finally impervious to his frenzied slashing and jabbing, and her body ceased twitching as her blood soaked into the white sheets.

She wasn't aware of the final indignity as he unzipped once more and urinated all over her, for by that time she was already mercifully dead.

The bells rang out joyfully that Easter Sunday morning and Peggy Dawes, up as usual with the lark, opened the front door of her lavender-painted cottage and picked up the papers lying folded on the step. She stood there for a while in her pristine quilted housecoat, sniffing the spring air appreciatively, imbued as it was with scent. Clouds of pink blossom, weighing down the branches of the cherry trees, floated around her like candy floss, littering the gutters with their carelessly strewn petals. Peggy clucked with automatic disapproval; Arthur would have to come out later with his broom. The forecasts had predicted unseasonably mellow weather, the hottest Easter on record, they said, since 1907. So far, although it was warm enough to stand out here in her night-clothes, the soaring temperatures had yet to arrive, which was probably just as well. What with global warming and the way the seasons had all gone haywire, they didn't need a heatwave yet, not with her seedlings newly potted.

Next door's papers still lay on the step; her neighbour was obviously not yet up. They weren't what they used to be in her day, these young women, keeping late hours and frittering away their lives. Peggy sniffed delicately as she closed the front door and shuffled back to the kitchen to boil the kettle. Upstairs Arthur was already on the move. He liked a cooked breakfast, and it was Easter, after all.

Once the toast was browning and the bacon beginning to curl, Peggy undid the heavy padlock and pushed back the wrought-iron security grating to let in some more of the balmy spring air. She stepped out on to her tiny patio to check up on yesterday's planting. She loved the evocative smell of damp compost and beamed down with approval on her row of tidy pots. You wouldn't believe you were in the centre of a city here; on Sundays particularly this small Kensington backwater was as remote and quiet as a rural village, at least while the pub was closed. Now that the hospital had gone from across the road and those fancy new Regency-style houses built in its place, the volume of noise had noticeably lessened without the scream of ambulances, which had moved off down to Chelsea. There was still that green glass monstrosity, of course, on the corner of the Cromwell Road, but Peggy preferred to ignore its existence and pretend it simply hadn't happened. Luckily the patients came and went in low-purring limousines, usually with smoked windows so you couldn't see inside. The less seen, the better was Peggy's opinion. Men with their heads wrapped in tablecloths, their women showing only their eyes. It wasn't that she was racist, oh no, just intent on preserving her territory. Keep London for the Londoners, was her cry, as if all those milling tourists weren't enough.

This curving enclave of pretty pastel cottages was in sharp and startling contrast to the development over the road. Built at the turn of the century as humble artisans' dwellings, they had rocketed in value over the years and were now worth an arm and a leg. Peggy and Arthur had lived here for fifteen years, since their children had left home and they'd needed something smaller. There were only two bedrooms and the interior was compact but that was space enough for just the pair of them and it did mean less housework. Also fewer visitors which was a blessing. Although she loved her grandchildren, Peggy knew from experience what a honey-trap fashionable Kensington could be to the casual caller passing through.

The Dawes's house backed on to the garden of the pub, as did all the houses on that side of the street, and a flimsy wooden trellis formed a rough partition between their patio and the one next door. Peggy raised herself on her toes and peered through the rambling honeysuckle. She couldn't help it, it was an in-built part of her nature, an insatiable curiosity about the doings of those around her. A folding canvas chair and a white wrought-iron table were all that adorned Miss McLennan's patch. Apart from an empty beer glass left out on the table. Peggy mentally tutted again; such sloppiness made her skin prickle. She noticed also that the patio door was ajar even though the newspapers were still neatly folded on the front step. Now *that* sort of carelessness verged on the positively criminal. Especially in an affluent area like this, it paid to take security precautions, what with the jungle of Earl's Court only yards away, just across the busy Cromwell Road. And the stories you heard, they grew worse by the day. Muggings and bag-snatching and people having their Rolex watches ripped from their wrists in broad daylight. They had caught the famed Notting Hill Rapist eventually but now there were rumours of a new one at large, committing copycat crimes around the Kensington area. It didn't cost anything to be over-cautious, especially for a single woman living on her own.

'Jinx is obviously having a lie-in,' she reported when Arthur came down. 'Though she went to bed and left the door ajar, silly girl. At her age she ought to be more responsible.'

Arthur, immersed in the *Mail on Sunday*, merely grunted. Years of habit had taught him to filter his wife's conversation effectively. Very little of what she said warranted his full attention, and these days she never even noticed that he wasn't listening. He did perk up, however, when she served him his bacon and eggs. Even folded the newspaper carefully and laid it aside for later.

'Nice day.'

'But no sign yet of that heatwave they promised. Just as well.' Too much sunshine was bad for your skin. These days those so-called best things in life grew fewer and fewer. You couldn't even leave your garden door open for fear of what might come in. She'd keep her eye on the house next door just to be on the safe side.

When they left for Evensong the papers were still there, so on their return Peggy made it her business to ring the doorbell of number 7. That's what Neighbourhood Watch was all about; no point having those meetings if you didn't rise to the occasion. No answer, rather as she'd expected. Yet the patio door was still ajar, the empty glass untouched upon the table.

'You don't suppose she's gone away for the weekend and forgotten to lock up properly?'

Arthur, never surprised at the vacuousness of women, merely
grunted. He was flicking through the television listings, entirely
uninterested in the doings of his neighbour.

'Could be. I don't know. Now come and sit down. *Antiques
Roadshow* is about to start.' He changed into his old tartan slippers
and poured them each a schooner of sherry which he carried into
the front room. But Peggy was fidgeting, unable to settle.

'It may sound silly,' she said in a minute. 'But I think I'll just
call the police.'

Two police constables, one a woman, were there in a matter of
minutes. Easter was quiet and the station not far away, just
round the corner in the Earl's Court Road. They had left their
panda car in Stratford Road in order not to block access to the
cul-de-sac. They tried the doorbell at number 7 and when there
was no answer, asked if they might come inside. Peggy, full of
importance, led them through to the patio.

'See,' she said, 'the door isn't properly closed. And it's not like
my neighbour to be so forgetful.'

The policeman looked at the fragile fence, and Peggy showed
him where he could climb up. There was a concrete post
supporting it at one end; he was up and over in a jiffy.

'Hello,' he called cautiously, peering in through the door.
'Anyone at home?' When no one answered, he pushed aside
the curtain then took a tentative step into the room.

'You'd best come and join me,' he said to his female companion.
'Just in case.'

Peggy was dying to go in there with them but wasn't sure
she could manage the climb. In any case, they were excluding
her now, talking quietly and seriously between themselves, very
much on the job. They disappeared. Six and a half minutes later,
after what seemed an agonising wait, the woman appeared with
an ashen face and her radio on the go, and told Peggy that they
had called for reinforcements. There had been an accident – that

was all she would say – and they would be round to talk to the Daweses later. No need for Peggy to hang around now.

Detective Chief Inspector Hal Burton of the Murder Squad stood in the Dawes's pin neat front room, a cup of tea in his hand. What they had found upstairs in the house next door almost defied description. He was trying not to dwell on it too much and was not about to share the gruesome details with the white-faced elderly couple facing him now. All he would concede was that their neighbour was dead and certainly not by accident or her own hand.

'Murdered, you mean?' said Arthur with goggling eyes, his full attention belatedly on the subject. 'Good God in Heaven, what a truly terrible thing.'

Her name was Jinx McLennan, they told Hal, and they'd known her for the six years since she first moved in. Alone; she had never shared the house and they didn't believe she'd been married. It was certainly something she had never mentioned and Peggy would have winkled that one out if anyone could.

'Nice girl,' ruminated Arthur, valiantly trying to get a grip on himself. 'Friendly and sociable. Good to have living next door.' Good grief, whatever next; what was this old world coming to? Slaughtered in her bed, they said, in the middle of the Easter weekend. As bad as Johannesburg and the terrible happenings in Kosovo. Maybe living in the heart of London at their time of life wasn't as sensible as it seemed.

'Age?' asked the detective, putting down his cup. His constable would take down the details later. First he needed to get the general picture.

'Recently turned forty,' said Peggy, piping up. 'Had a big party in October. Was nice enough to include us.'

'So you knew her well and you also knew her friends?'

'Not all of them. They were always coming and going. Hugely popular and social, she was. Always so much fun.'

'Jinx McLennan.' The name tripped off his tongue. Forty years old and a woman of the world. No husband, no children, no apparent live-in lover. Parents both dead, Peggy had already volunteered that, and no siblings either, an only child.

'Boyfriends that you knew of? Anyone special?'

Arthur and Peggy looked at each other then Peggy shook her head.

'There were a couple, one of whom we met. But he wasn't here much, and I think it was something from the past. She had loads of friends, though, of both sexes. Always entertaining, people forever dropping in.'

'She was a lovely girl,' repeated Arthur with more emotion. 'A real cracker. One of the absolute best.' The sort you would like your son to marry, the archetypal girl next door. Friendly, sweet-natured and squeaky clean.

'We did, as it happens, see her only just recently,' said Peggy. 'Out with a man we'd not met before. Wednesday it was, we were driving down to Dorking to deliver the eggs. They came out of her door at the same time as us and she wished us a Happy Easter.' She dabbed at her eyes. Just imagine, if only they'd known that that was the last time they would see poor Jinx alive.

'And the man?' asked Hal alertly, his fingers on his phone.

Peggy and Arthur looked at each other blankly. It was clear the old geezer had no recollection at all. 'Tall,' Arthur said vaguely, but Peggy was rallying.

'Dark,' she said decisively. 'With very good teeth and a well-cut suit.' Which didn't sound much like Jinx's usual sort. Those artist fellows she normally hung around with could hardly be described as smart. 'And a signet ring.'

'And his car?'

'No car. They were waiting for a taxi. Heading into the West End for a meal, they said.' There was some sort of an accent, though she couldn't be precise. He had said very little, Jinx had done the talking. Australian, possibly American; maybe even some sort of a foreigner. What Peggy remembered most was how happy they'd both seemed. Bubbling over with it, in fact, now she came to think of it.

Thank heavens for nosy neighbours, thought Hal as he pocketed his phone.

The murder scene was unbelievably upsetting and even the forensic team gagged as they went about their work. WPC Trudy Taylor had never seen so much blood. When they'd first been called to the crime scene, the curtains had been closed so she'd been spared the full enormity of exactly what had occurred. Now the curtains were open and the body had been removed. But the pretty blue walls were laced with a network of blood, and the ghastly, ravaged sheets were still there, stiff with gore and spattered with yellow stains. Also, there was the smell which caused her to press her balled handkerchief to her mouth.

'Beaten to a pulp, she was,' said the fingerprints man. 'We're going to have to identify her from her dabs.' They'd taken away the weapon that had been used, an art deco bronze and ivory figurine snatched, presumably at random, from the bedside table. By some miracle, it hadn't even cracked, though the weighty onyx base had done its deadly work with horrifying efficiency. Far worse, however, at least to Trudy's shocked gaze, were the police photos of what had been achieved with a broken bottle. How so much violence could exist in any human being was too terrible even to envisage. Whatever kind of an animal could it be who was out there now, prowling the Kensington streets?

Was it the work of a random intruder? That was the main question currently on their minds. There had been a series of local break-ins and rapes but nothing even halfway as awful as this. No one till now had actually been killed; the masked intruder had caught his victims by surprise then left abruptly after he'd robbed and violated them.

'It must have occurred in the early hours of Sunday morning,' said the pathologist. 'After the pubs had closed and the punters gone home.'

'And the odd thing is it appears that nothing's been taken. Not that we can tell for sure without an insider's knowledge. This room's a mess but mainly because of the struggle. The rest of the house appears untouched. Which is unusual with this sort of a crime.'

'You're not suggesting it could have been someone she knew?' Trudy's gorge was rising as the possibilities grew even worse.

'Could be,' said Hal, still nosing around. 'This sort of violent crime is more often than not domestic. Can't rule out the people she hung out with. Maybe it was someone from the pub next door.'

Who might well have sat there, drinking in the garden, able at leisure to case the row of cute sweetpea cottages. At this stage nothing could be discounted. Every possible angle had to be exhaustively researched. First, however, they needed to establish next of kin.

Peggy Dawes was unable to help them there. All she really knew about the dead woman was that she was popular and sociable with an enormous zest for life and an ever open door. Her friends were constantly coming and going. What a tragic waste.

'Threw herself into her work, she did. A girl that pretty ought by rights to have been at home having babies.'

'What sort of line was she in, do you know?'

'Graphic designer with her own small company. Just up the street in the mews. Nice offices. You should go and see them.'

Trudy made a note.

'What kind of a social life would you say she led? Bit of a raver, was she? Bars and clubs, that sort of thing? Picking up strangers perhaps?' Hal was being deliberately provocative, studying the effect of his words on this eminently respectable lady.

Peggy was genuinely outraged. 'Absolutely not,' she said indignantly. 'The very idea of it!'

Jinx, she told them, came from a solid, middle-class background, army folk as far as she could recall. Died quite early, both of them, leaving her on her own.

'Went to a private boarding-school somewhere in the West Country. And after that to art school here in London.'

She had always been an achiever, had worked her way up through various different jobs then started this business some years back. When she was still remarkably young. Doing extremely well, or so they'd heard, with a nice tight circle of business colleagues who had always remained loyal to her through thick and thin.

'Those are really the ones you should talk to,' said Peggy. 'More like family than work-mates, she always said. Nice people, too. We met them at one of her parties. They'll be able to fill in some of the gaps.'

Trudy made a note of the address. It was Bank Holiday Monday; the office would be closed. First thing tomorrow they'd go round and break the news.

2

First one in that Tuesday morning was Dottie Sullivan, a little after nine. She switched off the alarm and scooped up the mail then carried it through to the main office to sort, shrugging off her ancient waxed jacket on the way. The Easter break had been refreshing, though they still hadn't seen much sign of the scorching weather the forecasters had so confidently predicted. They had driven down to Frinton to visit her mother, and Sam, bless his heart, had presented the old lady with one of his recent watercolours, done specially for her as a surprise. He was like that, Sam, kind, thoughtful and always so caring. An affectionate smile creased the corners of Dottie's mouth as she dumped the mail and went into the kitchen to start the coffee brewing. They were all of them in this studio fairly fanatical coffee addicts, apart from Serafina, of course, who preferred her fancy teas.

Jinx's desk was for once pristine. It was odd to come in and not find her here, busy on the telephone amid a litter of opened mail. Five minutes later, Serafina came bursting in, uptight and seething as was so often her way.

'Bloody bus was late again. I almost ended up walking.'

Serafina Rossetti was tall and willowy and quite outstandingly beautiful. Dottie never ceased marvelling at how she managed to keep so immaculate, untouched by the ravages of everyday city living. Even after her fevered rush down the mews, not a hair was out of place, her makeup perfect. She slid out of her neat linen jacket and draped it over her chair, then booted up the computer while she flicked through her mail. All of them on the team were like that, especially right now: nervous and obsessive, under unusual pressure from a deadline they all considered crazy. And which, more seriously, they were worried they wouldn't meet. That was what happened when greed compelled them to lower their meticulous standards. But these days, alas, they no longer had total control. Anyone in doubt should hear Ambrose on the subject, provided they could stand the ear-blasting. It was a team that cared and pulled together, credit again to Jinx's brilliant leadership.

'Tea?' called Dottie from the kitchen. It was really supposed to be part of Wayne's job as office gofer and general dogsbody but he was rarely ever in on time and today she couldn't wait. After the long bus ride from Muswell Hill, that first shot of caffeine was like nectar. Sam, like Serafina, preferred tea first thing, though the old-fashioned workman's kind with leaves, brewed in an earthenware pot.

'Please,' said Serafina, scarcely bothering to glance up.

'What's it to be this morning then?' (The 'madam' was implicit though good-humoured.) 'Earl Grey or apple and ginger?'

'Apple and ginger.'

It was a joke among the rest of them how Serafina managed to maintain her reedlike figure. At five foot ten, she had a twenty-two inch waist which Jinx always said verged on the obscene.

'One of these days, my lady,' she liked to threaten, 'I shall bring in my little cleaver and slice you in half.' Like the ill-fated airman in *Catch 22*. 'We can't have you hanging around always looking so gorgeous. Bad for office morale.'

It seemed unfair when some of them had to struggle with their weight, yet Serafina, who normally ate like a sparrow, would occasionally indulge herself and without so much as a batted eyelid join them for cheeseburgers and chips at Sticky Fingers, their favourite local joint. Wayne had a theory that she probably had a tapeworm, such thinness just wasn't natural. One of these nights, he predicted darkly, it would slither out of her mouth while she was sleeping. Provided she left out a saucer of milk, a traditional cure, so he said.

What Serafina actually suffered from, which warm-hearted Dottie had deduced but was keeping to herself, was a chronic case of anorexia nervosa that had plagued her since childhood and still returned at stressful times. Part of her personality, Dottie was aware; a symptom of a manipulative nature which had on occasion to be watched. She needed to take better care of her health. All that denial and not bothering to eat was already taking its toll. Her bones were so slender they could easily fracture and with age other factors would set in. Osteoporosis, serious things like that. But Serafina would never listen so Dottie had learned to keep quiet. Might as well talk to the wall.

'How was the weekend?' she inquired now, carrying in steaming mugs.

'Nothing sensational. This guy I'm seeing had to work.' Serafina ran a nervy hand through her lustrous hair. She was usually seeing someone but played her cards close to her chest. Dottie had given up trying to pry but Jinx was constantly on her case.

'Come on, Serafina, spit it out,' she'd say. 'Don't be such an old meanie. Give us oldies a bit of vicarious living. Brighten our dull little lives.'

Which was, of course, nonsense. Jinx had more social life than the lot of them put together, was only ever home when she had guests. Or was here, in the office, feverishly working overtime, which was something she increasingly did. She was even more driven than the rest of the team but, then, it all belonged solely to her. She had taken a mammoth gamble when she set up on her own to get them all out of a bit of a spot. It was entirely due to her guts and determination that they were still under one roof and these days doing so well. They all had a great deal to thank Jinx for, not the least for refusing to be beaten when the odds were stacked against them. Something not one of them should ever lose sight of and probably never would.

Wayne Peacock was rolling up now on his swanky inline skates, bumping over the cobbles to crash in a heap against the door. Typical of Wayne, always out to play the fool. He couldn't make an unostentatious entrance to save his life. He sprawled across the doormat, unclipping the purple monstrosities and swapping them for luminous pink trainers.

'Hi there, kiddies! What's cooking?' Wayne had peroxided hair shaven close to his scalp, a tattoo on his right biceps and a silver ring in one ear. He always dressed very camp, in T-shirt and fatigues, but Dottie knew his best-kept secret which was that he had a girlfriend on the sly. Melody, she'd met her, nice and straightforward, a trainee manager going places fast. Like Wayne himself if he'd stop the horsing around. As Jinx had spotted right from the start, he was far too bright and talented for his own good. If he'd only apply himself that little bit extra, there was no saying what he might achieve. It was almost as though he were daunted by his gifts, a scholarship to the Slade at the age of sixteen. From Bradford too.

'No Jinx?'

'Not today, dimwit. Don't you remember, she's working at home this week.'

'Yeah, yeah, that's her story. Updating the accounts to the end of the tax year. Or so she would have us believe.' He trilled his luvvie's laugh. 'Bet she's having a lie-in, dozy mare. Go on, give her a ring and see if I'm not right.'

'You're so bad,' said Dottie indulgently, pouring him coffee. Wayne didn't change except for the worse. She knew full well what he was capable of but also that Jinx richly deserved this unscheduled brief break. If break it could be called with all those dreary figures to check. Dottie had offered to lend a hand but had been instantly over-ruled. Why should she have to sacrifice her Easter, Sam either, come to that? The Sullivans had a close family life with children they adored. They should enjoy it together whenever they got the chance whereas Easter was nothing of special significance to a habitual singleton like Jinx. She usually worked through it, as it was; this year would be nothing different. Yet Dottie truly valued her generosity of spirit. Not every employer would be so altruistic, but that was one of the things that made Jinx so special. Without her inspired leadership and effervescent energy, they'd none of them be where they were right now. If only these youngsters would learn to appreciate their luck and not take so much for granted.

Serafina leaned back and stretched like a cat, then languidly sipped her cooling tea.

'I doubt she'll be having much fun,' she remarked smugly, 'with those dreary old ledgers to sort through.' Though she'd do it herself like a shot, reflected Dottie, if she thought there might be anything there for her. Serafina's thrusting ambition was hardly a secret, certainly not in this office. And lately she'd been acting even nervier than before, deep in some unresolved resentment she had not yet cared to declare. Maybe not obvious to the rest of the team, but perceptive Dottie could always spot the signs. She was wasting away before their eyes, doing herself irreparable harm.

'Well someone has to take care of the boring details.' Ambrose Rafferty had entered unobserved and was now clumping up the curved iron staircase to the gallery above, which was dominated by his computer and drawing-board. 'One of the tedious things about being boss.' He chuckled. 'It's her own fault really for being so damned high-flying. Right out of the orbit of the humble folk like us.' Ambrose was Jinx's principal admirer. Everything she did looked good in his eyes.

'Ambrose!' said Dottie, delighted to see him. She adored this gentle humorous man, who preferred to stay out of the limelight but was actually the creative strength and backbone of the design group. He was straightening his papers and emptying his canvas book-bag of the volumes he was returning to the London Library. Ambrose worked steadily and consistently hard without ever making a song and dance of it. Dottie admired that about him. Quiet and self-effacing, he was reliable through and through. She poured him coffee and carried it up. Something about the man's air of helpless incompetence never failed to hit the right buttons with her. All Ambrose needed, she had always been convinced, was the love of a good woman to shape and define his life. Luckily for him, until that woman appeared, he would always have doting Dottie to worry and watch over him. With as careful a scrutiny as she did her own children. And Jinx.

'You all right?' Close to he looked a bit pasty, as though he'd had insufficient sleep or fresh air, and was shuffling his papers in a distracted way as if he had not yet fully surfaced. He stared at her blankly then gave his sweet smile, like a guilty schoolboy caught with his hand in the sweet jar.

'I guess so,' was all he said.

Dottie carefully cleared a space for his coffee then picked up the carelessly slung jacket to hang on the hook on the door. These bachelors with their casual lifestyles. She dreaded to think what his flat must be like.

'Nice weekend?' she asked as she fussed. He sometimes saw Jinx, they went shopping together when he wasn't embroiled in a chess-game with Wayne. Despite the fact she'd have been working all weekend, they were such good pals, harmonious as a pair of old slippers, that it was entirely possible they'd spent some of it together. Secretly Dottie nurtured all kind of fantasies about a joint future for them both. Sam, however, had forbidden her to speculate. Told her that it just wasn't right. When Ambrose failed to answer she had another go, knowing she was bugging him but unable to resist.

They liked to refer to her jointly as their den mother, which was precisely the role she played. Her own grown children no longer really needed her so she had extra worrying time to spare.

'Did you see Jinx?' she asked him boldly, but Ambrose said he had not. Nor even Wayne, for a change, he just hadn't been there.

'I was in Birmingham till yesterday at that computer thing.'

Which accounted, of course, for the pallor. Too much beer in a smoky atmosphere playing endless computer games with the lads. Dottie clucked, she just couldn't help it. She would have loved to be able to cook him regular meals, to dose him up with fresh vegetables and fibre. But by the age of thirty-nine he should be able to stand on his own feet. Or so her husband would sternly have her remember.

'He's not exactly a child, Dot. He's managed alone all these years.' In Sam's private view, Ambrose was a lot more smart than he ever cared to let on. That air of helpless ineptness worked like a charm with the womenfolk every time. Witness his own foolish wife. Dottie was forever fretting about him, wishing he'd find the perfect mate and settle down. But there weren't many flies on old Ambrose, in truth, and who in the world could ever blame him?

Adam & Eve Mews, which joins Kensington High Street to Allen Street, is a hidden thoroughfare right in the heart of the shops, a pretty, cobbled, other-worldish sort of place with Dutch-style houses and a feeling of timeless peace. Legend has it that the playwright and wit, Richard Sheridan, used as his regular watering-hole the pub on the corner that gave the small backwater its name. These days, despite opening on to one of the busiest high streets in central London, only the occasional gawping tourist spoiled its tranquillity, making it the ideal setting for a creative group like theirs. McLennan Graphics was halfway down on the left, an airy modernised building with smart spruce-green trim and slatted wooden blinds that could be drawn down for additional privacy. All of them loved it, it had such a good feel. Jinx, in particular, since she could reach it easily on foot and was thus enabled to rid her life of the frustrations and annoyances of commuting or driving through traffic. And the area was wonderful for restaurants and shopping, right there in the fulcrum of fashionable Kensington.

Dottie had donated painted wooden tubs which were placed on either side of the front door. At this time of year they were crowded with primulas and dewy-eyed pansies, even a sprinkling of miniature bluebells. These she lovingly tended, carrying home the bulbs when they'd passed their best for future nurturing in her own wilderness garden. She was often to be found pottering first thing in the morning, with her tiny trowel and shears and miniature watering-can. Wayne made all sorts of evil jokes and was currently scouting the nurseries for a tasteless garden gnome, but Jinx found Dottie's dedication endearing and had banned him from interfering.

'Leave her alone, she really cares. And it does add a certain elegance to the place.' Good for business and their own morale. That kind of thing was important.

Dottie, when all was said and done, really was the salt of the earth. Patronising though it might seem, Jinx had always been touched by her devoted support. It was Dottie who kept the store cupboard supplied, popping out at lunchtime to buy loo paper and coffee or to fetch them all sandwiches on days when they were particularly stretched. Wayne was supposed to take care of these mundane chores but his head was usually well in the clouds. And not only because of his hectic nightlife either. Ambrose, who'd been known to roll the occasional joint himself, was deeply attached to the bright young man and had lately been teaching him chess. He enjoyed his enthusiasm, found it fresh and appealing, and sincerely admired his spectacular talent. Envied it too. So in their varied and separate ways, this team was a clone of a true

22

genetic family. Looked out for each other at all times, one of the reasons they had lasted together so long.

'Anyone know if we're likely to see the Moon Monster again today?' asked Wayne flippantly from his corner, intent on the rapid-fire sketches he made look so simple.

'Damien?' said Dottie, clearing away the mugs. 'I wouldn't imagine so, not so soon.' He had already enraged them by crashing their pre-Easter lunch, seeming even crazier than ever. 'He should be safely back in Jersey by now, where he belongs.' Nursing his neuroses and worrying himself sick about paranoid fantasies in his head.

'Avoiding tax and accruing wealth,' added Serafina sniffily, with just a trace of acid bitterness. 'With dreary little Wifey ever at his beck and call.'

Damien Rudge was something of a bugbear to them all, but Wayne, who'd known him the shortest time, had even less patience for all that petty posturing. Who, when it actually came to it, did the creature think he was, Leonardo? Only the goose that laid their golden eggs, Dottie reminded him, which didn't satisfy sceptical Wayne one bit.

'He's hardly going to bother with the likes of us when he knows Jinx isn't here.' Serafina couldn't bear the man and made little attempt to disguise it. Her disdain was usually written plain upon her face, which hardly endeared her to their resident genius who had fleetingly tried flirting but been permanently rebuffed. These days he'd more like to strangle her but she couldn't care a hoot. She was a tough one, Serafina, with whom it paid not to tangle. Snobbish to her fingertips, she dismissed the artist as more of an artisan. More dangerously, she also allowed it to show. Jinx had occasionally had to caution her.

'Children, children,' said Dottie placidly. 'Please remember who covers our overheads here.'

'Rubbish,' said Serafina rudely, though actually it was true. 'All that nerd ever really did was come up with the seed of the original idea. Inspired by Ambrose with all that chess and embellished by the rest of us as a team.' She was very mean-spirited, Serafina. *'Damien's Bright Idea*, indeed. He's got about as much talent at Wayne.'

A lightning glance passed between Dottie and the young man, which haughty Serafina failed to catch. Wayne was enough of a trial as it was, teasing her and endlessly setting traps. The first thing she'd do, the minute she gained control, was fire the irritating little squirt. What she significantly failed to recognise, however, which the rest of them saw quite clearly, was that the unpretentious twenty-two-year-old northerner possessed more original artistic flair than all the rest of them put together. Which included Damien Rudge.

'It was Jinx who discovered him and encouraged him from the start.' Dottie believed in credit where it was due. They'd been students together, Damien, Jinx and Ambrose, taught for a while by her husband, Sam.

'Though don't overlook the source of the real funding. He who holds our lives in the palm of his hand.' Ambrose was listening from up above, his normally mild expression contorted into a scowl. When Ambrose took against a person it was for life as the rest of them well knew. When he had it in for someone, which was rare, he was inclined to bang on about it like a cracked record.

The doorbell shrilled loudly, interrupting their chatter, and Wayne, with his head stuck out of the window, reported that there was a police-car outside. First thing back after the Easter break. And still only ten to ten.

'*Now* what have you been up to, you bad, bad boy?' asked Dottie with an indulgent chuckle. But all merriment fled when she opened the door and saw the grim expression on their faces.

'Mrs Sullivan?' asked DCI Burton, consulting his notes. 'Mind if we come in?'

3

Dead. That one stark word, leaden and unacceptable, hung in the air, too terrible even to contemplate. Not when applied to Jinx, *their* Jinx. Jinx dead? Impossible, there had to be some mistake. Jinx, the golden girl, always with so much vitality, whose radiant smile was guaranteed to brighten any room. Jinx, with her gaiety and perpetual sense of fun; Jinx, the wit, with her rapid-fire repartee. They had all been together celebrating only five days before. She'd been very much alive then. Wayne, his mouth frozen half open imbecilically, hovered on the precipice of an irreverent quip. This was just some sort of wicked stunt, yeah? These jokesters were kidding, round here for a laugh. Any second now and she'd bounce in crying 'Gotcha!', triumphant because she had fooled them all so well. It was just the kind of caper he might have got up to himself. Dead? Not possible, not *Jinx*, pull the other one. But the police officers remained inscrutable, no sign of even a flicker of mirth. Was it possible, then, that they were genuine after all? Wayne thought better of it and quietly closed his mouth. *Dead?* Bloomin' heck, whatever next? The world must be coming to an end.

'What happened?' Predictably it was the poised Serafina who managed to regain her equilibrium first. She slid thin, nervy fingers through her over-abundant hair, apparently in perfect control though her usual pallor had increased to near translucence.

'We are not quite certain. Not yet.' The Detective Chief Inspector seemed almost apologetic while his WPC looked as though she might be going to cry. 'We'll need to talk to each one of you separately to run through some routine questions.'

Serafina studied him, approving of what she saw. Fit and well-toned with spiky, dark-red hair, and a nose that was almost too perfect for a real-life run-of-the-mill street cop. He looked rather as if he'd stepped out of one of the soaps, too groomed somehow to be genuine. She had lied when she told Dottie about the man in her life. That particular episode was history now. The position had just come up vacant again and Serafina was constantly on the lookout. She swung one elegant silk-clad knee nonchalantly over the other and watched the responsive flicker in his glacial eyes. This situation could prove promising, she liked a man with an iron will who was also a bit of a brute.

Trudy sighed resignedly as she saw the predatory gleam. Working alongside Hal Burton had its pluses but she was sick of women constantly throwing themselves at him. Especially, as now, when he was supposed to be on duty.

'Who's in charge here?'

They looked at each other in ashen confusion, then their eyes all shifted to Dottie. Though she'd be the last to claim it for herself, she ran the studio on a day-to-day basis, keeping an eye on this disparate group of strung out, creative individuals. Also she was by far the oldest. She twisted a paper tissue in her anguish, shredding it miserably as she fought the gathering tears. This was too awful even to take in. All she longed for was home and the comfort of Sam's arms.

26

'Is there somewhere private we can talk?' Hal glanced round at the spacious, open-plan studio, aware of the frightened, watching eyes.

'The conference-room,' said Dottie, leading the way. Then added, more from habit than anything, 'Would you care for some coffee? It's really no trouble.' Both officers declined. The sooner they got through this and out of here, the better. There were facts to check, people to locate. Plus a dangerous killer loose out there somewhere who might very well strike again.

Without wanting to go into too much detail, they outlined the salient points. The house had been entered and Jinx murdered in her bed; they avoided the gorier facts. Dottie wrung her hands and visibly shook, quite clearly in genuine shock. At least, if she were faking it she was a lot brighter than she seemed. Trudy drew a neat line through her name and reckoned they could safely eliminate her. Dottie did, however, have access to Jinx's personal records.

'Next of kin?'

'Now that I *can* tell you.' Only recently Jinx had set about making a will and Dottie had helped her with it. Furthermore, she kept a copy on disc. Jinx had no secrets, or so she regularly claimed, and her private data was easily accessible. A trusting soul, Hal registered mentally, alarmingly so. Might that have contributed to her untimely death? He made another note.

Marjorie Rawlings, a retired civil servant. Her mother's sister's unmarried daughter who lived in the Cotswolds. Dottie ran through the organiser and flashed up the address on the screen. Trudy scribbled it down. They would drive down tomorrow for a first-hand statement. In the meantime there were other things they needed to know.

'Boyfriends? Anyone in particular?'

Dottie considered then shook her head. There were a couple of fairly recent ones, one especially she didn't care to mention, but no one exactly immediate, nothing current. Certainly no one who mattered so much as to be likely to want to kill her, of that she was positive. Hal, however, had watched her falter. It was his decision, he told her brusquely, which of these leads he would follow up. Now, if Mrs Sullivan would kindly stop wasting his time, he would like all the details – and fast.

Hamish Cotterell presented no problem. There was his address in Hay-on-Wye and this she meekly handed over. Former lovers and long-time friends, they had both remained single so their relationship had been ongoing in a cosy, natural way. A nice man who occasionally dropped in at the studio, rather a good crime-writer with a penchant for fishing. He had once been very keen on Jinx – Dottie had observed it in his eyes – but these days they were little more than chums though she did still occasionally spend weekends with him. And when he was in London, he usually stayed over at her house. Poor man, this was going to hit him especially hard.

And the other? For a moment Dottie prevaricated, wondering frantically where her true loyalties really lay. But the inspector was far too canny for her, saw her floundering and pressed his advantage. Again, don't waste my time, lady. Final warning.

'Professor Norman Harker,' said Dottie at last, feeling a tiny bit treacherous.

'You mean the bod on the box?' said Hal, startled.

The very one. Pompous, over-bearing and what's more married, yet for several months the light of Jinx's life. She saw the incomprehension on Hal's face as she flicked through the organiser for the address and wordlessly noted it down. Not a nice man but a very big fish. Even Jinx was not always infallible. Hal glanced at it then passed it over to Trudy. They would interview the egghead as soon as he'd allow it. Interesting to see what such a high-profile public figure had to say about an illicit alliance.

'Anyone else?' Who might have had a motive? Dottie thought again then shook her head. The thing about Jinx was she always had had men, they'd flocked around her all her life and rarely wandered away. She possessed the kind of easy charm that drew them to her like flies. And yet she never seemed to give it a thought, was impervious to her own pulling power. Which was, of course, all part of her lasting allure, a gift from the fairies.

'She was spotted by her neighbours on Wednesday night with a tall, dark man in a well-cut suit. Any ideas?'

Dottie had one fleeting thought which she instantly dismissed as preposterous. She shook her head. Wednesday was the day before they'd all had that office lunch. Jinx had been right at the top of her form, bright and ebullient, her natural self, asking about their plans for the four-day break even though she'd be working right through. But that was Jinx all over. Everything to her was just another challenge, the end of tax year accounts just a dreary chore. A tall dark stranger, well that could be many people. Though if she'd had a date, it was not like her not to have said. Jinx kept no secrets, none that Dottie knew of. But that, as the policeman gently pointed out, was what secrecy was all about.

Someone was going to have the grisly task of identifying the body. It was so horribly mutilated, especially about the head, that it wouldn't be an easy or enviable task. There were, of course, fingerprints and dental records, but the formality was still something that had got to be gone through. Who the onus should fall on was not immediately clear. The cousin in the country was rarely around; Dottie had a feeling Jinx hadn't seen her in years. And neither current lover was close enough in status to have this unenviable duty dumped on him. Hal looked hard at Dottie and watched her visibly blanch. No, she couldn't, she'd really rather not. She would prefer to remember lovely Jinx as she had been. Of those in the office, apart from herself, Ambrose, as the second most senior, was clearly the obvious candidate. But here again Dottie shook her head. The poor man was in no shape at all to go through such an ordeal. He'd been closer to Jinx than the rest of them and she knew he'd not be able to cope. It would keep till later, there was no immediate rush. Forensic had not yet finished with the body and it was far more urgent that the killer be apprehended.

There was a best friend living in Bristol; they made a note. And of course the other neighbours in the street. Already the police were making a door-to-door check but the cul-de-sac was small and the houses few. They had shrouded number 7 with a plastic awning and taped off the entrance to the street. No one could either enter or leave without first identifying themselves and answering some routine questions, but so far nothing of any apparent significance had emerged. Behind their prettily painted front doors, the residents of this classy close preferred to mind their own business. It would be different in a proper village, as Peggy Dawes pointed out to Arthur. There the net curtains would be constantly on the twitch. Little would escape the neighbours' vigilance.

There was, of course, also the pub. Popular in this particular neighbourhood, it was regularly packed, inside and out. The garden backed on to the row of pastel cottages with only a low brick wall to mark the boundary. It would be no problem at all for an athletic person to vault it and gain easy access. Especially to the house with the French door left enticingly ajar. What possibly could have possessed her to be so lax?

'We're not getting anywhere very fast,' brooded Hal. 'Right, let's wheel in the rest of them one by one.'

Ambrose was seated with Dottie in the pub, not the one next door to Jinx but the Britannia at the end of the mews. They frequently lunched together but today neither could eat a thing. The jukebox was playing, though not very loudly, and only a handful of drinkers shared their space. Across the road the mellow stone columns of the United Reform church provided a dramatic backdrop to a creamy magnolia tree in full bloom.

Normally Dottie would have revelled at the sight, but her appetite for life had shrivelled entirely. The nightmare hung over them, growing darker by the minute. As the first numbing shock began to sink in, she wondered how they'd find the strength to carry on. Jinx dead, and she'd seemed so happy and fulfilled on Thursday, more so somehow than even her normal self. It was shocking how tragedy could strike like that, suddenly without warning out of a clear blue sky.

Ambrose raised his glass to his lips but his hand shook so badly he could scarcely hold it steady. The police had given him a right going over; he realised it was their job, but still. Dottie, aware of his increasingly fragile state, removed the glass and patted the hand instead. A capable hand but gentle too, that of a sensitive artist. She stroked his long, slightly spatulate fingers and for once he didn't recoil from her touch. She, perhaps more than anyone, was aware of the depth of his sorrow, had watched the two of them over the years and had a measure of how much he cared. He had idolised Jinx, thought the world of her. The best friend he'd probably ever had.

'No need to talk if you don't feel like it. Just sit there and be quiet awhile and try not to think too much.' What else could Dottie say; the man was in obvious pain. As, indeed, was Dottie herself. She had phoned Sam and told him the ghastly news and he'd immediately offered to come right over and fetch her, but she felt her presence was still required here. It was what Jinx would have wanted, she was certain, that business should continue as usual especially with the pressures on them now. Though how any of them could hope to do much work. She and Ambrose had slipped away when she'd noticed his eyes no longer focusing, the pencil dead in his hand. She had raised one quick eyebrow to Serafina, who had instantly taken it on board, then steered Ambrose gently over here. When he felt like talking she'd be here for him. If not, she was content just to sit and think.

'Why not go on home, lovie,' she said. 'There's really not a lot you can do here. I doubt that any of us will get any work done today. Maybe we should close the office out of respect.'

Ambrose looked at her despairingly. 'There's just too much work to get through,' he said. His worried brown eyes behind the rimless lenses swam with emotion and his hand still visibly shook. He was tall and wirily built with an amazingly Spartan physique considering the sedentary life he lived. Right now, however, he looked like a little lost orphan whom Dottie longed to sweep up and comfort. She could see one of his migraines threatening and soon he'd be out of action altogether.

'Go home,' she urged him again gently. 'If you like, I'll come with you.' But Ambrose shook his head. He lived in Battersea, just the other side of the river. He'd take the bus as usual, he insisted, but she went with him instead to look for a cab.

'She was always so vibrant, so overflowing with life,' said Dottie, at home in Muswell Hill. 'The kids in the office adored her, everyone did.'

Sam, in his comfortable jogging-pants, sat at the table watching her assemble the shepherd's pie. Nursing a beer, he stroked his beard reflectively as he contemplated the day's awful news. He knew from first hand, all too well as it happened, the power of the dead woman's personality. He had taught her years ago at the London College of Printing, along with Ambrose and Damien. One thing was certain; he would never be able to forget her. She had played far too important a role in his life.

'My old mum used to say that people divide into radiators and drains,' he said thoughtfully. 'Jinx was most definitely a radiator.' The world would be that much the poorer without her. There were things he still didn't talk about to Dottie, best left suppressed and unsaid. The time with Jinx was now so long ago that the pain was little more than just a memory. He closed his eyes and recaptured her as she had been then, bright and vivacious, constantly laughing, with her wild pink-streaked hair and outrageous clothes. The girl he'd allowed to disrupt his stolid life, the girl he had loved so intensely. A child of the seventies with that vast original talent, a born entrepreneur in the making. It had been quite a privilege to teach her.

'How do you suppose Ambrose will cope?'

'Badly, I should think. He already has a migraine. I made him go home to his bed, poor sweet, after the mauling he had from the police.' Dottie, sprinkling chopped parsley, shook her head. Bad times that could only get worse.

Sam had always liked Ambrose a lot and really enjoyed his company. The fellow was smart with a sly, incisive wit and a quiet way of watching things, not letting anything get by. He seemed hardly to have aged in the years since he left college, just gained a little in confidence and stature. He, too, was talented but maintained a deliberately low profile. The work he was doing now, with advanced computer software, was a natural extension of the draughtsmanship he was so good at. It was amazing how he'd adapted, and so quickly, once the axis of his working world had shifted. Yet there again, it all came down to Jinx. Her timely intervention, just when they'd needed it most, had saved the whole lot of them by keeping them in work, though she'd run a serious risk of losing everything. No wonder Ambrose was such a devoted fan.

'Gay, is he?' Sam asked suddenly, as if the thought had only now occurred.

'No, of course not!' said Dottie in swift indignation as she closed the oven door and rinsed her hands. The very idea!

'What, a bachelor of that age? Pushing forty?'

'I wasn't much younger when I married you,' she reminded him primly. 'Why is it people only ever say that about men? Might just as well think it of me.'

Her husband leaned over and fondly patted her bum. 'Get us another of these will you, lovie?' he said, flipping the beer can into the bin. 'No one could ever imagine you as a dyke.' Not with those curves and that mass of flaming hair. Even after all these years, he still liked the way she looked. Saw her as one of the voluptuous famed beauties, a Titian or possibly a Rubens. Dottie's personal tragedy was that she simply couldn't see it herself, would certainly not have believed it if she had.

'So how come in that case,' persisted Sam, 'does he never seem to have a girl of his own? Answer me that. He's a nice enough looking fellow and very entertaining. You'd think they'd be buzzing around him like wasps.'

Dottie considered. 'I really couldn't say. The ladies certainly love him. He is always hugely in demand as an extra man.' His dance-card was perpetually full, he need never eat alone, yet that one special relationship appeared always to elude him. He was a bit of a late developer, Ambrose, perhaps that was all it was. Though pushing forty was cutting it fine if he ever intended to settle down.

'If you really want to know,' she said, having thought about it constantly, 'I think he has always been a little bit sweet on Jinx. That's the plain truth.'

And now the tragedy too.

4

*I killed the bitch because she had it coming. As simple as that,
I had had it up to here. She had messed me around, taunted
me, made me look a fool, and now she was bloody well fucking
someone else. I couldn't stand it, neither would you. Women,
they're all the same, they let you down.*

*The thing you have to understand is this. She was mine, and she
knew it, right from the start, from that very first meeting years ago.
The first time I ever set eyes on her I recognised my soulmate just
like that. I had seen that smile too often in my dreams. And the fact
that our stars fitted confirmed it. She was standing surrounded by
the usual sycophantic group, all elbowing for her attention. She was
telling a dirty joke – I still remember the punchline – and when she
was through she cracked up with the rest, hysterical at her own wit.
But that was Jinx all over, tiresome but also adorable. It was hard
for almost anyone to resist her.*

Finally she deigned to notice my presence.

*'Hello,' she said. 'I know you, don't I? What's your name?' I told
her yes though actually it wasn't true. In my dreams, maybe, but I*

35

couldn't say that, nor that we'd been together in past lives. She simply nodded and took my hand and led me into the group. That's how she always was, friendly and upfront, naïve to the point of total idiocy.

'Probably at some party,' she said, and I went along with that. No point in making a big thing of it, after all. I prefer to remain out of the limelight. For this was the woman I'd waited for all my life, had been put on this earth just to worship. Finding her again, after all the empty years, felt like coming home.

She clung on to my arm as though she had always done so and led me around the group making introductions. It didn't matter, the clowns just nodded and grinned and I didn't give a toss about any one of them. Just being beside her was all that ever counted. I'd put up with the rest of the shit for the sake of her.

I knew I could never forget her and I never will. In this life nor in the next one.

5

The drive down to Moreton-in-Marsh next morning was fast and
uneventful. They left Earl's Court at a little after eight, and by
ten were banging the ornate brass knocker on Marjorie Rawlings's
weathered oak front door. They had debated whether to break the
news by telephone first or save it for the inevitable face-to-face. By
mutual agreement the day before, they had come down on the side
of humanity, with the result that the plain, slightly horsy face had
traces of recent weeping round the eyes. Her courtesy, however,
could not have been bettered. She ushered them through her tiny,
low-ceilinged hall into a minute sitting-room overlooking the garden,
with uneven, polished floorboards and crooked beams laden with
horse-brasses. Trudy looked round with frank appreciation.

'This is very nice.'

'Isn't it just. I bought it when I took early retirement from the
Civil Service. The fulfilment of a long-time pipe dream, the cosy
country cottage with roses round the door and all that.'

She offered them coffee, which she served in small exquisite
china cups, flowery and delicate like the rest of the cottage though

slightly out of keeping with her own bony frame. She was almost as tall as Hal, with squarish shoulders and a flat chest, thick ankles and sensible countrywoman's shoes. An overweight cat slumbered in one saggy armchair and she pushed it on to the floor to make room for Trudy.

'Jinx used to laugh and say I was getting old before my time, but I know she liked it really. Once used to pop down for the occasional weekend to unwind, though I'm afraid it must be years since I last saw her.' She sniffed and dabbed at her nose with a tissue. 'Actually, I've left it to her in my will. She never knew that but I think she would have been thrilled. Worked too hard, always did. She needed some outlet for relaxation.'

She turned away briefly to blow her nose, then handed round sugar lumps with tiny silver tongs.

'When did you last speak to her?' asked Hal.

'Let me see now. Oh, not for months. She sent a card at Christmas, of course, with a scrawled note saying it had been far too long and we really must get together some time. But I can't recall when we last had a proper jaw. Our lives are quite different, she was so much engrossed in her work.'

'Do you have any pictures of her?' asked Hal.

'Of course.' Marjorie crossed to the crowded windowsill, which was cluttered with china knick-knacks and photos in frames, and selected a couple that she handed to Hal.

'When were these taken? Approximately.'

'Oh, ages ago, both of them, though she never much changed over the years apart from the colour of her hair. I've probably got some more recent snaps somewhere but I like both of those particularly because they capture the real Jinx, so spunky and cheerful and full of beans.' She came to stand beside him. 'She was always such a lively little thing. Packed with energy and enthusiasm, throwing herself into everything with gusto. Not a bit like me, I'm afraid. I've always been something of a plodder. Jinx was always a high-roller, right from early childhood.'

Her voice wobbled but she continued manfully. 'I don't know where it all came from, her energy. Her parents were not like that at all.'

Hal studied both pictures with curiosity. He saw a skinny smiling child on a pony, her hair scraped back into short, untidy plaits, with bare, scarred knees and broomstick arms. In the second picture, taken about seven years later, she had matured considerably into a pretty, stylish girl with a wide, humorous mouth showing a gap between her teeth and friendly, warm butterscotch eyes. Her hair, in this one, was now dark red streaked with pink and fell shaggily over her forehead. So this, at last, was the fabled Jinx McLennan. She looked far more down to earth and approachable than he had imagined. But definitely fun.

'That was Jinx at art school,' said Marjorie. 'Lately she'd stopped all this playing around with colour and let it grow back to its natural shade. Brownish with fairer streaks. But, of course, you must already know that.'

Marjorie stared at them both in sudden horror and clapped her hand over her mouth. It was as if the true enormity of what they'd told her was only now sinking in, even though she had had all night to digest it. She looked quite peculiar, as if she might well faint, and Hal stepped forward and grabbed her by both elbows.

'You all right? Why not sit down?'

Marjorie blinked rapidly then shook her head. 'No, really I'm OK. It's just the thought of what happened to her . . . Was she very badly injured?'

Hal thought briefly of the bloody, pulpy mess they had found on the bed and shook his head. Since this woman would not be called on to identify her cousin, a small white lie was in order.

'Hardly at all,' he said. 'Scarcely even scratched.'

Bravo, applauded Trudy silently, surprised. Not like her boss to display such finer feelings. Not like him, come to think of it, to feel anything at all.

'So she wouldn't have suffered?'

'Not a lot I don't think.'

They resumed their seats and Marjorie poured more coffee. The colour was returning slowly to her cheeks. Trudy pulled out her notebook and flipped it open and Hal embarked on his questioning. There wasn't a lot she could tell them, though. Dates and facts about Jinx's parents, where she went to school, which subjects she excelled in. Stuff like that. An average life viewed through the rosy lenses of an admiring, less-achieving older cousin.

'Boyfriends?'

'Loads of them. Jinx was always popular. Not so much pretty as bursting with personality. And she didn't make distinctions between them; men liked that. No particular favourites and she kept in touch with them all. Some of them even after they'd married and moved away.'

'But no one in particular?'

'Not that I'm aware of. Though I really can't say why that should be.' Marjorie fell silent as she gazed into the past. 'She never seemed to want to settle, I think life was far too exciting as it was. Never met Mr Wonderful, perhaps because of her parents' marriage. Peter and Julia were very lukewarm.'

'Perhaps he was out there still looking for her.' Hal stared at her thoughtfully. And then, with consummate professional skill, he slipped in the crucial question. Her movements over the Easter weekend. What exactly had she been doing? Marjorie blinked but appeared not to take offence. She was a sensible woman with a calm demeanour. And the answer was very simple. She had spent the entire weekend with the Ramblers' Association, hiking in the breathtaking Cotswolds countryside, her reason for moving here in the first place. Surreptitiously, though with little surprise, Trudy drew a neat little line through her name.

Hay-on-Wye was less than an hour away so Hamish Cotterell came next; they could take in Bristol on the way home. He was waiting for them in the doorway of the pub, a pleasant-looking man in perhaps his middle forties, handsome in a faded way with longish, greying hair and washed-out pale blue eyes. He shook both their hands with a warm, firm grip.

'Good of you to come.' His monogrammed pewter tankard was waiting in the inglenook while his ancient labrador, Henry, slept peacefully alongside. He raised his hand to summon the barman but they both shook their heads.

'Not while on duty,' said Hal. Besides, it was barely past noon.

'I'm afraid I still can't quite take it in,' said Hamish. 'Not my lovely Jinx.' A writer of some distinction for many years, he had given up the academic day job when his trout-fishing detective had hit the small screen. Now he lived in some comfort in this pretty, book-infested town and, in an elderly tweed jacket and worn-out cords, looked every inch what he was. He wiped his eyes, unashamedly moved. Trudy was touched. *Byronic*, she thought approvingly. Poetic yet in a masculine way.

'She was always so very vivacious, so completely full of life. Generous with her company, too, altogether an inspiration.' The first of his many novels had been dedicated to Jinx. They'd been friends and, later, lovers for the best part of twelve years. No, he said now, it had not been love exactly but something very near to it; he was not ashamed to admit it. As it happened, he'd left her a message just a few days before, inviting her down for a spur-of-the-moment weekend. Only she hadn't even returned his call so he'd never got the chance to say goodbye. He wiped his eyes unabashedly on his sleeve.

'I suppose you might say she was my closest friend,' he said simply.

He turned the tables slightly on Hal by embarking on his own cross-examination. His forensic knowledge was remarkably sound and his questions so probing he was hard to head off. There were details Hal didn't want to tell him, not yet while the killer remained uncaught, but the things he did know were really quite startling. The hairs on Trudy's neck began to rise.

'Professional knowhow,' he explained at length, catching the stunned expression on her face. 'Remember what it is I do for a living. Research is the principal element.'

Which didn't exactly explain his first-hand knowledge of how the intruder had entered the house and the actual weapon he had chosen for the job. Or his observations on the paucity of traffic that Easter weekend in the early hours of the morning. But he'd spent a great deal of time in the neighbourhood, was a regular visitor to Jinx's home, knew Jinx's lifestyle and the sort of people she mixed with. Anyone with a writer's observant eye could, Trudy supposed, have garnered such intricate details. She certainly hoped so for the man was so nice. Warm and genuine with those really quite sexy eyes.

Hal's closing question, having regained his authority, settled the matter more or less conclusively. When asked about his movements on that Bank Holiday weekend, Hamish told them comfortably that he'd been off fishing outside Ludlow with a string of fellow enthusiasts who could, if called upon, vouch for his movements. With a small feeling of relief, Trudy crossed his name off the list. She believed in the basic decency of most people; unlike her boss she was not a cynic.

As they rose to leave and shook hands again, there was one other thing Hal wanted to know.

'What was it she had? Can you tell me that? Everyone we've talked to seems genuinely shattered. She must have been one hell of a gal.'

'So she was,' said Hamish, his blue eyes sad. 'A true free spirit, one in a million. Talented, original, generous to a fault. She just romped through life like one great adventure, a sassy Pied Piper drawing everyone along in her wake.'

'Rats and all.'

Hamish nodded. 'Wait till you meet the Professor,' he said grimly.

*   *   *

Veronica Phillips was waiting to receive them in her suburban villa on the outskirts of Bristol. She apologised for the appalling clutter as she ushered them into her huge kitchen. A cluster of chirpy ten-year-olds were messing about with makeup, and she asked them mildly if they'd move.

'Sorry about that,' she said with a grin. 'School holidays are always a bit chaotic.'

Yes, she told them, she had always been Jinx's best friend, right back to the time they had first met, just a few months older than her daughter was now.

'Our fathers played golf at the same club and they threw us together when we moved on to boarding-school. We took one look and hated each other,' she said. 'But that, I suppose, was inevitable in the circumstances. We got over it jolly quickly.'

She was a pretty woman with good skin and intelligent eyes, dressed in shorts and a T-shirt with the beginnings of a tan. She taught part-time at a local school, maths and biology with occasional PT.

'We were both on the netball team,' she explained, 'and later got the tennis bug in a big way.' Trekking up to Wimbledon to queue all night for tickets; fanatical club players while Jinx still had the time. 'She was always a wonderful server,' she said. 'With a killer backhand as deadly as Sue Barker's.' It was a blow to them both when the pressure of business began to impinge upon Jinx's leisure time, but then Veronica got married and moved to Bristol and Jinx set up the design group.

'And stopped coming down to us for tennis weekends when the work thing got in the way.'

Yet the closeness of the friendship had endured and the two of them continued to keep in touch regularly.

'Did she tell you about her lovelife?' asked Hal intently.

'Of course,' said Veronica. 'That's what best friends are all about.'

'So you know Hamish Cotterell?'

'I do indeed. He's a genuine sweetie who adores – adored – Jinx.'

'Why do you think, then, that they never quite got it together?'

'Well, they did in a way. They've been on and off for years.'

'But he never actually married her?'

'Correction. *She* never married *him.*'

'And why do you think that might be?'

'No particular reason. Except that Jinx wasn't ready to settle down. Not yet, at least.' Veronica sighed and shook her head. Behind her calm exterior she was really hurting a lot. She had tried so hard, for the past twenty-four hours, to be so brave but it wasn't an easy task. Life without Jinx was something she couldn't envisage. Even now, with this policeman's incessant interrogation, the fact of her best friend's murder was something she couldn't accept. Why Jinx, why now, for heaven's sake, just when her life had been coming together so well?

'He was not really strong enough to cope with Jinx. Too easy-going and lacking in mystique. Just too nice; Jinx always craved excitement.'

'And Professor Harker? Do you know him too?'

Veronica frowned and perched on the window-seat. Girlish giggles came floating down from upstairs and occasionally there was a stampede of platform soles on the stairs.

'I never exactly met him. And I certainly didn't approve.'

'Why was that?'

'Quite simply, the man is married. Even though he hardly ever sees his wife, or so he always led her to believe. So the whole thing had to be a bit hole-and-corner, almost as if he were ashamed of her. I couldn't accept it; Jinx was worth better than that.'

'So what was it that she saw in him?'

'Fame and brilliance, I suppose, and the accompanying glamour. Jinx was ever the romantic, never completely mature. Thirteen with plaits and glasses, she always claimed. I think I know what she meant.'

'The ultimate aphrodisiac?'

'Something like that.'

'But without the requisite commitment?'

'That too.'

'But didn't she ever really fall in love?' asked Trudy suddenly, interrupting. 'Among all those men there must have been someone. She wouldn't have been normal if there wasn't.'

Veronica swung round to stare at her; the two women locked eyes for a long moment. Then, 'Actually,' said Veronica slowly, 'there *was* someone new in her life. She had her heart broken when she was still in her early twenties and never really trusted anyone since. Safety in numbers was what she used to say, preferred to run several relationships at once. Was determined never to be caught out like that again. But recently she told me she thought she might be in love. Was quite giddy with excitement, though said she couldn't tell me more. Something to do with business, though that's all she would divulge. Promised to fill me in on my birthday lunch, though I wasn't to breathe a word when she did. Didn't want to risk spooking it before it got properly started. Jinx was always superstitious about things like that. As I've said, it happened once before and all went horribly wrong.'

'Someone in her office?' asked Hal alertly. 'One of her own team?' Surely not.

'I wouldn't have thought so,' said Veronica. 'Though she's always been close to them all, especially Ambrose. He's never been exactly a boyfriend, of course, just a very close buddy. More like a brother to her all these years.'

'Any guesses?'

'None whatsoever.' Although Jinx talked quite a lot about what she did, Veronica knew little of the life of a graphic designer and was therefore fairly vague about what it actually entailed. Apart from the team in the studio, there were millions of outside connections in ad agencies and software firms, constant lunches and partying, all part of her frenetic working life. Jinx, who took

45

care of the business side of things, was an ace networker whose Filofax was always crammed.

'She must have had regular contact with loads of people,' Veronica continued. But she made a firm distinction between real and business friends. Although Veronica had heard some of the names, she was vague as to who they all actually were and how exactly each one fitted into Jinx's life. She had heard many anecdotes about her team but had never met any of them, apart from Dottie once when Veronica came up to Kensington to shop.

'I'd talk to her,' she advised Hal now. 'Nice warm person and terrifically sound. She'll know if anyone does.'

They drove back to London in silence, Hal at the wheel, Trudy checking through her notes. Both were exhausted; it had been a gruelling day. All those questions, few with satisfactory answers. Veronica and her family had spent Easter at home, with her parents visiting and a party for neighbours and friends. So she was well and truly out of the frame. Not that she had come under any sort of real suspicion; she was clearly devoted to her friend. Yet everyone had to be considered seriously, that was the essence of this sort of inquiry. Most women are murdered by someone they know well, a grim but indisputable statistic.

'Well,' said Hal finally, lighting a cigarette, 'she must have been something quite extraordinary. Everyone seems to have loved her so much. I wish now I'd known her myself.'

Trudy flicked him a sideways glance. He was difficult, infuriating and very often misogynistic in his attitudes, but the stark truth was that she was more than a little in love with him. Had been for the two years they had worked together, if only he would view her as a woman and not just another uniform without a brain.

'So where do we go from here?' she asked.

'A few more questions to the rest of the team,' said Hal. 'Then on to the redoubtable Professor Harker.'

6

Professor Norman Harker kept them waiting twenty minutes. A man of his self-importance usually did. Hal had met others of his type before, was well versed in that particular brand of egoism. But the lounge of the Connaught was comfortable and quiet and he found himself suddenly exhausted.

'Coffee?' asked the waitress and Hal nodded. Let the bastard cough up for it, too.

They recognised him, of course, the minute he stepped out of the lift and came towards them rubbing his hands, a smile of forced affability on his jowly face but a giveaway mark of tension between the bushy eyebrows. Now what, they could see him thinking, was this latest minor irritant? A parking ticket left unpaid most likely. Hal saw the contempt in the familiar mocking eyes as he rose and introduced himself and Trudy. *Yes, yes* ... The professor was already glancing at his expensive watch when Hal's words wiped the condescension clean off his face.

'Is there somewhere a little more private we can talk, sir?'

'Say whatever it is right here and get it over with. I'm a busy man.'

Hal glanced round the lounge where a couple of tables were already taken. All conversation had ceased abruptly when Harker walked into the room. With his regular irascible appearances on television, these days he had become something of a house-hold name. He traded on his sarcastic superiority; the delighted onlookers were anticipating one of his fights. And Harker, ever aware of his public image, was more than content that they should witness it.

Until, that is, Jinx's name was mentioned, when the smile evaporated and a look of wariness crept into the eyes.

'Yes,' he said guardedly, 'I do know Jinx McLennan slightly. What of it?' He glanced round the room and fingered the perfect knot of his silk tie with suddenly shaking fingers. Well, *that* had succeeded in catching his attention and powerfully concentrating his mind. Concealing his triumph, Hal maintained a low, deferential tone.

'Bad news, I'm afraid, sir. The lady is dead.'

'What was it? A car crash?' asked Harker after a pause. Hal, watching carefully, saw no trace of emotion in his eyes.

'Worse, I'm afraid, sir. It seems she was murdered. Now wouldn't you prefer it if we went on up to your room?'

The ruddy glow faded from Harker's chubby cheeks. 'What, *now*? I have to be at White City in forty-five minutes. Won't it wait?'

'I'm afraid not, sir.'

'Oh, come on then. But I can't give you more than a few minutes. And I'll have to check in with my producer first.' Harker turned on his heel like a thwarted child and blustered his way grumpily back to the lift. Following, Hal flashed a complicitious grin at his passive WPC. The cracks were already showing and they hadn't even got going yet. This promised to be easier than he'd thought.

They had met, Harker told them, a handful of years before, at a party at the House of Lords to which they'd both been invited unaccompanied. Some fund-raising thing, the usual boring shit. He'd liked her bright smile and intelligent eyes, and had taken her for supper at his club. Since then he'd seen her, oh, half a dozen times. She was funny and spunky and helped him to relax. *I'll bet*, thought Hal savagely, immediately hating the man.

'And now you tell me she's dead?' It was as if it were only just sinking in. 'What a truly terrible thing. I can hardly believe it.'

'When did you last see her, sir?' *And where were you Saturday night?*

A shifty look crept into Harker's eyes and he turned away as though in elaborate thought.

'Oh, not for months. I'm pretty certain of that. My work means I'm forced to travel quite a bit. I'm not often in London and then only passing through.' His wife lived in Norfolk; he used this hotel as a *pied-à-terre*. Expensive, he told them smugly, but he'd grown used to a certain standard.

'We have access to her computerised diary. If you can't recall actual dates.' He'd seen her twice at least in the last three months; Hal had already checked. Harker's face grew red again and the unctuous manner fled. He looked as though he'd dearly like to thump him. Hal almost wished he would try.

'We occasionally met for a late-night drink,' explained Harker with reluctance. 'Television can be an exacting mistress and Jinx was always a good listener.'

Hal asked the routine questions and Trudy noted the answers but they seemed to be leading nowhere, to the secret disappointment of them both. The man was a jerk but too public a one to get caught. With his superior intellect, he'd be a fool if he fell into their trap. Yet stranger things had been known to happen – and vanity could be a powerful Achilles' heel. In the end he grew restless and kept glancing at his watch, so Hal softened his technique a little and told him they were through. At least, for now.

He asked how Harker had spent the Easter weekend and was sorry to discover he had been chairing a late-night discussion group. Live from Liverpool after midnight on Saturday night. It was available on video should the police decide to check. Trudy, somewhat reluctantly, crossed off his name, and Harker saw them both to the door.

'It won't hit the papers?' he virtually pleaded, and Hal told him coldly that that would be up to the press.

'Nasty piece of work,' he commented as they walked back to the car. 'Now what would a woman as wonderful as that—'

'See in a creep like him?' Trudy cut him short. 'Star-fucker, probably, you'd be surprised. It gets all sorts.'

They still had quite a number to interview; the list kept growing longer. There was famous artist Damien Rudge and someone called Julius Weinberg, whose name the bloke in the office – the boffinish one – had let slip. Weinberg lived abroad yet was one of their key investors. From the scowl on Ambrose's face and the way his lips turned white when he spoke the name, it was clear he didn't much care for the fellow. Which had instantly alerted Hal's interest.

'What did you make of him?' asked Hal thoughtfully. 'The quiet one, Ambrose Rafferty?'

'Nice,' said Trudy without much thought. 'Like someone's big brother. You felt you could trust him.'

'And he was certainly loyal to Jinx.' His blind devotion had been almost doglike; he had spoken of her in the hushed and reverent tones people used of Diana immediately after the crash.

'Well, they'd known each other an awfully long time. Practically grew up together, he said.'

'Do you think they were doing it?' asked Hal crudely.

'Absolutely not.'

'How can you be so sure?' he inquired, amused. He loved to rile her, particularly on feminist issues; she never failed to rise.

'I just know these things,' said Trudy indignantly. 'For one thing, he spoke of her with far too much deference, as if she were an icon, not a flesh-and-blood woman. It was "Jinx this" and "Jinx that" about the clever things she'd done and said, for all the world as if she were some sort of genius or saint. The man's infatuated but not on a physical level.'

'Poofter, is he?'

'No, not that either.' Why were men's minds always so crude and one-track? 'He just sees her as the girl next door, his ideal woman. To be honoured like his mother, not defiled. Centuries ago he would probably have been a knight. He'd lay down his cloak for her or even his life.'

Hal was impressed. Trudy was quiet and occasionally a little too uptight for his taste but there was clearly keen insight in that demure little head. He slanted a thoughtful glance at her and enjoyed watching her discomfort. She shifted in her seat and snapped her notebook closed.

'Where to next, guv?' she asked brusquely, straightening her chequered police hat.

Where indeed. They were doing the artist in the afternoon; he was booked on the noon flight from Jersey. The door-to-door inquiries in the cul-de-sac were very nearly concluded but so far nothing of obvious importance had emerged. It was essential that they move as fast as they could before the trail went cold. It was still mid morning; they had time on their hands.

'Back to the mews,' said Hal thoughtfully. There was still more to learn from that close little team, who joked and sparred like blood relations, covered each other's backs with amazing deftness and appeared to get on so well. He needed to do a little more gentle probing, to be certain they weren't inadvertently covering up some important piece of evidence they failed to recognise. That was the thing about vital clues; quite often they were literally staring you in the face.

*   *   *

'One thing's for certain,' Serafina was saying idly, exhaling a thin stream of smoke into the air. 'I'm in the clear and Dottie must be too. They can hardly make a case against either of us.'

She was dressed in a fine cream linen shirt this morning, with skin-tight breeches tucked into highly polished boots. There was nothing remotely sporty about her lifestyle but she certainly knew how to dress to the utmost effect. Her blue-black hair was swept sleekly behind her ears, revealing genuine pearl studs. Even Wayne was impressed. He privately sneered at her and found her pretentious but was bound to admit she had style. It was that groovy cop who was currently getting her knickers in a twist; with any luck he'd come nosing round again so that Wayne could enjoy another private smirk at all her ridiculous showing off. Serafina liked to pretend she was posher than she actually was, but Wayne, with his northern astuteness, was no fool. He had seen right through her from the very first day.

'So why's that, then?' he asked now from his post by the Xerox machine, where he was mindlessly copying contracts for Dottie. Serafina possessed not a jot of humour. He loved, more than anything, a chance to send her up.

'Obvious, dumbo.' She regarded him with scorn. Something about Wayne got up her nose so she continually felt the need to slap him down. Ambrose, up in his gallery, was vainly trying to work, but none of them was taking the slightest notice despite the ominous deadline hanging over their heads. Wayne looked back at her with innocent eyes and a look of blank incomprehension.

'The rape, you imbecile. Think about it. Or didn't your mummy explain yet about the birds and bees?'

Wayne was openly laughing at her now. As one who had his nose stuck into a crime novel at every conceivable opportunity, he was well versed in police procedure. And he loved more than anything to egg her on.

'Wouldn't be too certain of that, duckie,' he said darkly. 'Did you never hear of contract killing? It's the latest in thing, all over the papers these days, women knocking off affluent hubbies in order to run off with their toyboys. Easy as anything to hire an assassin, you can find one lurking in almost any bar. Provided, of course, that you have the necessary readies. And know where to look.'

'But rape?' said Dottie worriedly. 'Surely not?'

Wayne cackled evilly and gave a world-weary shrug. 'Goes with the territory,' he said as if he knew. 'Once the cash has been handed over it's up to them what they get up to. Call it job satisfaction, if you like.'

Serafina stubbed out her cigarette and regarded him with the purest distaste.

'So I'd assume nothing,' Wayne continued, feeding the documents into the copier like an automaton as he launched himself into his stride. 'The cops certainly won't. We're all of us potential suspects until we can prove our innocence. Mark my words.'

Dottie sighed and went back to her work. Someone had to keep the ship afloat, though no one was really interested any more. Her grief for Jinx kept choking her in spurts. The longer it was, the more keenly it hurt and she knew it was likely to get a great deal worse. If only they'd make a quick arrest and let them get back to normal living. But Wayne was into his stride by now. There'd be no stopping him.

'If you want my opinion,' he said as he collated, 'the most obvious suspect is the Moon Monster himself. Mad as cheese, it sticks out a mile. You have only to look at his work to see how weird he is.'

'Damien!' shrieked Serafina. 'He hasn't got the balls.'

But Dottie, never quite sure of Wayne's black humour, continued to look alarmed.

'But why would he even want to?' she asked seriously. 'Hurt Jinx who was always so good to him? He was devoted to her and well you know it. Look what she did for him over the years, spotted his unique talent right from the start and used all her energy to help him to develop. You could say Damien owes his whole career to her. What a terrible idea, you bad boy.'

'All the more reason to get rid of her, then. Kicking away the ladder that he climbed.'

'Wayne! Enough!'

'What?' He turned ingenuous eyes towards Dottie, whose tension visibly eased when she saw his sly grin and belatedly understood what he was about. So that's all it was, Serafina-baiting time. They were like a couple of squabbling kids, the boy couldn't leave her alone. Well, if all it was was just prankish fun they could certainly use a good laugh. Jinx would be the first to agree. Provided it didn't stop them working.

It certainly gave her pause, however, to reflect on what Wayne had just said. Damien had certainly been acting oddly lately, more paranoid even than before. He had always been something of a loner from the start, with a strong distrust of other people. She'd had lunch just recently with the poor put-upon Janey, who had sounded near the end of her tether. He appeared to believe that the world was conspiring against him to knock off his best ideas. And he'd acted pretty strangely at the recent office lunch. It had taken all Jinx's powers of persuasion to calm him down and alleviate his fears. And even then he had not been wholly convinced.

Up in the gallery, Ambrose threw down his pen. There was no point in trying to work with all this racket so he admitted defeat and went downstairs to join them. He needed a break from the pressures he was under, and welcomed a bit of lunacy from his colleagues. They were a good bunch, this team, and he was inordinately fond of them all, probably the best mates he'd ever had.

'You are overlooking somebody,' said Ambrose quietly. 'There's a far more likely candidate I can think of.' He glanced at each one of them, waiting for the penny to drop, but nobody had a clue what he was on about. His hair was shaggy and could do with a cut, there were egg stains on his jacket. He was like a benevolent teddy-bear but for once he wasn't smiling. He picked up a sharpened pencil from Serafina's desk and twirled it between his fingers as he searched for the answer he wanted.

'Go on,' said Wayne eventually, giving up, and the rest of them waited expectantly.

'Public Enemy Number One. To each and every one of us here. Mr Julius Fucking Weinberg, that's who. Who dumped us all in it once before if you recall.'

Ambrose's gentle smile turned into a snarl of rage and he snapped the pencil between his fingers in two.

7

It seemed he had had it in for her right from the start. That much had been obvious to Ambrose all these years. Since those early Weinbergs days when she'd constantly joked and poked fun at him, leading to a dramatic walkout of the staff. He might have thought he had crushed her then but look how quickly she'd bounced back – giving him the two fingers as she determinedly went about raising the capital to provide them all with new well-paid jobs and a brighter future than any they'd dreamed of before. Tired old Weinbergs, deprived of its creator, had foundered and later sunk altogether, unable to withstand the shock of that dastardly takeover. Jinx had possessed the wisdom and foresight to spot where the market was headed and risk all she'd got on that one great significant gamble. For twelve years now they'd been upwardly mobile while Mr Julius Weinberg was very soon gone from the scene. He had quit his highly paid job as the new supremo and retreated to New York to amass another fortune. He was still glimpsed occasionally in the society pages; he had married some Swedish starlet and they were a very high-profile pair. But never again in the hallowed halls of publishing. His single great talent had been to destroy; the tragedy was that he'd succeeded so well. Then just when they'd thought he was finally gone from their lives, he had suddenly and shockingly re-appeared.

That meeting at the IEP headquarters in January had turned out to be explosive in the extreme. They were there to give an update on the progress of their secret project, by far the most ambitious one to date. 'DBI-2000' it was code-named in the office, and had the potential, all going to schedule, to outsell even *Final Fantasy VIII*. Very big business indeed, in fact. More thrilling than anything they'd envisaged. Ambrose had been there in his role of software engineer, along with a very perky Jinx who was fronting the whole thing. She'd been looking especially gorgeous that day in a sharp little suit, with her hair newly streaked. Ambrose had been so proud of her, but when was he ever not? They had filed into the meeting place, seven suits and them round a table, to await the imminent but late arrival of the new *grand fromage* from New York. Jinx was in super sparkling form and soon had the lot of them eating from her hand. Ambrose sat back like a proud indulgent parent and watched her skilful schmoozing at which she had always excelled.

All the auspices looked excellent. IEP had guaranteed the necessary funding and had already handed over quite a sizeable cheque to get the creative part underway. A large slice of that, of course, was Damien's upfront fee, without which he couldn't have been persuaded to start work. The remainder was for basics like materials and overheads. Jinx herself would continue to pay their salaries in the usual way. Profits would not significantly kick in until the game was finally completed and out there on the internet and into the high-street stores. This meeting was pure formality – or so they'd been told by IEP – to allow this new guy from head office to get an overall picture for himself of how things stood.

'Great!' Jinx had said with excitement to Ambrose. 'With the CEO on board, the rest should be easy peasy.'

He had kept them all waiting a full thirty-five minutes but in an atmosphere both relaxing and calm. They were a nice bunch, these guys from IEP, unusually civilised for mere money men. So they were utterly unprepared when he finally stalked through the door. In one seamless movement the suits were on their feet as the tall, imposing figure entered their presence. Ambrose practically had a coronary and Jinx had the breath knocked right out of her as he briefly paused and offered them each his hand.

'Both Jinx and Ambrose are old pals of mine,' explained Julius Weinberg smoothly. What he really meant was enemies to the death. He was gaunter now and his hair was thinner but he still had the same ice-cold charisma and gleam of contempt in his eye. He had not forgotten and certainly not forgiven; premonition gripped Ambrose till he nearly choked and he wished that he hadn't come. Weinberg took his place at the head of the table and indicated all should sit. Then he flicked through his notes and embarked on a cross-examination that would put an SS interrogator to shame and practically brought tears to Jinx's eyes. After such an interval, this she did not deserve. What had happened between them all those years ago should now be water under the bridge. How had this Judas slithered back into their lives without the slightest warning or hint of shame? He was chilly, he was charmless and as dismissive as of old, and Jinx was unusually flustered as his questions grew harsher and more unwarranted.

'The worst thing was he made me feel so stupid,' she complained to Ambrose when they finally got away. He bombarded her with questions and expected detailed answers, even though, by this late stage, the project was well underway. When he ended up querying their actual deadline and insisted on bringing it forward, Jinx had finally flipped.

'That's a bloody stupid suggestion,' she screamed. 'You, more than anyone, should see that. The more you reduce the timescale, the shoddier will be the end product. You can't make silk purses out of sows' ears, not without spilling blood. Top quality is never achieved by skimping on man hours. Your uncle might have taught you that if you'd not been too much of a smartass to listen.'

A ripple of tangible terror ran through the group, and even Ambrose was now seriously alarmed. He was scared she had finally gone too far and provoked this proven bastard to pull the plug. As he'd done once before with gargantuan reverberations. Cross this man and you risked your whole career. But there was no stopping Jinx once her dander was truly up. She swept up her papers, with fire in her eyes, and stalked out of the boardroom with Ambrose trailing miserably behind.

'If you even so much as *think* of apologising,' she hissed at him in the lift, 'I will never ever forgive you. No matter what.'

Now Ambrose faced his colleagues like a slightly crazed terrorist, fury and thwarted love burning in his eyes.

'He could never bear her because she was so strong and magnificent. So now the bastard's gone that extra step and put her permanently out of the way.'

'You can't be serious.' They stared at him, aghast. The worst thing was that Weinberg was where their particular buck stopped just now. They needed his backing and goodwill to complete the project. Not to mention all the other ramifications. And he'd seemed so reasonable only a couple of weeks ago. Everything had seemed plain sailing then. Where had it all gone wrong?

'Hang on,' said Wayne reasonably, weighing it all up. 'How could he have done it when he hasn't even been around?'

'You said it yourself, contract killing. Easy if you have that sort of money and clout.'

Stunned silence all round as they considered this shattering theory. Then Dottie gently patted Ambrose's arm. He was white-faced with anger, quite spaced out with grief.

'Come along, lovie,' she suggested quietly. 'Let's take an early lunch and go across to the pub.'

Too late, she was interrupted by the swirl of tyres on cobbles. The police had returned for a further inquisition.

Damien Rudge was a surprise. Far from being the suave sophisticate Hal had been expecting, he was tall and awkward with a receding hairline and a disconcerting squint behind his contact lenses which made him look shiftier than he probably was. Strange that, the way vanity could affect even the plainest of men. Hal had no doubt at all that he would have looked better behind large, concealing horn-rims, the way he was portrayed in his earlier press photos. He led them into the huge double drawing-room of his ornate Mount Street duplex while a cleaning lady carried in coffee on a tray.

'I really don't know what you think I can tell you.' He was already on the defensive, uptight and ill at ease. He wore a blue-and-white-striped seersucker jacket over plain grey flannels with an immaculate crease. His cufflinks and watch were solid gold. Hal glanced around the room. Not the interior you'd expect of a fashionable painter; dark and formal with intricately swathed curtains and gold tassels adorning the overstuffed furniture. His wife's taste, no doubt. Even the pictures were traditional, and one of those fake log fires burned in the grate.

'We just need to run a few things past you, sir,' said Hal respectfully, playing the docile cop. 'How long were you acquainted with the deceased?'

Damien thought. 'Oh, years. Right from the time we first met at college, 1977 or thereabouts.'

'And that was?'

'The London College of Printing. In Elephant and Castle.

Dismal place but one of the best courses for graphic design in the country. At least, at the time.'

'And since then you have also worked together?'

'On and off. Though these days, of course, my projects are all my own.' Which Hal knew already was not entirely true. By everyone's account, Jinx's input had been considerable. She had encouraged and inspired him and enabled him to grow. Her energy and vision had more than complemented his unusual talent and unique way of looking at things. Without his genius, true, she might not have been able to set up her own business; without her inspiration, he would not now be a millionaire.

'How exactly would you describe your relationship?'

Rudge paced the Chinese carpet and looked distinctly rattled and out of sorts. The slightly popping eyes were cautious, a trace of South London still evident in his speech. 'Close, I suppose you could say we were,' he said reluctantly. 'In the old days certainly. Lately, for obvious reasons, we had grown somewhat apart.'

'Since you moved to Jersey?'

'That and other things. At the level of work I'm engaged in now I need isolation and to be left alone. Jinx had her uses and I'll always be grateful. She was a great facilitator and there were times when we had fun. But I suppose you could say I moved on years ago. The stuff she's producing now is fairly run of the mill. There's a market for it, mainly in the States, but I'm now concentrating on far more innovative images.'

'This computer game, you mean? The one that is so secret?' Rudge looked distinctly alarmed.

'Don't worry, sir. We don't have the details. Just the bare parameters of what McLennan Graphics are working on now.' The myopic eyes behind the lenses grew wider. He pulled at his tie in a nervous spasm, as if he were heading for a stroke.

'You must understand that I've already moved on. That was done for commercial reasons. Now I am back to pure art.'

'And where were you over Easter, sir?'

Rudge stared at him with barely disguised hostility and, just for an instant, appeared to be tongue-tied. 'Why, at home in Jersey,' he offered, after a while, sounding decidedly lame.

'Can anyone vouch for you? Your wife perhaps?'

Damien's eyes flew wildly round the room. He attempted an answer but his stammer got in the way. Trudy made a note. They could check it out later should it come to that. Meanwhile she did not put a line through his name, which gave her a perverse twinge of satisfaction.

'Another solipsistic loony,' commented Hal as they pushed through the massive double doors. How could she have abided them, that obviously big-hearted woman? She was, from all accounts, inspired at business as well as a mover and shaker *par excellence*. He supposed all these weirdos must go with the turf. After years of police work, not a lot surprised Hal.

8

It was not at all like Ambrose to bear any sort of a grudge, at least for no longer than it took him to sober up. Weinberg, however, was the exception. Since their paths first crossed in that earlier incarnation, the pair had locked horns and not got on. Just like Jinx. Weinberg was everything the Irishman was not, cultured, highly educated, chilly and aloof. He was also South African, which damned him even further. Anathema to Ambrose and that was that. Born with the traditional silver spoon in his mouth, or so Ambrose liked to believe, Weinberg had thrown his weight around in a fairly insensitive manner till Ambrose, beginning to seethe inside, had built up a body of steam. The man might be smart but he wasn't creative and one of these days he was going to come unstuck.

What happened, of course, was now a matter of history. There had been a major punchup and Weinberg had come out on top. Overnight he had betrayed them all by ruthlessly pulling the plug on the department, and they would have been up shit creek with a vengeance had it not been for gallant little Jinx. It was one of the many reasons that Ambrose continued to adore her and why even the mention of their major foe still made him break out in hives.

Some of this he shared with Detective Chief Inspector Burton, who invited him round to Kensington police station for a chat before making a formal statement. Of all the people he had interviewed thus far, in Hal's opinion this man came top for integrity, loyalty and insight, in addition to being the dead woman's closest confidant, certainly on matters other than personal. Hal was impressed by Ambrose's unswerving honesty. He told things as he saw them, which was rare.

'So where would Mr Weinberg be now?' he asked.

'Home in New York I would imagine. That's where he mainly hangs out these days.' He paused, as if about to add more, then let it go. Hal noted the hesitation but made no attempt to force him. He was in no hurry. Sooner or later he would get to the bottom of everything. He asked questions about the project they were developing and Ambrose explained it briefly, omitting the technical details. They had come a very long way since they first set up the design group in creating complex software for the masses. It was a far cry from publishing, as he was the first to concede, but in many ways more fascinating and intellectually challenging.

'A book is a book is a book,' he explained. Whereas what they were doing these days had virtually no limits. He had swapped straightforward design work in order to create the most advanced computer games. Their current project, the code-named DBI-2000, was strides ahead of all its competitors, making even *Doom II* look as infantile as *Snakes and Ladders*. They were still on the lookout for a really snappy title, something to draw in the punters in droves. Ambrose's pride in his work was apparent from the shine in his eyes as he talked. Apart from the one big drawback.

Weinberg was ever the bugbear, constantly in their way. He

had a kind of genius for popping up and upsetting them. And it wasn't as off the wall as it might seem to add his name to the list of possible suspects. He'd been on Jinx's case since their paths first crossed. For reasons of his own, he couldn't abide her.

'And when would that have been? When they first met?'

Ambrose did a swift calculation. Round about 1985. Good grief, half a lifetime ago. It remained quite clear in his memory, that fateful January when they'd still all been so happy and Julius Weinberg had first entered their lives.

'And why exactly do you think he might be involved?' Hal leaned back in his swivel chair, lightly tapping a pencil against his teeth.

'The man's corrupt, it's as simple as that. Greedy and ruthless, out for no one but himself.' He thought of Max Weinberg and what had happened in the end, the thirty pieces of silver tawdrily earned.

Hal and Trudy exchanged a rapid glance. The rage was visibly welling up again; this docile man was apparently balanced on a very fine edge indeed.

'How far do you think he'd go to get what he wanted?'

There was no prevarication, Ambrose was definite. 'All the way.'

'Even murder? Is that what you're suggesting?'

'I don't see why not He's never stopped at anything in the past. In my humble opinion, the man's a certifiable sociopath. Who always had it in for poor old Jinx.'

'Why do you suppose that might have been?'

'Jealousy and envy. She was close to his uncle. He feared she might stand in his way.'

'And did she?'

'She tried.' But Weinberg had proved too strong. Yet Jinx had been the victor in the end; it was that he could never forgive. Like all true cowards, he had to be the oppressor. Her courage had driven him wild. Trudy asked for a contact number in the States, and Ambrose hesitated before scribbling it down.

'The thing is,' he explained with sudden caution, 'I'm not sure we want him knowing about it yet. Jinx and all that,' he added awkwardly. From his earlier unfortunate experiences with Weinberg, he had learned to fear the man. Could not be certain even now that he wouldn't find some devious way of using her death against them. Snatch away their ambitious project, into which he had already sunk so much finance, and disband the team just weeks away from its completion. He had, after all, done it once before without giving any of them a thought.

'I'm afraid, sir, we have no control over that,' said Hal brusquely. The investigation had to take its course, as fast as possible before the trail went cold. The atmosphere needed lightening, so Hal moved swiftly on. 'Tell us about your work-mates,' he said.

He had already cross-examined each one of them, but would appreciate hearing the overview of this obviously shrewd, perceptive man. The raw anguish in Ambrose's face eased a little and they saw the tension of his jaw relax. They were a great crew, Ambrose acknowledged, smiling, and he was inordinately fond of each one of them. Dottie, of course, was solid gold and managed to keep her tabs on them all. Married to the doughty Sam, who was practically an honorary member of the team and had once been their tutor, back in the LCP days.

'He was very close to Jinx for a while,' said Ambrose, regretting it when he saw Trudy scribble it down.

'Oh?' said Hal in his tell-us-more voice, swinging his chair round to face him.

'Yes,' said Ambrose, momentarily nonplussed. 'He was sweet on her for a while.' He looked at Hal defiantly. 'Everyone knew about it, it was all out in the open. He wasn't married to Dottie at the time.'

'So what happened?'

'Sam made a bit of an ass of himself. Walked out on his wife and kids to move in with Jinx.' It had been a disaster. He could still remember the electric atmosphere at college with everyone whispering and taking sides. Dottie had been there too, in the wings, poor faithful adoring Dottie.

'But they didn't stick?'

Ambrose shook his head. Togetherness had never been Jinx's forte.

'She bolted,' he said. 'She was always a bit like that. On to the next one with never a backward glance.'

He minds, thought Hal, surprised and a little disappointed. So his golden girl had had clay feet after all. He had built up an image of some kind of paragon, the girl next door with the looks of an angel and a heart of purest gold.

'And Sam?'

'He never did return to the wife and family. His heart was broken so he mooched around for a while, drinking too much and developing bad habits, then fell on hard times and eventually landed up with Dottie,' – again, with the connivance of Jinx – 'who had always had a big crush on him but was far too timorous to show it.'

Again Ambrose smiled, reflectively, as if he understood. Poor Dottie, what a saint she was. And how she must have suffered through those dreadful months. It had meant the end of Sam's teaching career but she had valiantly supported him and helped him struggle through. Worked now all hours to supplement his earnings as a freelance illustrator of children's books.

'So Sam, too, has a reason to hold a grudge against Jinx?' The list was growing longer with each interview.

Ambrose considered, then firmly shook his head. 'No, never Sam. Far too big-hearted. Forgave her long ago and remained a good friend.'

Hal made a note then sat there thinking. Sam might harbour no resentment but how about his protective wife? It couldn't be easy to play second fiddle, especially to the person who was now her boss. Even a saint must occasionally feel resentment, but Ambrose was adamant in his denial. Dottie was an angel, pure and simple. She had never had a mean thought in her life. Especially not about her beloved Jinx. The two of them had remained the closest of friends.

'She's the glue that holds the team together. We'd none of us have made it without Dottie.'

'So now let's move on to Serafina Rossetti.' The cool exotic chick with the ruthless gleam in her eye.

Ambrose chuckled, at last relaxing. 'Serafina is, as the Americans say, a piece of work. Ambitious, calculating, out for all she can grab. Talented, too, in a limited way though not nearly as much as she'd like to think. Her vision is blinkered, she does not have an original brain.' He looked at Hal a little uncomfortably, embarrassed by his own forthrightness. It wasn't his habit to speak out quite so harshly. The policeman was leading him up avenues he'd sooner not tread.

'I don't want you to get me wrong,' he added hastily. 'She's a sweet kid at times as well as dead efficient. Give her a problem to solve and she'll get it done. Just needs the occasional slap in an office environment or else she gets up too many noses, which can prove very disruptive.'

Hal laughed. 'She fancies herself a bit of a femme fatale,' he said. She had clearly viewed him as a tasty bit of rough and, in other circumstances, he might well have gone along with it. He certainly wouldn't kick her out of bed. But she looked too nervy and unhinged to be taken seriously; these thin, neurotic women were usually trouble in the end. Apart from which, of course, he was on a case. Which wasn't, at present, developing as fast as he'd like.

'How was she with Jinx?' he asked.

'Adored and respected her like a big sister. We all did. You have to understand, Jinx gave us all she'd got and more. Leader, muse, wet nurse, earth mother . . . you name it. She had energy and guts and encouraged us all to aim high. And Serafina was the one who responded most.'

Yes, she had bouts of discontent when she felt herself slighted or unnecessarily held back. Sometimes she grizzled to Dottie or Ambrose, and each time they delicately attempted to defuse her. Before she could do herself harm. No point in trying to run before you can walk.

'It's mainly insecurity,' Dottie had always maintained, though Ambrose wasn't entirely convinced. The thing about Dottie was her ability to see the best in people. She had the sunniest, most docile of natures.

Hal moved on down the list. 'And Wayne Peacock?'

Again Ambrose laughed. 'Vain Wayne', his pet name for him. He had a particularly soft spot for the lad, both brotherly and protective.

'Wayne has more talent in just his little finger than the rest of us put together,' he said. 'And I mean that quite sincerely. Including, I might add, the eminent Mr Rudge. Though there's no way, of course, that *he'd* ever see it like that.' Even if anyone had the gall to suggest it. 'I'm teaching Wayne chess and he's coming on like a natural. I've never seen anything like it, a proper little Bobby Fischer in the making. And all in just a matter of months.'

'How long has he been with you, Wayne?'

'About a couple of years. Came to us for work experience while still a student at the Slade, and clever old Jinx saw his potential and snapped him up. Before he had even completed his course. He's a really sweet guy behind the brash exterior. If only he'd grow up a bit and stop all this clowning around.'

'How did he feel about Jinx?'

'Total gratitude. He was her slave. He's smart enough to recognise the break she gave him, notwithstanding any raw talent he might also possess. There's nothing he wouldn't have done for her, nothing at all.'

Ambrose fell silent and the renewed pain in his eyes showed

how much he empathised with the younger man. Time to end the interview; Hal knew when he was ahead. He had got far more than he'd hoped for as it was.

'And what was it you were doing over the Easter weekend?' he asked casually.

'I was up in Birmingham most of the time, at a computer software convention.' Ambrose's passion for computer games had long been a joke among his friends. Of course, Hal remembered that now, it was in their notes along with the drinking. And now, as it turned out, the chess. Typical pursuits of a fairly solitary bachelor.

Serafina sat in a corner booth of a famed Fulham restaurant, sipping chilled Chardonnay and picking listlessly at her salad. Since the news of the murder she had barely been able to eat a thing she was so keyed up, and the hand her companion was so fondly caressing was limp and nerveless and seemingly translucent.

'Is there something wrong? You're so subdued.' His voice was urgent with concern, his expression suitably adoring. He was new on the scene, she'd only recently picked him up, but already his interest was so obvious it was threatening to stifle her. These upper-crust public schoolboys with their strangled vowels and clumsiness between the sheets. But he still had a definite purpose to serve, so she'd just have to tolerate him till her mission was fulfilled. If only he would stop the puppydog pawing. She sharply disentangled her hand.

The radiance of her smile, as she raised her eyes to his, reduced his heart to instant rubble. 'I was thinking about Jinx,' she said, just the hint of a tremor in her voice, then ducked her head briefly to dab at her eyes. Contrition gripped his throat.

'Gosh, I'm sorry. I'd totally forgotten. How stupidly selfish of me.' After such a trauma he was lucky she'd shown up at all. Him with his big mouth, always getting it wrong. His ma had tried to teach him social finesse but so far to no avail. He waved ineffectually towards the waiter, trying hard to engage his eye. But as usual, he seemed to be invisible.

'If you'd like to talk about it . . .' He stumbled then stopped. Jolly embarrassing, these things. Serafina smiled rainbow-like through the mist in her glorious eyes, and her dark silken hair swung forward to frame her face. Merle Oberon, he was thinking with awe, with that high, smooth forehead and to-die-for bone structure. She was wasted in sordid commerce, he longed to snatch her away. Her destiny surely lay somewhere a lot more exalted. He was a lucky bloke to have run into her at all and still couldn't quite believe his luck. Though still fairly junior at IEP, his prospects looked promising and there was always the title. A girl like this deserved only the very best and he'd do what he could to provide it. If she'd only allow it.

'It sounds as though she was something quite special,' he ventured after a pause. Jinx McLennan, whom he'd known only slightly, was famed in the business for her originality and flair. It was a piece of amazing luck that their paths had crossed at all, and now this beguiling creature had him hooked. Wait till he took her home to meet the parents. He might stand more of a chance when she saw where he lived.

'She was like a big sister,' said Serafina with a wobble in her voice. 'Warm and giving and never too busy to listen.' She raised one imperious hand and the waiter was there like a shot, fussing around her, filling her glass. Offering warm rolls in a basket.

'So you're all going to miss her.'

'You can't imagine how much. I truthfully can't envisage life without her. And what's going to happen to the business now she's gone?' She was stricken.

He stroked her hand, at an absolute loss for words. She was being so brave yet he feared she still might crack. But she surely needn't be worrying about her future. A beauty like her had the world at her feet, though he was working up the courage to pre-empt. He might try asking her to the Red Cross Ball once the horrors of this murder had receded.

'She must have left a will,' he said. 'A canny person like that.'

'Not necessarily. She was single and untrammelled and, well, young.' Not nearly as young as Serafina herself but there was no need to point that out.

'But first and foremost a businesswoman. She has to have given it some thought.' Jinx's business brain was legendary within IEP. They'd be properly in the soup if she'd failed to line up her successor.

'I am sure you're right. I'm just not thinking clearly,' said Serafina, batting those incredible lashes which made him want to ravish her on the spot. If only he had the courage. 'It's just that it's all been so horribly upsetting. I can't think about anything till they've caught the monster who did it.'

So bang goes tonight, he thought resignedly. She was clearly not in the mood, but he could wait.

In the end, Hal decided there was no real need to involve Julius Weinberg just yet. A swift check with Immigration confirmed all he needed to know – that the man had not been in England at the actual time of the murder. Though he had, it transpired, been in and out on a flying visit just the week before, which was interesting.

9

'Go on, have a stab at it. Based on what we know so far, who would be your prime candidate for our murderer? I promise not to hold you to it.'

Hal and Trudy, despite the coolish weather, were settled with their beers in the stone-paved garden of The Devonshire Arms. It was early Thursday evening and the home-bound travellers were starting to straggle in. For this stage of the investigation, both had gone under cover, and Hal was surprised and not a little impressed by how well Trudy shaped up out of uniform. She was dressed deliberately casually in a sweatshirt and skin-tight jeans, which fitted her better than he ever would have suspected. Also her hair was an unexpected surprise. Let loose from the prim coil that normally nestled beneath her cap, it cascaded almost to her shoulders in a riot of curls which did much to soften her solemn little face. He felt quite proud to be seen with her, though not quite enough to let it show. This, after all, was a strictly work situation.

'Well?'

She sipped her beer and he watched her thinking. No prizes for guessing who'd come first if she had her way.

'Professor Harker.'

'You wish.' Harker had come up with the best alibi of them all, live on national television from a distance of two hundred miles. Unless he had an identical twin, there was not a lot they could pin on him. Unfortunately.

'Guess again.' Despite the chill, sitting out here was pleasant and gave them a view of the cottages behind. At just this spot the murderer might have waited, studying the layout and figuring out ways to break in. Hal glanced around. Just a handful of raucous Hooray Henries with a couple of insipid girls; Kensington was packed with them, one of the things he disliked.

'Not Ambrose, not Wayne, not Dottie. Should we talk to her husband, Sam?' His name was already on Hal's secret hit-list but he shook his head. That would wait.

'They were away for the whole of Easter visiting her mother. It's only her word against his at this stage but no doubt the mother can confirm it.'

'Serafina?'

Hal nodded thoughtfully. She was on the right trail, bright girl. He flicked through his notes. 'Serafina was holed up with a boyfriend. He has not yet come forward but we'll get to him in time. She seemed fairly cagey about their actual movements but that probably just means they were at it all weekend.'

Trudy inwardly winced; at times he could be so crude. Though she was tickled to death to be sitting here with him right now, relaxed and joking as if on a real date. He was wearing jeans and a black leather jacket and looking every inch the off-duty cop. She wasn't going to spoil it for him though. A girl at a nearby table kept shooting him covetous glances.

'Motivation?'

'Envy.' Trudy had no doubts about that. She hadn't taken to the glacial Serafina and not just because of her stupendous looks.

There was something withdrawn and calculating about her; the fact she had cut Trudy completely hadn't helped. 'I just didn't trust her. I'm not quite sure why.'

Hal grinned. They were all much the same, these women. Jealous as cats when it came to a passable male. Trudy caught the grin and was immediately incandescent. How *dare* he be so cocky, assuming all sorts of things.

'Well, supposing you're right, how do you think she did it? She looks pretty fragile to be battering someone to death.' Not to mention the rape. And those other vile atrocities. Trudy shuddered. No woman could possibly even think of behaving like that, not to any human being, let alone another female. Yet the fact remained that somebody had.

'The boyfriend,' she said firmly. The one they hadn't yet met. If he was as taken with Serafina as the DCI appeared to be, there was just no saying what he might be induced to do if the prize at the end was Miss Snotty Nose herself.

'Could be.' But Hal wasn't convinced. The fact that Serafina was beautiful and bright did not automatically make her a bad person. Possibly her chilliness concealed a warm and generous heart; for a second he thought wistfully of another opportunity lost.

'What about Arthur Dawes?' he said. 'The old cove from next door? Now, he had both access and proximity.'

'But what motive?'

'Lust,' said Hal promptly. 'Did you take a peek at his wife? Probably been panting for it for years.'

'If she'd only take her eye off him for a second.' They both cackled.

They weren't getting anywhere, that was the sobering truth. All those interviews and careful notes, yet no one obvious was staring them in the face. And the longer they left it, the harder it would get. What the murder squad called a 'sticker'.

'Maybe it really was just a random break-in. A burglary gone wrong.'

'Maybe. Only, in that case, why wasn't anything touched? No damage, no emptied drawers, nothing taken. Not as far as we can tell without corroboration.' Which, in view of the victim's single status, they were unlikely ever to get.

'So what do you think triggered it?'

'The open patio door.'

'Maybe.' And how come a woman as clued up as she was, a city dweller living in a high crime area, could have been so careless as not to lock up properly? It was warm that night, but this was ridiculous. That was not how he'd have expected Jinx to behave; canny and street smart, so everyone said. He was growing morose and there were things he had to do back at the station.

'Drink up,' he said abruptly as he counted out his change, and Trudy registered, with a sharp jolt of disappointment, that their subterfuge date was at an end.

'There's someone waiting to see you, sir.'

Hal sighed wearily and raised one cynical eyebrow. Just what he needed after a gruelling day's work, but the desk sergeant indicated it had something to do with the murder inquiry, so Hal instructed him to wheel the visitor in. A strange-looking woman in a maroon raincoat came warbling into the interview room with a cheery greeting. She was loaded down with Marks & Spencer bags and told him, without being asked, that she'd been late-night shopping and was on her way home.

'And since I live just round the corner,' she explained, 'this seemed as good a time as any to pop in and see you.'

She had a large, protruding nose and virtually no chin, with a shock of stiff white hair in an old-fashioned Raine Spencer sixties' bouffant. She resembled a cockatoo, Hal thought idly, down to the garish powder-blue circles around her eyes. He placed her in her early fifties, though there was something timeless and unreal about her. He asked her name.

'Myrtle Hobday,' she said, settling down comfortably as if for a social call and piling her shopping on an adjacent chair.

'And you knew Jinx McLennan?'

Myrtle's doll-like eyes grew wide and she lowered her voice to a whisper.

'She was my dearest friend.'

Hal was surprised. He flicked back through his copious notes. No mention of her anywhere here; how could they possibly have overlooked her?

'So how exactly do you fit into her life?' Veronica Phillips had claimed that role; she had certainly not mentioned this odd woman's name. Nor had any of the others they had interviewed.

'Oh, we've known each other for yonks,' said Myrtle cosily, not at all as if she had recently suffered such a shattering bereavement. 'Former colleagues, neighbours, friends. Jinx was as close to me as family.'

'So it must have come as a terrible shock?'

'Indeed.' The smile faded briefly; she composed her irregular features. She had, he noticed, in addition to her other defects, large, unfortunately protruding teeth. What a shame; these days any parent would, as a matter of course, have had them fixed at an early age. But she was obviously a good-hearted soul; for what other reason would she be here? He looked at her inquiringly.

'The thing is,' said Myrtle, leaning forward conspiratorially, 'I wonder what's happening to all her things?'

He stared at her in disbelief. Dead five days and already the vultures were circling. The eyes, now he concentrated, were pale, unblinking and icy cold. He had made the not uncommon mistake, it appeared, of assuming a plain woman to be blessed with a generous heart.

'There was one particular picture she always said she would leave me. It hangs in her bedroom and would look lovely in my flat.' Impervious to his sudden coolness, the woman prattled on and the smile returned, obscenely coquettish now. She had lipstick smeared on her teeth. 'By a great stroke of fortune, it goes with my sitting-room curtains. We always had a laugh about that. "It's obviously got your name on it, Myrtle," she used to say. "I'll have to remember to leave it to you in my will."'

Yet Jinx McLennan must have been a good ten years younger than Myrtle Hobday. And now he realised she was trying to flirt with him. She shifted in her chair and crossed her legs in a sad caricature of seductiveness. Beneath the old-fashioned mac, she was wearing a voluminous dress, in lavender-sprigged cotton with a lace-trimmed pie-crust neck. She was ludicrous. He was about to ask her if she had anything to contribute to their investigation when she dumbfounded him even further by asking for access to the cottage.

'I know Jinx wouldn't mind,' she said. 'I was in and out of there all the time. We lived practically in each other's pockets.'

No chance, he told her curtly, closing his file. The property remained very much out of bounds. The forensic team were still active there and the plastic tent they had erected firmly in place.

'Where were you over Easter?' he asked cruelly, aching to knock the complaisant smirk from her face. Oddballs were constantly popping up at crime scenes, confessing to all sorts to which they had no real connection. Any minute now he expected her to oblige. But Myrtle fluttered her eyelids demurely and told him she'd been in the country. With dear friends.

'Well, keep me posted,' she had the nerve to add, as she rose like a purposeful hen and gathered together her shopping. 'We wouldn't want that painting to fall into the wrong hands. You know what people are like these days, out for whatever they can get.'

Gobsmacked into silence, Hal showed her out. But once she had gone he allowed himself a smile. In a slightly macabre way, she had lightened his feeling of doom. This murder had got beneath his defences. And he hadn't even known the dead woman.

*　　*　　*

'Oh Lord,' said Dottie, when he checked out his visitor. 'Myrtle Hobday is nothing but a pathetic hanger-on. Worked here fleetingly about thirteen years ago and Jinx has never since been able to shake her off. Not, mind you, that she ever really tried. Far too good-natured for her own good.' Dottie recalled the countless occasions when the awful Myrtle had just turned up. At parties, at dinners, even office occasions. She seemed to have radar that led her unerringly to any free meal.

'She even had the nerve to keep inviting Jinx out for lunch then lumbering her with the bill. She would pick the restaurant – she has very specific tastes – then coolly make the reservation in Jinx's name. Can you believe that? We were always urging Jinx to tell her to get lost but she wouldn't do it. "She's lonely," was all she'd say, and leave it at that.'

Dottie looked sad. Remembering Jinx and her daft little ways brought her grief flooding back in a great torrent. Waifs and strays had always been irresistible to Jinx; bag ladies, beggars, you name it. They clustered around her like flies and she never so much as attempted to shake them off. Her attitude was that she'd been lucky herself and could therefore afford to extend a helping hand to others less fortunate around her.

'Myrtle has a good heart,' she was always saying, though Dottie wasn't at all sure that that was true. Still, she would even put up with the grotesque Myrtle Hobday if only the clock could be magically reversed and Jinx restored to them, safe and well. Alive.

And then they had what might be a minor breakthrough: the hairdresser came forward of his own accord. She had missed her regular appointment so he phoned the office and was baldly told the horrific truth. Tony was aghast and more than willing to co-operate with the police. They visited him at his Church Street salon and he answered their questions amid a clutter of brushes and bottles.

'She'd been coming here for years,' he told them. 'Every four weeks for a trim and touch up. Lovely lady, one of the best. Murdered, you say, how dreadful.'

He had seen her, it so happened, on the previous Thursday, for an unscheduled appointment. She'd been full of excitement, simply glowing with happiness. Wanted a last-minute trim and blow dry; the roots, they'd decided, would keep till next time.

'Going somewhere nice?' he'd asked and she'd told him yes but that she hadn't got very much time.

'Bless you,' she'd said when he had her in and out in forty minutes. 'Have a good Easter and I'll tell you all about it next week.'

He was dark and good-looking with that smooth androgynous charm that often goes with the job. Italian roots, maybe, with that warm seductive smile. Hal asked if he'd seen her socially but he demurred. Great friends, yes, always dishing together. And occasionally he went to her house when she had a crisis.

So he knew quite a lot about her lifestyle? A fair bit, agreed Tony, after all these years. Boyfriends? asked Hal but there the hairdresser went quiet. There were certain secrets between stylist and client . . .

'Do you think he's covering?' asked Trudy later.

'Could be,' said Hal, putting Tony's name on his list.

Soon something would have to be done about formal identification of the brutalised body, which still lay, in chilled solitude, on a slab in the police morgue. Cousin Marjorie was fretting about a funeral, and keen to announce the death in the *Telegraph*. Not that that was strictly necessary; the press had done their bit, though in minor key, due to certain restrictions imposed on them by the police. Hal had been hoping to identify the murderer before too much hysteria focused on the crime. Now he was having to revise his thoughts.

'Perhaps a funeral is not such a bad idea,' he mused. They

appeared to be getting nowhere. Nothing of any apparent significance had emerged from their doorstep questioning, and the trail appeared already to have gone cold. Some sort of an announcement might flush out more jokers but also, with luck, some real leads. In a life that busy there were bound to be loads of people they'd missed entirely, even people who'd known the dead woman well. For instance, they still had no idea at all who the smart-suited stranger might have been.

'It's very often a person really close to the victim. In all probability someone she liked and trusted.'

'Like the hairdresser?'

'Maybe. Or even a close neighbour.'

Hal found himself growing disproportionately involved, with a keener interest than was quite appropriate in a routine murder inquiry. The more he learned about the victim, the more he regretted not having known her in life. Her photographs showed a vibrant, ebullient woman, bouncing with vitality in the absolute prime of her life. The sort of woman he was pretty sure he'd have got on with.

It was Friday already; another weekend. He'd allow his team the space of two more days then throw open the publicity floodgates first thing on Monday. Time to come out into the open and see what the world could contribute. Time to arrange a much-publicised funeral and keep a careful vigil to see who turned up. Of one thing he was grimly determined; he'd nail that bastard if it was the last thing he ever did. The spectre of Jinx McLennan was really beginning to get to him.

10

D amien Rudge sat slumped in his plushy duplex in a state of near catatonic terror. What had just occurred was more dreadful by far than anything even he might have imagined, and he was still very much in shock. He had known all his life that he had to be careful, to watch where he was going and always keep on the alert. From the moment his smouldering talent began to blaze the hostile forces were out there watching him, and now he feared that they might gain access to his brain. These days he trusted nobody at all and that included his wife. Even his island studio was no longer secure. Alien eyes had been scanning his work, probably taking photographs. Despite all denials, it was something that he knew. Could tell by just looking at a piece of his artwork if other eyes had been there too. And now there could be no doubt, he had the evidence. He had tried defending himself by getting rid of the household retainers, but those wily Americans had devices of their own that could infiltrate no matter how strong the security. He sank his head in his hands and groaned. How he was going to manage in the future, he really didn't know.

Damien had always been a man of strong appetites, though found it very hard to relate to women. His gangling frame and myopic blink had proved unenticing to the girls he had grown up with. He had endured a miserable adolescence as an envious spectator on the sidelines of his youth. Until he'd met Jinx in his first year of college and she'd worked her magic on him. With her easy good humour and relaxed sexuality, she had recognised his talent and accepted him as he was. For that he had remained grateful though never able to express it. He had left all the social niceties to his wife.

Jinx had had the vision, Damien the talent. Together they had made an unstoppable pair. But now that was all ended, Jinx was dead. The magic might well be all spent. More than anything, he dreaded, with a chill of foreboding, having to go it alone in the future, unable to mask his inadequacies from the eyes of the world. Suppose he wasn't able to manage on his own, suppose, after all the spying, they found him out. Saw that the dazzling creativity had only been partially his, that Jinx had provided the underpinnings and let him take all of the credit. With no one now to protect him, to stand between him and his tormentors, they would easily break through his delicate defences and plunder the secrets in his head. He would have to be extra vigilant, they must be stopped. He could not allow his enemies to win.

At another table in a different part of town someone else was having similarly maudlin thoughts. Sam Sullivan sat at his drawing-board in their Muswell Hill dining-room, gazing across the garden into space. It was raining hard. He watched the heavy drops crash through leaves of laburnum and beech to flatten the irises and forget-me-nots beneath. Raining in my heart; an apposite title. Sam, if the truth be told, was well acquainted with mourning Jinx, had never stopped regretting her since that ill-judged early affair. Not that Dottie was aware of it, or at least he hoped she was not. What had happened twenty years ago was rarely mentioned between them now, at least not the most searing part.

He could see her now as vividly as then, bright and cocky with that beguiling gap-toothed smile, hair cut spikily like a raggedy doll's and streaked with a lurid pink. Jinx McLennan, one of his brightest students, twenty years old and going places fast.

'Hi!' she'd said, that first morning he'd really clocked her, looking up perkily like a bright-eyed little chipmunk as he stumbled in blearily and only partly awake. Tamsin had been the trouble at the time, cutting her first teeth and keeping them awake night after night. The journey in from Burgess Hill was grim enough but, hell, when he glanced at his watch it was still not quite nine. Whatever was this kid doing here so early? Students traditionally straggled in late, reluctant to leave their beds till the very last moment. Such beaverlike enthusiasm was, to his mind, an anomaly. Except among swats and other sycophantic smarmies, which a single glance told him she was not. She smiled when he shuffled round to see what she was at, standing aside from her easel obligingly so he could take a proper look.

Not bad at all, he was powerfully impressed. Brilliant neon colours shot off in all directions with an energy and vivacity that mirrored the spark in her eyes. A rough design for a stage backdrop, she'd explained when he raised an inquiring eyebrow. For the revue they were rehearsing for the end-of-year festivities. In which, of course, she was starring and also contributing sketches. Edinburgh next, she told him confidently, unabashed in her naïve self-belief. At that very first encounter his heart had quite gone out to her. From the battalions of drone-like student clones who were usually his dull lot, this girl's talent and originality marked her out as a star.

From then on he'd seen as much of her as was seemly, sucked willy nilly into the whirl of her life as forcefully as into a jet-stream. It wasn't so much that he found her seductive, her ease with her natural sexiness was unfeigned. Jinx appeared quite unconscious of the effect she had as she cut a swathe through her college course, strewing the corpses of suitors in her wake. Her eye was fixed entirely on the main chance and the glittering prizes that beckoned. She loved the work and threw herself into it with gusto while also managing to have a great social life. A model student whom no one appeared to resent. She was universally popular with both sexes, voted by her peers the girl most likely to succeed. And Sam, enchanted, fell instantly under her spell, approving and openly proud of his protégée's rapid rise.

All that changed dramatically when Holly developed measles, and Janet's life became a nightmare with the pressures of three under-fives. Life at home declined rapidly into something of a war zone and Sam sought solace within the college, most particularly with his darling girl. In those days he was younger and a great deal less obese and she was impressed by his knowledge and calm authority. The boys she mixed with were gauche and raw-edged. To have caught the attention of a lecturer of forty was flattering plus a feather in her cap.

They took the revue to the Brighton Festival and Sam went along in the role of minder. He had told his wife he might stay away all weekend, and ended up sharing a hotel bed with Jinx, who was beguilingly *comme ci, comme ça* about such things. Already, at twenty, she had had several lovers, while Sam, a traditionalist, was comparatively inexperienced. And it blew his mind. The actuality of realising a dream, of holding this wonderful girl in his arms all night, proved more than his sanity could stand. In a rush of emotion he ought to have been mature enough to suppress, he raced off home to his over-wrought wife and spewed up all his feelings on the spot. At which, understandably, she lost it entirely and ended up throwing him out. *Finito.* Three squalling babies was the most she was prepared to take.

Sam winced now as he remembered all the damage, the pain he had wrought upon his family. Simon and Holly were five and three and Tamsin barely crawling when he'd taken off into the night.

Jinx was sharing with others in the King's Road, so he'd rented a Bayswater basement he could barely afford and they'd lived out his idyll for two heady months before the tug of fatherhood had begun to make him ill, and Jinx had realised that she'd never loved him anyway, not in the measure that was required. To her it was nothing more than another youthful caper, to Sam the greatest passion of his life.

'Go home now,' she had advised him gently as he clung to her in his agony. 'Let Janet see how much you actually care and perhaps you will find that she'll forgive you.' The year was advancing, there were other excitements beckoning. She was hoping to break into publishing, had her job experience all fixed. The affair had been fun but he was twice her age; she was far too canny to tie herself down at this stage. There were plenty more pebbles on the beach when she was ready. Which was unlikely to be for quite a while.

'Marry me!' Sam had begged her in desperation, but nothing could have been further from her mind. Not at that stage, verging on twenty-one with excellent grades and the whole of her life still before her. Sam had looked into those bright, brown eyes and known that he'd lost her.

Now, twenty years later, he was facing going through it all again. He wiped his eyes with the back of his paint-smeared hand and lumbered over to the fridge for a beer.

The rain was still sluicing down when the time came for Dottie to go home. April showers, she reflected as she shrugged herself into her old mac, though unusually heavy for this time of year. It was almost ten, they'd been working right through, and now Ambrose thought they should call it a day. Wayne had zipped off on his fancy skates hours ago while Serafina was out somewhere on a date.

'Don't bother waiting,' said Ambrose, 'I'll close up.'

'You're sure about that, ducky? I don't mind hanging on a little longer. Sam won't mind.' There was that match he'd missed that he'd be deep into by now. If he felt a bit peckish he could always raid the fridge.

'No, you go on. We've done quite enough for tonight.' Try as he might, Ambrose couldn't help worrying and the deadline was horribly close.

'Do me a favour, then,' said Dottie, poised by the door. 'Give him a ring, would you, and tell him I'm on my way.' It was far too late for that leisurely bus-ride. Much though she hated it, she would have to brave the tube. Clutching her collar to keep out the rain, she tottered along the slippery cobbles of the mews and cut across Allen Street on her way to the Earl's Court Road. She would have to negotiate that narrow passage which was usually full of drunks and layabouts. Still, safety in numbers she supposed was the thing. Not late enough yet to be getting really scary. There was a row of small ethnic restaurants, teeming with life, and she waited at the crossing till the road was clear. This part of London was the bit she most disliked, only a stone's throw from the office but astonishing in its sharp contrast. The difference between the postcodes SW5 and W8 was vast, as the property pages were constantly pointing out. She scuttled through the driving rain and into the welcome shelter of the station.

As luck would have it, the lifts were out of service, definitely not her night at all. A bit of rain and everything ground to a halt. The whole of the London underground seemed to be breaking down, with endless holdups and escalator repairs which turned each journey into total misery. Stalwartly Dottie stuck her ticket in her bag and ventured timidly down that dreadful staircase. It was steep and narrow and made of iron on which her heels clattered and echoed. She was always reminded of the film of *The Third Man* with Orson Welles racing through the sewers. She shuddered and tried to speed up a little, which wasn't easy on this spiral staircase; she was obliged to hold on tightly and step cautiously for fear of falling and breaking her neck.

And now someone seemed to be right on her heels. Muffled footsteps, perhaps with rubber soles, were matching her own beat by beat and when she halted, hoping that they might pass, eerily they stopped too. Was it just an echo? She glanced behind her but could see no one coming since the bend was so sharp and so narrow. She soldiered on, moving a little faster, and the other footsteps picked up speed just as she had feared they might. She heard the rattle of a train below and willed herself forward, determined to catch it. The carriages would be bright and warm, no danger there at this time of night. She hated the tube, found it seriously spooky, but her husband was waiting and she must get home. It was one of the problems of living so far out, though it meant they had a garden and cleaner air.

She couldn't help thinking of Jinx's murder and the faceless stranger who had so savagely carved her up. The world got more dangerous by the day. She'd be happier staying at home but they needed the money. Her pursuer was drawing closer and now a huge dark shadow loomed in front of her on the wall, of a person tall and threateningly built with some sort of headgear pulled down low over his ears. She couldn't help glancing back again but he was still just out of sight, though gaining rapidly from the sound of his urgent feet. With a supreme last effort and almost missing her step, Dottie arrived at the bottom and shot forward on to the platform. Just as the doors closed and the train began to pull out.

There was nobody left on the platform, the exit was up the far end. Too scared now to look behind her, she walked rapidly ahead, praying that her pursuer was not a mugger or a rapist. You heard so many nasty stories these days, and look what had happened to poor Jinx. Almost crying now in a fit of sudden panic, Dottie plunged on in search of help. Her hair was heavy with the weight of the rain and shaking itself out of its pins. If she turned to confront him, he might still attack. She had nothing to steal but he couldn't know that. And then, as hysteria was turning her into a jelly, she heard the welcome rattle of another approaching train.

She was through the doors the second they opened, and for once went and sat near three men. Beneath their Rastafarian locks their eyes were warm and unthreatening. They'd look after her, she was sure of it, if her unseen assailant should strike. But once she was settled and dared to turn her head, she saw no one else had entered the carriage. And she still had that long walk up the hill to face. She would call Sam from the station but didn't want to disturb him.

He was slumped drowsily in front of the telly when she got in, beer can in hand, watching the re-run of the match. She dropped a kiss on his balding pate and he reached up fondly to caress her. He had loosened his belt by a couple of notches to allow his spreading paunch to sag out, but in Dottie's eyes he remained her hero, the centre of her universe all these years.

'All right?' he said vaguely, his eyes still glued to the game, and she shook herself dry and then dumped her mac in the porch. Her heart was still racing and there was a knot of fear in her throat, but she mustn't go alarming Sam or he'd make her give up the job. Though what it would be like without Jinx she couldn't envisage, too terrible even to contemplate yet.

'Won't be long, lovie,' she called from the kitchen as she turned on the gas for the oven to heat up. The cooker was ancient and they really needed a new one but Sam's going freelance had meant they'd had to cut back. Not that he wasn't doing well. Since Walker Books had signed up his nursery rhyme series, things in the Sullivan household were definitely on the up. Which was just as well since the kids were both headed towards college soon and they'd need all the finance they could raise. They owed it all to Jinx, who had been such a help. She watched him through the half-open door and wondered just how he was coping. These days he barely ever spoke her name but she knew that the hurt had gone deep.

'I love it when you let down your hair,' he said fondly as she loosened her mane. What she saw as an unruly mass made her, in his eyes, the Titian temptress who had first caught his eye. It was one of the things that had attracted him from the start, her voluptuous and quite unconscious beauty.

'Come and get it!' she called gaily as she untied her apron and piled a mound of greens and potatoes on to his well-warmed plate. Whatever he might think, she would always remain grateful to Sam for marrying her in the first place.

11

From that moment on our paths crossed often. I made it my business to know where she was and kept a beady eye on all her movements. And she always seemed delighted whenever I showed up. As if she were already sharing my dream.

'Hi!' she'd call out in that slightly affected way, and beckon me over to her side. Me the lapdog, well it actually didn't matter. We fitted together like a pair of clasped hands and I was happy to indulge her just for the hell of it. We had the same sense of humour, you see, were both avid people-watchers. I only had to catch her eye in a crowd and she'd smile and wink as if we were sharing a joke. She always knew I'd get it because we were on the same wavelength. How she put up with the rest of that dross, I never could understand.

It was cosy and intimate and made me feel good inside. Something I'd looked for all my life. Jinx was gregarious but I could put up with that. She was like a fallen angel from heaven, an angel with slightly grubby habits. In her way she was also a total innocent, which is one of the reasons I loved her. She just couldn't see, the stupid cow, the way her constant flirting was hotting up all the men. Flirting and preening like all the other bitches. Constantly on heat and making a show of herself.

She needed protecting from herself. She was lucky to have me to take control.

12

The police investigation appeared to be getting nowhere. A press conference had been called. Sharp at noon this coming Monday Hal would reveal to the public at large the current state of play, such as it was. He was cross and somewhat disheartened. None of their leads had amounted to anything and the trail had now definitely gone cold. Apart from the egg that would soon be all over his face, what principally concerned him was the fact that a maniac killer was still at large, liable to strike again. And since they had established no proven MO, it was hard for the police force to be effectively on their guard. The forensic team had packed their equipment and left, the plastic tent that had shielded the crime scene had been folded and taken away.

Peggy Dawes bobbed in and out like a weather woman, offering tea which was always politely refused. The officers on the scene had been brewing their own. Perhaps she would have more success with the press. She looked out her second best Royal Doulton and rinsed it off just in case. There were certain standards one had to maintain and she might yet get her picture in the papers. She paused before the mirror to fluff her hair. Was there time, she wondered, to fit in a perm before Monday? She had tried like anything to find out what was going on but answers to her questions had always been heavily censored. All in good time, the duty officer told her. But to get some peace he had leaked the time of the press conference. There couldn't, surely, be any harm in that. It might help to occupy the old duck's mind and with luck keep her off his back.

Arthur, too, was heartily sick of the whole damned shebang. Once the horror of the murder had ceased reverberating, his mind had wandered back to more mundane matters where it felt less uncomfortable. Peggy's eternal mithering was something he'd learned to live with but even she was starting to get on his nerves.

'Silence, woman!' he barked as he shook out the paper and turned it firmly to the stock-market reports. He was sad about his neighbour, whom he had genuinely admired, but it had been pretty nearly a week now and he'd had enough. He was tired of the endless speculation, the ghoulish elaboration of the few known facts. Perhaps, now the police presence was gone from the street, he would finally be allowed a little peace.

DCI Burton and his personable sidekick called one more time to go over the established facts. No, Arthur told them with gloomy resignation, neither he nor his lady wife had had any further enlightenment. Certainly nothing germane to this inquiry.

'No more details of her mysterious escort?' The well-dressed stranger with the excellent teeth.

Arthur shook his head. He personally had only the vaguest memory of the man. It was Peggy, as usual, with her infernal twitching proboscis, who had dredged him up in the first place, more's the pity.

'And what about the accent?' Hal was peering at his notes. 'Any further thoughts?'

All eyes turned to Peggy who thought hard then shook her

head. The stranger had scarcely spoken at all; her main impression had been one of suave good looks. Definitely not English, though, she'd stake her life on that. What she mainly recalled was the aura of happiness, the light of excitement in Jinx's eyes. A lovely young woman, dispatched to a premature grave. May they catch her destroyer before he could do it again. And lock him up for eternity, even hang him.

'Let's take a closer look at the hairdresser,' said Hal.

This time he produced his associate too, Pansy the colourist. She had bright fluorescent hair in two ridiculous little topknots, but a mind as gritty as her Stepney accent. Twenty-one and a goer, there were no flies on this young woman. She had been there already and seen it all. Even bought the T-shirt.

'She was everso nice,' was her immediate comment then she thought a bit and elaborated slightly. 'No side to her, know what I mean? Liked to have fun and was always good for a giggle. One of life's ravers was our Jinx. Though I don't mean that disrespectfully.'

Hal, taken aback, asked her to explain.

'Well, you know, darling, she was always one for the blokes. Didn't mind talking about it neither. Some people in her place behave like Lady Muck but Jinx was always one of us.'

There was that time, she expounded, when she'd really lost her rag, had spotted something in a glossy mag that had properly got up her nose.

'A while ago it was but she was beside herself with fury. Couldn't wait for Tony to finish the blow-dry, then stalked out of here without so much as a goodbye. Told me later she only been and picked up a bloke in a bar. And took him home with her just like that.' Pansy was clearly admiring; Jinx had been one of her ongoing heroines. But Hal was actually shocked, not sure if he wanted to hear more. Duty, however, prevailed; this could be a lead.

'Go on.'

'That's about it. Was full of it next time she came in, completely cheered her up it had.'

'That was one of the things about Jinx,' added Tony. 'Things rarely got her down for very long. A true free spirit, a marvellous girl. I can tell you one thing, we won't see the likes of her again.'

'And you've no idea who this guy might have been?'

'Search me,' said Pansy with an enigmatic shrug.

Hal and Trudy had taken to frequenting the pub. They dropped in haphazardly for the occasional snatched half-pint, to study the regulars and ask a few salient questions. The publican was affable, his bar staff eager to please. Yes, of course they were familiar with the dead woman. Living so near, she dropped in regularly, sometimes on a Saturday for an informal lunch with friends. Lovely she was, popular too, with that ready and radiant smile. It was shocking the atrocities that happened these days, even in a high-rent area like this.

The trees were still laden with blossom, there was a strong feeling of optimism in the air. Although full summer had yet to break through, shutters had been opened and windows flung wide. People whistled and shouted to each other in the street; residents in shirtsleeves were outside washing their cars. A few forlorn bunches of paper-wrapped flowers lay on the pavement across from the pink-washed cottage, already wilting in their sad little shrouds. The occupants of the exclusive cul-de-sac were shocked and horrified by what had occurred. It was a mini version of when the Princess died, a sea of trodden paper with the withering blooms inside. It was strange how people never thought to remove the wrappings. But it was a heartfelt gesture which showed that much of the world was still caring.

'I didn't imagine her picking up men.' Hal was still finding it hard to accept. This brought an altogether more sinister note to the inquiry. With behaviour like that, the possibilities became infinite. Trudy watched him steadily but didn't dare say a word. So his angel had flaws after all, she was pleased. As well as more empathetic. One of us, as the colourist had so rightly said. Though what in a magazine could possibly have caused her such grief?

With the forensic team departed, the house closed in on itself. Soon arrangements would have to be made for its future. First, though, Hal wanted to do some solitary wandering through its deserted rooms, getting as clear a fix as he could on what had occurred that night. He was a great believer in the power of the hunch, though he'd never admit that in a court of law. Or even to his sceptical WPC, who admired his results but not always his methods. Luckily he had a free weekend; time to explore and cogitate. There was one brand of psychopath they had not yet fully considered – the flamboyant type who enjoyed all the limelight and fuss and would not want the circus to go away. The type who, sooner or later, would slip up fatally by revisiting the scene of the crime.

The bedroom where the murder had occurred had been stripped to its bare essentials, the sheets carried off in a plastic sack for more detailed analysis in the lab. The walls, with their grim webbing of blood, were stomach-churning to look at, though had given forensics invaluable information about the sheer force of the attack. Hal mooched slowly around the pretty, feminine room, focusing on the watercolours and tasteful landscape over the bed. Which reminded him of the grotesquely greedy Myrtle Hobday; he wondered idly what she was all about. A hanger-on, Dottie had described her as, just one of many where Jinx was concerned. He marvelled at Jinx's capacity for compassion and wished yet again that he might have known her before she died.

The woman slowly emerging from the collage of random impressions had started off sounding too wholesome to be true. But a darker side was now appearing which he definitely needed

97

to explore. Perhaps there was a whole alternate life that her loved ones had never suspected. A person who could stomach an inflated ego like Harker's was certainly no Julie Andrews clone. Something in this complicated equation still didn't quite add up. And the deeper he dredged for the absolute truth, the more likely he was to unearth it.

The bedroom had a walk-in closet under the eaves, which revealed a neat row of colour co-ordinated clothes ranging in shade from purest white through beige to a couple of outfits in understated black. Plus a violet velvet trouser suit just screaming with attitude, zipped up separately in its own mothproof bag. An orderly person with a sharp sense of fashion. The shoes were all on trees and lined up with almost military precision. Her sweaters, each in its own clear polythene bag, were folded neatly on a shelf, while a cherrywood dresser held orderly piles of underwear, silky and seductive, luxurious to the touch.

On top of the dresser was a hinged wooden mirror, a large crystal atomiser and an old-fashioned jug and basin set. Hal distractedly picked up the atomiser and sprayed a blast of fragrance into the air. Armani's *Giò* – he recognised it immediately as the one worn by Trudy on the occasions they went undercover. A brass-trimmed mahogany casket turned out to hold jewellery, again neatly compartmentalised like the clothes. Brooches, neck-chains, separate compartments for earrings, tiny pearl and diamond studs, plain gold and silver hoops, all in the very best taste. Nothing here tawdry or lacking in style yet, strangely, it had not been disturbed. No rapacious fingers had dredged through this collection even though, to a casual burglar, it was the obvious place to start. So theft had not been the prime activator. The motive for this particular crime looked like being a lot nastier.

There were two more rooms on the upper floor, a bathroom and a second bedroom. The bathroom was plain, white walls and pine panelling, with mirrors and spider plants that gave it a jungly look. Hal opened the mirrored cabinet over the basin and checked through cosmetics and the usual female clutter. Vaseline, baby oil, cotton buds, tea-tree oil in a miniature size, aspirin, eye-drops, cuticle cream. He closed the door. Beside the basin, in a white ceramic rack, a toothmug held toothpaste and a single brush. Not surprising; Jinx McLennan lived alone. But the place was so orderly, something started to nag at the back of his mind. He opened the cabinet again.

No razor, no tampons, no condoms or contraceptive pills. From the statements he had taken, Jinx McLennan had not exactly been a saint, so how come her bathroom cabinet contained no intimacies at all? Hal stooped to the cupboard directly below the basin but all it revealed was disinfectant and cleaning materials. A wicker laundry basket stood just inside the door. He opened it – a single towel and a pair of tights. Perhaps she had done her washing the day she died. He knew he was splitting hairs but didn't know why. Something here didn't quite add up but he was at a loss to work out what it might be. He regretted he hadn't brought Trudy. For all his belief in his copper's nose, there were some things a woman could tune into that much quicker.

He walked along the narrow landing and into the second bedroom at the rear. Small and sparsely furnished with a single bed and plain pine desk, it had rows of books on white-painted shelves and a pile of ledgers stacked on the floor. He picked one up and flicked through its pages, composed of computer printouts. The company accounts she had taken time off to update, yet nothing appeared to have been done. The desk was bare, the computer switched off. A clean pad of paper lay there unsullied. Nothing here had been disturbed except by his own forensic team. Hal nosed around and opened the wardrobe, which contained winter clothing and a couple of bright cotton dresses. A canvas bag was folded in the corner. He checked inside and found an umbrella, a pac-a-mac and an old leather purse containing a role of five pound notes, some change and a travel card. And balanced on top, its brim squashed by the door, a somewhat unlikely straw hat.

The stairs were wooden and lightly varnished with the kitchen-cum-dining-room at the rear, leading on to the patio, while the living-room fronted the street. The kitchen was fairly basic, white with economy units, and a large fridge-freezer which he opened and peered inside. It was here the murderer had found the wine bottle that he'd later smashed and used for the mutilation. Just standing here, as it were in his footprints, sent a frisson of acute distaste down Hal's spine. Forensic had already been through here with a tooth-comb; he took a swift glance round then moved on into the annexe, where the wall had been knocked through to make one large room.

A pretty room this, with bright terracotta walls and bold flower prints framed in wood. Friendly and welcoming, the heart of the house, where visitors would gather to watch their hostess cook. The chairs and table were rustic and serviceable, set with straw mats all ready for a meal. Through these double glass doors the intruder had entered. The bolt had been dusted with fingerprint powder then firmly pushed back into place. Hal could still see traces of it on the floor. He had a good look around.

A quaint old-fashioned sideboard held china, glass and cutlery, indicating a person who liked to entertain. There were expensive linen napkins and several sets of candle-holders as well as a ceramic oil and vinegar set. An electric hostess trolley was pushed into one corner, piled high with cookery books and a wooden bowl of fruit. Hal liked a woman to be handy at the stove, then dismissed the thought as unworthy in the circumstances. He could imagine what Trudy would have said, had he voiced such a sentiment aloud. He was here to investigate a murder, not to speculate too much about the victim's private life. Not that the two things were unconnected. The more hard evidence he could amass, the more likely he'd be able to revitalise the trail.

He retraced his footsteps along the narrow hall, back into the elegant living-room. This, the most formal room in the house, had tall sash windows which overlooked the street. She had certainly had taste, not only in her clothes, but then he recollected her profession. But where the office studio was stark and ultra modern, all functional glass and tubular steel, this room was the essence of understated style, straight out of the pages of an interiors magazine. Off-white sofas were set against wintry walls with a narrow black table between them, displaying one solitary orchid in a glass. Very minimalist, very chic. Too pristine and tidy to relax in. A wafer-thin television, black upon black, stood close to the window on a lacquered black cube. The single detail that did not fit in was the clutter of photos over the fireplace.

Photos of friends in informal poses, at dinner or on a tennis-court. He recognised Veronica with what was presumably her husband, and an older snap of the two friends together, beaming with youthful confidence in front of the Eiffel Tower. Hal was intrigued as he peered at each one, wondering why the forensic team had failed to point them out. He sorted through them slowly, squinting to catch every nuance, occasionally carrying one across to the light for a better look. Hamish Cotterell on a riverbank, smiling with those sad, soft eyes as he dangled a trout. Dottie Sullivan, with that burning aureole of hair, alongside a jovial bearded man he supposed must be her Sam. No sign at all of Norman Harker; at least she had shown some judgement there. But there was one of a tanned and smiling stranger, nobody Hal had encountered so far. They were standing close together in an obvious party setting. Their eyes were bright and red from the flash, and they were laughing and holding up glasses.

Central to these smaller pictures was a larger group, framed in silver. Here they all were, unmistakably, the team on some sort of office outing. Dottie, Ambrose, Wayne and Serafina, their arms round each other, smiling bravely into the breeze. And right in the centre, a laughing Jinx, her hair blowing wildly and her collar turned up. It was on this particular picture Hal now focused, all of them together having fun. He scrutinised each smiling face. The elite little group that made up her inner circle, probably her closest buddies in the world. Beautiful Serafina posing as always, her sunglasses shoved up into her hair. Ambrose grinning benignly at the camera, Dottie quite radiant with delight. And zany Wayne, the office wag, with his dyed blond hair and glittering earring. Wayne Peacock; something stirred in the recesses of Hal's brain.

Wayne the comedian, Wayne the trainee. He picked up an omission he'd so very nearly made. Wayne the chess prodigy of whom Ambrose was so proud, with a sharp intelligence which was why they had snapped him up. Wayne who'd been with them the shortest time of all, yet who was already one of the trustys. Wayne whom Hal had barely bothered to question, assessing him as too recent and too young. Glad that, after all, he hadn't brought Trudy along to witness his potentially dangerous oversight, he slid the group shot out of its frame and hotfooted it back to the station.

13

There was not a lot his team of investigators could dredge up on Wayne Peacock, not even working overtime on Sunday with Hal breathing down their necks. Eventually they were rewarded with a couple of brief police reports, one for abusive behaviour while a student when supporting Leeds against Manchester in a cup final, the other for being in possession of cannabis but let off with just a stern warning and fine. They checked with the Slade and got only glowing reports. Regular attendance with consistently high marks plus points for originality. A young man with a very bright future was the bursar's considered opinion. They sought hopefully for accounts of loutish behaviour but again drew a blank. A model student with impeccable references, apparently nothing to hide at all.

'There has to be more.' Apparently not. Not if you're twenty-two and only recently left the parental home. Hal beat his forehead with his hand in frustration. Less than twenty-four hours before the world found out just how royally he'd screwed up. He regretted now calling that press conference.

'Sexlife?'

'None that we know of. Certainly nothing spectacular.' Melody, the trainee manager, still remained Wayne's little secret, smart boy. And there the police were obliged to leave it. At least for the while.

'Knight to D3.' He would then move on to attack E5 while protecting B4, then playing C4. It was first thing Monday morning but Wayne, for once, was in early and already absorbed in his game with an imaginary opponent.

'What are you doing?' asked Dottie, bustling around him with mail and mugs. Wayne remained silent. Stuck into a chess-game he retreated from the world. She really believed it was possible he didn't hear her.

'What's that piece with the horse's head?' asked Dottie, unperturbed. She had never had time for cerebral matters since she spent her life clearing up after people. She came and stood beside him, craning to study the tiny ivory pieces. Unlike Ambrose, Wayne was unfazed by interruption.

'My knight,' he said, moving it two places to protect his queen.

'Why does it move in that funny way?'

'That's what knights do. One step forward and a jump to the side. The most devious piece on the board. One to be watched.'

'What's its function?'

'To defend the queen. Against all assailants.'

Breaking his own powerful concentration, Wayne beamed up at her. He was in this early as a ploy to defeat Ambrose with whom this battle had been raging for several days. He had thought out his next moves as he roller-bladed to work. Now he was working them out on the board in anticipation of the next round. Seeing what Dottie was doing, he remembered his manners.

'Right,' he said energetically, heading for the kitchen. 'Who's for coffee and whadja all want in it? Last call.' His shaven head was bleached an acid yellow and his rather good legs were

swamped by khaki game warden shorts. He was incorrigible.
Dottie watched him go with wonder. It was the first time ever
she could remember him volunteering to do anything off his
own bat. Especially at the start of the week. Ambrose, shuffling
in with a mammoth hangover, was instantly aware of the ditsy
smile and over-bright eyes. He was forever marvelling at the
lad's resilience while also wondering how he could possibly
afford the habit. There was certainly no family trust fund to
cushion this Bradford babe and he scarcely earned peanuts in
this job. Perhaps he was moonlighting but where did he find the
energy? Wayne's weekend raves were a topic of regular fascination
among his colleagues, the in-joke being to leave him alone on
a Monday. The lights might be on but there was likely to be
no one home.

'Tea for me,' said Serafina languidly, pushing back her heavy
hair as she pored studiedly over her mail, smoothing an eyebrow
with one skeletal finger.

Me for you and you for me, mouthed Wayne silently from
the kitchen doorway, camping it up complete with extravagant
gestures in a parody of Serafina at her arrogant worst. His
colleagues erupted in silent mirth. The lad was a riot.

But Ambrose had more worrying matters on his mind this
morning. He had checked the calendar and pointed out the
date. Twenty-one days to go until D-Day and they were still
nowhere nearly there. Right from the start, when they'd first
accepted the backing from IEP, the projected deadline, brought
forward by the financiers, had made no sense at all. If you
speeded up finely-tuned creative work like theirs, something
along the line was bound to suffer. As Jinx had so presciently
pointed out at that meeting, the one that had ended with
her storming out. And to be ready in time for a media fair
in Cannes meant busting an unnecessary gut since a project like this, only one of its kind, was set to dazzle the
games world no matter what. Particularly with the name

of Damien Rudge attached. But try explaining that to the money-minded middlemen. Which was something someone urgently needed to do.

'So who's going to break the news?' asked Ambrose grimly, wincing in the bright morning light. One thing was suddenly horrifyingly clear. Jinx's demise could no longer be concealed. New York would have to be told and fast. Though what would happen once the bastard Weinberg got on the case didn't bear contemplation.

'Must he know at all?' asked Dottie anxiously. He had been here so recently and seemed so suddenly compliant. Pity in a way to sabotage that mood of truce. Ambrose nodded. And as fast as possible before the shit hit the fan. There were big American bucks tied up in this project.

'Or,' he added for emphasis, 'he's likely to pull the plug. And then we'll all go down the pan.'

'He'd never!' said Dottie, shocked. After all their endless effort and grinding hard work. But he would and Ambrose knew it.

'You'd better believe it,' he told them all ominously. This was genuine danger looming. They all knew this man of old.

Damien was the one to draw the short straw. He was, after all, the star of this show, the 'name' who had attracted the seed money in the first place. Without his track record and mega-selling games, DBI-2000 might never have made it off the starting-blocks. So he, with his money and clout, was the obvious choice to take on their adversary. Damien was, into the bargain, an equally miserable curmudgeon, like standing up to like. If they could only persuade him to see things their way and not simply drop them in it and walk away. But he had as much to lose as they did – more in fact. It was now just a question of who'd be the one to convince him.

Not Serafina though she would actually have leapt at the chance. She'd already offended Damien with her too obviously curled lip and they were lucky still to have him on their side.

She'd be all too eager to confront the boss herself but that would be inappropriate in the extreme. Dottie recalled the way she had purred at his last appearance in the office. Stick such a predator in the presence of a man of power and she went on heat as predictably as an alley cat. Serafina, as it happened, was working to her own agenda but they weren't to know that yet.

'Why not ring Damien and see if he'll come over.' He'd been in London at the end of the week, with luck he was still here now. Then they could approach him committee-wise and share the onus of gaining his co-operation. It did seem a workable plan. Dottie made a cautious phone-call then waved to the others in triumph.

'He's coming,' she told them as he checked his diary. 'Quick, nip round to the patisserie, Wayne, and get something fancy to help sweeten him up.'

Wayne's wild weekends were nothing to Serafina's though she went about organising hers in a slightly more devious way. The keen young accountant she had recently been seeing was a sprig of the aristocracy and part of the IEP team. Which was the bit that really turned her on for down-at-heel stately homes were two a penny these days. She had stumbled upon him fortuitously in a bar while cruising the area for a glimpse of the CEO. He was gangling and awkward and to her not remotely appealing but that was a minor glitch when balanced against his potential usefulness. This was partly why she was keeping him secret from her colleagues, scared of their discovering she had a foot in the enemy camp. And now he was getting all soppy and clingy as men were apt to, at least at the start. She played him along like a particularly ticklish trout, using every subtlety to keep him on the hop. And although he bored her, put up with his amorous fumblings, determined to use him for her own Machiavellian purposes before eventually casting him aside. That, after all, was the name of the game played by the modern day seductress. She delivered the goods, up to a point, while he got to pick up the tab. Every time. And got a real buzz out of doing so, poor sap, honoured to be her willing slave.

Which could not have been in sharper contrast to all Serafina should have learned from working alongside Jinx. Jinx, eleven years older, had grown up a dyed-in-the-wool feminist who had got where she had on merit alone, allied to solid hard graft. She came from a background of middle-class toilers, with a father whose military career had also instilled discipline in her. Straight from college she had plunged into the workplace and, with dogged determination and the occasional shrewd shift of direction, had shot skilfully upwards and through the glass ceiling into financial independence in her thirties. By forty she had acquired all the trappings of success – the business, the house, plus a professional reputation that was the envy of her peers. Younger women, scrambling up behind her, respected those achievements and viewed her career as their yardstick.

But not so Serafina who, by twenty-nine, was no longer prepared to wait. She wanted it all and she wanted it now and her methods of going for it were straight out of the seraglio. A man appreciates a woman who makes him feel like a man. That was the sickening chant of a whole new generation of slackers who'd do virtually anything to get what they wanted but work. Work was for suckers like Dottie and Jinx. It drained their energy and sapped their looks and, in Jinx's case, see where it had ended. Serafina's over-riding ambition was to achieve her long-term goal with the least possible effort. Which was where young James fitted in.

Damien strode irritably up and down the conference room, fear and consternation stamped visibly on his face. Not a happy bunny, as Wayne had remarked before being shunted off to organise coffee. Serafina's reading of Damien had been correct. He mistrusted and felt ill at ease with the team who always appeared to be sharing a secret joke that kept them smirking behind his back. A fairly warped view of things though not entirely inaccurate. They found him increasingly ludicrous these days with his inflated ego and newly found grandeur.

'He was just another oik from "Sarf" London,' said Ambrose. 'With a squint and a stammer and no social graces at all.' Who stayed too long at parties because he lacked the manners to know when to leave and always allowed someone else to pick up the bill. Never a joiner, always stuck there on the sidelines, it was only Jinx's gift for friendship that had helped draw him out of himself. And released that stupendous talent on an unsuspecting world, the basis of all their current fortunes. So it somewhat stuck in Ambrose's craw to see him spruced up in a Paul Smith suit and those ridiculous tinted lenses he now affected. Lording it over the rest of them as though they were merely his subservients.

Wayne brought in coffee and gave Dottie a heavy wink. He had dug out a battered tin tray and covered it with a tea towel on which were arranged three mugs and a sugar bowl. Plus the fancy florentines he had bought out of petty cash and would doubtless wolf himself once Damien was out of the way. Ambrose was being persuasive. Specially for this confrontation, though why he wasn't even sure himself, he had flattened his schoolboy haircut with water, polished his specs and made an attempt at shining his shoes. He hated to crawl but if needs be. But his ancient tweed jacket was wearing at the elbows and his shirt had seen better days. Beside the overdressed Damien he looked shabby and down at heel but Dottie knew which of the two had the bigger heart.

They were squaring up to each other now, two old muckers divided by a simple quirk of fate. Despite their regular chess-games since those early art school days, Damien still managed to disdain him. Ambrose came swiftly to the point.

'If we don't make him see our point of view, we risk losing everything we've worked for. The commission, the funding, your contract even.' He inserted that point craftily to hit Damien where it hurt, he knew the right buttons to press. If money and prestige mattered so much to him these days, it would do no harm to let him squirm. They needed his paranoia right now. It would help them to fight.

'My contract!' said Damien predictably, his eyes bulging wide with alarm. 'How on earth can that be affected?' They had paid him all that money, there were further projects signed up.

'The deal was with the design group,' said Ambrose casually, as if he were calm underneath. 'Without which, namely Jinx, the financiers could easily cancel it and just pull out. They'd be well within their legal rights. I've checked.'

Damien looked as though he were about to spontaneously combust. His face turned purple and a vein throbbed in his forehead. What was this absolute rubbish Ambrose was spouting now? Everyone knew whose genius was responsible for the coup, whose name and prestige would adorn the finished package. What had that to do with McLennan Graphics or the surefire success of his game? The money men hadn't even seen it yet; that had been one of his main conditions.

'Quite simply,' said Ambrose gravely. 'Act of God.' *Check.*

Damien drummed his fingers on the table and stood for a moment in silent shock. He had known he had enemies mustering against him, this treachery was really no surprise. Finally he cleared his throat and turned back to face them.

'So what is it exactly you want me to do?' He was obviously in an advanced state of jitters, had always been fairly unbalanced. How on earth they were going to handle him in the future, without the calming influence of Jinx, didn't bear thinking about now.

'Talk to him rationally, show him you're not going to walk. That you still have total faith in what the team is doing. Let him know you're confident that we're right on target, that you're still with us one hundred per cent of the way.'

Drums were beating in Damien's head now and his eyes were visibly flickering. He had always known not to trust anyone at all and now all his fears were proving well-founded. The forces of evil were gathering around him and rapidly closing in. He stared at Ambrose as if he didn't know him and Ambrose waited patiently until he returned to earth.

'And who exactly is this guy?' asked Damien vaguely after a long pause. Which showed how much he had listened in the past.

'Julius Weinberg,' said Ambrose patiently, trying not to lose it and thump the dolt in the face. 'Remember him – our old nemesis from the past? Now CEO of IEP and second in the hierarchy only to God. And, lest you really have forgotten, one of the world's greatest bastards. There are no depths to which he wouldn't stoop, you'd better believe it.'

'Christ,' breathed Damien as if only now understanding. 'Not that animal again.' He took out his handkerchief and mopped his face, quite visibly shaking and looking ill. Dottie refilled his coffee mug and shoved the plate of biscuits towards him. Couldn't have him falling to pieces now, they needed him far too much.

'I'll do it for Jinx,' he said pompously at last. 'In memory of all she contributed over the years.' Just as though he didn't have as much to lose as the rest of them.

'Thank you,' said Ambrose with feigned humility, actually extending his hand. *Checkmate.*

The second Damien was out of there and had stalked away up the mews, Serafina jack-knifed out of her desk and was up those stairs to the conference-room.

'Well?' She really hated being excluded in this way. Wayne, of course, was there already, loitering as he collected the coffee mugs and nibbling surreptitiously at the few remaining florentines. It was still not long past eleven. The meeting had been brief and to the point. Ambrose, looking quietly pleased with himself, was industriously polishing his glasses while Dottie gave her a cheerful thumbs up.

'We managed, I think, to convince him. He finally sees our

point of view. Ambrose was fabulous, terribly firm and grown-up.'

'So what happens now?'

'He's going to talk to Weinberg once Ambrose has said his bit. Preferably as soon as poss to avoid any drastic repercussions.'

'Where *is* Weinberg? Does anybody know?' Serafina was keen to hear the answer. He had been in London just a few days before but where was he now when his presence was really needed? No-one knew the answer to that.

'So what are you going to do?' she asked Ambrose, even though she had a plan of her own.

'Call him in New York, I suppose. Assuming that's where the blighter is.'

'Well, you'd better get on with it.' Serafina consulted her watch. 'In less than an hour the police are talking to the press. And you don't want him hearing it first on CNN.'

Ambrose groaned. The net was closing fast. 'Anyone got his number?' he wanted to know.

Right at that moment they heard movements from below, the distinct sound of a key in the lock and a taxi pulling away. Everyone looked at each other, startled. Surely not even the police would be this intrusive. To begin with, how did they come to have a key? Swift, light footsteps crossed the downstairs hall and they all peered over the banister rail as the door to the studio was flung wide. There stood a slim young woman in creamy linen, with a golden tan and glowing smile.

'Surprise!' called out Jinx McLennan, putting down her suitcase. 'I'm back! Is there anyone about?'

Part Two

14

'Well, thanks, guys, for a truly terrific welcome,' she said.
Nobody uttered a sound. Just stood there staring down
at her like a row of dumbfounded zombies, too shocked and
uncomprehending to take it in. Dottie's head was in a spin; for
one brief giddy moment she thought she might be going to faint.
Ambrose let out a single hollow moan then clapped his hand over
his mouth in pure horror. Serafina gripped the rail so tightly her
fingers visibly blanched.

'What's up? It's as if you'd all seen a ghost,' said Jinx. She looked
marvellous, relaxed and radiant, the familiar smile brighter than
ever. Wayne was the first of them to get a grip on himself.

'You don't know?'

'Know what? I'm just off a plane. Has something happened?'
Jinx looked intently at each of them in turn, her smile beginning
to waver, anxiety taking its place. She had never seen them like
this before, a flock of terrified sheep who had lost their Little
Bo-Peep.

'There's been an . . . accident,' said Wayne diplomatically, tripping down the stairs to greet her in a sudden great rush of emotion. He pulled her clumsily into his arms and kissed her on both cheeks, and this simple human gesture activated the others who slowly began to breathe again. One by one they followed Wayne's lead and awkwardly greeted Jinx like a stranger. She was still looking puzzled and increasingly apprehensive. What terrible news could she be about to hear? She had never seen anyone look more poleaxed before.

So, falteringly, Wayne, since the others remained tongue-tied, started to tell her about the murder, and now it was her turn to grow ashen and clap her hands hysterically to her mouth.

'Oh my God, *Susie!*' she cried. 'My poor little Susie. Whatever have they done to you, my love?'

She had, she now explained, been off playing hookey on a Caribbean island with a friend. An impulsive last-minute decision made on that final day. And Susie Chandler, an old work-mate from way back, had stayed in the house while she was gone. Lived in Somerset, worked freelance as a picture researcher, loved these occasional breaks in London when she needed to do some checking.

'*Susie Chandler!*' exclaimed Ambrose, white as a sheet. This nightmare was continuing.

'I probably should have told you,' said Jinx, tears now streaming down her face. 'But there honestly didn't seem any point.' The truth was she hadn't wanted them to know at all. It was still all supposed to be hush hush.

'Hang on!' said Serafina, finally finding her voice, at the same time remembering the time. Just fifty minutes to the police press conference. They needed to reach Hal Burton – and fast.

Hal was as shaken as the rest of them, confronted unexpectedly by the embodiment of his dreams. They sat facing each other across the conference table and both were still quite breathless from the shock. Close to, Jinx McLennan was as gorgeous as she'd been painted, less a classic beauty than a vibrant, sensuous woman. Someone to be reckoned with, by nobody's standards a disappointment. She had shaggy, blonde-streaked hair, brushed neatly behind her ears to reveal tiny turquoise studs that looked well with her tan. The eyes that stared frankly back into his were warm and humane, the wide, somewhat sensual mouth had deep creases etched at the corners, a sign of someone who saw the funny side of things.

She wasn't, however, laughing now, and the brightness of her eyes was unshed tears. Susie had been a friend for years, since the days, way back, when they'd worked in the same office.

'She lived alone in the country,' she explained. 'Too close to her mother for comfort. She liked to pop up to town on the odd occasion, to do research but mainly to get away. We were roughly the same age and, I suppose, the same size. I've never really given it any thought.' They had played together on the company netball team. It had all been a bit of a lark when they were younger and they'd remained in touch, though these days rarely met.

'She was mostly only here when I was away. Liked having the place to herself for the occasional breather.'

Jinx rummaged in her bag for a tissue and dabbed at the corners of her eyes. If she let herself go now she knew that she'd be lost. The enormity of what had happened was just beginning to sink in.

'She wanted to get away this Easter to avoid an influx of Canadian aunts. She must have left the patio door open, poor sweet, because of the unseasonable heat. She just wasn't clued up to the dangers of city living. Where she came from they don't ever bother locking their doors.'

'So why would she have been sleeping in your bed?'

'The second bedroom was full of ledgers. It's where I work when I've got stuff to do at home. It just seemed that much simpler to change the sheets than to have to lug all the office

117

clobber elsewhere. It was all arranged at the very last minute. A sudden mad whim you might call it.'

'And where exactly were you?' Not that it was any longer his business, though she had to be cleared as part of the inquiry. Ironically, her name must now be added to the list of possible suspects. For the moment Hal couldn't quite get his mind around that.

'Abroad,' said Jinx abruptly. 'With a friend.'

'Can you tell me where?' he asked carefully.

'Anguilla. In the Caribbean. The flight got in at nine.'

'Can you prove that?'

She looked shocked but bit back her indignation. 'Call the hotel if you really must. I am sure they will confirm it.' Then, remembering something, she thought again and dived back into her handbag instead.

'Here,' she said triumphantly, proffering her passport. 'Any proof you need to have I'm sure you will find in here.'

Hal stared at his notebook and wanted to ask her more, but a wary look had come into her eyes that warned him to watch what he said. This forceful woman was nobody's fool; she knew her rights and he dared not risk offending her. Not now when she was still so shocked and there was so much he needed to know. He had managed to cancel the press conference and needed now to get his head together before he could think it all through. Could she bear to face the scene of the crime? he asked. Jinx shrugged wearily, suddenly resigned. Where else was she to go?

Trudy joined them for the short walk to Stratford Road, fascinated to be meeting in the flesh a woman she felt she already uncannily knew. Jinx was smaller and more finely boned than her photos had suggested, with a bouncy confident stride on her three-inch heels. The suit she wore was clearly designer cut and, despite the ten-hour flight from the West Indies, as fresh and unsullied as though she had just put it on. One of those enviable creatures who always manage to look good. Jinx had natural style and an ease of manner that made Trudy feel lumpy by comparison. And she could see the open admiration in the DCI's eyes.

Hal stepped forward and unlocked the front door, forgetting for a second that he was in the presence of the owner. He indicated to Jinx that she should enter, and he and Trudy followed her inside.

'Take a good look round,' he said. 'And see if there's anything missing or out of place.'

Jinx stood motionless in the centre of the hall, practically sniffing the air like a hunting dog.

'It all looks pretty OK to me,' she said. 'Susie was terribly tidy. The perfect house-guest.' She stepped into the kitchen and glanced around. Immaculate, wiped-down surfaces, a clean dishcloth folded across the taps. The forensic team had been tidy too. Hal was thankful there was no visible evidence of their presence here. He didn't want her upset more than was necessary. Together they mounted the stairs.

Jinx inhaled sharply when she saw the state of her bedroom, especially the walls, and Hal reached out to her with a steadying hand. Attempts had been made to clear away the blood, but those walls and the stark bare floorboards told her more than she cared to know. Also some of the furniture was missing. She looked around.

'My lady,' she said, pointing to the empty night-table.

'Don't worry, we've got it safe,' he told her. 'A crucial part of the evidence when it comes to trial.'

'Was that the weapon?' Jinx paled at the thought, Susie's innocent skull crushed with such force. She had not yet been shown the gruesome police photos; the nastier details were still to come. Hal wanted to spare her as much as he could, at least till she'd come to terms with the horrible tragedy. She backed out of the room in obvious shock and into the second bedroom instead. The ledgers were still piled neatly on the floor, the desk apparently as untouched as she'd left it, though the invisible fingers of the forensic team had already been thoroughly through it all. She opened the wardrobe and glanced inside, tenderly touching the bright cotton dresses.

'Susie's things.' She picked up the straw hat and held it close. Her friend had always dressed the way she was, a simple out-of-towner up on a spree. She drifted into the bathroom and checked the cabinet. With a flash of insight Hal answered his own question, the absence of intimacy among her more personal things. She had taken them with her, he saw that clearly now. What was left here were the strictly non-essentials.

'She even scrubbed out the bath.' Jinx was starting to shake. He longed to put his arm around her, saw that Trudy could see it in his eyes. They returned downstairs and finally into the sitting-room where the single wilting orchid was looking a little sad. Jinx had another good look. Then swiftly crossed to the mantelpiece and fingered through her pictures.

'Two missing,' she announced in surprise. 'Now why on earth would anyone take those?'

'You're certain of that?' Hal was uncomfortably aware of the one in his desk drawer. Soon he would have to come clean but first he needed the facts.

'Of course I'm certain. There was a big group picture of the lot of us on the ferry and a smaller one taken in Lille last year.'

'And what was it like, this smaller one?'

'Just a snap of me fooling around in a street on one of our annual outings. I only displayed it because I liked the frame. *Art nouveau* with lovely intricate engraving. I found it in a junkshop once with Ambrose.'

'Valuable?'

'Not particularly though I suppose a burglar might think so. What a shame, I was fond of it.' Her hand was beginning to shake.

120

'Come on,' said Hal, regretting now that he'd left the car. 'Time to be getting back. You need a rest.'

'Back where?' asked Jinx, looking despairingly round at her home.

'Back to the station with me, I'm afraid. You can't remain here.'

'But it's where I live.'

'Nevertheless.'

For much of the day he continued to cross-examine her, painfully aware of her increasing pallor and the fading of the light from her warm, expressive eyes. Susie's death was quite clearly hitting her hard. He watched the sorrow mounting in her the way it had earlier with her friends. Sudden death is never easy to accept. Combined with obscene brutality it is something the mind can barely absorb at all.

'Had she any enemies, do you know? Anyone close to her who might bear a grudge?'

'Susie? I certainly wouldn't think so. She was the dearest, sweetest, gentlest creature alive. Terribly family-minded even if her mother did get on her nerves. Lived extremely quietly in the village she grew up in. Her father had been a clergyman.'

'So no skeletons?'

'Not that I'm aware of.' Susie had never been actively sexy, men had not seemed to matter to her that much. A good girl who sang in the choir and helped with the flowers, she was an unlikely friend for the wild and worldly Jinx. Yet friends they had been and for seventeen years. Amazing how rapidly time streaks by.

'I still can't believe she's gone,' said Jinx, tears once more clouding her expressive eyes.

'I'm afraid this will mean a new investigation.' More interviews, more pavement pounding, more tracking down possible suspects. More false trails and dead ends. Hal felt indefinably crushed at the thought. Unless, in some way, it could all be short-circuited.

'How many people knew she knew you?'

'Very few.' Since Jinx had quit the book world to start her own design group, their lives had radically diverged. A handful of acquaintances from the old days might remember. Right now she couldn't summon up a single one. Other, of course, than her own immediate team, but even they hadn't seen Susie in years. Or even remembered her, Jinx suspected.

'And who precisely knew you were going away?'

'No one at all.' She was adamant. 'Except, of course, Susie.' Whom she'd told at the last minute while she was busy with the ironing, along with the secret reason for the trip.

'Not even the people next door?'

'Most certainly not.'

He smiled at the definiteness of her statement. He could well imagine how irritating Peggy Dawes might be as a neighbour. Well, she had a big surprise coming, her husband, too. He had better get round there and put them in the picture, it was the least that was due them after all their initial help. It might also help to jog their memories. Which reminded him. Hal was on the point of asking about her Wednesday night companion, then realised with a jolt that she was not obliged to say. She'd produced a solid alibi, the passport stamp was conclusive. Jinx was alive and in the clear; the questions would now have to cease. Certainly until they had dredged their dreary way through the life and times of Susie Chandler, deceased.

'You really ought to come home with me,' said Dottie firmly, taking command. 'You've got to sleep somewhere till the police have done their job and it's certainly not healthy for you to be alone. Not now.' She remembered with a shudder those awful chilling footsteps that had followed her that night at Earl's Court station and was filled with alarm at the thought of continuing danger. Sam, she registered quickly, would have to be told.

Though not right now with Jinx still sitting there listening. Not quite appropriate, she wouldn't have the words.

'Thanks but I really couldn't,' said Jinx wearily. 'You are chock-a-block as it is. It's simpler just to check into a hotel.' The thought of having to rub shoulders quite so intimately with Sam filled her with inexpressible fatigue. She had to be on her own to think, to sort it all out in her mind in order to grieve.

'Well then,' said Dottie brightly. 'Why not go to Battersea with Ambrose? He's got the room.' And adored her so much there was surely nothing he wouldn't do to help.

Ambrose, unusually, had remained more or less mute since Jinx's astonishing resurrection. He'd not even hugged her nor addressed her a single word. If she weren't so familiar with his delicate psyche, she might even believe he was indifferent. Shock, thought Dottie tenderly, observing his lack of expression. With, from the looks of him, one of his beastly migraines imminent.

'The last thing poor Ambrose needs in his life is girlie clutter,' said Jinx. She stretched out one foot in its elegant sandal and lightly touched his instep with her toe. But Ambrose failed entirely to respond. She remembered that time she'd had a routine D and C and he had not been seen for dust. No flowers, no visits, no communication at all. Not even so much as a card to wish her well. He had thought she was dying, it had finally transpired, when all she was trying to do was spare his bachelor blushes. There were certain matters, her mother had always told her, that you didn't discuss in front of the menfolk.

'No,' said Jinx, gathering strength and getting up. 'I'll check myself into the Kensington Close and try and catch up on some sleep.'

15

Jinx was in bright and early next morning, way ahead of the others, in fact. She was already settled and immersed in her work as they stumbled in one by one. She flashed the familiar megawatt smile; it had not been a dream, she was real.

'Nice of you to join me,' she remarked with some of the old acerbity.

'I really am sorry,' said Dottie, close to tears, and started to explain about the bus. Jinx cut her short. Dottie looked quite dreadful this morning; she hadn't slept in days and it was starting to show in her face. She was wearing an old navy cardigan with a moth-hole in the sleeve, the buttons wrongly done up.

'Don't you worry,' said Jinx more kindly. 'Relax. The kettle's almost boiled.' This morning, by contrast, she looked cool and elegant in a simple slimly cut beige linen dress with a fine gold chain round her throat. The epitome, as always, of casual chic.

'Lucky I had it with me,' she said. 'Else I'd be reduced to a couple of dirty shirts and a pair of crumpled shorts.' The hotel would do her laundry if she asked but at this stage she really couldn't be bothered. The sooner she could gain access to her home, the better. She hated having to live this way, like a gypsy. If only the police red tape would go away.

Yesterday's trauma already seemed fairly remote. Today she was calmer and back to functioning normally. You couldn't keep Jinx McLennan down for long; she always had been more or less invincible. She exuded a quiet inner radiance, remarkable considering what they'd all just been through. Something about her had subtly altered, though Dottie was hard put to know what. Maybe nothing more than just a week away from work. She'd not had much free time off in years.

Jinx was skimming through the backlog of mail and jotting down notes on a pad. 'I've still got those bloody accounts to sort out. That'll teach me to do some last-minute skiving.'

'No problem, I'll help you,' said Dottie, rapidly rallying. 'The minute I've got the coffee out of the way.' She could, of course, always leave that to Wayne. It was, after all, part of his job description. But that wasn't Dottie's way, she liked to fuss, so Jinx merely smiled and returned to her papers.

'I can do it,' said Serafina hurriedly. The accounts she meant, not the coffee. She was as pale and translucent as a stick insect this morning and wearing off-white which didn't help. Her hair, for once, was dull and lifeless and a spot was fast developing on her chin. Not like her customary chipper self at all. She looked as though she'd had a rough night too.

Jinx observed her caustically. It was quite unknown for the younger woman to be quite so quick to oblige but she did, for once, appear perfectly sincere. Maybe the shock of the murder had done the trick. She needed the occasional shaking-up though this had been unnecessarily drastic.

'That's all right,' said Dottie hurriedly. She wasn't having Madame taking advantage like that, no telling where that might lead. Serafina was nothing if not pushy, contriving always to be teacher's pet. Then a sudden thought struck her and she gave a small cry of alarm.

'Now what?'

'Damien. Did anyone think to let him know you're safe?'

Jinx was astounded. Had news of her murder really spread so fast? It had only been a matter of days with Easter intervening. She was sorry they'd thought to disturb their unbalanced genius, especially since the reports of her death had been grossly exaggerated. She looked to Dottie inquiringly, awaiting an explanation.

'The police,' was Dottie's faintly defensive reply. 'They interviewed all possible suspects. Simply doing their job.' And Damien's name had been on that list? Surely not.

Dottie still looked uncomfortable. 'I think I'll just ring the poor fellow to put him out of his misery. We can't have him going on believing you've been murdered.'

So now Jinx had to be told about the meeting and the way they had shoved all responsibility on to Damien. Ambrose had been worrying about that dratted deadline, afraid that without Jinx around the financiers might pull out. Which reminded her.

'Where *is* Ambrose?' Nobody knew. Serafina offered to phone but Jinx said to leave him in peace. He was bound to show up in his own good time and secretly she had an inkling of what he must have been through. Poor Ambrose, with his ultra-sensitive feelings. He had always been such a rock in her life, she was touched by this evidence of devotion. Then she glanced around at the other strained faces and a huge wave of love swept right over her.

'Come here,' she said impulsively, holding wide her arms, and hugged them all to her like children.

The right way to do it seemed to be for Dottie to make the call and then to put Jinx on the line. They daren't risk upsetting him, knowing how neurotic he could be, though both were in agreement that he needed to be told rightaway. Damien sounded thunderstruck, almost incoherent with shock, but then he had always had a bit of a stammer. As she made the right sort of soothing noises, it slowly began to dawn on Jinx the full horror of what had occurred. She was lucky to be alive, she saw that now, and to them the whole thing had been horrible in the extreme. There she'd been, cavorting on silvery sand in a romantic idyll, while her loved ones back here were coping with misery and shock. She felt suitably humbled. For almost a week they had believed her dead. You couldn't just shrug off a trauma like that.

Dottie then produced a scribbled list and Jinx saw, with a sinking heart, that she'd only just got started. Dottie was still looking guilty.

'I'm afraid I gave some names to the police,' she said. 'They rather insisted and I didn't know quite what to do.'

'Like who?'

'Like Hamish. And also Norman Harker.'

'You what!' For a second Jinx was stunned then she shrieked with genuine mirth.

'Well,' said Dottie, quickly on the defensive. 'I didn't really have much of a choice.' Jinx gave her a hug and told her not to worry. Of course she had done exactly the right thing in trying to help the police.

'I'd love to know what he told them,' she said. 'I bet he was mad as hell.' Always deep in some conspiracy, was Norman, taking his phone-calls behind closed doors. Dottie said she'd have to ask the police and Jinx said she certainly would. The whole ghastly business was verging on the macabre, albeit in an increasingly sick way. Then she remembered her friend Joel in the Notting Hill bar and wondered how long it would take them to track him down. Perhaps she should warn him though it hardly mattered now. The whole point was that she hadn't been murdered. So Joel was really not relevant.

*　　*　　*

The disruptive police presence had been temporarily withdrawn while Hal and his team were in Somerset investigating poor Susie's final days. So work resumed in the mews as they scrambled to meet that time-bomb deadline relentlessly ticking away. Round about noon Ambrose finally made it in, grim-faced and taciturn, not at all his amiable self. Wayne was starting to rib him a little until Jinx quietly shook her head. Leave the poor blighter alone. He had clearly been going through hell. Serafina, jumpy as a nervous cat, fidgeted constantly and couldn't seem to settle. Wayne eyed her shrewdly from his corner of the room, wondering what was up with her now, though Dottie recognised displacement activity based on her deep-seated insecurity. One of these days, when the pressure was off, she determined to get Serafina to open up. Whatever had happened in her childhood could not have been healthy, though she clammed up instantly if anyone tried to probe.

'You can help me with this copying,' offered Wayne, but for once Serafina failed to rise.

'Tell you what,' said Jinx comfortably, seeing the time. 'Let's all take an early break and go round the corner for a pizza. My treat.' She was always doing things like that, distracting them when they were trying to work. Serafina rather despised her for it, but Jinx was less of a fool than she thought and knew what she was about. Keep them alert and keep them keen. It worked every time as it did with men. Eating together brought them that much closer and helped them to communicate. It was only a couple of weeks since that Chinese feast but whereas that had been a celebration this would be more of a wake.

Ambrose refused pointblank to join them and burrowed resentfully back into his work. Jinx had the feeling she had somehow overstepped the mark. This was her good old buddy who was rejecting her, not like him at all. She stared at him thoughtfully then lightly touched his shoulder. It wasn't her fault that he'd had such a shock but she'd do what she could to atone.

'We won't be long,' she promised as she left. 'Keep the flag flying and repel all invaders.'

Wayne and Serafina bickered their way through the meal while Jinx and Dottie looked on like indulgent parents. They were nearly always at it, these two, scrapping away like kids, but Jinx still found it amusing much of the time. They were natural sparring partners, in many ways evenly matched, and Wayne in particular was smart as a whip. He usually got the upper hand though Serafina didn't always see that. Which simply added to the fun; he was a scream. Eventually Dottie interjected and brought the conversation tactfully back to Jinx. How was she feeling now? Dottie wanted to know, and Jinx replied not great.

'I still can't get to sleep at night, for thinking of what happened to Susie.'

Dottie nodded. She felt the same. Sam was always having to calm her now when she jerked awake in sheer fright. She knew she was lucky to have him there. Poor Jinx had to face things alone. The worst bit of all was what he'd done with a broken bottle. She tried hard to get the image from her head.

'It's hard to imagine pure hatred like that. To inflict such injuries on another living person.'

'You don't think then that he did it just for kicks?' said Serafina ghoulishly. She appeared to have no heart, which was no surprise.

'It doesn't much look like it,' said Jinx. 'Not from what the police said.'

They had told her that instances of stalking were on the rise and that seventy per cent went on to kill or maim. She shuddered. It really didn't bear thinking about. That her old friend's death might be all her fault. Though, for the life of her, she couldn't imagine who in the world might have wished her so much ill. She wasn't aware of having any enemies.

Dottie remembered the footsteps on the stairs, and the hair on her neck began to prickle. She told them briefly about the scare she had had and warned Serafina not to walk home alone.

'Nonsense,' said Serafina briskly. 'There are always loads of people about where I live.'

'Doesn't make any difference,' said Wayne. 'Look at all the ram raiders and time bandits.' This conversation was not at all healthy, they were nervous enough as it was.

'Tell us about your holiday,' said Dottie. 'Where've you been and who with?' And why so much secrecy? she also wanted to add.

A soft look came into Jinx's eyes. There was still so much thinking she had to do. For all sorts of reasons, she was not yet ready to talk, though Dottie would be one of the first she would tell. And Ambrose.

Pas devant les enfants, she mouthed silently, then called for the bill and said they'd best be getting back.

Marjorie too was in a right old state and so, predictably, was Veronica. Again, Dottie made the initial call then put Jinx on the line to reassure them. Tears were shed but they hadn't a lot to say. This Lazarus-like rising went beyond all rational thought. One thing Jinx was discovering, though: it certainly let you know who your real friends were. She promised them both that she'd see them very soon then left them to come to terms with it in their own way. She skimmed her eye down Dottie's list – Hamish next and then the worthy professor. She grinned at the thought of his baffled and outraged confusion. The man was so self-centred he'd be bound to blame her for his discomfort. Well, she couldn't help that. Norman was no longer a part of her life, or wouldn't be once they had spoken. She could no longer imagine what she had ever seen in him, pompous, inflated and self-serving. Not even handsome and only passable in bed, his prowess restricted by all that self-love. It was something she had occasionally observed in other men. Meanness of spirit was something that went right

through like the writing in seaside rock. A man who was tight
with his money was equally likely to be ungenerous in bed.
The professor had been one of her more improbable flings. She
supposed that at the time she'd found him charismatic.

But now she was permanently withdrawing from the chase.
Things had recently happened to change her outlook on life.
No more casual couplings or meaningless one-night stands nor
trifling with other people's feelings. She had not been a saint but
was determined to reform. If at forty it wasn't too late.

By late afternoon Ambrose was looking a bit more human, and
Jinx succeeded in luring him to the pub. Not the Britannia at the
end of the mews, but her own far jollier local, unaware it was
now a haunt of undercover police. She might, for the moment,
be exiled from her home, but she could at least sit and observe
it. She'd spent so many convivial evenings here with Ambrose,
she hoped it might help him to thaw. Certainly the life had
come back into his eyes and when she cautiously took his arm
he didn't resist.

'Right,' she said once they were settled with their beers. 'Tell
me what's on your mind.'

Ambrose stared glumly into his glass, back in the doldrums
again. His shirt, she noted idly, was not entirely clean and he could
have done with a better shave. She wanted to reach over and touch
his hand but was wary of pushing her luck. He had always been
predominantly non-tactile, fastidious about his personal space.
This man required a special sort of handling at which Jinx was
probably the world expert. So she sat and drank in silence until
he was more in the mood, happy just to be with him again.

'Bloody wanker,' he said at last, banging down his glass to
emphasise his point. Here we go, she thought warily, guessing
where things were heading. Ambrose could never leave a gripe
alone, and this particular one had been bugging him for years.

'That fucking deadline is ludicrous and he knows it. He's only

moved it forward in order to screw us up.' It was bad enough
that the slimeball was back in their lives. Now he was starting to
wreck things again. 'We're never going to make it. Not as things
are now.' His face was full of anguish again, he looked on the
verge of tears.

'Why's that?' She was curious.

'Because . . .' said Ambrose, his sentence tailing away. All that
had happened in the past few days was still just a blur in his mind.
He was struggling helplessly in a sea of tormented thoughts. 'Oh
Jinx,' he said brokenly. *'Jinx.'*

He pawed her arm clumsily, all out of words, and she saw
he was far too emotional to speak. She just leaned forward and
lightly kissed his cheek, and he clutched her for a moment before
pushing her away. She slipped away discreetly to allow him to
recover his cool while she went in search of the ladies'.

Later, when he was calmer, Jinx talked a bit about Susie, whose
savage slaughter was still reverberating in her head. She doubted
she'd ever again have a night's unbroken sleep, the images were
so terrible.

'I can't get rid of the feeling it was all my fault. If I hadn't suggested she stay in the house, none of this would have happened.'

But Ambrose, unusually, appeared unsympathetic, brooding
upon problems of his own. 'Nonsense,' was all he said brusquely.
'All she was was in the wrong place at the wrong time.' Which
tallied with what the police had said though it made it no easier
to accept.

'She was one of the sweetest people I ever knew.'

'Not my type.' Ambrose sorted through his pockets for change.
She'd been a little too insipid for his taste. He far preferred a
woman with an earthy sense of humour who could match him
drink for drink. Like Jinx.

There was no point arguing since Susie was dead. It was
growing late and Jinx suddenly felt wiped out.

'Come on,' she said. 'Let's call it a day.' At least she'd discovered what was currently on his mind and would try to sort things out as soon as she could. Jinx was by nature a peace-maker and the team depended on her strength and commonsense.

Marloes Road was still awake and throbbing even at this late hour. The great thing about London was it never properly slept and it made her feel invigorated to be back. The streetlamps illuminated the fine quadrangled building that was all that remained of the old hospital, its grounds now developed into modern housing. It looked like a stage set with its heavily foliaged trees or part of a great cathedral close transported to the city. As they strolled along towards the hotel, she inhaled the heavy summer scents. Kensington was still where her heart really lay, no matter what else might be happening. It was where she had lived for most of her adult life.

'Listen,' said Ambrose suddenly, halting in his tracks. 'Do you hear the nightingale?'

And above the buzz of traffic from the busy Cromwell Road they heard quite clearly the soaring disembodied voice, heart-stoppingly moving in its purity. Jinx slipped her hand through Ambrose's arm and they walked on in comfortable silence. They had been through so much together, good and bad, but this, the ghastly murder, was the worst. Ambrose might be confused just now but she'd make sure they didn't fall at the last fence. Their precious DBI-2000 was at the beta testing stage and soon would be safely out of their hands and off into the marketplace. Then they'd be able to take a bit of a breather before they decided which project to turn to next. And all going well, the world should be their oyster. Another rattling triumph for McLennan Graphics.

She remembered nostalgically her mentor, Max Weinberg, and wondered what advice he would give her now.

'Go for it, girl,' she distinctly heard him say in that gruff, attractive voice that had never lost its heavy accent. 'And show the world what you're really made of. Aim for the stars and never look back. You know you can do it if you try.'

16

Weinbergs, the distinguished firm of art-book publishers, in those days was based in two tall rickety adjoining houses situated in Great Russell Street close to the British Museum. Max Weinberg himself, a wartime refugee, had started it on a shoestring in 1949 and the world had watched it flourish ever since. A small, peppery man in his late sixties, he remained a fully hands-on publisher, working long hours well into the night and tyrannising his staff with relish. Without exception, he was regarded with awe and respect. Plus an element of terror befitting one with such outstanding talent who had survived the Nazis and had a fuse as short as his own chewed thumbnail. He had been known to fire people on a second's intolerant whim.

Jinx joined Weinbergs for work experience at the end of August the year she finished college. She loved it so much and worked so hard that they rapidly offered her a permanent position in the art department. Within just a few months, with a little coercion, Ambrose had followed her there too and they'd settled harmoniously into a group of kindred spirits with whom both had instantly bonded. Back in the early eighties, publishing was under fewer strictures and fun could still be had beneath its ramshackle roofs. The talent and erudition of Weinbergs' distinguished staff was legendary. Even the post-room, so it was widely rumoured, was staffed exclusively by PhDs.

They earned very little but were more than compensated by the privilege of working as part of such a creative team in a rarefied atmosphere of scholarship and culture. Ambrose did layouts, at which he excelled and which led him quite naturally to designing the computer software that he did so brilliantly now. Jinx was part of the publicity team, writing ads and catalogues and helping promote the books. She enjoyed the work so much that she often took it back home with her at night. Her father joked that the firm was a sweatshop, but nothing could have induced her to give it up. By the end of the first year she was already so firmly entrenched, she succeeded in persuading Damien too to join them.

So there they'd been all together again, Jinx and her merry men, the tight little trio from college, more firmly united than before. And when Sam Sullivan, really down on his luck, had falteringly embarked on an illustrated children's book, it was Jinx who carried it personally to Max and charmed him into giving Sam his first real break. Max looked increasingly on Jinx with indulgence and very much liked what he saw. She was feisty, hard-working, with opinions of her own and never too scared to challenge him when she thought he might be wrong. More and more he trusted her judgement and encouraged her to have her head. Because of the European catastrophe at a time when he might otherwise have been putting down roots, he had never got round to marrying or having children so that these bright young people, with whom he now surrounded himself, became his surrogate family. He gave each one space to develop their own potential, was disappointed when they failed to make it work. How proud he'd have been, had he still been around, to see how well this trio had turned out.

Jinx's friendship with Susie also harked back to those days. Susie, the country vicar's daughter, fresh from her cloistered convent school, had worked with them in the art department as a picture researcher. She was quiet and studious, roughly Jinx's own age, and they'd quickly started to like each other in the free and easy atmosphere of the office. Susie hung out in the basement, in a gloomy room filled with map-chests and bulging files, and escaped on forays whenever she could to the different picture libraries. Jinx became fascinated by Susie's work – that was what initially drew them together. They got into the habit of regular lunches, in either a winebar or the courtyard of the British Museum.

They could not have been more different, chalk and cheese: Jinx was ever Miss Popularity, with scores of boyfriends and a buzzing social scene while Susie seemed never to have a date at all. She was shyly attracted to Ambrose, with his loping, slightly awkward charm, but was never quite able to get him to focus on her. At times when they were all together in a group, Susie would valiantly steel herself to laugh along with the others but invariably Jinx's more powerful personality would swamp her. Not that it was in any way contrived; Jinx would have been mortified had she ever realised.

Sam occasionally had to come into the office, so his and Jinx's paths inevitably crossed. He was grateful to her for her timely intervention, had so low an opinion of himself at that time that he was convinced she must have swung it entirely on charm. He underestimated Max Weinberg, however, who supervised personally every project they signed up and would never have allowed special favours to be done. High artistic concept and originality were what counted; Weinbergs was known throughout the world for the distinction of its list. Sam had a rare, crude talent for primitive drawing that was an instant success with the 5–9-year-olds. Max's eagle eye spotted this flair at once. He signed Sam up on a three-book contract, uncharacteristically rash from a man who was usually so cautious.

The first time Sam and Jinx came face to face he lowered his gaze and tried to shuffle past her, acutely ashamed of what she would perceive he had become. It was over a year since the end of their relationship and Jinx hadn't seen him since then. She had heard that his attempts to mend the marriage had failed, that he was drinking more than was good for him and living in digs on his own. She felt superficially sorry but uninvolved; her life had moved on since those days. So she was quite unprepared for the startling change in the man she had fleetingly fancied she loved. He had put on weight, quite a lot of it, and the beard he now sported was fast turning grey. Gone were the slightly arty suits, in keeping with a lecturer with definitive dash and style. What he lived in now were jeans and fraying sweatshirts that did no sartorial favours to his increasing paunch. Jinx was shocked.

'What on earth has happened to Sam?' she asked Ambrose.

'He's down on his luck,' came the slightly acid reply. That's what happens, he might have added, when you take up with a flibbertigibbet half your age and allow it to wreck your life. Flighty Jinx had moved on without so much as a backwards glance while Sam had landed firmly in the mire. He had forfeited his family life in an attempt to recapture his youth and, when his end of the seesaw hit the ground, had found he had lost them irrevocably. Janet had instantly changed the locks and was now remarried, whereas Sam, deprived of his erotic dream, started hitting the bottle with a vengeance, ending up without tenure or even a job. There could be no going back. A classic parable with a suitably downbeat ending. A dispiriting rake's progress of modern times.

Jinx was appalled, as well she might be. She hadn't loved him enough to want to stay but had no idea till now he had sunk so low. Poor Sam. Her immediate instinct was to take him back as a friend, till Ambrose acerbically warned her off. Enough was enough, leave the poor wretch alone. It was quite bad enough that he'd loved her and lost, too humbling to imagine to have Jinx now trying to help him. At times she could be so unthinking that Ambrose despaired. They worked in the same room so he was aware of her day-to-day shenanigans, and he winced and mentally ground his teeth at some of her more thoughtless antics. Jinx was, and remained, a natural flirt. No man was totally safe from her mindless coquetry. She had no idea of the power she possessed, which was a major part of her charm.

Yet in the end it was Jinx who led Sam back to Dottie. A kindness he had blessed her for ever since.

Dottie was working for the British Council when Jinx ran into her on a bus. They'd lost touch since the London College of Printing days, and Jinx at first had difficulty in remembering who she was. So much had been crammed into the intervening years and her work at Weinbergs absorbed her thoughts. Yet suddenly here was Dottie smiling weakly, with faintly mauve shadows beneath her fine eyes and skin that had acquired a slightly puttyish hue. Long hours working in badly lit spaces, she explained apologetically over a glass of wine. But the hair was still a radiant fireball and when she smiled the beauty came creeping back. She liked what she was doing well enough, more of the thankless administration she had coped with so effectively at LCP. But she missed the fun of the good old days. There was a hint of wistfulness as they talked.

'Come for supper,' said Jinx impulsively, scribbling down the Islington address. She would round up some others and have an impromptu supper party. She'd knock up her special Bolognese sauce, and the guys could contribute the wine. She was putting together a neat little list when she bumped into Sam in the street. And a sudden lightbulb went on in her head. Dottie and Sam, the ideal pairing; both of them older and each alone. She was still feeling bad about what she'd done to Sam so this might be the moment to atone.

'Don't go and ruin it,' warned Ambrose over-sharply, so she didn't explain when she issued Sam's invitation, just let him believe he was still a part of the old gang.

It was never exactly fireworks but moved along smoothly from that point and pretty soon Sam had moved in with Dottie and even began losing weight. They had been together now these sixteen years with two fine children to show for it. The Muswell Hill house was a haven of contentment, untidy and down at heel though it might be. Jinx always got a buzz whenever she went there. To her it represented harmony and security, precisely what family life should be.

Yes, those had been the good times right enough and they'd all had a lot of fun, like a bunch of silly students not yet in the real world. Warmth came back into Ambrose's face as Jinx started reminiscing. She had always been such a ball of fire with her parties and revels and madcap schemes. But they'd also worked quite prodigiously hard and produced some memorable books. And were now reaping the rewards of that draconic apprenticeship by applying the same skills to the work they'd moved on to now.

'If things hadn't changed,' mused Ambrose, 'we would doubtless all still be there. Hanging around in the Museum Tavern, grumbling about the regime.'

'Meeting surreptitiously in the British Museum when the heat was really on.'

'Overworked and underpaid. Constantly threatening to quit.'

'Funny how the old days are always the best. We're beginning to sound like our parents.'

Jinx squeezed his arm as they strolled on through the night and leaned her head comfortably against his shoulder. Pals from the start, she felt safest in his company, able to talk about anything, more or less.

'Remember the jokes we used to play on Julius?'

'Usually thought up by you.' The phoney letters with their meticulously forged headings, right down to the postmark on the envelope. The telephone calls from two offices away purporting to come from abroad. How they had loathed him, that cold and arrogant man, and done all in their power to undermine him. Remembering that gave Ambrose sudden hope. He had idolised her then and continued to do so now. His main problem was that she never seemed to see it.

They reached the entrance of the Kensington Close Hotel and Ambrose daringly chanced his hand. How about one more drink for the road, he suggested. Now that he'd got her back again he was loath to let her go.

'Do you really think we ought? It's a school night after all.'

'That's never stopped you in the past.' The pain in his soul was rapidly abating and he suddenly couldn't bear to say goodnight. 'Just a quick one at the bar,' he wheedled. 'And then I promise I'll call it a night.' She was looking awfully good despite all she'd just been through and her head fitted well against his shoulder. He gave her a clumsy pat then ushered her up the steps and she laughed in resignation as he propelled her towards the bar, ever the sucker for Ambrose's persuasion. He bought them both malt whiskies and carried them to a booth as a feeling of sudden exhilaration swept through him. He felt proud and happy to be with her, the old magic had returned. The voice of the solitary nightingale had certainly touched his soul. Maybe, with just a bit of luck, he was still in there with a chance.

In 1984, at the age of seventy-two, Max Weinberg suffered a slight heart attack and was warned by his doctor to ease off. He rarely ever took time away, had never been known to have a proper holiday. Jinx, who had just turned twenty-five, by then worked hours pretty nearly as long as his. He had recently promoted her to dealing with co-editions in addition to the design work she was anxious not to give up. He was impressed at how well she coped with it all, had even promised her a trip to the Frankfurt Book Fair.

'That young woman has a fine head on her shoulders,' he told his colleagues admiringly, praise indeed from one whose standards had always been so exacting. He felt she was wasted in the publicity department, had plans of grooming her for greater heights. Though he didn't let on. He believed in effort and letting the best candidate win, and Jinx's dedication almost matched his own, though she managed to fit in a whale of a social life too. Burning the candle at both ends was something he privately approved of. His own youth had been blighted by that terrible European war. He rejoiced at Jinx's endless *joie de vivre* and secretly envied those younger chaps. But then he was struck by ill-health and everything changed.

For over forty years he had carried the burden of Weinbergs alone and had now reached an age when he ought to be taking things less strenuously. Or so his doctors told him. Jinx had great potential but was still far too young for the added responsibility; maybe some time in the future if she stayed on. Max looked around for a more immediate solution and found one right under his nose. His nephew, Julius, thirty-one years old and currently employed by a city merchant bank. His brother's son, born and raised in Cape Town but packed off to England for a fancy education. He had all the main ingredients for the successor Max desired, perhaps the most important of which was blood.

By the time the workers got to hear, it was already a *fait accompli*. Julius, it transpired, was weary of peddling money. Uncle and nephew had a leisurely dinner from which Max emerged triumphant having succeeded in securing his future. Julius would leave the city and join Weinbergs for the start of the new year. His title would be Managing Director and he'd be in day-to-day charge of the running of the firm, while Max would upgrade himself to Chairman. Chairman and CEO, of course, but at that stage it wasn't spelled out.

'You'll like him,' Max assured them when he broke the news to his startled team. 'He is clever and knowledgeable with a sound business brain. He can teach us all a thing or two about modern business methods. And he won't be involving himself at all with the publishing side.' A proper education was what emigré Max admired more than anything, in this case Eton and Oxford. His brother had made a fortune out of gold and had invested in his children in a way that Max approved. It seemed a neat solution to a problem that had long been nagging. He would sleep that bit more soundly knowing he had his nephew to back him up.

The staff were curious though not especially concerned. They trusted Max who looked after them like a stern father. If putting a money man in charge of the nuts and bolts meant freeing Max to concentrate on the creative side, it would surely be to everyone's benefit. He wasn't, after all, getting any younger and would still continue to front the firm. It was vital that Weinbergs continue to be privately owned.

Ambrose alone remained sceptical.

'He sounds a bit of a berk,' he said. The fact he was South African already weighed against him in the Irishman's eyes. 'I hope he doesn't come in here throwing his weight around.'

'Wait and see,' said Jinx soothingly, her mind already on other matters. Ambrose had always been an alarmist; he clung to the status quo, couldn't bear change. The book fair was rapidly approaching and she would be there this year as the Weinbergs' standard bearer. She was working long hours, late into the night, perfecting the book dummies she would take to elicit orders. For a firm like Weinbergs, that relied on international sales, this was the key event of the year. Much depended on Jinx's success; she was determined to gain Max's approval.

But then nephew Julius came crashing into their lives and everything suddenly went wrong.

142

17

The news story broke the next morning and was plastered all over the national press. The phones in the mews went on overdrive as they all coped with hundreds of calls, exactly what they didn't want now while working under such terrific pressure. Jinx, however, was touched and humbled by evidence of so much unsuspected love. She'd had no idea at all how much people cared; it was almost like reading her own obituaries.

Next the doorbell began to ring and the mews filled up rapidly with reporters and camera crews. They clustered outside causing quite a disturbance and trying to peer through the windows and letterbox. Dottie swiftly adjusted the blinds while Ambrose bad-temperedly paced the studio then told them belligerently to buzz off. Jinx didn't dare go out at all so good old Dottie popped round the corner and brought them all back sandwiches for lunch.

She was just arranging the sandwiches on a plate when someone rapped on the glass and an all-too-familiar voice called cooee. Dottie looked between the slats to see the avian features of Myrtle

Hobday peering in. Amazing how the woman's radar never let her down. She was contemplating hiding but Jinx was there before her, opening the door cautiously and beckoning her quickly inside. Myrtle liked nothing so much as a spot of self-glorification and was adept at muscling in on other people's lives. She didn't appear to have much of a life of her own.

'Goodness, such excitement!' she panted now with relish, after she'd pinched a sandwich and accepted a beaker of wine. 'So who do you think would have wanted to kill Susie?' Jinx shrugged.

'Just an unfortunate accident,' she said. 'Of that I remain convinced.'

'Lucky you weren't there then,' said Myrtle as she nibbled, her protruding front teeth resembling a hamster's. 'How's that delectable detective?' she purred hopefully but they hadn't seen him for a couple of days.

'He's down in the West Country following up clues.' Wayne, the amateur sleuth, would have dearly liked to be with him.

'I oughtn't to be saying this,' said Myrtle coyly, all dimples and lowered eyelids, 'but I rather think he took quite a shine to me.'

'Whenever did *you* get to meet him?' asked Jinx, astounded, throwing Myrtle into confusion, to Dottie's delight. Talk your way out of that one, dearie. Always sticking your ugly nose in where it isn't wanted.

'Oh,' said Myrtle, affecting nonchalance. 'I just stopped by to offer what help I could. Heavens, can that really be the time? I must be off.'

They laughed like mad as they watched her scuttle away, pausing to chat to the newsmen, hoping for a little of the limelight.

'I wonder why she really came,' said Wayne thoughtfully. 'The murderer revisiting the scene of the crime perhaps.'

'Don't be absurd,' said Jinx quite sharply. A joke was a joke but this was going too far. He would get them all rattled and then where would they be? Things were quite upsetting enough as it was without him sowing seeds of hysteria in their minds. And Myrtle, well Myrtle was pathetic. He'd be pointing the finger at Ambrose next.

'You never know,' said Wayne undaunted. He had never liked Myrtle, didn't trust her one bit. And until the police came up with a solid lead, every one of them remained a possible suspect. The profile of your average killer showed they'd never knowingly leave a job half-done. And if Susie Chandler had been the wrong victim. Well, you just never knew.

Hamish was so emotional he drove straight up from the country to check that Jinx really was alive and well. He arrived unannounced in mid afternoon and Dottie, who'd always approved of him, let him in. Jinx merely waved at him from her desk. She was on one of her interminable phone-calls which showed no sign of ever ending, but Hamish walked straight over to her and gathered her into his arms. Dottie watched with her customary bemusement; she found Jinx's lovelife confusing and chaotic. All these men mad for her yet still she remained detached. An utter and tragic waste of someone so special. Jinx would have made a spectacular mother yet the biological clock was racing away and she still wouldn't settle or make up her mind.

When Jinx was finally off the phone, Hamish asked urgently if they might go for a short walk. He needed to talk to her in private, he said. Jinx declined.

'Sorry, I really can't. I am up to my ears in it as it is. Won't it wait? I'll be through by seven, we could grab a quick meal. I'd ask you back to the house if that was allowed.'

But no, he said, he had to be getting back. From the slump of his shoulders and dejection in his eyes, Dottie had a shrewd suspicion he'd been leading up to something momentous. Though not, poor man, today. What a tough little cookie Jinx could be at times. With the wind knocked completely out of his sails, Hamish wished them a subdued good day then pushed his way back through the photographers to his car. A few flashes went off but only half-heartedly. The story was already growing stale. By tomorrow they'd be hounding some other poor unfortunate.

Down in Nether Stowey, Hal and Trudy were getting nowhere fast. Susie's mother lived alone in a rambling slate-roofed house on the edge of the village where her late husband had been vicar for so many years. There was a married daughter with children just up the street and a couple of sisters hovering nearby. All of whom had to be interviewed, none having anything very interesting to contribute except what an exemplary daughter/sister/niece poor Susie had been. Much hand-wringing and shedding of tears – it seemed being murdered had been the highlight of her life. Having already been through it so recently, Trudy felt sickened by the misery of it all. The effect a murder could have on innocent lives was turning out to be quite an eye-opener, though the more cynical Hal took it all in his stride. Just another day's work to a busy policeman. The sooner they ticked them all off the list, the faster he could return to his main obsession. Tracking down a violent killer before he could strike again.

'You don't believe Susie was the intended victim?' asked Trudy on the long drive back.

'No.'

'How can you be so certain?'

'I can't. Just doesn't smell right. She seems to have been such a mouse of a woman, there was nothing apparent to murder her for. No secret liaison or undisclosed skeletons, not that anyone knows. Just a virtuous woman with quiet tastes, living the life of a virtual recluse.'

'So it really was a case of mistaken identity?'

'I would guess so.'

The two women were roughly the same size and weight, five foot five and around eight and a half store. In the absolute darkness of the curtained room all that would have been discernible was the shape of the sleeper in the bed. And unless the intruder had disturbed his victim first, she would have been overpowered and semi-asphyxiated before he realised his mistake. If he ever did. By which point it would already have been too late. Once he'd started to batter her, he'd be obliged to finish the job. He must have been deranged and out of control. Hal recalled those sickening photos and a nasty taste came into his mouth. They were dealing here with a dangerous nutter. The faster they got him, the better for everyone's sake.

'Have you ruled out completely a random break-in?' They had still not yet caught the Kensington rapist. There was always the possibility that his crimes were simply growing nastier.

'Not entirely. Though this sort of perverted brutality would appear to be personally motivated.' The anal rape and vaginal injuries pointed to someone settling a personal score. Added to the fact that he'd urinated over the body, a clear sign of contempt and the desire to degrade. It was hard to imagine that amount of pent-up hatred or what might conceivably have unleashed it.

Soon they'd be able to release the body, once the Susie statements had been checked and processed. The stricken mother was already arranging the funeral in the small country church where her husband had once officiated. With so much press attention, it would cause a bit of a stir, and Hal determined that the pack should give something back by publishing the details and helping him bait his trap. There's a class of extrovert killer who does what he does for pure kicks and sooner or later returns to the scene of the crime. And when he did, he would find Hal waiting. He would sprinkle the church-yard with out-of-uniform cops and see what swam into his net.

'The statistics on stalkers show that only one in fifty actually kills. And that's usually when there's been some sort of sexual involvement.' Another good reason to rule out Susie, who appeared to have had the morals of a nun.

'You think it was a stalker?' Trudy was startled. This was a new angle he'd not come up with before.

'Could be,' said Hal. 'It shows all the signs. It would certainly account for the savagery of the attack.'

'I thought that stalkers were obsessive fans. Why would one want to see her dead?'

'Look what happened to John Lennon,' said Hal grimly. 'Not to mention all the other recent attacks.' A whole range of celebrities from Madonna to Anna Ford had reported being harassed by someone they knew. It was turning into a designer crime, something of a growing epidemic among the rich and famous.

'I blame it all on the internet,' said Hal. 'Without computers, there'd be less invasion of privacy.'

And a lot harder work to follow the different trails.

The funeral was on Thursday. Jinx was driving down alone. She was wearing a simple black linen dress, with heavy gold bangles to make it a touch less sombre. Dottie watched her fidgeting at her desk and sensed she was reluctant to get going.

'Go with her,' she hissed at Ambrose suddenly, and watched him reel at the very idea. He was not at all good at handling emotional stuff. The thought of all that public grief was more than he could face. He hadn't really known Susie well and normally wouldn't be seen dead at any funeral. It would all be too excruciating for words, he felt quite panicked at the thought. But Dottie was seriously on to his case, he could see from her stern expression.

'I'd go myself, lovie, but I never really knew her.' She glanced down at her shabby old denim skirt and scuffed shoes. There simply wasn't time to get all the way back to Muswell Hill to change, though she'd certainly have done it if she could. She glared at Ambrose like a militant schoolmarm and he shifted his eyes uncomfortably.

'I can't,' he whispered. 'It's really not my scene.' Though he'd walk through fire for Jinx were it anything else.

'Actually,' Jinx said brightly, stuffing things into her bag, 'Marjorie is going to meet me there. Isn't she a brick?'

Marjorie hadn't known Susie at all but pure sentiment prompted the gesture. It would give her something constructive to do. After what they had all just been through themselves, she could imagine a little of the Chandler family's grief. Also she was keen to see Jinx in the flesh to prove to herself she was safe. For similar reasons, Veronica was also coming. Solidarity at a time of real crisis.

Dottie glared at Ambrose. He really was a dolt, there were times she could clout him.

'I'm hardly dressed for it,' he mumbled lamely but she assured him briskly that he would do. He kept a faded woollen tie in one of his drawers for just this sort of emergency and these days funerals were a lot less formal, especially in the country. It wouldn't hurt him to put himself out. She saw Jinx eyeing him with sudden hope.

'We needn't stay long,' she wheedled gently. 'Just a few words with Susie's mum and perhaps a quick cuppa at the house.'

'All right, then,' he said resignedly, unable, as always, to resist her. These past few days had been purgatory. The drive down to Somerset would do them both good.

The funeral was quiet and moving in its dignity. Despite the attention it had received in the news, most of the mourners appeared to be genuine locals, village folk who'd known Susie all her life. There was a handful of reporters and a single camera crew, but for once they had the delicacy to keep a low profile and not thrust their presence into everybody's face. The plain pine coffin was heaped with wild flowers, which Jinx found acutely moving. Somehow they summed up her lost friend's whole spirit. She clung to Ambrose's arm, glad of his support as they shuffled along the narrow path and through the lych-gate of the ancient Norman church. Marjorie and Veronica greeted them from the porch and Jinx ran ahead of him to hug them. It was a highly emotional reconciliation and the tears flowed freely all round. Ambrose, stiff with embarrassment, turned away to study the moss-covered stones.

From twenty yards off, in the shadow of a giant yew tree, Hal and Trudy were watching too. The churchyard was dotted with men in anonymous suits, notable by their haircuts despite an attempt to blend into the scenery.

'You have to be careful on this sort of occasion. Not everyone's a villager and those are the ones to watch.' Hal nodded towards the lych-gate where a party of three was arriving. A plump young woman with a determined jaw and hair cut short like a man's was accompanied by a couple of men in suits, looking decidedly awkward and out of place. Jinx gave a cheery wave and went to greet them. Susie's work-mates, she reported to Trudy. The picture editor from the publishing house, plus two of the guys from production.

'Nice of them to come,' said Trudy.

'Susie was very much loved.'

The bereaved mother arrived with a posse of aunts and preceded them bravely into the church. There was a pleasing scent of beeswax and lilies, and the lectern had been polished till it shone. A well-kept church in a prosperous village, bidding a dignified farewell to one of its own. The choirboys and clergy processed in slowly and the congregation rose to the opening bars of 'Eternal Father'. Jinx pressed her arm against Ambrose's tweedy elbow.

'Thanks, pal, for being here,' she said.

Hal stood observing from the rear of the church, feeling, in his blazer and flannels, conspicuous and slightly ill at ease. Trudy, let off the leash again, had gone slightly wild and was wearing a hat. Not the sort he might have expected either – a mufti version of her official cap, but something daringly high and swirling with a dramatically flattering brim. It set off her eyes, he was bound to admit, and helped her blend in with the mourners.

Hal swept his gaze over the rest of the thickly packed pews. The front two were filled with the family, mainly women with a couple of children and a gnarled old man who looked like a farmer in his Sunday best. Susie's mother was wearing an elderly straw hat and staring unflinchingly at the altar. What a terrible thing it was, to be sure, to have to witness the burial of your own child. Even Hal's toughened heart was moved. She seemed to be bearing up admirably, brave woman. Flanked by a mass of caring neighbours.

As soon as they reached the final verse of 'Abide With Me' and the pall-bearers were shouldering the coffin, Hal and Trudy slipped out of their seats and through the side entrance to the graveyard. The plainclothes policemen had also emerged and were loitering self-consciously among the graves. They awaited their instructions without so much as a flicker. But Hal for once was stumped.

'Let's get back to London,' he said. 'We're wasting our time down here.'

'I'm afraid you're going to have to face it,' said Hal. 'There's absolutely no doubt at all that you were the intended victim.' They were seated in his Earl's Court office, cramped into a small space that was tightly jam-packed with files. It was mid morning of the following day and he'd invited Jinx in for an update on their progress. The keys to her house lay between them on the desk and these he now handed over.

'You can move back in whenever you like,' he told her. 'Only please be extra careful and remain constantly on your guard.'

Jinx, faintly amused, regarded him quizzically. He was awfully nice-looking, if he'd only smile more, but he was being slightly absurd. As if he had watched too many police soaps and was modelling himself on David Caruso. She was aware that he quite fancied her but that gave her little thrill. She was well used to male company, enjoyed their admiration, but refused to be either bullied or manipulated.

'I'm serious,' said Hal curtly, seeing the humour in her eyes. Dammit, lady. She was treating it all as a joke. 'Whoever it was who did it is more than likely to return to finish the job. Unfinished business and all that. I can't underline that too much.'

Jinx looked suddenly uncertain. The sparkle went out of her eyes. 'Aren't you being a tad pessimistic?' she said.

'I'm afraid not.' At least he'd caught her attention. 'If you look at what little evidence we have, the murder was obviously premeditated.'

'Not the Kensington rapist, then, or another of that ilk?'

'Highly unlikely. A random intruder would have been out for what he could steal, yet nothing apart from the snapshot appears to be missing. No mess, no destruction, no ransacked drawers. No vandalism just for the hell of it. Which is sinister.'

'Why?'

'Think about it. You have some very nice stuff in your house, highly stealable. Jewellery and pictures and other obvious collectibles. So why would an anonymous intruder, having gained such easy access, murder a stranger without filling his pockets too? Doesn't add up.'

'So you're suggesting it might have been someone I actually know?' The thought was almost too terrifying to contemplate. Hal nodded. Finally she was hearing what he'd been trying to tell her all this time.

'And why that particular photo and not the others?' He had already come clean and returned the borrowed group shot. 'It can't have been simply the frame.'

Jinx shrugged, very much sobered. 'I give up. You tell me.'

'The answer is we don't know, but there was nothing random about this killing. And if we rule out Susie, the intended victim was you. Please take on board the point I am making and continue to keep on your toes. You can call me any time. I'll give you my direct line.'

She took the card he handed her and tucked it into her wallet.

'It could be almost anyone you know, not necessarily part of your own circle. The man from whom you buy your newspaper, the petrol-pump attendant at whom you always smile. A shop assistant, the window cleaner. Even, perhaps, your hairdresser. Anyone with whom you have even a slight degree of acquaintance, you never know what's going on in their head. Don't let anyone in without identification and always keep your door chained and the windows locked even when you're at home. I'm serious. I don't want to scare you but I'm pretty certain he'll be back. Sooner rather than later, I would guess.'

'You're the boss,' said Jinx, suddenly meek, beginning to be seriously shaken. The appalling murder had been bad enough, but a stalker had seemed too far-fetched. But the dashing DCI seemed to think she was still in danger so maybe, at least for the time being, she should listen.

18

And then I found out what I'd done and my world fell apart. Fucking hell, I had really screwed up. You have to believe me, I am not by nature violent, only when things get out of hand. I had done what I felt was my God-given duty and stopped the stupid cunt from making a further fool of herself. She had stepped out of line without ever letting me know and now it was up to me to settle a score. I might have got a bit carried away but what the hell. She had provoked me beyond all endurance and deserved to die.

Look at it my way, if you will. After years of frustration, of her flaunting her body before me, the flirting, the constant come-ons, the teasing and the jokes, here she was suddenly in the arms of another. It was more than anyone fully red-blooded could take. I am truly sorry about Susie Chandler, who was, from all accounts, a good and virtuous woman. They say that all cats are grey in the dark and I guess I simply got carried away.

But now I am faced with another huge imponderable. She's back and I don't know what to do. Do I allow her to live and expunge all *her sins or should I exterminate her now? In a way I suppose I've been given a second chance and I haven't decided how to handle things. One thing is certain, I shall watch her like a hawk and she won't get away with it again.*

The thing about women is they are fundamentally sluts and need to be protected from their own lascivious natures. Or not be too surprised if they end up in bad trouble.

Like Susie.

19

The phone rang but when Jinx answered it no one appeared to be there. She'd been in already for the best part of an hour and was still engrossed in reading the morning's mail. It rang again; again silence. She glanced with irritation at the answering machine to check she'd switched it off when she first came in. It was just after nine, the time in the morning she most valued, the mews outside a riot of bright spring colours. A little piece of paradise was what it seemed to Jinx. How smart she'd been to snap up this lease, pricey perhaps but worth every penny. Exactly the sort of tranquil environment conducive to creative work like theirs. The phone rang again.

'Yes?' said Jinx impatiently. She hated to have her private time interrupted and usually calls didn't begin quite this early. The whole point of her being there was to get her head sorted before the others got in. But nobody spoke and, after a brief pause, the receiver was softly replaced.

Serafina burst in then in a flurry of real aggravation, reminding Jinx vividly of her own impetuous younger self. Unusually, the glossy hair was in disarray and her normally waxen complexion flushed with anger. Jinx was intrigued. It was rare for Serafina to lose her cool. She stomped across the studio without so much as a glance at Jinx and thumped down her handbag on her desk. Something was clearly bugging her extremely. Jinx hoped it was not going to turn into one of those days.

'What?'

'Foolish boy,' Serafina was muttering through gritted teeth as she slammed through her drawers in search of something elusive. She tossed back her hair as she booted up her computer. Whatever it was looked like more than a lovers' tiff. Though it was up to her if she wanted to discuss it, Jinx really couldn't have cared less. She returned to her reading with a private smile and left the younger woman to simmer down.

Dottie blew in breathlessly, clutching a carton of milk. She was full of her usual apologies, blaming the lateness of the hour on the tardiness of her bus. Jinx waved her excuses aside, please not now. All she wanted was good strong coffee, not another litany on the horrors of London Transport. It was a well-known fact that the traffic in central London was a disgrace and growing more constipated daily. What the city required was a competent mayor with the necessary grit to sort it out. She wondered why Dottie didn't take the tube instead, then recalled she'd had a fright down there just recently. The city was growing more dangerous too as evidenced by what had happened to Susie.

'Tea, Serafina?' called Dottie from the kitchen, quite calmed down. But Serafina didn't grace her with a reply. Dottie glanced at Jinx who simply shook her head. Don't ask me. When Serafina was in one of her dark moods they were lucky to get a civil word out of her all day. At times it lasted even longer, depending on the cause. Jinx thought it rude, though Dottie was far more tolerant. It all had to do with that difficult childhood which had made her so thin and unstable. Attention-seeking was usually the manifestation of something that went a lot deeper. Pure psychobabble in Jinx's eyes. To her it was just plain brattish behaviour, and the sooner Serafina snapped out of it, the better for all of them here. This was a place of work, not a kindergarten. Serafina, after all, was very nearly thirty though you'd certainly not think so when she acted up in this way.

The phone rang again. Dottie picked it up but there was no one there. 'Hello,' she said a number of times, but a listening presence just hung up. She shrugged and returned to her work. People had no manners any more. A simple word of apology was all that was called for if you happened to keep dialling a wrong number.

Jinx was planning a meeting for later in the day, there were things she had to discuss urgently. But she needed them all there and in the right mood. Didn't want to get anyone rattled. Perfect teamwork was an absolute essential if DBI-2000 was to continue to be on target. With so much investment capital tied up in its development she dared not risk anything going wrong at this stage. So Serafina had better shape up. Or else she'd be in serious trouble.

Serafina was in a genuine bate to a state of positive savagery. That idiot boy, James, in whom she had placed her trust, had still failed to deliver what she'd been angling for since they first met. Worse, he had now been summoned to head office and was leaving town almost immediately. She had slammed the door of the Jaguar when he told her and flounced off wordlessly up the mews. She didn't have feelings for him, not even the remotest, but he'd become a crucial part of her master plan – her passport into the precincts of IEP where her real quarry was located. Now she was awaiting, with unfamiliar apprehension, the grovelling apology she was sure was bound to come. She was unaccustomed to being treated in this way. Especially by a nobody even if he were an Hon.

'So what's biting you?' asked Wayne eventually, sick of her

nervy jumping each time the phone rang. Serafina, with her constant theatrics, was more than he could take as early as this. It had been another hard night and his head still wasn't quite clear. She totally ignored him as she was wont to do and this added greatly to his irritation. So he sauntered over, hands in pockets, and settled down matily on her desk

'Don't!' she said snappishly as he unsettled all her papers, and gave him a great shove. Wayne studied her thoughtfully for a second or two, then suddenly leaned over and ruffled her hair. Serafina reacted by punching him hard in the face; Jinx was obliged to intervene.

'Cut it out, you two!' she commanded sharply. 'And both get on with your work. Wayne, if you've nothing better to do, go and help Dottie with the filing.'

Wayne pulled a face, though not at Jinx, and sauntered off amiably to do her bidding. He was a good kid, Wayne, talented and good-natured, whereas Serafina could be a right little bitch. Jinx took in the scowl on her face, then popped up to the gallery for a private word with Ambrose, who had come in late, having been to the London Library, and only caught the end of the spat. This childish acting up had got to stop before it started getting in the way of their work.

'Tell me, please, I was never like that,' groaned Jinx. She was perched on the edge of Ambrose's desk, one foot swinging while he worked. 'Was I?' she added anxiously when he failed to respond. Ambrose leaned back thoughtfully and slowly stretched, then took off his glasses and gave them a careful polish. She laughed with relief when she spotted the twinkle in his eye. He loved more than anything to get a rise out of her.

'You always were a bit of an uppity little madam,' he said slowly. 'But no, not ever quite like that. The thing about you, Jinx, is you always spit things out. None of this brooding or flouncing.' He raised one arm affectedly to toss back an imaginary curtain of hair in accurate imitation of Serafina's mannerisms. 'With you there's never the slightest doubt of what's going on in your mind.' He gave her an affectionate smile. 'For that I suppose we must be thankful.'

Jinx chuckled and gave him a rapid hug. Ambrose, bless his heart, was always spot on. Little ever escaped that needle-sharp eye.

'I have given her everything she could possibly want including paying her way above the odds. So why does she behave like a silly spoilt child? Please explain that.'

'Maybe because she is one.' Ambrose shrugged and turned back to his work. His screen was covered with hieroglyphics that Jinx had given up trying to understand. The problem these days with so many young people was they wanted it all on a plate. He thought back regretfully to their own early start when they'd all slaved uncomplainingly for a pittance.

'But we did have fun, didn't we,' said Jinx, reading his thoughts. 'Though the Old Man certainly made us work for it.'

'That was all part of his brilliance,' said Ambrose. 'He allowed us to develop our own special talents and at our own speed.' And had not interfered like his scheming, ruthless nephew who had caused more damage in just a few months than could ever have been envisaged.

Max Weinberg was a genius, in the most literal sense of the word, the last of the truly great Viennese publishers. His vision and understanding had been unsurpassed as evidenced by the outstanding books that were his lasting legacy. They no longer made gifted entrepreneurs quite like that since the book world had started to self-destruct. Once the accountants came in and took over the running of publishing houses, brilliance and originality had rapidly gone to the wall. These days they no longer cared about quality and integrity but only cost-cutting and that miserable bottom line. Jinx was correct to lament all that lost fun. There wasn't much of that around now.

*   *   *

The truth of the matter was, had Serafina been honest, that recent events had thrown her into such a spin she was finding it near impossible to adapt. Always ruthlessly ambitious, she had her eye constantly fixed on the main chance so that Jinx's apparent demise had rocketed her giddily into a new dream. In which drippy young James, with his calf-eyed adoration, had been just one more weapon in her armoury. With Jinx no longer in her way, she'd had a sudden glimpse of an undreamed-of future come tantalisingly that much closer and almost within her grasp. Only to have it jerked away again when Jinx came strolling in, alive and well. And now the super-nerd appeared to have vanished too, over to New York indeed which was where she most wanted to go too. Without, it appeared, so much as a last goodbye. It was almost too vexing to think about sanely. It meant she was back to square one.

'Anyone care for a sarnie?' asked Dottie at lunchtime, preparing to pop round to the post with some parcels. For once, unusually, she had no takers. Jinx was headed for a business lunch in Soho while Ambrose muttered something about a haircut. And Wayne was off on some mysterious errand of his own. Only Serafina remained frigidly silent. She swept away to the cloakroom and returned with brushed hair and lipstick freshly applied. Once again, without so much as a word of explanation, she stalked off out of the door and up the mews. Her colleagues exchanged looks of frank amazement but nobody bothered to comment. Life was too short for the moods of Serafina. They were tired of her sulky child behaviour. She needed a sharp slap and very soon.

Serafina headed home, crossing the flyover at Baron's Court and walking the fifteen minutes to her flat. She had got a mortgage when she first joined McLennan Graphics and was slowly and fastidiously improving her new home. None of her work-mates had yet been allowed round to view it, though they dutifully forked out contributions whenever an occasion presented itself. Christmas and birthdays, once even Valentine's Day when the object of her desire had been cranberry glass. Jinx was always very free with her largesse and enjoyed the obsession of the younger woman with feathering her neat little nest.

'Easier to get married,' she had remarked. 'Then you could fit it out all in one go. You could always dump him later.'

'And have to return the presents,' Dottie reminded her, ever the stickler for correct behaviour. Jinx laughed. She had personally never had to bother with any such problem. All she owned had been paid for outright at the time and solely by herself. She prized above everything her financial independence, was proud of her careful management, which meant that she had no debts. Not so Serafina, however, who was getting quite hot and bothered by what she increasingly saw as her humiliatingly single state. She had even had reckless thoughts of applying to 'Blind Date' but was too proud. Yes, they'd take her, were bound to do so because of the way she looked. But she wasn't about to go flaunting herself on television as a sorry sad sack who couldn't catch a man. Young James had not remotely appealed to her physically but his solvent status was more than a little attractive. And now even he had defected, leaving her back on the shelf. Apart, of course, from the ultimate dream which she still refused to give up. All the eligible single men appeared to have evaporated, leaving only wimps and gays and sad no-hopers like Ambrose.

She reached the red brick building into which she'd sunk her savings and trudged on up to the second floor. Her door opened straight into a tiny cramped hall with a dinky kitchen and living-room attached. Really only large enough for one and even then it was a squeeze. She stared with disenchantment at the unmade bed and the unwashed breakfast dishes in the sink. She definitely deserved much better than this, it was a waste of her style and her beauty. She studied her reflection in the mottled antique mirror and tidied the blue-black hair with distracted fingers. Thirty heralded the advent of her fourth decade, and once past that watermark it was downhill all the way. Jinx was the obvious glaring example.

She checked her answering machine for messages and saw, with a jolt of relieved delight, that she'd had seventeen already this morning. So the wimp hadn't deserted her after all, was obviously frantic to explain. The steel re-entered Serafina's soul. Let him wait for her forgiveness till she had eaten. She opened the fridge seeking culinary inspiration but found it virtually bare. Just some hardening pitta bread and half a carton of ageing hummus. She wasn't at all hungry, her usual state, so just nibbled an anchovy-stuffed olive while she anticipated the pleasure of hearing him grovel. This was how it always had been; the second she grew remotely emotional, all appetite fled. Dottie was constantly fussing and saying she didn't eat properly. But what did placid old Dottie know about the more sensitive side of life? Dottie was like some tired old dray-horse, overweight and uninspired, while Serafina was more of an embryo dragonfly, aching to be set free.

Seventeen messages, well that was overdoing it, even for someone like him. She licked her fingers then pressed the replay button, smiling with relish at the thought of what he would say. He would have to display an enormous amount of contrition if he wanted to crawl back into her good books. She'd forgive him, of course, once she'd played it to the hilt because she was anxious to join him in New York. But there were no messages, only a string of sinister hangups though she distinctly heard someone breathing on the line. She ran through them all, growing more and more alarmed, until she reached the last one and heard a single word, barely audible. 'Bitch!' it spat at her in a voice that positively hissed. An icy shiver of terror ran down her spine.

Jinx returned from lunch at three thirty and summoned Serafina abruptly to the conference-room. The drawback of these open-plan offices was their absolute lack of privacy. She didn't mince words but came swiftly to the point.

'What's up with you? You've been impossible all day.' Acting like a petulant schoolgirl, getting up everyone's nose.

Serafina's face was deathly pale but she stood there in silence with tightened lips. She was more shaken than she would care to admit by the vitriol in that unknown voice but hesitated to tell Jinx about it yet. For that would entail spilling the beans about James, which might prove fatal to the next stage of her plan. But she might go and discuss it with the dishy DCI, assuming she could convince him to be discreet. For something dark and incredibly disturbing appeared to have entered all their lives. What had happened to Susie might well be only the start, there was something very eerie going on.

'Well?'

Jinx's eyes, normally warm and smiling, right now were as chilly as chips of amber. She had had enough of this aberrant behaviour and it showed.

'I'm sorry,' said Serafina in a low, low voice. 'Lately I've been finding it hard to cope.'

'With what?' Jinx certainly didn't pull her punches. Serafina was suddenly almost scared.

'With how things are at present,' she explained almost pleadingly, fingering her perfectly matched pearls. 'I find I can no longer sleep at night. Keep running over the details of the murder.' And now the menacing hangups on her own unlisted phone. Where were they coming from, what on earth did it all mean? She knew that James was essentially pathetic but had not put him down as a vindictive fool.

'Oh my love, I didn't think. How selfish I have been.' In a trice Jinx had her arms about her, was cradling her head to her chest. She smelled disconcertingly of soap and expensive fragrance but Serafina fought an urge to pull away. She allowed Jinx to comfort her for a seemly couple of minutes then broke away gently and found that her tears were real. So it did work with women as effectively as men; she knew now to add it to her repertoire.

'I ought to have been more thoughtful,' said Jinx, still with one hand on her shoulder. 'While I was away whooping it up in the sun, the rest of you poor loves were going through hell.'

With the awfulness of the murder and all its attendant horrors. The police inquiry, the endless repeated questioning. That incisive detective with his chilly, invasive eyes. Not to mention the sheer mental stress of appalling grief and the shock of the violence of it all. Poor Serafina, no wonder she was cracking.

Serafina made a sudden decision and told her about the phone-calls but secretly, in her heart, she was starting to crow. What a ridiculously soft touch Jinx was turning out to be.

Jinx was appalled when she heard Serafina's story and told her she really must talk to Hal. He'd mentioned a stalker but she hadn't really listened. And now it appeared that someone was closing in. First Dottie on the station stairs and now these silent calls. Not to mention the recent hang-ups in the office.

'Has this ever happened before?' Serafina said no. She had had her fair share of admirers and hangers-on but this was the first time ever she'd been spooked. How had the caller known she wasn't there or got hold of her number in the first place? Perhaps because he'd been watching the flat or even followed her home. Mollified by Jinx's concerned attention, she allowed herself to be led back down the stairs.

The others all looked up in surprise. About time. Ambrose was relieved, he loathed any sort of disharmony, while Dottie was frankly delighted that the intervention had obviously worked. Only Wayne remained cynical but he kept it to himself. So she'd managed to pull it off again, the scheming little puss, and still come out of it smelling of roses. Well, she'd better start watching her back from now on. He, for one, had had as much as he could take.

20

No, Jinx had most assuredly never been like that, for moody was nowhere in her nature. Outspoken, maybe, and occasionally even wrong-headed, but she always possessed the humility and good sense to back off the instant she sensed she might be overstepping the mark. In the days when she was still Max's golden girl, able to twist him around her little finger, she still never failed to listen and absorb, learning as much from the master as she could. Which, in the long run, had stood her in excellent stead. Much of the business knowhow she now relied on had come from Max, a genius with vision far beyond his time. That first book fair had turned out a resounding triumph and she'd waltzed back to London with a bulging order book. Plus a Filofax crammed with all kinds of new contacts, still the fulcrum of her power base now. Max was fulsome in his praise and she'd basked in the warmth of his approval. She was popular and successful and now she was going places. The future was starting to look very rosy indeed.

Until that afternoon in late November when she barrelled back, late, into her office to find a stranger looming over her desk. Jinx stopped dead in the doorway, guiltily aware of that extra glass of wine, and waited for him to look up from perusing her papers. Eventually he raised cool eyes to hers and appraised her with all the cuddly charm of a male Medusa.

'Can I help you?' she asked rather tersely. Who the hell was he and what was he doing here? And how had he managed to sneak past the watchful receptionist?

'I assume you're Jinx McLennan,' he said without so much as a smile, coolly taking in her uncombed hair and faintly alcoholic flush. 'I was hoping to catch you before I left.' And then unabashedly he went on snooping, leaving her still standing there, boiling with frustration, like some backstairs skivvy at his beck and call. He finally had the manners to introduce himself, but by that time Jinx was ahead of him. Julius Weinberg – who else could it be? – heir apparent and their new MD. Come to make trouble before he was even in there.

Her first impression was that he was tall, unusually so; six foot three or even more. With the ramrod backbone and supercilious bearing of the not-quite-gentleman with more money than class. His thick dark hair was slicked back, Gecko-style, his eyes so black she could hardly distinguish the pupils. His cheekbones were classic and his nose slightly hooked. She loathed him profoundly on sight. He was wearing an immaculate city banker's suit along with the obligatory striped shirt. He looked down at her as though she were something nasty on his shoe, and told her briskly, before he swept out, to be sure to close the window before she left. Jinx collapsed like a punctured balloon, then immediately tried Ambrose's number. Too late. She could tell immediately that the eagle had already landed. Ambrose was incoherent to the point of total silence.

'What on earth are we going to do?' she groaned despairingly in the pub.

'You were the one who had such high hopes,' Ambrose

reminded her. 'Teacher's pet who can do no wrong. I've no doubt you'll soon have him suitably emasculated and eating out of your hand just like his uncle.'

'Not a chance,' was all she would say. This was a man who clearly didn't like women, certainly not in an office scenario unless they were making coffee or typing letters. She loathed the idea of him being constantly around, of having to deal with him every day. After Max, with his warmth and accessibility, his pig of a nephew was like an icy shower.

Julius started officially on the fourth of January, the beginning of the new year. He was very much in evidence right from day one and they gave him an office at the top of the main staircase from which he could keep an eye on the staff straggling in. His door was always open except when he was in conference and he managed to pick on Ambrose as he crawled in at twenty past ten.

'Morning,' called Julius brusquely from his desk. His papers were sorted and a tape already being typed. He had had his coffee and was searching for trouble to create.

'Hold up on the underground, was it?' he asked. Ambrose embarked on a stumbling explanation, then brushed the whole matter aside. In his hand, as it happened, he was carrying a load of work he had taken home to do over Christmas. But this rotten outsider was beneath his contempt. He couldn't be bothered even to answer.

Late that following summer, Max suffered another heart attack. Not too serious, provided he took things easy for a while, but enough for his doctor to warn him to go slow. But what else was a man to do in his situation? Wifeless and childless, the business was his whole life. Apart from opera, to which he was addicted, he really had nothing else. Except now for his ambitious nephew who had really got Weinbergs fully on course and was beginning, against all the odds, to show startling results. Even Jinx and Ambrose were obliged to give him grudging credit, though they still couldn't bear him, resented his over-bearing manner. Both avoided him as much as they could. On the whole, things worked better that way.

'He remains a jerk,' was Ambrose's opinion, adding out of fairness, 'though a bloody effective one.' What Julius lacked in experience of the fine art of book publishing, he more than made up for with his killer market instincts. Bringing him on board had turned out to be a stroke of genius. He had dragged Weinbergs into the present, got the accounts and shipping departments fully computerised and sent a handful of key personnel off on management courses.

'Editors,' he had been heard to say, 'don't know their arses from their elbows when it comes to business. Show your average publisher a balance sheet and he hasn't a clue what he's looking at. No wonder the industry's fast going down the drain.'

Jinx always bristled at his superior condescension, especially his treatment of women. But she had to concede that he did have a point. Since she'd been selling international co-editions, her own commercial knowledge was developing in leaps and bounds. Which even Julius eventually came to notice. If they'd only got on better, they'd have made a brilliant team, which is why, when Julius broached it, Max gave him his full support.

'Just hear me out,' he told Jinx gently, over an early evening whisky in his office. 'I know your heart is still in design but what you are showing all the signs of becoming is a truly gifted salesperson. And that's rare.' He laughed at the instant clouding of her brow and patted her hand. They had grown very close in recent years and he viewed her more like a favoured daughter. She was bright, she was innovative, had guts and would go far. Further if Julius allowed her to have her head. So his latest proposal seemed like a step in the right direction.

'He wants you to move over and work directly beneath him. Recognises your potential and is keen to give it a go. It's a rare opportunity, trust me.' His wise old eyes watched her shrewdly while she considered. The idea of working closer to Julius made her skin prickle with distaste. He was bumptious and opinionated with a scathing scorn of women. She doubted they'd last even a day without coming to blows. But on the other hand . . . She loved her design work and always would but was more turned on by the buzz of the marketplace. It gave her a kick just to get out there and sell, brought all the adrenaline surging to the surface. Under Julius's direction, there was no saying how far she might climb. For all his flaws, he was a consummate businessman with a brain like a computer behind the appraising eyes. She saw Max watching her and gave a sudden smile. He was a wily old so-and-so and had known all along he had her hooked.

'Go on, then,' she said reluctantly. 'I'll give it a go just for you. But don't imagine it will be easy.'

'I know that my dear.' He freshened her glass. 'That's exactly why it will probably work. I know full well that my nephew can be a handful and still needs some of his corners smoothing off. I blame it on South Africa,' he added. 'But please don't ever quote me on that.'

He showed her out and returned to his reading while Jinx burst excitedly in on Ambrose.

'Guess what!' she cried as she told him the details and would not be put off by his glowering reaction. Ambrose was a pet but also a bit of an old woman. He preferred the tried and trusted, was fearful of rocking the boat.

'Come on,' she said briskly, switching off his desklamp. 'Time to stop working and get out of here. You know what they say about all work and no play. And you'll only end up ruining your eyes.'

Jinx's new office was in the main building, in the hub of where the real action was. It opened directly off Julius's own which meant he had continuous access to her. He rapidly developed the irritating habit of addressing her loudly as though she were his personal slave.

'Coffee, Jinx!' he would call out when he had a visitor, or, 'Tidy your desk, there's a good girl.'

Jinx would bristle and try hard not to bite but found him detestable and wasn't sure how long she'd stand it.

'Is my nephew minding his manners?' Max would occasionally ask, but she was far too fair-minded and smart to risk telling tales out of school. Running to Uncle Max would get her precisely nowhere. She would simply learn to deal with him in her own way. He threw work at her as though he were constantly testing and she gasped with the pressure but refused to complain or give in. She was damned if she'd let him get the upper hand. And, little by little, she started to win his respect.

Julius was always immaculately turned out, in sharp contrast to the sloppy attire of his colleagues. He still dressed as if for the city and his range of suits was enormous. Whatever Max was paying him had to be considerable. But he did look good, even Jinx had to grant him that. She admired a man who wore his clothes well. And he was, after all, their Managing Director and figurehead of the firm.

'You're not getting sweet on him?' challenged Damien when she mentioned this, while Ambrose just muttered and wasn't amused. Nor particularly was Jinx. He might have his moments, with his height and superior bearing, but wasn't at all the type to turn her on. Too cold and supercilious, with a manner designed to repel. He rarely made direct eye contact or any concession at all to the fact she was female. And that really bugged her to the extent she wanted to pummel him. Who the hell did he think he was, with all his ludicrous affectations? The expensive suits, the handmade shoes. The swanky restaurants and superlative theatre seats. When all he actually was underneath was a slick, colonial, fast-talking salesman with no creative talent or flair. Or, come to that, manners either.

But at business, where it counted, he was undeniably a wiz, and there he had all of them dazzled. His reputation in London was already soaring and soon the Americans, too, beat a path to his door. He was sharp and canny with a mind like a razor and made split-second decisions that alarmed even Jinx. She admired his cool nerve and clarity of vision. She liked his gambling instincts, too, which she found quite sexy. And if he weren't so vile to her, she might even have let him know. But he swept in and out, scarcely noticing her at all, and when occasionally she happened to answer his phone, it was often some needy-sounding woman, exactly the sort she'd expect of him. She once saw him out after hours with a woman, in Shaftesbury Avenue at theatre time. Just as Jinx might have imagined, she was slender and leggy, decked out in dazzling designer clothes with limp, dark debutante hair. She was clinging to his arm as if welded there while Julius looked preoccupied and grim. Good luck to the pair of them, thought Jinx with a grimace. And ducked away before he saw her to meld rapidly with the crowd.

In the early autumn, just before the run-up to Frankfurt, Max finally conceded defeat and announced that in future he would be taking things a lot easier. His staff were horrified; Max *was* the firm. But he'd made his decision, though with real regret, and was handing over his majority share-holding to Julius who would now take his place in the driving-seat. Ambrose and Damien were thoroughly dismayed whereas Jinx, although grudgingly, could well see the sense of it. Max was into his seventies by then and no longer a totally fit man. He deserved some respite after so many years' hard labour and was fortunate in having an able heir to whom he could hand the reins. It meant that at last he'd be able to relax while keeping an active interest in the firm.

'He'll still be here for the important things,' Jinx explained. 'Which is really all that matters.' His mind was unclouded, his vision unimpaired. He maintained his warm contacts in the galleries and museums and was held in deep respect throughout the art world. The books would still continue to roll in. Max could do the fun part knowing Julius was handling the business. Which was how it had actually been since Julius's arrival except for one vital change. His control would be no longer merely nominal.

The Frankfurt Book Fair, in the second week of October, turned out another resounding success for Jinx. She was really into the swing of it now, even Julius was impressed by what she achieved. She spent cripplingly long hours on the company stand and the orders came flooding in. Along with her outgoing personality and cheerful smile, she could pack a very hard punch indeed, then carry it off with her infectious charm till the publishers were rolling at her feet. She always managed to look good, too; bandbox fresh while the rest were already bedraggled. And despite her many admirers, she remained aloof, putting her professionalism ahead of all the partying. Julius, aware of this, watched her with growing respect. What a dynamo she was, this spirited young woman, with her warm personality and winning smile. She also possessed amazing resilience and could stay on her feet for twelve hours at a stretch without ever complaining or asking to take a break.

He cornered her one night in the bar of their hotel and casually asked if she'd care to join him for dinner. Jinx was astonished but genuinely not free. She was meeting a Finnish publisher, she explained, with whom she was working on a deal. That, after all, was the purpose of this fair. She could gossip with her boss at any time. Julius, a man quite unused to rejection, wandered off in search of other company. He admired her integrity and was starting to like her looks. She drew people to her like a magnet.

In the early hours, he returned to the hotel after a dullish dinner in the centre of town with an overbearing American bore. His head was still humming with all that trade gossip but he didn't feel quite ready to turn in. He was too charged up. The bar was packed and the noise from the disco deafening. It seemed as if the whole of the publishing world came to Frankfurt specifically to party. Julius got himself a brandy from the bar, then went to look in on the dancing. A heaving mass of indistinguishable bodies was gyrating to a heavy metal band. He loathed the music, found it jarring and discordant, but enjoyed seeing so many colleagues making fools of themselves on the floor. They were dancing with such uninhibited abandon, he sneakily rather envied them. Julius found it hard to let go, was constantly on his guard. Part of his public school façade he occasionally wished he could shed.

The flashing strobes cut like searchlights through the throng, illuminating uncannily white clothing, eyes and teeth. And right there in the midst of them, whirling around like a creature possessed, was the woman who had lately become the focus of his thoughts, the enigmatic and elusive Jinx McLennan. If that was the Finnish publisher, she'd not mentioned that he was dishy, and if that was how she concluded her deals, it was way beyond the call of duty. All of a sudden he felt tired and dispirited, a rank outsider in this throbbing, intimate place. He turned away quickly before she could see him, aware that he didn't fit in. They viewed him, he knew, as an arrogant outsider without the charm or talent of his Uncle Max. He knocked back his brandy in one swift swallow, then carried another up to his room as consolation.

21

Dottie would willingly have accompanied her but Jinx felt it was something she needed to do by herself. Territorial stuff, almost a rite of passage, repossessing her beloved home, now so obscenely defiled. All the happy memories, the laughter, the parties, the pulling together of things, stood in serious danger of being ruined by the horror that had occurred. Whether she could possibly face living there again still remained to be seen. Even the recent presence of the anonymous forensic team, which had scoured the house thoroughly yet managed to leave it immaculate, added to her innate sense of violation. This was the house she had slaved so hard to acquire, the pinnacle of her material achievements, her fortress, her safety blanket. From a crumbling shell she had created a magical sanctuary and sunk whatever she had into its restoration. Its market value had lately more than doubled but she'd never ever thought of selling it, not till now. It represented, quite simply, everything she was. Her worst repeating nightmare was that she'd somehow lost the house. She would wake up sweating with a hammering heart and calm down only when consciousness returned fully and she recognised her own familiar curtains. So now she approached it gingerly, like a lover caught once *in flagrante*, praying it wouldn't betray her a second time.

She had told them in the office she'd be in a little late, reckoning it would take a couple of hours at least to come to terms with the house. It was one of those bright summer mornings, full of optimism and light. The blossom was virtually over but the trees were still thick with luxuriant foliage, and a score of intrepid city birds were singing their hearts out unseen. At the pub next door they were sluicing down the yard and lugging heavy beer-crates to the cellar. The barman called out a cheery greeting which Jinx acknowledged with a wave. Business was almost back to normal and she'd be in there later, once she'd exorcised the bogeymen and made her peace with the place.

She wandered through each of the silent downstairs rooms, opening windows and checking that all was in order. In the dining-room-cum-kitchen she flung wide the doors and ventured outside for a look at the patio before ducking back out of the range of inquisitive eyes. The last thing she wanted, while she was feeling so iffy, was any intrusion at all upon her precious space. Silence and privacy were what she craved, time to lick her wounds and come to terms with it all, to encourage the return of the good vibes.

She switched on the kettle for coffee before steeling herself for the daunting excursion upstairs. The sooner she got back to a normal routine, the more able she would be to take up residence here again. The fridge was virtually empty so she started to make a list. Once she'd sorted things here she'd pop round to the supermarket for a big, therapeutic shop. And also pick up fresh flowers from the corner barrow to kill the grim memories and bring back some life to the place.

Dottie had been on at her since she first moved in to do something constructive with this patio. A pity to waste all that open space, though she'd never been remotely interested in gardening. The furthest she'd run to would be a couple of terracotta pots to tone with the dining-room walls, nothing more. Something hardy and cheerful, requiring minimal attention, that could be ruthlessly disposed of as soon as it passed its best. Jinx's throwaway philosophy, her breezy approach to life. The same had applied to relationships. Up till now.

When, all those years ago, she had chanced upon that photograph, it had driven a dagger through her heart and practically done in her head. She'd been coping quite well, concealing her pain, doing her song and dance routine for the world who didn't know what she'd been through. Few had ever known of that disastrous alliance and they all assumed she was over it long ago. Jinx was so pretty, so popular, such fun. She could have whoever took her fancy and practically always did. It never occurred to anyone at all that she might be concealing a secret.

Then just when she'd thought she had got it right out of her system, there he was suddenly in the pages of *Tatler*, suave and sophisticated, at some charity do in New York. With his wife on his arm, the part that truly gutted her. She had blown a mini fuse and stormed out of the salon, to the consternation of Tony and Pansy. She had leapt blindly on to a passing bus, without an idea of where she was going, and ended up in a Notting Hill bar, drowning her long-suppressed sorrows. With Joel the magnificent, of the chocolate eyes and warm seductive smile, who had plied her with cocktails and allowed her to let it all out. And then, as a final solace, come home with her to her bed. What a man.

They remained great friends, even after all these years, though she rarely ever shared him with her set. A girl needed to have the occasional secret tryst, and Joel was where she went when she felt fragile. When she needed a hug or a shoulder to cry on or simply a jolly good laugh. Joel, in fact, was much more than just a barman. He had his own rock group which was rising fast. But that first night he had been both Samaritan and friend. For that she would always adore him.

When at last she felt strong enough, she ventured upstairs to confront the crime scene, or what was left of it now the police had picked it clean. It took a major effort of will to open her bedroom door, tightening her stomach against rising nausea as she once again saw the grotesque webbing of blood on the walls. How frenziedly that animal must have attacked and with apparent superhuman force. Just the idea made her queasy again. The blood-soaked carpet had been destroyed and the old Victorian boards creaked and shifted when she trod on them. This, her private sanctum, had always been her most cherished room, though she was not sure she could ever face sleeping in it again. She recalled, with a sudden chill of horror, Serafina's story of the silent telephone calls. Whatever terrible thing had happened that night to Susie they had not heard the end of – of that she was suddenly sure. Violent death had sullied her pretty home. And until the evil was exorcised she could never feel safe here again.

Her Victorian nursing chair, which she used while blow-drying her hair, had also been hauled off by forensics for closer lab testing. She knew she could never ever face it again, spattered by Susie's blood. Her bronze and ivory dancing lady, an original *art nouveau* piece, was also missing though only temporarily, safe in police custody as part of the crucial evidence. Despite its use as the actual murder weapon, this was one item she would eventually be obliged to reprieve. She had bought it on an extravagant whim at a time when she could barely afford it, to commemorate a particular landmark, a turning-point in her career.

Most of this stuff she had picked up piece by piece and was all the more precious for that. Nothing new or discordant or too glossy. Jinx, with her educated artist's eye, had a passion for pretty yet serviceable antiques and the cottage provided an ideal showcase for what she had gathered over the years. On quiet Sundays, often with Ambrose in tow, she would trawl the junk shops for the occasional rare treasure that could still be picked up reasonably if you knew where to look.

The doorbell shrilled, disturbing her contemplation, and she knew before she opened it just who would be standing there. Not like her neighbour to have kept away so long. Jinx steeled herself resignedly as she answered the door.

'My dear,' said Peggy breathlessly, bursting with self-importance. 'I saw your windows were open and came straight round.' She was peering inside with that prurient curiosity Jinx always found so distasteful. Hang on a minute, she wanted to protest. Susie Chandler was my friend. Instead she stood impassively as Peggy pecked her cheek, then stood aside to let the intruder in.

Over yet more coffee in the pristine kitchen, Peggy cross-examined her just as Jinx had known she would. Questions, questions, they all came tumbling out. Who and why and what and how; she was greedy for each little detail. Besides underlining her own contribution as the one who had noticed the fatally unlocked door, the good citizen who'd alerted the police.

'I knew things weren't quite as they should be, my dear. You can't be too careful, not even in a neighbourhood like this.' Peggy's eyes were bright with excitement, calamity always brought out the worst in her. But Jinx knew that basically she had a good heart. Just didn't always let it show.

'I said to my Arthur, that's not like our Jinx. Going away and leaving the house not properly locked. That young woman's got a good head on her shoulders. Exactly what I told the police.'

Jinx smiled and patted Peggy's hand. Lucky, for once, she'd been so much on the ball or Susie's ravaged body might have lain there for a week. Better, of course, if she'd snooped a little sooner, which Jinx managed to restrain herself from saying. She might well have stumbled on the crime while it was in progress and then they'd have had two corpses instead of just the one.

'So who do you think might have done it, dear? Any ideas at all?' Peggy was practically panting with sordid relish. Jinx merely shrugged.

'Your guess is as good as mine,' she said. 'Some poor demented loony wandering the streets who ought to have been safely sectioned long ago.' The health service had a lot to answer for by closing the mental wards. There was a beggar she saw occasionally on Marloes Road, shambling and softly spoken, unshaven with doleful eyes. He didn't look dangerous in the least but she supposed you could never really tell. She would certainly far rather put her money on him than on some vengeful acquaintance out to kill her.

'No one from Susie's past, then? A cast-off lover or even a casual pickup?' Peggy had certainly spent time with the DCI. Her probing was starting to resemble his. Jinx laughed.

'You obviously didn't know Susie,' she said. 'To imagine she had any sort of past.'

But Peggy's insatiable appetite for gossip had been seriously whetted and now a gleam came into her eye. She clapped one hand to her mouth in excitement and pinned poor Jinx with a bayonet stare.

'So tell me, my dear, who was that man with you that night?' The one with the excellent teeth.

Jinx stared back at her blankly. *Now* what was the silly woman on about?

'Only the police were asking us, they were keen to find out. The last known sighting of you alive. With a man we didn't know, as it happened.'

Jinx stopped her curtly in her tracks. This really was an intrusion.

'But I'm *still* alive,' she said cuttingly, causing her neighbour to blink and look confused. Jinx knew precisely what she was trying to say but for once wouldn't help her out. Let the busybody be embarrassed. At times she could be funny, today she was not.

'And now,' Jinx said shortly, 'I really must get on.' And before Peggy could get in another word, she had whisked away the coffee mugs and dumped them in the dishwasher.

Dottie, quite obviously, was similarly curious, though Jinx was able to head her off. Not wishing to face another barrage of inquiry, she had called Dottie secretly from the house and asked if she'd meet her for lunch. There was a nice fish restaurant they occasionally went to when they felt in the mood for some pampering. Dottie arrived in a matter of minutes, flushed and triumphant at the prospect of time with Jinx alone. Jinx was already seated with a glass of wine. All this stressful sorting things out was starting to tire her. What she needed more than anything was a bracing dose of Dottie's commonsense. With no more unwarranted interrogations; she had had it up to here with the police. Though she was on her guard with Dottie as she had been with her neighbour. Even between the closest of friends there can be off limit things.

So she talked instead about the condition of the house, the damage that needed fixing and her plans for a major overhaul. Dottie smiled. Jinx was constantly improving her home. It was rare indeed when she didn't have workmen in.

'Sometimes,' she had speculated to Sam, 'I think she likes having them there just for the company.'

'That or their tight little bums,' said Sam, who knew his Jinx, then winced when he found it still hurt.

'Your bedroom is so lovely,' said Dottie encouragingly. 'It's a shame to have to change it all again.' But then she hadn't seen the disfigured walls. Or smelled the rusty residue of blood. Or been shown those terrible photographs of Susie's battered corpse, an image Jinx knew she would carry with her for life.

'There is absolutely no way,' she said with heavy emphasis, 'that I could consider moving back in without everything first being done.'

Wallpaper this time instead of just pastel paint, which would mean new curtains and bed linen too. And, now she came to focus, of course a new bed. Dump everything immediately and start all over from scratch. In her current mood she would just as soon hand over the keys to a jobbing builder and tell him to get on with it regardless. Dottie, seeing that familiar spark, simply smiled and scrutinised the menu she knew off by heart. Jinx on one of her mad crusades was best not being challenged. She would do exactly as she wanted and as fast as she possibly could. She made snap decisions, then followed them through, one reason for much of her success.

'So how's your policeman friend?' Dottie asked. Jinx shrugged.

'I've no idea. I would guess he's got tired of the case. It must be pretty dispiriting with all that hard work and dead ends.'

Added to which there was not a lot more he could do, not till new evidence was forthcoming. She recalled their final meeting when he had handed over the keys and the chilling warning he had given her then which was still striking horror in her heart. She had mentioned it to nobody, certainly not Dottie who would panic. But she couldn't help thinking of Serafina's silent caller and the ominous awareness of someone watching.

'Come on,' said Jinx, suddenly businesslike, 'tell the waiter what you're going to have and let's get this show on the road.'

Ambrose laughed when she told him her latest resolve. His Jinx all over with her bouts of frenetic spending. He was used to her wild impetuous ways, loved the enthusiasm, such an integral part of her.

'Wait a second,' he said as he fended her off. 'How were you thinking of paying for it all?' The wallpaper, the carpet, the fancy new sleigh bed. Another antique chair to replace the ruined one.

Curtains and bedcover and fine Egyptian cotton sheets. Better throw in a new television, just for luck. One of those fancy slimline ones, like the one in the living-room only smaller. And a fridge, why not, for ice cream in the middle of the night. For a hard-nosed businesswoman she could be amazingly feather-brained. Which only increased his affection.

Jinx sighed but didn't attempt to explain. Deep down they were all much the same, these men. Especially this one with his ingrained bachelor habits. She had given up years ago even trying to make him see her point of view. Could *you* live with blood-stained furniture? she wanted to ask. Or sleep in a bed where a corpse had lain? But Ambrose was too sensitive and wouldn't be able to cope with it. So she simply grinned and gave him her madcap smile and they were off again, looking through wallpaper samples.

'I'm free at the weekend if you want to go shopping.' Jinx beamed and gave him a jubilant high five. There was nothing like a shopping spree to calm her troubled spirits, and Ambrose had always been her favourite partner in crime. The two of them had put this house together. Many of her purchases had been his choice. He was firmly proprietorial about the things she bought, providing it was her money they were squandering. After all, it made sense; what was hers was also his. He spent almost as much time in her home as she did.

Tired but exultant after a long hard day of pavement-pounding, Jinx and Ambrose lay sprawled on her front-room sofa. Around them were stacked a mountain of carrier bags, goodies she'd bought which he'd helped her carry home. She had opened a bottle of the best champagne to toast another binge of overt consumption. There was nothing to equal this wonderful feeling. She felt almost human again.

'Do you think,' she asked idly, 'I should also change the cooker? I've always rather fancied one in green.' Kensington green, that was, to go with her posh address. Once she really got going it was difficult to stop her. He knew from long experience not to try.

'You know me when the spending bug bites.' She flopped back on the cushions and kicked off her shoes. 'Remember that attic I used to have in Islington? Straight out of college when I'd only just started to earn.'

It was right after Sam, too, though neither of them mentioned it. She was so careless with people's feelings, she had doubtless forgotten that now. But Ambrose hadn't, not a second of it. The pain was still etched into his brain. He remembered that attic as if it were only yesterday, a chilly fifth-floor walkup with a leaking roof and a bathroom on the half-landing, shared with the occupants below. They'd none of them had any money in those days but that had in no way deterred Jinx. She had sunk her meagre savings into a tiny, draughty box rather than share with others like the rest. But they'd certainly had some good times there, as he always did with her.

'Remember that time we painted the kitchen?' Bright yellow like the worst kind of hangover. 'And somebody managed to kick over the emulsion so we ended up having to paint the floorboards as well.'

Like yesterday. Sunflowers on the window blinds and geraniums on the ledges. She was every bit as spontaneous now as she had been in her youth. And equally as much fun.

'And those vast plastic mirrors I got for the bathroom, to double its size so they said.' Cheap mirrored vinyl stretched over wooden frames, surprisingly effective though flimsy and impossible to clean. Though of course she'd moved on by the time they'd lost their shine. That was how Jinx always ran her life. They had started working at Weinbergs by then. Lord, it was almost twenty years. He had once, somewhat stumblingly, tried to kiss her one night. Luckily she'd dismissed it as a joke.

'Where did it all go?' he asked. 'The time.'

She fetched another bottle. 'Living,' she told him gravely. 'And putting all of our energies into staying ahead of the pack.' There had been that time, when they'd both been fairly pissed, that she'd thought he was coming on to her but had managed to head him off. It wasn't that she didn't fancy him, just that she preferred him as a buddy. Sex was easy but friendship like theirs all too rare. She wasn't going to risk spoiling things and it had turned out she'd been right. The friendship had endured and they'd done well together over all these hectic years. McLennan Graphics was now the best in its field. Whereas Weinbergs had virtually ceased to exist, victim of a rigorously changing world.

'That bastard!' spat out Ambrose, Pavlovianly primed, just as she'd known he was bound to. Bless his heart, he was immutable with his funny, old-fashioned feuds. Once the record stuck with Ambrose, it was hard to convince him to change it. Jinx, in her wisdom, these days never tried.

'But,' she said calmly as she wrestled out the cork, 'think where we all might still be now if it hadn't been for him.'

22

For several years Max had been promising Jinx a selling trip to New York. Time, he told her, to get herself known over there. But the arrival of Julius had effectively prevented it. A frequent visitor to the States himself, he saw no point in over-burdening his budget. But Max still retained some powers of his own and now Jinx was on her way. Before she left London, he took her aside and primed her with some of his more prestigious connections, luminaries of the publishing world she might not otherwise get to meet.

'Try and fit in some fun as well,' he told her sagely as they said their goodbyes. She was concerned about his shortness of breath and a worrying new frailness that was lately becoming apparent. He looked and moved like a far older man, as if the accumulation of years was finally catching up.

'You're sure you'll be all right while I'm away?' Jinx hugged him and planted a kiss on his gnarled old cheek.

'Don't worry about me, child. Get out there and enjoy. And be sure to leave behind you a little trail of stardust so they'll know exactly who's been through.'

It was the week after Thanksgiving and the countdown to Christmas had started. Jinx was thrilled by the noise and bustle, the shrieking of the traffic, the aroma of roasting pretzels on the streets and the nip of frost in the air. In between appointments she just walked and watched. Anything in the world seemed possible now. The New York publishers were warm and welcoming, showering her with invitations, too numerous to fit in. She'd begin each day with a working breakfast, followed at hourly intervals with appointments right through till the offices closed. By the time she returned exhausted to her hotel she was usually knackered and aching for a nap. But for that there was rarely time. The evening would continue with cocktails followed by dinner, and meant still talking business, sometimes till the small hours.

They loved her book proposals and the orders readily flowed. With one she found she had an auction on her hands and resolutely proceeded to up the bidding while resisting an urge to call London for advice. If she was good enough to be here alone, she was more than capable of making her own decisions. Even when they involved quite colossal sums. She was damned if she'd let Julius stick in his nose.

He'd seemed oddly withdrawn just before she left town, hadn't properly talked to her in days. Something was clearly gnawing at his mind. She'd expected his interference, which never came; he hadn't even bothered to say goodbye. Several of the publishers she met along the way asked her slyly about Julius. Max was a hugely venerated man but about his nephew they were still a lot less sure. And being plain-speaking New Yorkers, they expressed their opinions baldly. A stiff in a suit seemed to be the general consensus. Brilliant on the business side, aggressive, hard-hitting and bright. Yet they also found him unbending and hard to assess. Too driven, too chilly and lacking in basic humour. Not an easy man to be about.

Naturally Jinx defended him but secretly she exulted. Julius hadn't been making things easy for her, yet here she was a roaring success and the books were selling like hotcakes. They liked her for her warmth and open-mindedness; she fitted in comfortably, better than some of her compatriots. One even offered her a permanent job, promised to sort out the immigration problems if she'd stay. She was hugely flattered and, for a second, almost tempted but her heart still remained with Weinbergs. For as long as Max was alive and still functioning, that's where she intended to stay. The very least she felt she owed him was that.

She got back to her hotel one night weary and sore-footed, glad for once not to have a dinner date, longing only for a leisurely soak then room service in front of the telly. As she passed the entrance to the crowded downstairs bar she glanced briefly into its dim interior in case there was anyone there she knew. She had almost reached the elevator when she thought she heard her name called but dismissed it as unlikely. She was too tired even to turn and check. Just as the doors were opening she heard the voice again, this time directly behind her. There was no mistake.

'Julius!' she exclaimed, startled, when she saw who it was. 'What on earth are *you* doing here? I had no idea.'

He looked tired and worn, with shadows beneath his eyes, but every bit as elegant as ever.

'I arrived this morning. There is something I have to do. I was hoping you would join me for dinner.'

There wasn't a lot she could say in the circumstances; if she made up some prior engagement he'd be bound to catch her out. Besides, that wasn't Jinx's way, she was usually totally upfront. She saw the longed for evening of personal pampering dismally sliding away as she promised to meet him in the bar in half an hour. Just time for a rapid shower and change of clothing. Her mind was in a spin as she got ready. *Now* what could be up with the ungracious bastard? Couldn't he stay off her case even here? She changed from her chic little suit to a softer silk dress. It was, after all, after hours, at least as far as she was concerned. And he

was trespassing on her time. She spritzed herself liberally with a
healthy dose of *Giò*, ran critical fingers through her short, streaked
hair and returned to the bar with a heavy heart to meet him.

He took her to a really nice French place, dim and exclusive, in
the lower East Sixties. Hotel dining was all very well, he said, but
he felt they could do a little better than that. Jinx was surprised.
From his initial mask of weariness she had assumed he'd want
to keep things brief and to the point, to eat without fuss in the
hotel dining-room and get away as fast as he could. He had, after
all, important things to attend to otherwise he'd not be here. But
with a couple of bourbons inside him he revived a little and
a spark reappeared in his eyes. He inquired politely how the
trip was going but showed no interest in the actual details – all
that would keep until they were back in London. She had never
known him so strangely detached before. Maybe it was just jetlag.
He also let slip that he wasn't actually staying in her hotel but up
the road in the far more exclusive Pierre. Jinx was surprised; she
had supposed their encounter was accidental.
    'However did you find me then?' she asked. And what is your
real agenda?
    'I knew where you were staying so I hung around.' He seemed
quite unabashed at the confession.
    'What if I hadn't come back?' she asked.
    'You were bound to sooner or later.'
    Unless, of course, she'd had an all-night assignation, but he
probably knew her well enough to be aware that was not how
she behaved. Not while on official company business, she was far
too straight for that. He was looking at her now with such intense
concentration she started to feel uncomfortable and quite at a loss
for words. She quickly asked after Max, as though she'd been away
for months. Not so bad, he said, in the circumstances, and then
the conversation dried up altogether. He awkwardly fingered the
stem of his wineglass and muttered a few banalities about the

ambience and the food and his hope that she really liked this kind of place. Jinx responded with stultified politeness as though they were strangers meeting for the first time.

She started to wonder what he was up to, it wasn't at all like Julius to be remotely tongue-tied. In place of the usual swaggering bully, he was acting almost like a nervous suitor fumbling inadequately for words. Suddenly she was alarmed. In a flash she thought she was on to him and suspected she knew what was up. He'd come to New York specifically to fire her, out of reach of his uncle who he'd know would protect her. What a dastardly way to behave. The sheer bloody nerve of it shook her with a terrible rage. He had been on to her case since he'd first appeared on the scene, couldn't stomach the fact that Max favoured her so much. That he treated her almost as a daughter. Jealousy could be a terrible thing but unfairly applied it was also criminal. She was on the point of telling him, right to his face, that she found him despicable and his actions underhand when he put down his wineglass and gently touched her hand, sending a visceral shockwave right through her.

'This isn't at all easy,' he said slowly, reaching inside his jacket for a cigarette then remembering that this was New York and they wouldn't like it. 'Now that I'm actually here, I'm not quite certain how to say it.' His eyes were so incredibly dark she could barely discern the difference between iris and pupil. It was like gazing into two black holes that were drawing her irresistibly towards him. So do it, she wanted to shriek, and get it over. If you're here to sack me, just get on with it. Act like a man not a creep. She could imagine how Ambrose and Damien would react; told you so they'd say when they heard. She wondered if they'd stay there after she had cleared her desk. She knew she could always rely on their loyalty and support.

'Jinx,' said Julius, 'what I'm trying to say is I'd like you to give me a second chance.'

You what? She stared.

'We rather got off on the wrong foot,' he said. 'I guess I underestimated you because . . .'

'I'm a woman.'

He grinned now. 'And a pretty one too. Well, yes.' He looked rather sheepish and laughter came into his eyes. When he smiled he suddenly became quite beguiling; strange she hadn't been aware of that before. There were deep laughter creases at the corners of his mouth, and his teeth, which she'd rarely seen displayed before, were white and straight and strong. He even had the grace to look embarrassed.

'I'm not doing this very well,' he said. 'Let's start again. I was a fool who thought he knew it all. Only now, after all these months working together, do I suddenly see the light. You are bright, you are loyal and my uncle adores you. I must have been crazy not to have rated you better before.'

Careful, she thought, let's not overdo it.

'And you're a bloody good publisher too, what's more.'

Jinx stared back at him with wide amused eyes. Wait till she told the boys about this. But Julius was rapidly getting a grip and the waiter was pressing them to more wine.

'What I would like to propose,' he said, 'is that we spend a little time together while I'm here. I've got a couple of important meetings but they should be over by tomorrow. How about giving me the benefit of the doubt and spending the rest of the time with me?'

He was serious. She was stunned.

'Can't. I have appointments.'

'So cancel them.' Crazy too.

'No, I really can't. There are things to be concluded, ends to be tied up.'

He smiled now with real warmth and reached for her hand. 'I'm sorry,' he said softly. 'I was forgetting how committed you are.' But he wasn't poking fun. 'Don't get me wrong,' he said. 'I didn't mean it to sound that way. I truly respect your dedication, wouldn't dream of screwing up your trip. It's just that I'd like to get to know you better and this seemed the perfect opportunity.'

He really did mean it; she softened and allowed her hand to rest in his. Seen this close, or maybe it was the lamplight, he really was a lot more attractive than she'd thought, in a gaunt, ascetic way. Funny she'd never seen that before; she'd been far too busy making jokes behind his back. But the dark, tempestuous eyes were getting to her now and her hand, still lightly clasped by his, felt good.

'There's always the rest of this evening,' she said boldly. 'After all, the night is still young.' All of a sudden her fatigue had melted away and she was aware of the quickening of her pulse. His touch was affecting her breathing too. She longed for the meal to be over and paid for, and them out of there right away. Julius called for the check.

They skipped the corny romantic things, like a horse-drawn carriage or the top of the Empire State, and went straight to the Pierre and upstairs to his room. Suddenly neither of them could wait. Once Jinx made up her mind, she didn't hang about and there was no point playing the prissy virgin when that, most definitely, was not what she was. She wanted him suddenly with an urgent need and it was a race to get out of their clothes. He had a lean, tanned torso with a fuzz of dark hair and she went into his arms with relief. His skin was warm and he smelled so good it felt as natural as coming home. He was into her almost immediately, then apologised for his unseemly haste.

'I just couldn't help it,' he said as he stroked her damp hair. 'I can do much better than that. Just give me a second and I'll show you.'

Jinx was content just to lie there in his arms, quivering with excitement and rising lust until she felt the stirring in his crotch again and they were back into the arena for round two. This time he retained almost superhuman control, and coaxed her and teased her till she was panting with desire, no longer the temptress but the vanquished prey. He touched her everywhere except that one wet place, kissing her, nibbling, driving her to the edge.

'Please, please,' she begged him, writhing beneath his weight, but the skilled manipulation went on and on until she thought she was going to go out of her mind. She had never known love-making as sensual as this, he seemed to know her body better than she did herself. If this was an art then Julius was a maestro. On a scale of one to ten he was a twenty. She could not get enough of him, wanted it to go on all night. Eventually, temporarily sated, they took a breather, but still were unable to sleep. They lay there in a tangle of sweating limbs, and kissed and kissed until her mouth was bruised and swollen and the bristles of his cheek were grazing her skin. She dared not even think of how she'd look in the morning but that was of no importance right now. May morning never come.

The grey dawn light was filtering through the curtains when Jinx, exhausted, finally dropped off to sleep. Soon, too soon, she would have to get out of here, back to the hotel at a decent hour before other guests began to stir. Not that she was a prude in any way, but Weinbergs' reputation still figured first in her mind. But she needed just a few minutes' sleep before she could even move. She cuddled up closer to Julius's warm chest and drifted off into oblivion. To be shocked awake by the phone ringing close to her ear.

For a moment unable to recall where she was, she lay there in a stupefied daze, conscious of Julius leaning across above her to grab the receiver before she woke.

'Yes?' he barked in his formal corporate voice then listened for a while in rigid silence.

'When?' he asked, less stridently. 'And just how bad is it? Right, I'll be with you as soon as I can sort out my flight.'

'What?' asked Jinx sleepily, reaching out for him, but Julius rolled away from her and started pulling on his clothes.

'It's Max,' he said. 'He's had another attack. And this time it sounds pretty serious.'

'So you're leaving?' She couldn't completely take it in but now he was rapidly dialling.

'Just as fast as I can get out of here. I hate to have to leave you this way but I know you understand. There are things I still have to do over here. Urgent things.'

Jinx understood, of course she did. This was sudden paradise but it was his uncle who was sick. Her beloved employer but also his flesh and blood. 'Should I come with you?' She was up now herself, wrapped demurely in the sheet.

'No point. And we don't want to scare him. With luck, it will blow over, it has before. I'll give him your love and tell him what great things you're up to. That's the best thing you can do for him. Get on with the job and make it work.'

Once he was dressed and immaculate again, he took her in his arms for a lingering kiss. Jinx snuggled up against his chest, safe at last and content.

'I love you,' he said simply. 'I think I always have.'

And then he was gone and she was left to get dressed, anxious about Max, her emotions in a whirl. She still had a great deal of thinking to do, to work out what had happened and how she felt. She badly needed a hot shower and to pull her head together, but first she had a breakfast meeting and a string of appointments throughout the day. On with the job, that was why she was here. She'd have to leave the matter of Julius till later.

23

As the days ticked by Hal grew more frustrated. They seemed to be no closer to solving the murder and he now couldn't think of anything else. He could not believe that the trail had gone so cold. They had spoken to almost everyone in the neighbourhood and delved in minute detail into Susie's and Jinx's lives. Yet all this intense police activity had dredged up no new leads. They were right back where they had started from, a total dispiriting blank. There was now nothing for it but to open it all up again and repeat their house-to-house inquiries in the hope of finding new witnesses. The problem with a touristy area like Kensington was the number of itinerant visitors pouring through. Not that Hal believed for one second that the killing might have been random. He remained convinced, from what little evidence they had, that the victim had been carefully staked out. That much savagery denoted terrible anger motivated by reasons that had to be personal. Not just the casual sadism of a passing psychopath. Whoever had done it had been settling a score. A grim retribution as cold-blooded as an execution.

He kept a careful eye on Jinx to check on her personal safety. If his hunch was correct then the murderer would return to try to finish off what he had begun. She resisted Hal's suggestion that she move somewhere safe and told him pig-headedly that she really wasn't scared. Her life was in enough of an upheaval as it was. She refused to be intimidated by a nutter.

'You'll catch him soon surely,' was all she would say. Hal wished he could share her confidence.

Trudy was still brooding over the detestable Professor Harker. She hadn't liked the man on sight, mistrusted his shifty eyes. If she could pin it on anyone, it would have to be him despite the watertight alibi. A man like that shouldn't be allowed to get away with it. Lecherous, pompous and vain.

'Motive,' Hal reminded her each time she brought it up. 'Unappetising though he may seem, why would he ever want her dead?'

'Fear of discovery?' said Trudy thoughtfully. 'Didn't want to risk his reputation by being caught out in an extra-marital fling?'

Hal smiled. 'So why then draw attention to it?' Bombastic he might be but the fellow was by no means a fool. He checked with Jinx and found that Harker was travelling, a lecture tour of Australasia which would keep him away for the best part of six weeks.

'Not that I see him any more,' she said. She was a bit ashamed of that particular liaison, embarrassed that Hal had to know her more intimate secrets, like having him burrowing through her underwear drawer. Norman had been a mistake, she saw that now. But she'd found him sexy at the time, doubtless enhanced by his brain and huge success. It was true what Henry Kissinger had said, power *is* the ultimate aphrodisiac, certainly where Jinx was concerned. Why this should be she had no idea. Just found it exciting to be seen with a household name and have people swivel their heads in the street. Also every cab driver and waiter recognised him instantly and felt obliged to engage him in argument. When you made your living as a professional cynic, sparring with the public was simply par for the course. She had revelled in it and the reflected glory and wasn't ashamed to admit that now. Part of her misspent youth, maybe; something she'd not repeat. Things in her personal life had changed fundamentally so that these days Norman was just an uncomfortable memory. Best left that way.

'And Hamish Cotterell?' asked Hal, re-reading his notes.

'Nope,' said Jinx frankly, with a little shrug. 'Have only seen him once in quite a while. But, then, we haven't been really close in ages. Separate lives, you know, with conflicting priorities. It was really only ever a matter of time.'

Not exactly what Hal had observed in that painful interview with the gentle, sad-eyed man. He would reckon Cotterell still carried a massive torch though whether it was reciprocated was something he wasn't to know. Could it be that Jinx protested a little too much or did she really mean all she was saying? Why bother, after all, to lie to him? He was simply a policeman doing his tedious job. DCI Plod, more's the pity. He would like to believe she could see him as a man, then dismissed that thought as purely fatuous. The case was what mattered, he must concentrate his mind. And instead of being charmed by this electrifying woman, keep remembering that violated body on the bed.

'Are you certain there's no one you've overlooked?' he pressed. 'Someone with a viable motive who might simply have slipped your mind?'

Jinx shook her head, she was positive. She'd been through everyone in exhaustive detail, had even made meticulous lists of the vast numbers of people she knew. Not an easy task after so many years; her personal Christmas card list alone ran to well over three hundred.

'A business opponent?' supplied Hal encouragingly. 'Someone on whose toes you might unknowingly have trod?' He was still somewhat vague about what she actually did, just knew it involved an awful lot of socialising.

Again Jinx shook her head. 'It's not that kind of a business,' she explained. Not arms-dealing nor drugs nor anything else remotely dodgy. Except for the confidentiality of their project, the shit hot secret computer game they were shortly going to unveil to the world. Involving undreamed-of billions in revenue if it touched the pulse of the peer market the way she had planned. After a moment's hesitation, she told Hal a little about it, sketched it in general non-specific terms to show him the sort of thing it was. Nothing terribly revolutionary, just a brilliant new concept for an adult computer game. What could a mere copper do with such classified information? Provided he never let Damien know, she was safe. It was in its beta stage, she explained. The final edit before they showed it to potential purchasers.

'And is there a lot of money involved?' asked Hal.

'Loads. But only a fraction of what we hope to recoup once it's finally launched and into the retail outlets.'

'Might someone be interested in trying to block its progress? By eliminating you, the leader of the creative team?' That thought had only occurred to him this minute, a whole new angle. He jotted down a note. But the anger didn't fit; competition surely couldn't account for all that rage. Though money can be a powerful motivator. And greed.

'Wouldn't think so for a minute though Ambrose is not so sure. To begin with, how would anyone know?' DBI-2000 had been cloaked in the utmost secrecy right from its moment of inception, months ago. 'Damien's Bright Idea' was what the acronym stood for, a simple office code to cloak its content. It wasn't only Damien who had occasional attacks of the vapours. Jinx knew from experience how ideas can get passed through the ether without any conscious breach of confidentiality. Hence the constant race in nuclear science, with the big nations competing to keep abreast. What one solitary scientist might be dreaming up in Moscow could, in a blink, be flashed instantaneously to Washington. That was what was so exciting about this business, especially with the recent advances in the world of electronics. Not like the book world which still ambled along, stuck in the nineteenth century. Here decisions were made and things done in just seconds, otherwise projects could be out of date before they were even launched. But a traitor in their midst, she was sure not. It was a small, closed world and she knew most of the major players. Everyone had their hands so full, plagiarism was scarcely an issue. Getting things done before they became obsolete was what counted.

Hal was still not entirely convinced. This could well be the elusive lead he was after, the true *raison d'être* for the whole sick affair. Jinx was marvellous but perhaps just a tad naïve. She allowed far too many people to get too close. Just the memory of the creepy Myrtle Hobday made his skin crawl. If Jinx was that indiscriminate in the selection of her friends, how sound could her judgement be of the others who crowded her life? Or was he allowing it to get too personal? His main function now was to keep an eye on Jinx. She could be in more danger than she realised.

What Hal was also keen to know, along with Dottie who could scarcely contain her curiosity, was what could be giving Jinx that added glow and the extra spring to her already jaunty step.

'You don't suppose there's someone new in her life?' Dottie was unpacking groceries in the kitchen. She'd been thinking about it on the long bus-ride home, was consumed with curiosity.

'She'd have surely told you first if there was,' countered Sam from the dining-room table where he was carefully colouring in sky. The two women had been virtually joined at the hip all these years. The first to hear Jinx's innermost secrets was almost always the non-judgemental Dottie. Sam usually tried to steer clear of the whole subject but this time, against his will, was similarly intrigued. It wasn't like Jinx to be so apparently manless yet, according to what she had told the police, she had now given even Hamish the push. A fact for which Dottie could personally vouch. Her heart had gone out to the poor, defeated fellow that time he'd dropped round to the mews and had been publicly rebuffed. Jinx could be very cruel at times in a casual, unthinking way. Not that she ever meant it unkindly. She just didn't trouble to think things through, never had.

'You don't suppose it's that policeman johnny?' Sam had been pondering it too.

Dottie thought for a second then firmly shook her head. He certainly had an eye for Jinx but she didn't appear to have noticed. Now Serafina was another matter entirely, was always at him, flaunting her charms. Not that she'd stand a chance against Jinx despite the ten-year age gap in her favour. Serafina was beautiful but brittle, like a piece of fine china liable to crack at the slightest touch. Any man with any sense would stay clear. She was a dangerous siren with a storm warning over her head.

'We still don't know what that trip was all about. Why so sudden and why still so secret? And where, come to that, did she go? Do you think she's trying to hide something? If so, what?'

'You don't think it might have been him? The cop.'

'Not a chance. Apart from anything, he didn't appear on the scene till after she'd gone. To investigate the murder, remember? By which time Susie was already dead.' Sometimes Sam could be quite obtuse but she loved him all the more for it.

It still hurt Sam to think about Jinx's lovelife, even after so many years of contented marriage. What he'd found with Dottie was steady and enduring; with Jinx that roller-coaster ride had been turbulent and destructive. But exciting, yes – in those days he'd been fully alive.

Dottie gave him a thoughtful glance as she set about starting the supper. What went on in his innermost heart she still really wasn't quite sure. She cursed the day he had ever met Jinx, even though it had resulted, in a roundabout way, in bringing the two of them together. But only after a long, sad gap, far later than Dottie might have wished. But might-have-beens got you nowhere. Look how content they were now. She picked up the beetroots he had dug up for her and ran them under the tap. Beetroot was one of Sam's favourite things. She'd make him some nice fresh borscht for supper, as a treat to go with her home-made bread.

Dottie tried probing Ambrose too but came up, as always, against a wall of cold steel. Where Jinx was concerned he remained inscrutable, finding any personal gossip distasteful. The truth was he preferred not to know. But Dottie was far less circumspect, was determined not to let her off so easily. It was time, she felt, that Jinx opened up, at least to a good friend who cared only for her welfare. Look at how she always plagued Serafina, never off her case. And if it turned out to be an affair of the heart, they would all be so happy for her.

'Come on, sweetie,' she coaxed her over lunch. 'What's this big secret you're not telling? I swear I won't breathe a word to a soul.' Other, of course, than her beloved Sam who'd be likely to pass it on immediately. He meant well, bless him, but could never keep it stoppered. Jinx flushed slightly and looked a trifle confused, then a radiant smile lit up her face.

'Oh, dearest Dottie,' she said in a lowered voice, impulsively squeezing both her hands. 'I'm dying to tell you, I really am, but just now my lips have to remain sealed. It's too amazingly wonderful, beyond my wildest dream. As soon as things are sorted and I'm free to spill the beans, you, I promise, shall be the first to know.' Along with Veronica. 'Trust me.'

Dottie absorbed all this with interest. So there was some sort of a secret after all. She was naturally disappointed that Jinx didn't feel she could trust her now but quite resigned to waiting. If it had anything at all to do with Jinx's lovelife, which seemed obvious, then Dottie would be right there for her as she always had been.

Goodness, how exciting. She quite perked up. A bit of juicy intrigue was always good for the soul and Jinx was long overdue for some lasting happiness. She had always had lovers but rarely one that mattered. Dottie's main concern for her was that she might well have left it too late. All the best men were spoken for, like her Sam. A tiny shiver of apprehension ran through her as though someone had stepped on her grave.

'One thing I can tell you, though,' added Jinx with shining eyes. 'I have never ever been this happy before.'

And it showed. Her skin was glowing, not just with her tan, and her short, springy hair was glossy with health. She was still as slim and supple as a woman half her age, which was something Dottie had always secretly envied. It seemed not to matter how many glasses of wine she knocked back or the jokes she was constantly making about the rail-thin Serafina. Somehow Jinx managed to maintain her youthful weight without ever becoming gaunt or scraggy. She claimed the secret lay in her genes but Dottie thought it was more likely to be because of all that energy she burnt up. A right little dynamo was Jinx when she got going. She left the rest of them standing.

Jinx suddenly waved and fluttered her menu. Ambrose was hovering outside. She caught his eye and beckoned him in to join them and he threaded his way bashfully through the other lunchers and dumped down his book-bag by their table.

'Anything wrong?' she asked anxiously but he simply shrugged his shoulders and pulled up a chair.

'One of those for me, too,' he instructed the waiter as their second glasses of wine arrived. He glanced rather hungrily at the menu and Jinx insisted he had at least a plate of chips. He hadn't eaten, had been at the library and had spotted them quite accidentally as he headed back.

'There's not really time for a proper meal,' he fretted, but Jinx assured him that the world wouldn't come to an end. She beamed at him fondly as he ordered himself a burger, happy and content in his company. Dottie watched them together; the bond between them was practically tangible. What a shame they couldn't find a way to share their lives. Which it seemed must be quite out of the question now in view of what Jinx had just told her.

Yet Dottie was still perplexed. Whatever it was that was giving Jinx so much joy she should surely be able to talk about with her friends.

24

What James saw romantically as the intervention of the hand of fate was actually nothing of the kind. That chance first encounter with Serafina had not been the fortuitous accident it appeared but the result of a bit of nifty stealthwork on her part. Something had happened just days before that had unsettled her outlook and moved the goal-posts forward. She'd been led on then snubbed, at least in her own perception, all in the short space of a few days and was now hellbent on a blaze of furious retribution. She had always been one for aiming at the pinnacle but this was the ultimate challenge. If anybody crossed her she would not rest until the balance of power had been restored. Plus this time the target in her sights was irresistible. She had tasted blood, there could be no going back.

Since shaking off her roots in suburban Wembley she had come a long way in record time. She'd been christened Shirley Anne (the family name was Stubbs) but had changed that the day she hitched up with Mikey Rossetti, whom she'd met as a student at the tech. Total reinvention was Serafina's forte; blink and she was likely to have transmogrified. Mikey was overweight but essentially good-hearted, the son of an Acton pizza parlour owner with his career path already clearly designated. He was comfortable and kind but lacked the necessary oomph to keep pace with the flighty Serafina. But he'd idolised her from the second he first saw her, and she had gone along with it mainly through lethargy. Blind devotion had always been her turn on, though their impetuous marriage at the end of their final year was as much to acquire his exotic last name as her longed-for disconnection from her past. With her pale, pre-Raphaelite beauty and silky ink-black hair, she could easily get away with Rossetti as her birthright, and these days even hinted at refined Venetian ancestry instead of the plodding truth she had managed to shed. The marriage had been over in less than a year. She no longer even knew where Mikey lived, nor cared.

She had shot up socially, moving from man to man, each time bettering herself and helping to feather her nest. She was not particularly discriminating about whom she chose to seduce. The only real requisite they all had in common was money. Class as well, if that could be arranged, but she intended to stop being self-supporting as soon as she possibly could by whatever means came her way. Which is how she came to pick on the unsuspecting James, though certainly not by accident.

She'd been hanging around in St Martin's Lane one rain-sodden evening in March, casing the offices of IEP as she progressed to the next step of her master plan. What she currently desperately wanted was bona fide access to that austere building, with its corporate slogan etched discreetly into the stone. Her sights were set firmly on their American financiers. She was heartily sick of being part of a tinpot setup and wanted to get herself to New York and a lucrative job in head office. For New York, to Serafina, represented the ultimate challenge. International Electronic Publishing, the giant conglomerate that was funding Damien's project, had offices worldwide all doing exciting and innovative things. But New York was its power base and that's where she wanted to be. A natural and timely stepping-stone, she felt. Close to the current object of her desires.

She was wondering whether to make a dramatic entrance when a group of braying young men in dark suits came bowling out of the building and into a nearby bar. Closely followed by Serafina, never one to let a chance slip by. Wearing a shiny black silk trenchcoat, belted tightly to set off her minuscule waist, with huge black sunglasses even in the half-light, she moved silently in beside them and settled herself at the bar. It was the work of a second to nudge James's elbow and knock his beer into her own lap. As he sweated and apologised and dabbed at her sodden clothes, she had slowly raised the eclipsing shades and given him the benefit of her heart-stopping smile. To which he succumbed as so many had before him. Poor babe, he never really knew what hit him. Swimming in a tank of piranhas might have been a more benign fate.

At first she told him nothing about herself, allowed him to believe her simply a passer-by, a fascinating stranger of independent means. But she pumped him subtly for details of what he did until, flattered inordinately and unable to believe his luck, he had blabbed out everything she wanted to know. Still in his early twenties but a fully trained accountant, he had landed one of the plum jobs with IEP. And his prospects looked good, they were grooming him for head office. Sprigs of the aristocracy went down well in the States. Serafina, having gleaned all she needed to know, demurely accepted a second glass of wine and an invitation (postponed) to dinner, then excused herself abruptly and went triumphantly home. He was a bit of a twit, still with adolescent spots, but the perfect foil for her manipulative purposes. Which is why she was incandescent now that he seemed to have jumped ship and left town without taking her with him. Or even, unbelievably, bothering to say goodbye.

* * *

On the way home that night she dropped into her health club for an intensive workout followed by a leisurely swim. Temporarily without anyone to wine and dine her, it was good to have an excuse to dawdle before returning to her pokey flat for an uninspiring evening of bad television. The club was more expensive than she could really afford but Serafina would not be seen anywhere but the best. She had, after all, a lifestyle to support that pretended to be better than it was. She shopped like a wild thing, running up credit in all the major stores, had her hair and nails cared for by an exclusive West-End salon and swanned around like a rich man's daughter instead of the nine-to-five worker she actually was. Her secret role model was actually Jinx though she'd die rather than admit it. She admired her style, her poise and personality, envied her popularity too with women as much as men. Jinx was rarely at a loose end socially, her telephone never stopped ringing. Serafina cared little for female company but a friend or two might have been nice, especially now.

There was no one very inspiring in the club tonight, just a bunch of out-of-town businessmen horsing around. Serafina disapproved of this corporate membership stuff, felt that it lowered the tone. With her willowy figure in her neat little St Tropez bathing suit, she knew she was an eye-catcher as she poised on the side for a dive. Not that it was worth doing for a rowdy mob like this, just hard to give up the habit of a lifetime. She hit the water in a perfect curve then swam very fast to the other end. If this was all that was on offer tonight, she wouldn't hang around. She did a few underwater leg exercises then became aware of the man grinning at her from nearby. A leprous, toad-like, yellow-skinned figure with rolls of fat descending from a pendulous jowl. He was seated in the shallow end making no attempt whatsoever to be doing anything more than just gawp. He looked her up and down in insolent appraisal then hawked noisily in his throat and spat out a great gob of phlegm into the pool.

Scandalised, Serafina leapt out of the water and headed for the jacuzzi to relax before she went home. She lay back luxuriously in the foaming froth, and absorbed the healing properties of the life-enhancing salts. In a perfect world, she'd be doing this every day, preferably in the privacy of her own home. She stretched out her foot and encountered another's, the bloated Iraqi she'd just fled from in the pool. He grinned at her lasciviously through a row of tobacco-stained teeth then farted like Vesuvius erupting.

Feeling shocked and violated, Serafina walked rapidly home. It was dark already and raining hard, and her heels tapped briskly on the sluiced-down pavement. Everyone else must be sheltering indoors, there was hardly a soul to be seen. After all her careful manoeuvring, her life had turned upside down and everything seemed to be suddenly falling apart. She had felt so secure as she swung through a jungle of men but now appeared to be losing her touch. First the dreadful snub she preferred not to dwell on and now even drippy James had gone away. She knew Jinx had a fairly low opinion of her, considered her wayward and spoilt, while even good old Dottie occasionally clucked. Even Ambrose had lately been looking at her askance though his adoration of Jinx remained undiminished. It wasn't fair, they hadn't given her a chance. She knew she could have done Jinx's job if only she hadn't come back.

Tears of self-pity began to gather in her eyes. She had always been able to summon them at will. It was time to move on, to shape-shift again, and haul herself upwards, before it was too late, to another dimension of prosperity. She knew exactly where she wanted to be and for that reason had been cultivating James. But now, on this cold wet miserable night, she also had a longing to be loved. To incite in some man that besotted admiration that to her meant exactly the same thing. Which is when she remembered the delectable DCI and the spirit came back into her stride. Not quite the type she would go for out of choice but a good enough substitute for a stopgap. Her eyes gleamed and she began to smile. She would have quite a story to tell him when he next came round.

The phone was ringing as she stuck her key into the lock and she rushed to open the door and get inside. It had to be James, she had known he couldn't resist her. And after she'd played with his feelings a while, she might even end up forgiving him. He was bound to come up with some plausible excuse and she needed him on her team. Right now.

'Hello,' she breathed into the phone, at her most seductive. But all she heard was the pregnant silence of someone listening then hanging up.

The next day Serafina finally did strike lucky: Hal inquiring politely if he could speak to her. Her heart beat a little faster when she heard his clipped tones though she managed superbly to retain her cool. After some lengthy prevarication and pretend consultation with her diary, she consented to meet him the next evening for a drink. He suggested, for convenience, that he saw her in the office but could tell from her tone she wasn't keen. She always played better on a one-to-one basis, knew the presence of others would detract from her limelight. So Hal suggested the pub round the corner but again heard the chill creep into her voice. Serafina had an antipathy to pubs; they were noisy and squalid and crawling with *hoi polloi*. More to her taste was an intimate cocktail bar, but Hal hadn't reckoned on going to so much trouble. Finally they compromised on the flashy Olympia Hilton. Not exactly what Serafina called class but at least one notch up from a bar. She agreed to meet him at seven, and Hal rolled his eyes as he hung up.

'Better come too,' he said to Trudy. 'This dame could turn out to be quite a handful.' He remembered the predatory gleam in her eye but by now had lost all interest in that game. Privately Trudy agreed but kept it to herself. Hal often had this effect on silly women but was old enough surely to take care of himself, his fault in the first place for leading them on.

'Are you crazy?' she said. 'That's the last thing she'd want. You'll be sure to get more out of her on your own.' More, if you don't keep your wits about you, than even you might be bargaining for.

Hal sighed theatrically then flashed his roguish grin. Trudy felt her stomach muscles contract but maintained an impassive expression. He was looking especially dashing today, with a sharp new haircut that enhanced his boyish appeal. On the whole, she loved working alongside him, but at times like this found it tough.

'Dirty work, I know,' he said, half reading her mind. 'But someone has to do it. And it seems I have drawn the short straw.'

He sat in a shadowed corner and watched Serafina's *grande dame* entrance. Either she'd been home to change, which seemed on the whole unlikely, or else she was always this well turned out for the office. Impressive. A short tight skirt with an ice blue silk shirt and large Gucci sunglasses shoved up into her hair. Her Prada bag was this season's hottest buy and her shoes had the fashionable kitten heels. How he came to know these things he really couldn't have said. A policeman dredges through so much dross daily a lot of it sticks in his head. She allowed the doorman to swivel the door then stood there dramatically peering around for Hal.

She reckons she's some kind of starlet, he thought, rising and crossing to greet her, yet he couldn't control a small flicker of pride at being seen publicly in such company. Whatever her attitude, this was one classy dame. Trudy had been right not to tag along. Egos such as this only functioned one to one. He was reminded, slightly oddly, of Norman Harker.

'Detective Chief Inspector,' purred Serafina silkily, extending one delicate hand. She demurely allowed him to pull her up a chair then settled herself to the best effect, displaying a great deal of leg. Hal ordered drinks – a spritzer for her – then fell back on chitchat while they waited. This looked like being fairly tricky since he didn't quite know what he was after. As with many routine interviews, probably nothing at all, but it had to be gone through for the record.

He need not have worried. Thrilled at the opportunity of a cosy *tête-à-tête*, Serafina was giving it all she'd got. Their drinks arrived and she was away, milking the occasion for all she was worth. She fixed him with those huge almost aquamarine eyes, smiled bravely then settled right into the part. These past few days, she told him with a shudder, had been the most horrific of her life. All the incessant questioning, the bombardment from the press. The suspicions, the possible motives, the sinister implications. It had thrown their small group into a terrible frenzy from which they had not yet recovered. Each one suspecting the others and constantly wondering. And then, of course, there were the phone-calls. She gave him a sketchy account of the sinister hangups and that voice full of vitriol hissing the single word, *Bitch*. She placed her hand lightly and trustingly on his knee and lowered her voice to a little girl whisper. *Protect me,* those eyes were beseeching him, and for one nanosecond Hal felt himself swayed. He cleared his throat and slightly shifted his chair. Business, a stern voice reminded him.

'Why do you suppose,' he asked in his best copper's voice, 'that you might be the subject of anonymous calls?' She had told him about the Iraqi too and the disgusting way he had behaved. Par for the course was Hal's private thought. If you can't stand the heat and all that.

He tried another tack. 'Is there anyone at all you can think of who might have been motivated to attack Ms McLennan? With sufficient antagonism, even unresolved hatred, to drive them to premeditated murder? Think hard.'

Serafina sipped her spritzer and artfully lowered her gaze. Her elegant legs were crossed at the knee and one wrist jangled heavily with bracelets. This, he accepted, was a seasoned seductress. But his mind right now was firmly on the job and the memory of the atrocity. When she failed to answer immediately he gave her a mental nudge by making some suggestions of his own. He had been through this routine so endlessly by now, he more or less had it off by rote.

'Boyfriends we don't know about? Who might have slipped her memory? Or even casual acquaintances. A woman like that must have a lot of admirers.'

Serafina thought hard, then shook her head. She rarely socialised with Jinx outside the office. She had met Hamish Cotterell and knew about Norman Harker but other than that was fairly vague. Except that, just lately, she'd had the strong impression there might be someone new in Jinx's life.

'She's been taking a lot of calls in the conference-room,' she said. 'Normally she has no secrets, let's all of us hear what's going on.'

She raised her glorious eyes to Hal's and gave him her helpless female shrug.

'But why don't you simply ask her?' she said. The obvious course of action.

'Any information,' he said, 'that she prefers not to divulge is covered by her citizen's rights. She is not obliged to reveal it, not to us.' He was interested to hear that Jinx might have a new admirer in the offing. She hadn't given a hint of that in any of their meetings. But there was still the mystery of the well-dressed stranger seen with her shortly before the crime. She'd been oddly evasive about that one, almost as if she were covering something up. Hal switched to a different tack.

'So how do you get on with her?' he asked. 'Good employer would you say?'

For one fleeting second, Serafina looked startled then the mask slid smoothly back into place. 'Brilliant,' she said in that smooth and honeyed whisper, her eyes positively shining with sincerity.

'She really is the most inspiring boss, generous, encouraging and kind. Talented too,' she added after a beat. 'It's a privilege to be working on her team.'

Oh yeah, thought Hal, alerted, aware of the phoniness of her reaction. She sat there like a schoolgirl now, earnestly clasping both knees, all attempts at sultriness suddenly fled. She recited a list of some of Jinx's successes and the way she so generously shared the credit with them all.

'And you'd like to follow in her footsteps one day? Perhaps when you reach her age?' Even inherit the business some day, though he didn't actually say that. Right on target, he could see it in her eyes. He sensed within her a gnawing envy combined with fierce ambition.

'Jinx didn't have my advantages,' she explained with a touch of hauteur. And gave him a swift précis of the well-heeled Italian parents and the place at Oxford to read fine arts, achieved when she was barely seventeen. He might even have believed her, she certainly looked the part, but his cynical policeman's heart was far too fly. But he let it pass unchallenged nevertheless. Serafina was not a major suspect, at least not yet, though he was curious about her current motivation.

'I've had one other thought.' She lowered her voice to a whisper. She sensed he was losing interest and wanted to detain him. 'It may sound far-fetched but I think it worth considering.' She fidgeted slightly as if embarrassed.

'Did it ever occur to you,' she asked, 'that the murderer might be Jinx herself?'

No, it most certainly hadn't. Hal's expression continued inscrutable but inside he was slack-jawed with amazement. How ever had she come up with a crazy idea like that? It was totally off the wall.

'Think about it,' said Serafina smoothly. 'Nobody knew she was going away and we have only her word for the way things turned out. Maybe she set Susie up.'

'For what reason? We need a motive.' The creature was clearly deranged.

'Who's to say,' said Serafina archly. 'It's your job to find that out. But I definitely think you should take it seriously. She would make a plausible killer because she's always so nice.'

Hal closed his notebook and rose to his feet. Now he had heard it all. He thanked Serafina for her co-operation and promised she'd hear from him if he needed her again. She didn't like Jinx one bit, that was clear. But did she hate her enough to kill?

'She was on the pull, it's obvious,' said Trudy. Men could be so gullible, it made her want to laugh. Hal looked at her quizzically, caught off his guard.

'You think?'

'I know. I've seen the way she looks at you. She'd gobble you up if she ever got the chance. Wait and see.'

For once he was slightly disconcerted and uneasily shifted his gaze. He was fond of baiting Trudy just for the hell of it but all of a sudden the boot had swapped feet. She considered him shrewdly with a flicker of amusement and knew why he was always so much on her mind. There was something about him so deliciously naïf it belied the tough cop with all the answers. She felt the urge to hug him but instead turned abruptly away. No point in getting ideas about her boss, though she was damned if she'd let some other woman grab him. Especially one as transparently fake as Serafina Rossetti.

25

Women are all the same, the slags, with their grizzling, self-centred ways. They witter on about their personal hygiene problems and whine if their hair gets wet. They piss and moan and generally waste time and expect some poor unsuspecting male to take care of them. They flaunt themselves and tell coarse jokes, smoke and drink and fornicate. Then scream and yell if you so much as touch them and run to the police crying rape. This is not how things were supposed to be. Not what I was raised to expect.

They are rubbish, the lot of them, and I can't be doing with them, but I plan to keep a closer eye on their antics. No more making a fool out of me. I'll kill a second time should it prove necessary.

So I watch them more closely, to see that they behave, and will be waiting out here in the darkness to get them the second they step out of line. They need to be culled, there are too many of them about.

They appear to be taking over the world.

26

The light had long faded to a murky grey but Ambrose, lost in a world of his own, was oblivious. He sat hunched in front of his personal computer, zapping the enemy for all he was worth, his jaw locked grimly in rapt concentration. Far too much of his time was passed in this manner, though there was no one now to know or chide him. Dottie would have clucked and called it unhealthy, bad for his migraines with that sporadic flickering light. But Dottie, although an absolute pet, was not his mother, and he was plenty old enough to do as he liked. He finished the game and glanced at the clock; twenty to ten and he still hadn't eaten. And now he found that he was ravenous.

The hard bright strip lighting in the kitchen hurt his eyes as he sought in the fridge for inspiration. Not much choice, one egg and some fairly ancient bread, so it would have to be baked beans again tonight. Luckily he had stockpiled tins for just this sort of emergency. He usually ate out, at the chippie on the corner, when he wasn't stuck in a pub somewhere with friends. He scraped the mould from a couple of thick slices and stuck them under the grill. He hadn't cleaned that for a year or so, so the kitchen filled with acrid smoke which added to the discomfort of his eyes. While he waited for the beans to heat, he switched on his tiny black and white telly. It was a castoff from Jinx, donated years ago, which she'd doubtless forgotten all about. He had never known anyone go through material things like she did; he smiled to himself as he scooped out the beans and sloshed them onto the toast. Jinx believed in the consumer society while Ambrose had been raised far more frugally. Waste Not, Want Not had been his mother's favourite axiom, along with Make Do and Mend. Both of which had rubbed off on Ambrose, who rarely threw anything away.

He stood at the counter while he gobbled his beans, keen to get back to the computer. Nothing much was happening on the news, apart from the Kosovo atrocities which still dragged on. Ambrose was impervious to the suffering of strangers; his world was encompassed by his job and these four drab walls. Yet Dottie, had she had her wish and managed to infiltrate his territory, would have got an unexpected surprise. Despite Jinx's jokes about the squalor of bachelor life, Ambrose was actually fanatically neat and kept his home thoroughly shipshape. The curtains needed cleaning and were fraying at the edges but the bed was made, with hospital corners, and his washing was soaking in the sink. Every Sunday he scrubbed the kitchen floor with carbolic and dosed the basins and lavatory with bleach. Jinx would not be surprised. She knew him so well and laughed at his little eccentricities, like always demanding clean glasses with each fresh bottle of wine. No one else she knew was quite so fastidious; she found it endearing, a symptom of his Spartan upbringing. Like Jinx herself, he came from an army background, one of the things he believed helped bind them together. Though where Jinx's father had passed through OTC, Rafferty senior had remained in the ranks, a sergeant and proud of it until his demob.

Ambrose poured himself another beer and took it back with him to the computer. The room was now almost completely dark but he still didn't bother with the light. He preferred it like this, a cocoon of fuggy blackness with just the lighted screen on which to focus. He started another game of *Doom II* and was soon happily zapping away, lost in his alien world. He found these adult computer games enormously challenging and unwinding, a release from the petty frustrations of the day. Wait till the world saw their own brilliant DBI-2000, which was set to blow even the list-leaders out of the water.

Later, as he rinsed out his washing and hung it on the drying-rack in a neat, straight line, he thought about Jinx and her extravagant refurbishing, and smiled with real tenderness at her impetuousness. Most people in her situation would be crushed by what had happened. Not Jinx, though, she was already bouncing back, an attribute he found most endearing. He loved her to death, had done so all these years, but only ever conceivably at arm's length. Which was the principal tragedy of Ambrose's life: he was seriously, cripplingly inhibited on account of how his mother had let him down.

Bridget, her name was, though his dad had called her Bridie and worshipped the ground on which she trod. Not that she'd trodden very far, at least since Ambrose was quite a small child, because of her persistently failing health. She was fair and wan with eyes like stars and the softest Galway lilt to her voice. She would read to the young chap often, and from that his voracious love of books had been born. He had such happy memories of being cuddled up together, in a hand-knitted patchwork shawl in those freezing Belfast winters, alongside his mam on her lamplit low couch while she read to him stories that had remained with him ever since. Of witches and make-believe and hobgoblins and the rest, of talking animals beside a quiet stream, of beautiful young damsels being rescued just in time by the buccaneering heroes of their dreams. She had only been able to have just the one baby so Ambrose's childhood had been solitary but blessed. He'd had quite an early gift for drawing, and at this she had encouraged him, sitting beside him at the kitchen table until the pain grew bad and she'd been forced to return to her couch.

His father, Frank, had often been away on army business, leaving the family at home. Bridie was far too delicate to travel; besides, she had wanted a proper home for the boy. So Ambrose had developed under his mother's gentle rule, assisting her around the house on the days she was too weak to carry on. He had learned to make scones and help her stir the stew, to turn the handle of the heavy iron mangle and drag the wet sheets out to the line. 'My little man' was what she always called him and rewarded him with biscuits for helping so well with the chores. Those, looking back, had been the happiest years of his life, till the second stage of the cancer set in and she lived in a state of continual suffering, shrieking out in agony at even the slightest touch, unable any longer to allow him too close for fear of the excruciating pain.

Ambrose frowned as he remembered those days and tried hard to dismiss them from his mind. Her soft translucent beauty had drastically faded till the bones of her face stood starkly out while her eyes receded into their sockets. He was no longer allowed even a proper goodnight kiss and had to make do with one simply blown. When Frank returned and saw the state she was in, he banished the boy altogether. At nine years old, in short trousers and an oversized cap, he'd been sent away to school in Limerick, to a cold, grim place that was little more than an institution. And when Bridie had died, an agonising eighteen months later, he'd not even been allowed home for the funeral. Deprived of the chance to say his last goodbyes, he still saw her face at night. Sorrowing and tragic like the Blessed Virgin Mary, in whom he had never quite believed.

How Dottie would have wept for him if only she could have known, Jinx too, but these were matters he never discussed; they were kept locked away in his heart. His father had married a second time and was retired contentedly now back in Galway. Ambrose rarely visited him for he found that these days they had nothing at all in common. He respected Frank for his toughness and rude health but there was very little else about him he could respond to or admire. Whereas Bridie remained the lost angel of his dreams; it was her picture in an ornate frame that he still kept beside his bed.

If tattered remnants of that early love had been bestowed on anyone, it was Jinx. Ambrose first encountered her at the London College of Printing where she was already into her second year. Bright and ebullient as a pixie on speed, she had romped all over his sensibilities, thereby enslaving his arid heart forever. Entirely unwittingly, which was how she did most things, and this had made the resulting sensual ache that much more difficult to bear. Ambrose, in those days, was shy and unassuming, especially awkward with women though they showed an interest in him. Uncertain, after the motherless years in the bleak institution, exactly how to deal with this unknown, slightly alien other sex. Which was perhaps why he had palled up with Damien, whose social insecurities, for entirely other reasons, had been as pronounced as his own. For the first couple of terms they lurked on the sidelines, observing and admiring yet usually too bashful to approach. Together they had joined the photographic and chess clubs, and sunk their basic lack of confidence in totally amorphous activities. They got along, they scored high marks. They developed a private code of humour that saw them through the more difficult days. They were model students who slowly carved out their own niche.

And Ambrose had learned to relax and enjoy and slowly grow into his adult self. He became less scrawny and began to fit his clothes, to look people in the eye when he was speaking. The minute Jinx got onto his case she made him get rid of the awful National Health specs and invest in a pair of stylish designer frames that made a world of difference to his appearance and confidence.

'Why, Mr Rafferty, you're beautiful!' she joked, snatching them off him when he first appeared wearing them and reaching up on tiptoes for a kiss. Ambrose blushed heavily and backed away, yet was pleased, nonetheless, by the attention. He was a nice-looking chap with a beatific smile, and the girls began to notice him until he became a bit of a star. Witty and insightful when they took the time to listen, he soon had his own little following of fans who would hang around him hopefully in the pub. Yet none was able to get beyond first base, since Jinx alone was the keeper of his heart. Not that she ever realised the depth or extent of his passion. That he was always most careful to keep under wraps. Now that he'd caught the photographic bug, he got into the habit of snapping her a lot, usually when she wasn't aware he was doing it. He never tired of watching her, to him she was quintessentially female. He only wished his dead mother might have known her.

He had witnessed her progression through the rest of her college years with the benign and smiling approval of a parent. Bright though he was, she was quicker off the mark and kept him constantly amused with her facile wit. A real scream, as Damien pronounced her, with her easy laughter and careless unthinking charm. And then, when she finally flew the nest and ventured out into the real world, she had faithfully kept in touch with them and found them both jobs alongside her at Weinbergs. What more could anyone wish for in a friend?

Damien was in town on one of his flying visits, so the two men met up at Ronnie Scott's where the Count Basie orchestra was booked. Damien was irritable, as he was so often these days, complaining about the position of their table as well as the slowness of the service. Ambrose, well used to him, simply sat back and drank and unwound. He loved the smoky atmosphere of this famous Soho jazz den and sank himself into the music, ignoring the constant fidgeting of his companion.

'Damn traffic,' Damien was muttering. 'Blocked solid right the way through. Had to get out and walk halfway down Piccadilly. This city is getting too crowded.'

Ambrose nodded without really listening. He had come on the tube which was always the simplest way and would take a night bus back to Battersea. He loved the city in the small hours best of all and would roam for miles, whenever the mood took him, working out his problems and releasing ugly tensions. He rather despised Damien for having copped out to Jersey. Being a tax exile was all very well but he surely risked losing his talent along with his soul. The players appeared and so did their second round, so for a while even Damien shut up. Their mutual passion for jazz still united them in an ongoing camaraderie that had not really changed much over the years. Despite the gap in their current fortunes and Damien's annoying habit of treating Ambrose as an underling. This he put up with stoically; it simply wasn't worth the hassle. He had more important things on his mind than Damien's petulant whining.

At the end of the first session Damien started to fret about his game. He had more or less completed his own creative input. It was now into its beta testing stage and up to Ambrose and the team to perfect the finished product. They had yet to come up with the brilliant selling title but that should be only a matter of time.

'Are you still getting grief from those buggers in New York?' Damien was such an obsessive neurotic he could not let any gripe alone for long. He made even Ambrose appear laid back as he chewed his cuticles and squirmed around, his wild myopic eyes darting back and forth like hyperactive goldfish in a bowl. Ambrose wanted to tell him to shove it but instead just shook his head. What was actually happening was really quite weird though he didn't want to go into details now. They had had a sudden unscheduled visit from the big cheese himself, after which everything had gone suspiciously quiet. No calls from New York, not even an e-mail or fax. It seemed as if the heat were suddenly off. Which was even more unsettling since the deadline was so close. He privately feared it might just be the calm before the storm. That IEP were considering pulling out. After all, their nemesis, Weinberg, had done it before. Nothing was too drastic for that man. Though he hesitated to mention that to Damien.

'Why does that bastard keep cropping up in our lives?' Damien loathed him as much as the rest for pulling the rug from under their feet. He had always believed, and was probably right, that it had something to do with the jokes. The biting satire of an acid-tipped pen sliding unsigned caricatures under doors. Max Weinberg had chuckled and collected them, had occasionally had one framed, but his arsehole nephew was less benign. He had hated their humour and the fun they'd all had, had done everything in his power to split them up. So that any little hiccup Damien had encountered in his career ever since he had usually attributed to Weinberg. Such was his paranoid nature, getting worse, though it did appear to be rooted in possibility.

'I've really no idea,' said Ambrose, reluctant to get into the discussion. 'It is almost as if it's a sort of personal vendetta, him against us until the end. If we weren't so tiny and insignificant, a gnat compared to the dinosaur IEP, I would almost believe he saw us as some sort of personal threat.'

'How so?' asked Damien, alarmed and beginning to twitch.

'Vanity,' said Ambrose. 'He loathes the lot of us because we knew him when.'

'When he sold us all down the river and left us unemployed.' Damien's fists automatically clenched and the eyes continued to dart uncontrollably. Fame and huge fortune had done nothing at all to calm him. If anything, he was more manic than before.

Ambrose wondered how poor Janey managed to cope. He had noticed he rarely mentioned her these days.

'Is there nothing we can do to escape his clutches?' In a minute, Ambrose saw, he'd be calling his lawyers.

'Sorry, old chap, not a bloody thing. They own us lock, stock and barrel. Or at least the project.' Then seeing the distress in his companion's eyes, he tried his best to calm him down.

'There's no point starting to panic now, what is done is done. We'll just have to keep a watchful eye out to see he doesn't fuck us over again.'

The last time had been bad enough. This could prove catastrophic.

27

It was clear to almost everyone that Max was on his way out, and the first thing Jinx did, on her return from New York, was drop off her luggage then rush straight round to see him in his private room at the Lister Clinic. He looked awful. Smaller and somehow shrunken, with pallid cheeks and bright, feverish eyes. He was banked up against pillows and surrounded by cards and flowers, and the nurse warned her quietly not to stay too long.

'Jinx, my darling. Come here and give me a kiss.' He was obviously bucked to see her back and held out his arms for a hug.

'Well, you're a bit of a silly old thing,' she said. 'Can't turn my back for one second.' She was appalled by his pallor but tried hard not to show it. She'd always assumed he was indestructible, had relied on his wisdom for so long.

He laughed. 'Anno domini, my dear. Sooner or later it happens to us all. Now come sit right here and tell me all about it. Rumour has it that you took the city by storm.'

Since it was clear that his delight was genuine, she did as ordered and gave him a detailed account. Omitting the night spent with Julius, of course. She still hadn't quite sorted that out in her head. She told him about the people she'd met and passed on the messages they had sent. Max was respected but also greatly loved; she'd been struck by the huge esteem in which he was held by the New York publishing world.

'Everyone sent their love,' she told him. 'Without you behind me I'd not have had half as much fun.'

He chuckled. The nurse stuck a disapproving face round the door but Max imperiously waved her away. He was paying through the nose for this cramped little room so he'd damn well do as he pleased while he was here. He insisted on chapter and verse on all her sales and adventures and whooped with appreciation as she described how she had scored. Only now, telling him, did she really fully realise how much she had actually achieved. Max had always done this for her, raising her morale enormously by letting her see things through his eyes. Oh Max, whatever would she do without him – but now was no time for such sombre thoughts.

'And you really liked the city?' he eventually asked.

'Loved it! It thrilled me to bits.'

'That's my girl.' He patted her hand but his touch was faint and clammy. She looked at him more closely and saw death lurking in his eyes.

'I ought to go.' So far Julius had not been mentioned. Jinx wondered at that but could not bring herself to speak his name. She felt self-conscious and afraid of somehow betraying something. If Max preferred to be discreet she ought to follow his lead. Perhaps Julius had held off telling him because of the state of his health. She wondered why he wasn't here now; had been aching to see him from the moment she got back. It was possible he was somewhere in the hospital, respecting their privacy for this *tête-à-tête*. Now that she knew him better, she saw that he did have finesse. She would never have believed it of the man she had thought she knew. Her heart swelled with tenderness.

'Don't go,' Max pleaded, clutching at her arm, but the officious nurse was back in the room and this time she really meant business. She took a thermometer out of her starched pocket and stuck it abruptly into the old man's mouth, effectively silencing his protests. In spite of his condition, Jinx couldn't help but smile. The doughty old warrior had finally met his match. She started to leave and blew him a kiss from the door.

'I'll be back to see you tomorrow,' she promised. 'In the meantime, do take care.'

'What's happened to Julius?' she asked Ambrose the next morning and was surprised when he merely looked blank. It was the first time he'd known her show any such interest. Back five minutes and already up to her tricks. He grinned with real relief at having her under his scrutiny once more.

'It's really great to see you,' he said. 'Without you London is just not the same.'

'Yeah, yeah.' She ruffled his hair. In recent years he'd taken to wearing it longer, which gave him a raffish, almost beatnik look. With the tinted lenses he had also now adopted, he had the air of a Teutonic intellectual or a Mahler-like musician with his head well into the clouds. But he still hadn't told her what she was dying to know. It was four whole days since she'd been in Julius's arms. She was starting to wilt with the continuing deprivation. But was careful not to let Ambrose see her concern.

'Julius,' she asked again casually. 'Where is he?'

Ambrose looked at her blankly, at a loss. 'How the hell should I know?' he said grumpily. 'Who cares?'

This wasn't as easy as she'd hoped; he clearly didn't know that they'd both been in New York. And, fearful of gossip, she decided she couldn't proceed. She skipped back to her own office next door but Julius's room was deserted. A clear desk, an empty waste-bin, no shouted orders or strident phone-calls. His ashtray was clean, no hint in the air of his aftershave. Not even his umbrella hanging on the back of the door; she checked. It felt like the *Marie Celeste* with everyone gone. Now her desire to see him grew desperate; she needed the reassurance of his arms. Perhaps it had all been a crazy, impossible dream. A symptom of her hormones running wild.

'Where's Mr Weinberg?' she finally dared asked his secretary, as casually as she could muster without giving the game away.

'New York,' said the girl without ceasing to type. 'He had to go over there urgently on business.'

Not back yet – how could that possibly be? She had heard him on the phone arranging his flight. Anxious not to ask too many questions, she withdrew into her own office to attack the great backlog of work. But she couldn't escape the confusion in her brain. He'd been rushing back to London to see Max, yet Max hadn't mentioned him at all. She remembered the look in his eyes before he left. He had told her he loved her and she had believed him. Yet now he seemed to have vanished. What on earth was going on? Or was she simply losing her mind?

Julius eventually put in an appearance three days later. Ambrose saw him first as he was loitering in the post-room when Julius burst through the main front door looking tired, harassed and cross. He had his raincoat slung over one shoulder and a suitbag and briefcase in his hand.

'Good trip?' asked Ambrose robotically, though truthfully he couldn't give a toss. The return of the tyrant meant more fluttering in the hencoop and Jinx acting oddly again. Julius, barely acknowledging Ambrose, took the stairs at his usual rapid stride and vanished abruptly into his office.

'Betty!' Ambrose heard him scream and instantly the curfuffle recommenced. 'Coffee!' he ordered. 'And a list of my messages. Look sharp. I'm expecting an urgent call from New York so be sure to interrupt me when it comes through.'

Ambrose smiled grimly and sloped off back to his den, where

Damien was quietly slaving over something quite breathtakingly intricate.

'He's up to something, you mark my words,' said Ambrose darkly as he perched on the edge of the desk.

'How's that?' asked Damien abstractedly, pausing to pick invisible fluff from his nib. It was amazing what this man could achieve; Ambrose never tired of watching him at work. He had the patience and artistry of a Fabergé craftsman, at odds with his rather uncertain temper.

'Instinct,' said Ambrose. 'I feel it in my gut. He's been gone too long and we don't know where.'

'Or care,' observed Damien calmly as he drew.

The first intimation Jinx had that Julius was back was the arrival of the memo on her desk. By then her cuticles were gnawed and bloody and she'd dropped a good five pounds in weight. It summoned her curtly, along with the rest of the staff, to an emergency meeting in the boardroom at half past four. Jinx had been out all morning seeing the wholesalers so had missed the pomp and circumstance of his return. Her first action was to stab the buzzer frantically to see what Ambrose might know. Something was clearly going on; Jinx was keen to find out what. But Ambrose, for once, hadn't a clue. Nor did he appear very much to care.

It was unlikely to be Max, she reasoned, since she'd checked already with the clinic and they'd told her he was resting and still holding his own. What disturbed her most was the fact that she hadn't even had a glimpse of Julius. She'd been pacing the room for almost an hour and he still hadn't emerged from his meeting. She occasionally heard his raised voice through the door, which for once remained firmly closed. It was not like him to be quite so secretive; Julius was very much a hands-on MD. She was beset by a terrible premonition Something had to be radically wrong, though she had no idea at all what it could be. She didn't, as it happened, have very much longer to wait.

They all shuffled in and stood grouped around the room and Julius brought the meeting to order then came swiftly to the point. In view of the current state of his uncle's health, he had sold the company, lock, stock and barrel, to the German giant Holtzbrincks, of international fame. The takeover to be effective as soon as the small print had been resolved, which he hoped would be very shortly, before the end of the year. Stunned silence all round while everyone reeled. No one had seen this coming.

'But why?' Jinx dared to ask, after a frozen pause. He was looking divine, though tense and tired and unwilling apparently to meet her eye.

'Progress,' said Julius curtly, as if they were barely acquainted. 'They are, as you know, at the top of their field and among the biggest in the world. They already have strong holdings here and want to expand. They have recently taken over Art Editions and now want to merge us with them. Makes sense considering the size of their turnover and the up-to-date technology they have recently installed.'

He glanced round the room for any other questions but no one but Jinx had the guts to speak out. Until Ambrose, ashen-faced, asked how it was likely to affect them personally, and Julius told him briskly that business would continue as normal. There was no need for anyone to worry, drastic changes would not be made. Definitely not in the foreseeable future. It was almost Christmas and they would all find in their end-of-year pay packets an extra bonus as a mark of goodwill. For their loyalty and industriousness; Weinbergs would not let them down. The meeting ended and they all trooped out, Jinx along with the rest, too shaken to want to linger or talk.

She was home that night but he didn't call, and somehow that didn't surprise her. The man she had trusted and found that she loved had quite casually sold them down the river. Far worse, this treachery must have been half resolved by the time of that rapturous night in New York. He must have known, as he held her in his arms, that he was about to sweep the rug from beneath her feet. In no mean way. For a day and a half later, when the news broke in the press, it was announced that Weinbergs was moving into the Art Editions premises, the two separate companies to be absorbed under one single management and roof. First to be dispensed with would be the art and production departments. There was no point in duplicating existing services, for rationalisation was the name of this game and cost-cutting top of the list.

'Bastard!' said Ambrose, as if he'd proved a point, while they thumbed their way through the newspapers. All those lost jobs and he'd known all along yet had not had the decency to warn them. Fuck the sodding bonus, he had snatched away their livelihoods. And in a couple of days it would be Christmas.

'Well you're still sitting pretty,' said Damien accusingly, but Jinx simply shook her head. There was no way she was going to abandon her friends now. A great wrong had been done and she refused to condone it. She was willing to bet that Max didn't know a thing. There was no way he could have agreed to the takeover, particularly now while he was hovering at death's door. Weinbergs represented all he had ever worked for. He would not have let it go just like that. The worst irony of all was that he'd survived the holocaust only to be sold out to the Germans after all.

She thought of going to see him to plead the case of her colleagues, but the poor man was already fighting for his life. Of one thing she was sure, though, and nothing could alter her mind. If her friends were going to be thrown on the scrap heap, then she was joining them too. All for one and one for all after so many years together. The least she could do was show some solidarity; she had expected it of them, after all.

Her phone rang, Betty trying to locate her urgently.

'Mr Weinberg was hoping for a word,' she said, 'before he leaves for Germany tonight.' Forget it, she was far too incensed to confront him. If he'd been all she'd thought, things would not have turned out this way. The man she had started to love would have had some integrity, would have honoured his uncle's trust and not played Judas.

'Tell him to stuff it,' said Jinx succinctly. And followed Ambrose and Damien to the pub.

28

What Jinx had achieved all those years ago was ground-breaking at the time. She had fearlessly, not to say reck-lessly, jacked in an excellent job to join the masses of the unemployed, thus chancing her future to the gods. All the promise and the years of slow advancement were sacrificed in that single noble gesture. It was the start of 1987, a cold, raw January with a cutting Arctic wind, and she'd walked straight out because that's what Julius wanted, pausing only to pick up her personal things. They'd had one explosive final confrontation when he shouted at her like the old days and she'd called him a traitor to his face. At which he had totally lost control and ordered her out of the building forthwith. No word of intimacy, no reference to what they had fleetingly been to one another; they might just have been enemies trading insults. Jinx had turned and gone without another word, clenching her heart against the certain pain, keen he should not detect the tears in her eyes. All these years she had searched for her one great love and just when she'd thought she had finally found it, it had crumbled away into ashes. Never, she determined, would she be caught that way again. Never trust a man, they were liars, the whole breed.

Ambrose and Damien were filled with delighted awe, impressed by her ballsy attitude, touched by such loyal support. But then they'd no inkling of what lay hidden in her heart, of the real sacrifice she was making on their behalf, a loss far more devastating than just a job. She shouldn't have done it, her position had been secure whereas jobs for designers were thin on the ground and they'd only got limited work experience on their CVs. Jinx assured them that they were bound to be all right. Training by Weinbergs was about as good as it got, and degrees from the London College of Printing prestigious. They were all back together in the same boat now and she'd do what it took to see that they triumphed in the end.

First thing after quitting the building, she'd been straight round to see Max at his home. He'd been ordered by the clinic not to work any more which, from the way that he looked, was probably wise. The German takeover had hit him exceptionally hard; he was blue-lipped and indignant when Jinx rang his Hampstead doorbell. A housekeeper led her to the book-lined study where Max, engulfed in a shawl, was crouched by a single-bar electric fire. Jinx kissed him warmly but was privately appalled; she had never seen him look so fragile. She felt terrible about what had happened, she said, but he cut her short with a peremptory wave of the hand. Sorry wasn't good enough, Max was bloody furious. That scoundrel, his nephew in whom he had put so much trust, had sold his birthright for a paltry mess of pottage. The moment his back had been turned.

'I suppose he thought I was not long for this world,' Max croaked grimly, agitation making his breathing painfully short.

'Then you had no idea?'

'No, of course I didn't. I handed over my shares as a matter of trust. Who do you turn to if not to blood? He was supposed to be the guardian of the interests of you all. Instead look how treacherous he has turned out.'

He coughed chokingly and hard, and Jinx was alarmed. She recalled all the New York well-wishers who loved and revered this old man. All that wisdom and publishing experience just thrown away on an avaricious whim. Exactly what Julius had hoped to achieve, apart from big money, was imponderable. She had known him as a canny businessman, not taken him for a fool. For he had been designated sole heir to a grand old institution and apparently chucked it unthinkingly away. She squeezed Max's hand, which was trembling with fury.

'Try not to let it get to you too much,' she urged. 'I'm confident Julius has your interests at heart. He is not a dishonourable man.' Yet he had pursued her and wooed her that memorable night in New York, made love to her in so many ways and she'd allowed him right through her defences. He had treated her gently and told her that he loved her and she had gone along with it and taken him at his word. But she knew now for certain he had lied.

She stayed with Max for another few minutes then let herself out with a promise to return. But she was never to see her beloved mentor again, for in just a few days he was dead. Dead of a broken heart, she always felt, an embittered old man who had survived two world wars to see all his achievements simply swept away by his own nephew's greedy hand. The publishing house he had laboured decades to create was seamlessly absorbed into a faceless conglomerate, destroyed overnight by his German adversaries in a fire of another nature.

It turned out not to be as easy as Jinx had predicted for any of them to find jobs in a market that was on the shrink. They tramped the wintry streets in answer to many ads, for the promised Christmas bonus would barely see them into the spring. But Jinx was a natural fighter with a great weight of anger to unload, so she made a precipitous and harebrained decision to set up in business on her own. Undeterred by the fact she had neither job nor savings, she marched boldly into the bank one day and demanded an interview with the manager. Though just twenty-eight, she asked for a substantial loan and ended up risking her sole security by taking a second mortgage on her flat. Crazy, said Ambrose and even Damien was scared, but once Jinx set her mind to something she inevitably saw it through. She had promised to look after them and that's what she'd damned well do. Unlike another whose name she'd never mention again, Jinx always stuck to her word.

She found the nice open-plan offices in the mews and by the end of March they were in there and up and running. McLennan Graphics was the name on the door but Jinx saw it more as a consortium. She had raised the money so she'd carry the financial can but relied on the others' talents to make it work. So they put their heads together and did extensive market research and in the end decided, by unanimous consent, to give the world of publishing a miss. They had been there, done that; it was time to move on. What had happened to Weinbergs was repeating itself all over with the small independents being swallowed by faceless giants.

The field of electronics was where they were headed now. They were young and bright and adaptable, and that was where the future lay. Computer-related technology was taking the world by storm and first CD-Is and then CD-ROMs beginning to make their mark. Infotainment was the new buzzword and they couldn't wait to get into it and started. Both Ambrose and Damien were experienced graphic designers while Jinx had the proven flair and chutzpah to take care of the marketing side. Backed, of course, by the stalwart Dottie, without whom none of them ever could have coped.

Dottie was inclined to worry quite a bit about Jinx's lovelife, which seemed to her both erratic and unsuitable. Put it this way, she'd not like her daughter to be milling around with quite so many men, certainly not by this age. She couldn't recall when she'd last seen her with someone suitable; the way she was headed did not look good at all.

'Love is for wimps,' Jinx had been heard to say. 'Why dirty your hands in the kitchen when there's fast food on every corner?'

All well and good but she wasn't getting any younger. If she ever intended to settle down, she should surely be thinking about it now. Especially if she wanted kids. Which she declared emphatically she did not.

'I'm one of those fortunate women,' she bragged, 'who's not had a maternal urge in her life.' Yet with other people's children, animals and young friends she was the epitome of patience, generosity and fun. She was a special favourite in the Sullivan household where the children had known and loved her all their lives. On any of the rare occasions that she could be enticed to join them for supper or Sunday lunch, they would both instantly cancel other dates, preferring to stay at home with the grownups.

'I don't know what your secret is,' said Dottie, 'but you can have both of mine any time. They are models of good behaviour when you are around.'

Nevertheless, she still felt it was a shame. Jinx had all the requisites to make a wonderful wife and mother, and was wasted on this wild and profligate lifestyle.

'You worry too much,' was Sam's sole comment, trying to block his mind to the past. Jinx would survive, she had managed miraculously till now, and he'd no doubt whatsoever that she'd win through.

All she really lived for in those turbulent early days was work and the pursuit of new business. They fitted together brilliantly as an integrated team, which was part of the secret of their instant success. The offices were expensive and so were the day-to-day running costs. Jinx, impulsively, had committed herself to finding them all employment, and the biggest headache she faced every week was how to cover their salaries and overheads. They lived on a financial knife-edge that kept them all on their toes. The single scariest moment of Dottie's week was having to face the bank statement and watch how they were haemorrhaging money for what might turn out to be just a dream. Life was a roller-coaster of fiscal dread yet so heady and exciting it kept them all buoyed up with the pure exuberance of being free, away from the tyranny of the German jackboot. Never again. The strong lasting friendship of Jinx, Ambrose and Damien was put to new tests but survived.

Then Sam, too, came unstuck when the brash new Weinbergs' regime decided, in their wisdom, that the quaint, old-fashioned charm of his drawings was not what they wanted for the future. Too ossified for the current proactive market were the words they actually used, whatever that meant. Sam, long accustomed to rejection, was stoic about it, until Jinx intervened and with her customary magic introduced him to Walker Books, the best of the emerging children's publishers. Since when he had not looked back.

The boys worked well as a harmonious team, quietly getting on with it at opposite ends of a long table. Dottie sat downstairs and did the donkey work, billing and chasing money and keeping the accounts. While Jinx was out on the road for the most part, drumming up business in a field she scarcely knew. But she rapidly learned to adapt. She spruced up her outfits for the smarter clientele and carried around a slim portfolio instead of the bulky dummies she'd had in the past. As Max had foreseen, she was a natural at selling. Charming and gossipy yet keen and to the point. She bluffed her way through many a closed door to emerge triumphant with lucrative orders to fill.

Christmas cards, brochures, even menus. Once the entire décor for a Hallowe'en party. Not what they were aiming for but work nonetheless and some blessed cashflow to keep them afloat. Nothing was too small for them and they prided themselves on their fast efficiency. Added to which it was fun.

'I don't miss the meetings at all,' said Ambrose placidly. All that time wasted when he could have been getting on.

Eventually the big breakthrough arrived when Jinx wormed her way into a computer software firm. She watched what they were doing and made some constructive suggestions and pretty soon they trusted her enough to unload some of the routine design work on to her. They learned the basic requisites as they actually did the work and began to have brainstorming sessions of their own. Ideas came easily, it was how to apply them that counted. Once they'd got the hang of the market requirements, the rest followed pretty naturally.

Their reputation grew rapidly and they took on more staff. Serafina first, to mop up some of the design work while she learned to shadow Jinx on the marketing side. And eventually Wayne, who was too good not to snap up and provided them all with entertainment as well as the benefit of his youthful input. It had worked; they had survived twelve years. It seemed incredible now, looking back. Jinx got the credit for having the initial vision and the courage to set it all up, but they all pulled together quite magnificently as a team. A consortium, that was the right word.

And throughout all the years they heard nothing more of Julius, who appeared to have vanished off the face of the earth. He had sorted out the Holtzbrinck takeover, then quit the job and moved permanently to New York. That much Jinx did know from reading the financial press. Always a high flier, he was now apparently soaring. Without the confines of the family business his ambition had no ceiling at all. Ambrose continued to hiss about him occasionally but even his venom had been drawn.

What had seemed at the time like an act of betrayal could now be considered their deliverance.

'Funny how things work out,' said Jinx. 'We might still be sitting in Great Russell Street designing catalogues. He actually did us the favour of our lives.'

Part Three

29

Minutes after they had arrived back in the mews after that disruptive meeting in January the phone started ringing from IEP. Julius Weinberg urgently for Jinx. She shook her head angrily and refused to take the call.

'He's already rung three times,' said Serafina. 'What's going on?'

'What indeed. You might as well ask him that.' After all the hollow years spent trying to forget him, what was it still about this man that bugged her? She'd succeeded in getting him out of her life but not her head. It seemed he was unable to let her go. A vainer woman might have given that some thought. But the team was looking perplexed, she had to explain. The meeting hadn't really gone off very well, she admitted. Something of a catastrophe in fact. Ambrose, grinning broadly, gladly took up the story. Having weathered the initial shock he was really, really proud of her for standing up to the bully once again.

'You ought to have seen them,' he reported with a chuckle. 'Real David and Goliath stuff. Glaring at each other across the room like pit bull terriers about to scrap. Well, he got no more than he deserved.' Jinx had ousted Julius again.

Jinx smiled ruefully, grateful for his backing. It had been quite funny now she thought about it rationally. His attitude had been outrageous, an echo of the tyrant she'd first known. And she didn't intend to be treated like a minion any more, all that was well in the past.

'But I ruined it all,' she admitted. In the end she had gone too far. So Ambrose provided a blow-by-blow account and soon had them cheering on her behalf.

'It was the cross-examination that finally did it,' Jinx confessed. 'It felt like he was using a rubber truncheon.'

'Quite right,' agreed Dottie, he'd been way out of line. Treating Jinx like a four-year-old when she was the mover and shaker behind the whole thing. Though she was a bit apprehensive nevertheless. Suppose he were to withdraw their financial backing. They had more to worry about than just this immediate victory. Months of hard work and Damien's entire project hung in the balance of one man's vindictiveness, a man who appeared to have become Jinx's implacable enemy. The thing about running your own small outfit was the terrible risks it incurred. IEP had contributed the development money for DBI-2000 and could just as easily snatch it away without warning. And then whatever would McLennan Graphics do? It would mean facing almost certain ruin.

'You'd think he could leave us alone after all these years.' Dottie had never really known him but had heard him endlessly discussed. Sam, whose opinions she treated like the gospel, always said he wouldn't trust him further than he could throw him.

Ambrose, still grinning, merely shrugged. He was thrilled by the way Jinx had leapt again into the fray. She had properly shown the bastard where to get off.

'He'll not get the better of us,' he chortled. Though he wished he could really believe that.

The phone rang again and Serafina waved. Him again, she indicated to Jinx. Jinx shook her head. Nothing would persuade her to speak again to that man. He had humiliated her publicly like a recalcitrant child. She wasn't putting up with any more.

'You take it,' she hissed, seeing Ambrose's uncertainty. He had been there, after all. He could cope.

'I can't,' he pleaded, as uneasy as Dottie. Giving a humorous account was one thing, having to face up to the bastard something else altogether. And Ambrose famously avoided confrontation even though he knew that Jinx was in the right. Despite the brilliance of their recent track record, this was the big one which they could not afford to screw up. Jinx had got them into this scrape, only she was capable of resolving it now. It was finally time for her to pause and face the music, despite how much she might loathe this particular adversary.

So she took the call. Alone in the privacy of the conference-room. She was not going to be seen as a coward or defeatist and she knew in her heart they were right. Besides, she was far too angry to be afraid. She snatched up the receiver with a curt hello and felt her stomach take an involuntary dip as she heard the familiar voice.

'Jinx,' said Julius in a calm and reasonable tone. 'I really think we should talk.'

His choice of venue surprised her. Nothing brash or too opulent, which she once might have expected of him, but a friendly family-run Italian trattoria just off the King's Road. *La Famiglia* was warm and enticing with blue and white tiles and crisp linen tablecloths. A smiling waiter led her to a corner table where Julius was already ensconced. He rose and solemnly offered his hand then waited until she was seated. Not wishing to appear as if she'd gone to any fuss, she was still wearing the sharp little suit of the afternoon meeting, though she had, of course, slipped it off and pressed it before indulging herself in a long and sensuous bath. And why not? If this was to be the battle of the Titans, she needed all the ammo she could muster.

Alvaro, the owner, came over and shook Julius's hand then slapped him on the shoulder, as if they were old pals, and chatted about obviously mutual friends.

'Are you going to be here for the millennium?' he asked. 'It promises to be something of a party.'

Julius, more human than Jinx had ever known him, laughed and said that was too far ahead for him to be sure.

'You know how it is with Pia,' he said, and Alvaro obviously did. 'Long-term plans have to be fitted around her schedule. Social commitments become very last minute.' Which was when she remembered the wife. Since she'd seen that photo in *Tatler* that time, she had known all her dreams were finally torpedoed. Not only had he abandoned her but he'd damn well gone and married a socialite Swede who was also a rising starlet, exactly what she'd expect of him from his track record. Suddenly she was scowling and both of the men picked it up. Alvaro shook hands with both of them this time and said he was needed in the kitchen.

'But do make a note about New Year's Eve,' he said. 'We are already taking bookings.'

So there they were facing each other, just the two of them again, and suddenly both were tongue-tied. What words do you use to a person you once loved but have not spoken to properly in twelve years? Just shouted at fiercely in a boardroom battle and then, much to your chagrin, flounced out. Julius asked what she'd like to drink and gave his order to the waiter. Then sat there looking uncomfortable for a moment or two, obviously searching for something anodyne to say that wouldn't risk setting her off again.

'You're looking well.'

'Why, thank you.'

He was looking pretty bloody good himself, though the face

was thinner, the cheekbones more pronounced; there was a touch of silver in his hair. And on his left hand, the one without the signet ring, a narrow gold band that made her wince. Leave her by all means, be untrue to his promise, but marrying another was going a bit far. Now she saw him again properly, without the business trappings, she knew all too painfully why her life was such a mess. Dear old Dottie had been right all along, and Jinx was a one-man girl. And now she was face to face with that man she knew that her case was quite hopeless. She could run and run and divert herself but her heart could never ever forget. It was more than a decade and look how both their lives had changed, but deep down, beneath the veneer of sophistication, she was still the same girl who had loved him. Damn you, Julius Weinberg, she thought, and gave the huge menu a savage scrutiny.

He was watching her intensely while she read, she could feel his eyes on her face. And when she glanced up he made no excuse, just continued to stare and admire.

'You were marvellous this afternoon,' he said. 'I longed to ravish you on the spot. You certainly got the financial guys twittering. They were every bit as impressed as I was.'

'Really?' She stared at him, startled.

'They like a fighter who can hold their corner. What you said made good sense, every word of it, and they saw you were not to be lightly dismissed.'

His dark, dark eyes were pulling her in, a smile played at the corners of his mouth. Jinx's heart was thumping, far faster than it should be, but she wasn't going to allow him to sweet talk her again.

'You've done so well since we were last in touch. I am proud of all your success.' She looked at him sharply but he seemed sincere, was giving her a look that was distinctly fond.

'But, then, you always did have the ability. I spotted it right back when I first came into the firm. That's the reason I promoted you so quickly, why I was sorry when you left.'

Jinx was speechless; she had thought it all down to Max. Though, of course, she only had Julius's word for it now. For all she could tell he might be lying. The food arrived and she busied herself with her pasta. Let him continue this tortuous dialogue. It was he who had manoeuvred it in the first place.

Julius ate placidly, with obvious enjoyment, and toasted Alvaro when he came back into the room.

'*Eccellente, signor!* The veal is out of this world as always. There's nothing in New York that quite equals this.'

Alvaro bowed then moved from table to table. Julius was obviously a known and favoured customer.

'I've a small *pied-à-terre* round the corner in Chelsea Harbour,' he explained. 'We got it a couple of years ago when Pia was doing *Hedda Gabler* at the National. All that travelling was too exhausting but then she got this three-movie deal and moved out to the Coast.'

So not just a starlet, her informant had been wrong, but a fully-fledged classical actress. Jinx silently gritted her teeth. It ought not to matter, not after all these years, but she found to her chagrin that it did.

'That must be nice,' she said politely, flashing him a smile that was only pasted on. But Julius brushed it aside. They were not here to tittle tattle about his private life, there were far more urgent things he needed to say.

'Tell me more about the design group,' he said. 'How did you luck into Damien Rudge?'

Jinx was surprised that he even remembered the name but, then, Julius had always been focused when it came to work. She reminded him that they'd all been together at Weinbergs, though skirted diplomatically around the walkout. Julius grinned.

'It's amazing how talent can sometimes be so latent. Though I'll bet you were the one responsible for bringing him along.' Which was true though she could hardly agree. 'I remember him as a rebel with a hefty chip on his shoulder. Perhaps that is what makes him so creative now. They say there's no such thing as a happy artist.'

So he did remember Damien; he had certainly acknowledged Ambrose. After so many years and his stratospheric career she was softened by the realisation that he hadn't entirely forgotten. And then she recalled his treachery and the smile disappeared from her face. Julius, watching her closely, grew attentive. Was she about to go for him again?

'I still can't believe you did it,' said Jinx, emboldened by the wine. 'Dropping us all in the shit like that. Breaking your uncle's heart.'

A slight frown clouded Julius's eyes. He looked down at the table for an uncomfortable minute then back at her candidly with full force.

'Max was always a dreamer,' he said. 'He needed to move with the times.'

'But what you did killed him,' said Jinx, getting upset. 'He trusted you and you let him down.'

'What killed Max was his dicky heart. Plus a lifetime of bad habits and overwork. Weinbergs wouldn't have lasted another six months. You have to believe me on that.'

They ate in silence, Jinx suppressing her rage, till Julius skilfully turned the subject and brought it safely back to a discussion of the design group. He asked intelligent questions with such courteous and informed interest that pretty soon she was sparkling again as she launched into the topic she most loved. She sketched for him the steps she had taken to set it all up in the first place and then her methods for bringing business in. Julius astounded her with his grasp of what she was doing. She had thought of him always as simply a money man, now she saw he was a lot more.

'I've watched your progress over the years. I admire what you have achieved.' And when she looked startled, as she immediately did, he laughed and explained where he stood. 'Why do you suppose the IEP finance was so readily forthcoming?

I wasn't quite in the saddle then but I did have the overall say.'

Jinx stared back at him, thunderstruck. What was this, blood money? But he seemed sincere. He ordered a second bottle of wine and launched himself into the evening's agenda which was business, as she might have guessed. He had come to London for a number of reasons but the Damien project was paramount. He had asked those crucial questions and she'd acquitted herself well. He hadn't meant to be harsh, he said, it was just his method of getting things done. He was more than satisfied with the progress they were making and admired the way she controlled her team.

'So you can move your deadline if it's really important. The decision's entirely yours,' he said.

'Just like that?'

He nodded. 'I would have told you sooner if you'd bothered to stick around. But that's never been your style, has it, Jinx?' He was hugely amused and she felt herself flushing then joined him in a hearty laugh at her own expense. When he let himself go, he was enormously attractive. She looked at the eyes, now alive with humour, and the finely curved mouth that she so much wanted to kiss. And he caught the look and held it for a second till a shudder ran through her and she felt quite weak. No, not that again, not after all these years. He was out of her reach and she knew that now. She was far too intelligent to risk getting hurt all over again.

'There's just one condition,' he said as he paid the bill. 'I'm leaving tomorrow but plan to be back quite soon. And I'd like to get together with you for another evening like this. Just for old times.'

She looked at him, frozen, and he saw her surprise.

'I want to get to know you better,' he said.

'But you're married.' The words were out before she could stop them. Foolish, bungling, how inappropriate, she thought. Don't let him see that you care, but it was too late.

'We'll talk about all that then,' he promised. 'Now let's go down to the King's Road and find you a taxi.'

30

Serafina heard it first, the low, understated throb of an expensive engine, and peered out of the office window in time
to see the Daimler drawn up outside. A tall, dark stranger was
standing at their door. Ambrose, right behind her, saw him too
and his heart went plummeting into his boots. Retribution upon
them already and it was still just a shade after nine.

'Who's that striking-looking man?' asked Serafina with immediate interest, craning to get a good look.

'You'll discover soon enough,' said Ambrose darkly as Dottie
rushed forward to let him in.

Julius, suave and immaculate as ever, appeared, all things
considered, to be in surprisingly good form. 'So this is where
you hide,' he said with interest. 'Is Jinx about?'

Dottie was appalled. Caught on the hop so early in the
morning and she still holding a carton of milk in her hand.
She fussed around him and offered him coffee but Julius waved
it impatiently aside. He was on his way to the airport and
hadn't a lot of time. He had hoped for a quick word before

he left. Ambrose and Dottie exchanged a doom-filled glance. Ominous.

'She'll be here any minute,' said Dottie optimistically, hoping sincerely that she was right. They couldn't have Jinx compounding yesterday's bad behaviour by keeping this notorious killer waiting longer than absolutely necessary.

Serafina preened and stepped forward to shake his hand, agitating her cloud of silky hair with a pert little toss of the head. 'I'm the team member you haven't yet met,' she said. 'Serafina Rossetti.' Wayne wasn't in yet and besides he hardly counted. Not to a bigshot like this.

Julius was even more impressive than she'd imagined, tall even for her and wearing an Italian suit. His tan was just right and his eyes like black coals. She could tell he appreciated her on this very first glance and a thrill of anticipation shot right through her.

'Take a seat in the conference-room and I'll happily show you whatever you want to see.' She was bang in her element, flirting with a stranger, though Julius appeared impervious and glanced instead at his watch. Right then, to everyone's vast relief, except perhaps Serafina's, the street door opened and in bounded Jinx, clutching an armful of yellow tulips.

'Hi!' she said sunnily at the sight of Julius. 'I see you've already met the team. Now come upstairs.' And led the way as though they were the best of friends, still clutching her flowers and chattering as she went.

'I hadn't realised you were dropping by. I thought you were catching a plane.'

'At one,' he said, 'so I need to be there by eleven. Just thought I'd look in and see where you work and get an impression of what goes on.'

'No problem,' said Jinx, leading him into the conference-room and firmly closing the door.

Ambrose and Dottie were speechless with amazement and Serafina disappointed at being deprived so soon of her prey.

He had definitely given her a lingering look, of that she had no doubt at all. It would feature in her dreams in the weeks to come and spiral off all sorts of craziness.

'Well,' said Ambrose. 'Pigs might fly.' He couldn't believe this sudden unexpected rapprochement. Something momentous must have happened since he'd last talked to Jinx. This was not the behaviour of a couple of sworn foes. But what on earth could it mean? One minute the pair of them were at each other's throats, the next as warm and comfortable as friends. Ambrose was uneasy unless he knew the full story and normally Jinx told him everything first. He was hurt.

'Has she said anything to you?' he asked suspiciously, but Dottie was as much in the dark as he was.

'She said she'd fix it,' was all she could come up with. And that was what Jinx invariably did.

Behind the closed door Jinx was a lot less welcoming. She had always mistrusted him and did so still. She stuck her mass of tulips into a wide, clear, waterless vase then turned to face him without the smile.

'I didn't realise you were planning to drop in. I thought we'd cleared up our misunderstanding.'

'So we have.' Julius remained benign as he strolled round the big spacious room, admiring its aspect. 'I just wanted to see your setup and meet your colleagues. I'm impressed by what you've achieved, I've already told you.' He appeared quite sincere so Jinx relaxed. She opened the door and called down to the others.

'Stick on the answering machine, then all bring your coffee up here. I'd like you to get to know our Führer better.'

So up they all trooped, bearing mugs of coffee, Dottie with a tray on which she'd set china cups for Julius and Jinx. Only the best when the money man was in. If she'd known in advance he was coming she would have bought biscuits too.

*   *   *

253

Julius today was as sleek and contained as a jungle cat, never so much as flexing his claws as they each did their bit like children invited to perform. Ambrose was amazed. Somehow, since yesterday, the man had been mysteriously de-fanged and that made him very uneasy though he wasn't sure why. Jinx appeared relaxed and calm, chic and slim in a lavender silk shirt and leather skirt. All signs of animosity between them had fled. She encouraged her team to display their skills and looked proud and happy as each of them did just that. But soon it was time for Julius to leave and he shook hands all round and pecked Jinx on the cheek.

'Keep up the good work,' he said as he climbed into the waiting car, 'and I'll hope to pay you a visit again next time I'm here. Don't forget your promise.'

'Well,' said Dottie with a great sigh of relief. 'All's well that ends well, I suppose. Or so it would appear.'

'What exactly is going on?' Ambrose asked Jinx suspiciously as she waved Julius off in the mews. 'What promise?'

She turned and smiled, her eyes dancing with light, and said that she thought she had fixed things for now. There wasn't time to go into details but it certainly seemed that she had Mr Weinberg tamed. If only for the moment while they wound up their project on time.

'Hm,' said Ambrose dubiously, returning to his gallery. He was by no means satisfied but would have to leave it at that. At least for now. The best thing was the deadline had not been mentioned, though that didn't mean they could now slack off. He still had a deep mistrust of Julius Weinberg, not the least because of the way he had looked at Jinx.

'He's gorgeous,' said Serafina with stars in her eyes. 'Why did no one ever tell me that before?' Her cheeks were glowing, her smile was radiant. She was as winsome and charming as a woodland nymph. Dottie regarded her balefully. Interesting what a bit of flattering male attention could do for a woman's looks.

'Handsome is as handsome does,' she said primly, echoing Sam's mother. 'You wouldn't have thought him quite so enticing if you'd been at Weinbergs twelve years ago.'

But Serafina's mind was on other things. This was the big boss, controller of all the power, and furthermore he had said he would soon be back.

'How old is he?' she asked casually as she started to open her mail.

'Old enough to be far beyond your reach,' said Dottie sternly.

'And married,' said Wayne who kept up with all the glamour mags. He had crept in late while the meeting was in full flow and managed to infiltrate without drawing Julius's fire. He too was impressed by the man's charismatic presence and the razor-sharp brain behind the unfathomable eyes. Julius Weinberg didn't miss a thing, even his own late entrance. Today he'd been passive, for some reason humouring them, but Wayne wouldn't like to be there when he lost his cool.

'He's married to a Swedish filmstar called Pia Lindström who's making a movie in Hollywood with Robert de Niro.'

'Why are all the best men always taken?' It was the cry of a whole generation of women, Serafina's curse.

'Because he's far too old for you and also out of your reach. Now please get on.' Jinx's patience was suddenly wearing thin. She was sick of Serafina and her endless bleating about men. More unsettled, too, by recent events than she cared to let show and Julius's unscheduled appearance had really thrown her off balance. It was almost as though he were stalking her, not the first time she'd privately thought it. He appeared to have an uncanny knowledge of what went on in her life, as well as an updated grasp of their current progress. Though what his motives could possibly be, she was quite at a loss to know. It couldn't be just Damien's Bright Idea, he was far too high in the hierarchy for that.

She longed to confide in Dottie but wasn't entirely sure she could trust her to be discreet. It was bound to get back to Sam as things always did. They were constantly on at her about her irregular lovelife. One whiff of this and Dottie would be on Cloud Nine. Only she wouldn't, of course, approve of his married status. Very moral was Dottie, part of her quaint old-fashioned charm.

'You should have seen her,' said Dottie with a chuckle. 'Salivating all over him as if he were Harrison Ford.' She'd been startled and scared at the unexpected reappearance of the Antichrist, Julius, then hugely amused by the effect he had had on Serafina. It did the girl no harm to lose her cool occasionally; normally she was so tightly controlled that she couldn't relax. But Julius Weinberg was nothing if not bad news. After all these years he was sleeker and cooler but that dangerous gleam was still in his eye. Even Dottie had picked up on that and she had scarcely known him in the old days other than by repute. She wondered if she ought to be cautioning Serafina, then decided it was safer to stay right out of it. Serafina was, after all, a fully grown woman. She must make her own mistakes and learn by them, provided she didn't get too badly burnt in the process.

Sam appeared only mildly interested as he pottered around in the kitchen, cleaning his brushes with turpentine, splashing paint all over the sink.

'Keep that filthy rag off my pastry counter,' warned Dottie. If she took her eye off him for half a second he was soon creating havoc. As bad as one of the kids, even messier. She fussed around him, screwing the tops back on his tubes, laying down newspaper to avoid any more damage.

'How did Ambrose react?' asked Sam. 'And Jinx?' He was pretty sure of his own behaviour, he'd have thumped the bastard and not before it was due. But Jinx had had several clashes with him over the years and he feared now for her safety. He would never mention it to Dottie, of course, but her welfare was ever on his mind. She should watch her back when dealing with a villain like Weinberg, who had amply demonstrated in the past exactly how ruthless he could be.

'Ambrose isn't happy at all,' said Dottie. 'But there's not a lot he can do about it. Weinberg has the right to walk in whenever he chooses. Until we're shot of the game he's our lord and master. It's up to Jinx to keep the pressure off us and hope that things go smoothly from now on. It certainly looked today as though they were hitting it off.'

But she'd glimpsed the strain in Jinx's eyes and guessed at her inner turmoil. After all this man had put them through, it must be hard for her to keep her temper in check. He might be a reformed character now he was older and settled, but Dottie still wouldn't trust him as much as an inch. Always fretting, that was Dottie. Sam said it was bad for her blood pressure but somebody had to do it, it went with the job.

Serafina was in a lather of excitement as she scrabbled feverishly through her crowded closet and flung all her clothes on the bed. One look at Julius Weinberg and she was lost. Here, right in front of her, was the embodiment of all her desires done up in such a breathtaking package she had practically swooned at his feet. All these years she'd been slicing her way through men it seemed in readiness for perfection such as this. He was tall, he was gorgeous, he was well-attired and she loved the stern imperialism in his eyes. 'Take me,' she'd felt like crying, but then Jinx had come in and spoiled it. She knew she could have scored with him if it weren't for that jealous bitch.

All, however, was not yet lost. He had said quite clearly that he'd soon be back and when he did she would be waiting. But first she needed to perfect her image to ensure he didn't slip through her fingers a second time. And, as usual, she seemed to have nothing appropriate to wear. A man of his calibre would have an eye for cut and style so she needed a new designer wardrobe no matter what the cost. Luckily she had loads of plastic and could put it all down to investment. He might live abroad but he travelled a lot and, if she played her cards right, she'd soon be travelling with him. The fact that he was married concerned her not at all. A wife away in Hollywood was not the same as one constantly there with her eye on him. And Serafina would back her own sultry allure any time against the milk-white insipidity of the legendary Swede. It was the sort of challenge she took up with relish. Despite the nagging insecurities of her childhood, in the beauty stakes she knew she could hold her own. This was the man she'd been searching for all her life. When it came to the chase she could be relentless. And almost always got her man.

So she needed to start preparing and that meant a lot of work. The main part of being a flawless beauty was maintenance so the sooner she got started, the better. Who could tell when he might be back? She also needed to do some basic research to find out first-hand what exactly she was taking on. The more you knew, the better prepared you were and Serafina, a practised street fighter, was accustomed to getting her own way. Nothing and nobody was going to stop her now. She would even kill for him if that's what it took.

31

Out of the blue Dottie received a postcard from Janey Rudge. Explaining that she was planning to be in town and wondering if they could meet up for lunch. Easter was almost upon them, there was urgent shopping she needed to do. They usually took a spring vacation somewhere exotic in the sun though it grew increasingly harder these days to prise Damien away from his work.

'Rather you than me,' chuckled Jinx, generously allowing Dottie the whole afternoon off. They were working flat out but these things had to be done. And keeping the clients sweet was a large part of the job. Which included humouring the wives.

They met at Harvey Nichols the following Thursday. Janey was wearing a brand new mink, too warm for the time of year. She was certainly bolder than Dottie would have dared be, with fur being such a political issue, but maybe she simply didn't know. She was already firmly settled in the Fifth Floor restaurant, surrounded by classy shopping bags and drinking a gin and tonic, when Dottie flustered in a little late. Janey had had her hair done in a hard, unbecoming bouffant that sat uneasily above her pinched uncertain face. But then she had never been much of a looker, she was lucky to have caught herself a husband when she did. For just a passing moment, Dottie almost felt sorry for her. Marriage to Damien couldn't be a barrel of laughs, even with the cushion of all that money. But then she took in the Cartier jewellery and understated Hermès bag and succeeded in hardening her heart.

Both ordered salad and then cod with puy lentils, with a smear of some sort of saffron-based sauce artistically daubed across the plate. Too good to consume, said Dottie as a joke. It should by rights be hanging on the wall.

'Maybe Damien should try his hand at something like this,' she said. Janey merely grunted. There had been a time in the early days of the marriage when her husband had done most of the cooking, enjoyed it too. Then she had been the main breadwinner, teaching a bunch of malevolent kids in South London, while he worked contentedly at home and shared all the chores like a true New Age man. No more.

'He only goes into the kitchen these days to get ice for his whisky,' she complained. 'Too much the bigshot artist to do anything so ordinary as cook. Or even stack the dishwasher, come to that.' Which set them off giggling and discussing their tiresome husbands, and Dottie confided about the mess Sam made, turning her dining-room into his workspace. If he'd only learn to clear up before she got home. Janey was luckier, they had so many rooms. Her chief complaint was exclusion.

'There was a time,' she sighed, 'when he told me everything. But these days he shuts me out. Treats me no better than a housekeeper, in fact, except that I don't get paid.' Dottie glanced at the jewellery again but didn't dare say a word. Janie ordered herself another gin while Dottie stuck prudently to water. The Rudges had never succeeded in having kids. Perhaps it was just as well.

* * *

'Tell me,' said Serafina confidentially. 'How do you find addresses and things on the internet?'

'Why?' asked Ambrose, instantly suspicious. She was always interrupting him when he was trying to do his work.

'Just thought I'd like to know,' she said brightly, beaming him one of her melting smiles. When Serafina was on a high, she could be very appealing. If only those dreadful moods didn't intervene. 'One is always reading about it these days in the papers. It seems you can find out anything if you try.'

'But why should you want to?' He refused to be led. She shrugged.

'Just thought it might be useful some time,' she said.

She had combed the phone book but the number was unlisted and had even tried hanging around in St Martin's Lane. If she could only trust Ambrose it would make things a lot easier, but she suspected that his loyalties still lay firmly with Jinx. Not that it was any of her concern either. What Serafina did in her spare time was nobody's business but her own.

She was going to the health club on a regular basis now, avoiding the pool where she usually languished and working instead on toning herself up. She pumped her muscles till they screamed with pain and worked on her abs till she could scarcely sit up. Too much exercise, Dottie was always cautioning her, had as detrimental an effect as none at all. But Serafina, as usual, refused to listen. She had bought a floating grey Ghost dress that she was aching to be able to show off but wasn't intending to unveil it except for one very special man. If only she could manage to locate him.

She had tried phoning his office, pretending to be somebody's secretary, but all she ever came up against was a stone-walling flat-voiced PA. Mr Weinberg was currently out of town. She could leave her number if it was really important and maybe they would get back to her. Provided she also left her name.

'Try the websites,' said Ambrose wearily, anxious only to fob her off. If she was after a popstar, though surely she was too old, it shouldn't be too difficult if she had the patience to track him down. 'Otherwise you may be able to check him out via his credit rating. Strictly illegal but what the hell. Everyone's at it these days.' You could work miracles with a computer if only you had the knowhow and the time. He wondered what the minx was up to now but was far too over-burdened really to care.

Damien wasn't there to meet her when Janey got off the plane so she had to get home in one of the island's clapped-out taxis. Disgruntled and irritated that he valued her so little, she stuffed her many carrier bags on to the back seat then gave the Portuguese driver her address. She was in no mood for idle conversation though the day out with Dottie had been fun. What Janey lacked more than anything else these days was regular female company. Once Damien had been her best pal and she hadn't felt the need of anyone else in the early years of their marriage. She'd been the principal earner, he the delicate talent, and she'd got quite a buzz out of taking the lead and making it possible for him to concentrate on his art. But things had changed radically since those carefree days and he'd dragged her into isolation here the moment his accountant told him he should leave. For years they had barely maintained a subsistence level, then Jinx had negotiated that mammoth deal and here they were.

The islanders were friendly enough but not really Janey's type. Affluent women of a certain age who liked having lunch and dressing up. They had been to a couple of dinner parties, then Damien had rebelled against what he considered their mindless chatter and from then on had insisted that they turn all invitations down. With the result that Janey had no friends, not a single kindred spirit to lighten her days. She read a lot and gardened but pined for the bustle of London. And got away just as often as she could for a bit of recharging of her batteries. Dottie Sullivan was a real tonic though she envied her her job and fulfilled life.

Those children had turned out a credit to the pair of them and now Sam's new book career looked to be burgeoning too. Depression descended on Janey again. She still had the supper to cook.

They reached the beginning of the mile-long drive that led to their house on the cliffs. Damien had bought the property without even consulting her, and it was far too big for just the two of them. The taxi bumped along the potholed cart-track and their pantiled roof came into sight and beyond it the marvellous view. It was after six and she was dying for another drink. She was not by any means a habitual boozer but occasionally went off the rails. Living with Damien was harrowing enough. At times she felt driven to it, at least that was her excuse.

There was no sign of Damien as she lugged her bags inside and she called to him through the unlit downstairs rooms. He was probably shut in his work-room upstairs, listening to modern jazz. How he could work amidst all that racket was something she'd never understood. Creativity, in Janey's mind, demanded absolute stillness. But then she was a writer manqué and he just a jobbing artist. Even if his latest success had brought all this. Once she'd poured herself a gin and taken out a casserole to defrost, Janey carried her shopping upstairs and hung the mink carefully away. She knew it was over the top but didn't care. Material things had lately become important to her, in place of the babies she had always longed for, which seemed to have passed her by. She was too old now to be likely to conceive; besides they rarely did it any more.

There wasn't a sound from Damien's studio, and when she tested the handle, it was locked. Oh nice. Not only had he not bothered to meet her but he wasn't even here to welcome her home. Before she started cooking, she had better find out where he was. She was damned if she'd go to all that trouble if he'd absent-mindedly left the island, which he occasionally did without telling her. Off to the city and his beloved Jinx without a passing thought for his wife. She hadn't been joking when she'd complained to Dottie that she was nothing more than an unpaid housekeeper. She often thought that he'd hardly notice if she vanished from his life altogether.

Serafina had had no success at all with the internet. She had tried every possible website she could think of yet still could find nothing that led to Julius. Maybe because he lived abroad she had consistently drawn a blank. She had even tried tracking the famous wife but all she'd come up with was a list of her movies and occasional stage successes. No personal details at all, not even an address. It was all becoming a bit of an obsession, she couldn't think rationally at all. She had started plaguing Ambrose about the past but he'd swatted her off like a fly. He hated Weinberg and didn't want reminding. They were under enough of a threat again as it was.

Dottie was kinder but it was mainly second-hand. She really only knew him through Sam and he had stayed out of his way. Not a nice man was her overall impression and certainly not one to be trusted. She ran through with Serafina the details of his treachery, how he'd sold them down the river without warning. No wonder he and Jinx had always been at daggers drawn. She, more than any of them, had excellent reason to hate his guts.

'Yet they seemed so cosy the other day.' Serafina was fishing. Dottie didn't notice.

'Don't believe it. Leopards don't change their spots. Jinx was simply buttering him up because of his financial involvement.' A consummate businesswoman, she always did the right thing. Though it must have really stuck in her craw to have to be quite so nice. Still, the immediate danger appeared to be past and with luck they'd be shot of him soon. Then they'd be able to breathe again and find other backing for the future.

Being warned off Julius had quite the opposite effect. Serafina tingled at the thought of all that ruthlessness and just couldn't wait for an opportunity to test her own charms on the brute. She had changed her hairstyle in a subtle way and Dottie suspected she was also losing weight. And the clothes she started wearing to the office were quite amazing, a new expensive outfit every day. How she could afford it Dottie couldn't guess and actually didn't really want to know. She despaired of Serafina and felt she would come to no good. She should take a leaf out of Jinx's book and learn to pay her own way.

His car was still there so he'd obviously gone for a walk. Janey got out her own little run-about and headed towards the cliffs. Normally she would have walked herself but time was growing short. And if she found him, she could drive him back before the casserole burnt. Bloody men, they were scarcely worth the bother. She wanted to be relaxing with a drink and *Coronation Street* instead of running after her husband like a mother.

The sky was on the brink of an incredible sunset when Janey spotted Damien on the headland. One of the pluses of living here in Jersey was its glorious natural effects. Damien loved all this rugged scenery and the quite unequalled light. He had built his studio with that in mind and could spend whole days up there, locked away, without once coming down for a break. Now she could see him outlined against the sky, hands sunk into his pockets, gazing out to sea. She got out of the car and waved frantically to him but he didn't once turn his head.

Janey set off to walk the two hundred yards towards him, curbing her sense of injustice as the beauty all around her calmed her soul. If she'd been able to write poetry, this place would have sparked it off, though Janey was sadly aware she lacked the talent.

'What?' he said, startled from his rapt concentration, obvious annoyance crossing his face when he saw her. 'Oh, it's you. Now what do you want?'

Not a word about how her day had been or if she was feeling worn out. Not a smile or inquiry about all she had achieved, not even a peck on the cheek.

'Supper's almost ready,' she said and started to walk back to the car. If only he'd carry a mobile like nearly everyone did these days, she'd not have to waste all this energy. She expected Damien to follow her but he didn't even move.

'What?' she asked, stopping and repeating his question. It couldn't be the sunset, it was already past its best.

Damien stood with shoulders slouched, a scowl of discontentment on his face. When he looked at her, his eyes were flickering; rampant paranoia at its worst.

'Have you been into the studio?' he asked. Janey simply shook her head.

'How could I? The door is locked,' she pointed out. These days he even hid the key. *And why should I want to?* she silently added. She was sick and tired of all the endless secrecy.

'Someone's been looking at my work,' he said accusingly. 'And the obvious person is you.' Rightly so. He had sacked the daily at an early stage and even the window cleaner. Janey had to do it all herself with no help, and the house was almost too big for her to cope with. But there was no point even discussing it now; Damien's mind was perpetually closed.

'Come home and eat,' she said, attempting to take his arm, but he backed off irritably and shook her away.

'You can't trust anyone these days,' he said, genuine hostility blazing in his eyes. 'The world is full of spies trying to rip off my ideas.'

Janey sighed. She had heard it all before so many times, and lately his ranting had grown much worse. She had even tried suggesting that he went to talk to a doctor, but the eruption that had caused had been frightening in the extreme. Sometimes she felt that the callow youth she had married had disappeared altogether, leaving this loon. If this was the price of his huge fame and fortune, then deep in her heart she knew it wasn't worth it.

'Come home,' she begged again, starting to walk away, but Damien hadn't finished with his grouch.

'Those bastards in New York,' he said, 'have started sending over spies. They are cloning my ideas and selling them cheap. I blame it all on the Chinese,' he added irrelevantly, though why he didn't bother to explain. The light was fading and they were stuck up on this headland. Janey didn't want to have to negotiate that steep winding path in the dark. Again she reached out to tug at his arm but this time he practically leapt on her.

'Traitor!' he screamed, grabbing her round the throat. 'You are just as bad as the rest of them. Selling my ideas to Sega.' His eyes were wildly rolling now, he looked like a creature deranged. She had seen him crazy in spasms before but never as frantic as this.

'Calm down,' she tried to say as she pried away his fingers. 'Come home with me and have some supper. You'll feel a lot better then.'

'You and Weinberg both,' he continued to shout. 'You're all of you in it together. Jinx too.'

They were rather too close to the edge, she thought, to risk getting into a fight. She wished now she'd worn her proper hiking-boots, these shoes had slippery leather soles.

'Damien,' she said as calmly as she could manage. 'Come home and we'll talk about it there. It's getting dark and we don't want to be stuck up here.'

'Get off!' he yelled hysterically, giving her a sudden violent shove, and Janey, in total disbelief, felt herself slipping backwards towards the drop. Now it was her turn to scream with panic as she battled with her balance on the slippery sandy grass.

'Damien!' she cried wildly as she slithered and tried to hang on. 'Help me . . .'

And then she was gone.

32

*L*ately *she's been behaving in a positively skittish way, which I put down to her over-active hormones. They are delicate creatures, these women, all of them cyclically unbalanced, and it looks as though she's being affected by the spring. She is positively radiant and even more gorgeous than ever and I'm hoping I may still be in there with a chance. Provided I play my cards right.*

I shall tread very carefully, learning from past mistakes, and hope to worm still further into her favour.

I know she likes me, there's no doubting that, so I'll build on what we already have and see if I can finally win her. It's time for her to settle, she's been flighty for far too long, and I will really take care of her forever if she'll let me.

My love has never diminished, not over all these years. She remains my soulmate, my goddess, my muse.

My nemesis and my destiny.

33

The call came far sooner than Jinx had expected, well before she was properly prepared. He was still in New York but aiming to fly over at the weekend. Any chance, he asked, of dinner on Friday night? Jinx was confused, uncertain of how to react. It had only been a matter of weeks and her emotions were still pretty much in turmoil. He'd been absent from her life all these years yet suddenly seemed to be battering down her door. She didn't know what to think or how she felt. She said she would see if she could clear him a window and left it vaguely at that. There was, after all, still the question of the wife.

She was actually supposed to be seeing Norman. He had tickets for a fund-raiser and wanted her there as his date. But given a choice between Norman and Julius there really was no contest at all. Making a snap and possibly rash decision, she dropped a line to Norman to say she'd been called away. Her affair with him had long ago lost its lustre. She'd been close to letting him go for quite a while.

Dating a married man was not something Jinx really approved

of. Less for moral reasons than because it was such a mug's game. After her heart had been brutalised all those years ago, she had gone through a brief phase of sleeping with anything with a pulse but that behaviour had rapidly palled and she'd soon cleaned up her act. She had known since early youth that she could pull any man she wanted, so where was the point in continuously proving herself? Married men might have their virtues – more considerate, more attentive, inclined to be more grateful. But you couldn't rely on one to keep his word, to be readily available or turn up punctually. And the worst part came when it was time for him to leave and you waved him off in your bathrobe, feeling used and essentially tacky.

None of that was behaviour she cared to continue now. Norman had somehow infiltrated her life and she'd kept him around out of lethargy. It was nice to have someone occasionally to doll up for and Jinx had a healthy sexual appetite. She wasn't exactly proud of the Norman episode but at least his feelings were unlikely to be dented. It was time to move on, not only because of Julius. She needed the breathing space to sort herself out and try to decide what it was she really wanted. Workwise as well as romantically.

Just the thought of Julius still made her uneasy though there was absolutely nothing she could do about that. She called herself a fool, knew what a chance she was taking. Remembered the last time she had hit the deck and the scars that had taken so many years to heal. But she couldn't always be in control of her feelings or running away from commitment. This man was beckoning and she badly wanted to follow. Despite the danger; despite the wife. She shut her mind to the consequences.

'Have you heard from Julius recently?' asked Serafina surprisingly, almost as though she were psychic. Now why would she come up with a question like that just now? Had Jinx given anything away? She started to answer then instead just shook her head.

'With a bit of luck he will leave us alone.' But that was hardly the answer Serafina wanted.

While Jinx was being cautious and indecisive, Serafina was so frenzied with desire she thought she might be going out of her mind. Julius Weinberg was all she'd ever dreamed of. Rich, successful, handsome, impeccably dressed. Tall, too, to match her willowy five foot ten. What a couple they'd make as they swanned around the hot spots; the fact he was married didn't bother her one bit. She thought about him incessantly and at night he embroidered her dreams. For starters he'd offer her a plum job in New York with a Park Avenue condo thrown in. After that, the sky would be the limit. He would dump the wife and devote himself to her, adoring her madly and indulging her slightest whim. She liked the image, it made her preen. She could hardly wait to see him again so that she could embark on her campaign.

She was pretty certain she'd have no competition from Jinx. Ambrose had told them all often enough how the two of them clashed at every meeting. Besides which, Jinx was far too old for him now. At forty, she was pretty much over the hill. Serafina pestered Ambrose for as much information as she could get, while he grew surly and snappish with her, bored and irritated by her perpetual girlish questioning.

'Forget him,' he said in exasperation, 'the man is a louse and a pain.'

'Serafina getting on your wick?' asked Jinx later, having caught only the tail end of the exchange.

'I wish she'd go and find herself a proper boyfriend,' sighed Ambrose. 'And give me a little peace just once in a while.'

Jinx gave him a slant-eyed look but made no comment. She'd decided to keep the news of Julius's imminent arrival secret from the rest of them for the time being. She couldn't risk Ambrose getting all het up again, not with the disc in its final stages.

She planned not to tell them anything, in fact, until there was something worth telling. And that included Serafina who was behaving in a very flighty fashion and walking around with a foolish grin instead of her customary tight-lipped scowl.

By the time he rang again she was feverish with excitement, nervous only that he might have changed his plans. She just couldn't help it, it was way out of her control. She found it hard to concentrate on anything she was so keyed up with nervous anticipation. He called from the airport, which showed a measure of keenness, having come in early on an overnight flight.

'All set for tonight?' he asked breezily, and she found herself meekly complying. 'Why not come to Chelsea Harbour around eight,' he said, 'and we'll have a natter and a couple of drinks first.' He gave her his address then rang off abruptly leaving Jinx all washed up and wondering how she was going to get through the rest of the day. She hadn't felt this skittish since she was a silly teenager, angling for the attention of one of the sixth-form boys. Her limbs felt shaky and her bladder unreliable. She needed to get her act together and prove to herself she didn't care.

She managed not to mention him in the office though that wasn't easy to do. She longed to scream it from the rooftops that Julius was back in town, that she'd be seeing him in less than ten hours' time. Dottie asked if she was free for lunch but Jinx felt she didn't dare risk it. She explained there was something she needed to do at home and fled there at one to rake through her clothes and decide once again what to wear. And all this for a man she knew she couldn't trust, who had proved himself a bastard time and again. Pathetic really, she told herself fiercely. Get a grip on yourself, girl, or you'll only end up hurt.

The phone was ringing as she let herself into the house but when she rushed to answer it nobody spoke. For a second she thought it might be just a fax machine but she definitely heard human breathing then the receiver being replaced. She shrugged and put it out of her mind as she raced up the stairs to her room. Perhaps she ought to rinse out a silk shirt or would something more formal be better? She checked to see that she'd got fresh tights. The phone started ringing again.

'Dammit!' she said crossly, picking up in the bedroom, but again there was nobody there. Someone playing silly buggers or maybe a foreigner with an insufficient grasp of the language. Though usually they at least said hello or gabbled away in gobbledygook. She refused to be rattled, there were better things on her mind and tonight – tonight – she would see him. She left the phone ringing as she scooted back into the street and hurried back to the office and her work. If some deranged pervert had nothing better to do than plague a total stranger, then she pitied them. She thought about having her number changed but decided it really wasn't worth it. Obscene calls were one thing and could be upsetting but a poor pathetic breather didn't bother her.

She knew she'd made a mistake when she rang his bell and he ushered her into the vast open space that was his penthouse overlooking the river. All shades of pale in wood and chrome with filmy curtains pulled wide to display the spectacular view. She walked to the window, searching for something to say, and he came and stood beside her, almost touching.

'What can I get you?' he asked her after a while and she turned and saw the Krug already on ice.

'That would be nice,' she said as he twisted off the top. Let them start as they intended to go on. There was caviar, too, in a delicate silver dish, and slivers of smoked salmon on triangles of thin brown bread. For one heart-stopping moment she suspected his wife might be here. Such dainty hostessy offerings were hardly the handiwork of a man. But when he took her on a rapid tour of the place it was clear he was its sole occupant. Pristine bedrooms, entirely untouched, with just

273

his one bag in the master one. Impressive, maybe, and spacious, but lonely too.

When she finally took a seat he came to sit beside her, clinking glasses in a toast before savouring the crisp champagne.

'Your health,' he said solemnly, gazing into her eyes, and she knew in that single second she was doomed.

They set off for Chutney Mary, within easy walking distance, and by then Jinx had begun to relax her guard and enjoy him all over again. He had aged quite a bit, was leaner and more lined, and the thick black hair was thinning a little on top. But that only added to his air of authority, his imposing bearing as he strolled along at her side. Away from his desk he was affable and witty, obviously keen to put her at her ease. She found herself laughing at one of his marvellous anecdotes, and when he drew her arm within his, she didn't mind.

'I must say, you're looking particularly fetching tonight.' She had on a mint green suede jacket and skirt that fitted her neat figure impeccably. She'd hardly aged in twelve years. She saw his admiration and was pleased.

The airy, glassed-in restaurant was very nearly full but they welcomed Julius with the utmost deference and showed him to one of the best tables.

'It's clear you're not a stranger here,' said Jinx.

'It's my local,' he replied. 'On those rare occasions I make it over to London.'

Once they were settled face to face, with the wine poured and the food in front of them, she knew they were going to have to talk seriously at last. There were things between them that could no longer be pushed aside, not if they were to remain courteous, if this rapprochement were to develop. But since she felt the wrong was all on his side, she sipped her wine silently and left it for him to start. At the very least, he owed her an apology for breaking his promise and, incidentally, her heart. He couldn't just act as if none of that had happened. She studied his hands, with the thin gold band, and steeled herself to resist him.

'Well,' he said intimately, 'so here we are again. Back to where we were, I hope, with a great deal still to discuss.'

Jinx stared at him, faintly alarmed. He was suddenly moving far too fast for her liking. Much had happened since that night in New York to alter the way she felt. And she wanted him to back off a bit. They needed the time to get to know each other again, to rekindle the feelings they'd once had.

'If only you hadn't been so silly about the job,' he remarked, crumbling his chapati in his fingers. 'You're a right little firecracker when you get your temper up. As my IEP colleagues can endorse.' He chuckled admiringly but his dark eyes mocked her. There wasn't a hint of remorse in his cocky demeanour.

Hang on a second, this wasn't the right scenario. He was expected to grovel and acknowledge his terrible sins. The way he'd so ruthlessly shafted them all and driven his uncle to his death. The way he'd pursued her and declared his hollow love before vanishing completely and marrying another. Not that she'd ever refer to that now, she had far too much pride. But here was this man, smiling and relaxed, getting on with his meal with obvious enjoyment as if there were nothing on his conscience at all. He asked how she liked the food and she told him fine, though it was clear to see she was barely touching it. Her throat was constricted and she felt her temper rising. How *dare* he make light of her boardroom outburst when he'd already admitted she'd been totally in the right.

'What's up? You're hardly eating?'

'You know what's up. You're doing it again. Treating me like some featherbrained halfwit. Some bimbo you can dispose of once you're through.' Now she was almost choking with emotion and wanted to slap his face. Julius laughed out loud and reached for her hand, but Jinx snatched it back in irritation. She would not be treated like this by this arrogant man. He had lied and been devious, all for his own selfish ends. The fact that Weinbergs had ceased to exist appeared not to bother him at all. He'd flushed his uncle's legacy down the plumbing as lightly as he'd tossed aside her love. She suddenly wanted to be out of there, and fast, but dignity glued her to her seat.

'Seriously,' he said in a gentler tone, 'you were most impressive at that meeting. You certainly succeeded in putting me in my place.' He laughed at the recollection.

'So you've already told me several times.' If she went to the ladies', would he think he'd upset her? It would certainly give her a chance to recover her cool. And him, maybe, to see the error of his ways, though by now she knew that was unlikely.

'Excuse me, please.' She left the table and almost ran to the loo, wishing she had the courage to leave altogether. This wasn't going to work, she'd been crazy to think it could. People of his age didn't change and neither apparently did Julius. He'd always been arrogant, self-assured and fairly smug but this new benevolence was more than she could take. Angry tears came into her eyes and she scrubbed at her mascara to ensure it didn't run. That would be the ultimate shame, letting him know he could still get to her.

By the time she got back to the table she was once more composed, radiantly smiling, cool and fresh as a flower. He half rose to his feet and solemnly kissed her hand. She'd had him worried if she did but know it, but Julius was as practised a dissembler as she was. She took her seat gracefully and accepted more wine. And nodded to the waiter when he went to clear her plate.

'You've eaten nothing.'

'I don't have much of an appetite.' Her initial nervousness was still cramping her digestion, not helped by the indignation coursing through her. Which at least was healthier than the love she'd felt before. If she got out of here without blowing her top she wouldn't care if they never met again.

'Jinx,' he said in a more subdued tone. 'I can't tell you how good it feels to be back here with you. In all the years that we've been apart, I never ever forgot you.'

She found the intensity of his eyes upsetting. 'Mind if I smoke?' she said.

He slickly flipped open a solid gold case and offered her one of his own. Watch yourself, Jinx was telling herself sternly. The man's not trustworthy, you'll only get hurt.

'You remember that night in New York?' he now asked her.

'I wasn't sure that *you* did,' she shot back through a wreath of smoke.

So that was what all this was about, it appeared she must be still smarting. Julius was secretly thunderstruck; he had always imagined that to worldly Jinx it had all been something of a lark. She was always so soignée, so cool and level-headed with men hanging round her in hordes. He recalled that time at the book fair long ago when he'd first begun to realise how he felt. He had never been able to relax with her in those days, had felt he was too stuffy and uptight. Jinx made everything seem such fun, she could teach him a lot about relaxing. He remembered how he'd felt as he watched her dance that night. He'd been unable to shake off the memory ever since.

'It was fun,' he said. 'Or maybe you don't think so.'

'If fun is the word,' she said stiffly.

He had lost her again, her eyes had gone hard and she stubbed out her cigarette half-smoked.

'I told you I loved you,' he said softly. 'Which was true.'

'Then went behind our backs and sold the firm.' All of a sudden she wanted badly to cry, but her emotion just poured out as brittle laughter. Right at that moment she loved him more than ever before but hated him as well for what he had done. He could see that she was itching for a fight and mentally squared up.

'The two things were unconnected,' he said carefully. 'I had hoped you might have realised that by now.'

277

'I never heard from you again. What was I supposed to think?'

'I did try calling but you wouldn't pick up.'

'Can you blame me?'

'If you hadn't behaved like a hysterical schoolgirl . . .'

'God, that's enough!'

All of a sudden she was up and out of her chair, shaking with fury as she reached around for her bag. The man was insufferable, there was no point continuing this fiasco. The sooner she was out of here, the better.

'Thanks for the meal,' she said through tightly clenched teeth, then turned abruptly and stalked out of the restaurant. Leaving him devastated and feeling an utter fool.

34

Wayne's bishop was so strong he knew that if he could force Ambrose to move a rook or his queen to the back row, he might be able to force checkmate. He sat in the cramped corner of his Hackney rented room and chewed his lower lip reflectively. Normally he moved like lightning but this was a crucial move. The more time he took, the more Ambrose might be lulled into complacency. Ambrose may have been playing the game all his life but Wayne was learning largely by studying his opponent's tactics. As well as his thought processes, which was highly instructive.

'I'll call you back,' he said into the phone.

Ambrose was startled, this wasn't at all like Wayne. He knew he'd got him pretty well cornered, just couldn't quite see how. Not right now. So the brief remission was actually a lucky letout. If Wayne had to call back then he couldn't be as confident as he sounded.

'Take your time. Meanwhile I'll fetch myself another beer.' Ambrose shambled across to his fridge. Playing from the kitchen table was fine because the light was so bright but the hard chair took its toll of his back after several hours' solid concentration. He was no longer as young as he liked to believe. He grabbed another can of Fosters and jerked off the metal tab. Then stood by the window with his back to the board and stared out into the darkness while he thought. He had no need to study the position of the pieces, knew Wayne's every move off by heart. He glanced at the clock; getting late. He was dying to eat but refused to admit defeat. Once this game was finally over, he would call a temporary truce and pop out to the chippie for some sustenance.

It was Sunday night and they'd been at it all weekend. Wayne's remarkable aptitude for chess was starting to edge on the phenomenal. Ambrose had never seen anything like it and was uncomfortably aware he was beginning to lag behind. He had always seen that the lad was bright as well as a super fast learner, but this revealed more than just a retentive memory. At times he seemed almost psychic with his flashes of pure intuition. And he was growing almost as fanatical about the game as Ambrose was himself. Their battles to the death, for that was what they had become, were no longer confined to the pub or slack moments at work but were beginning to encroach on all their available time. Witness this game. They had taken to doing it over the telephone which Dottie and Jinx thought was creepy. What was the point of a game at all if you couldn't even see your opponent? Games playing had surely something to do with team spirit.

Damien had long been Ambrose's preferred sparring partner but Wayne was slicker and more inventive, with a far faster brain and defter approach. Besides, while Damien was growing slack, Wayne was keen as mustard and always available. He represented an intellectual challenge that was all too beguiling. Ambrose was hooked. They both played avidly against the computer, which was like hitting tennis balls against a wall. But a human assailant was that much more inspiring. It was fun to witness your opponent squirm.

The phone rang. Wayne on the offensive.

'Queen to G5.' Thus taking the pawn. Then move the bishop and then the rook with a straight run through to the king. *Damn.* But at least he could finally eat. Ambrose grinned and reluctantly called it a day. Work tomorrow so he needed to get some sleep, though he felt invigorated by all this mental exercise.

Wayne lived in Hackney and Ambrose in Battersea, which was inconvenient, to say the least. The fervour of their enthusiasm grew such that Jinx suggested they move in together and save all that wasted commuting time. Not to mention the gigantic phone-bills. She recalled the pocket set she'd been given as a child. At fifteen, fleetingly, she'd been similarly hooked, playing endless games on the bus and in the library and on long winter evenings in an alcove under the stairs. The craze, like jacks, had lasted a couple of terms but then she'd matured and moved on to other things. Like boys and dating and experimenting with makeup as well as working hard on her GCEs. Chess, along with netball, was relegated to childhood. Real life was so much more challenging as it was. Yet she couldn't help pausing when she came upon them playing, to admire their dedication and the interminable battle of wits.

The trouble with the pub was all the noise and the smoke. Ambrose was so pernickety he found he couldn't concentrate, not when amassing his forces against an antagonist as tricky and unpredictable as Wayne.

'Why not just join a chess club?' suggested Jinx, but that smacked too strongly of pensioners and retirement. They were content to pit their skills against just each other. Provided they could find the right place. Wayne's cramped digs were sordid and unsuitable. And he wasn't yet ready to share Melody with the rest of them. But Ambrose was still a footloose bachelor with a pad of his own in Battersea. With only a little persuasion he was convinced that they should start meeting there. Wayne said he didn't mind the travelling and at least it should save them both a crick in the neck. Not to mention all that solitary drinking which couldn't be good for their souls.

'There's no need to cook me Sunday lunch,' he said cheerfully. 'Just a few beers and some pub nosh will do.'

Ambrose smiled. He rarely ever ate at home, except for the odd can of beans, and liked the idea of companionship on a Sunday. Normally he just stayed put and watched old movies unless, of course, he was seeing Jinx. Those weekends were the magic ones. All too few as far as Ambrose was concerned. They agreed to meet at eleven o'clock and fit in a game before eating. Or at least get one started. The way things were going since they'd really got to grips with each other's play, games were running into hours, even days.

'I can't see the point of it myself,' said Dottie. It almost gave her a headache just to think of it.

'Boys will be boys,' said Jinx significantly but Serafina merely sniffed. There seemed to be something on her mind just lately. She had suddenly turned into a scatterbrain.

It was too far for Wayne to get there on his skates so he took the train to Clapham Junction and walked, and was on Ambrose's doorstep at the appointed time. He climbed the five flights of steep, narrow stairs and was fairly puffed out when he reached the top.

'How do you manage this every day?' he asked but Ambrose merely grinned. These youngsters didn't necessarily know it all. Walking and climbing the stairs had kept him fit. He was still as wiry as he had been in his youth whereas Wayne, half his age, was already showing signs of decline. Decadent living was what did it; drugs and beer and not enough exercise though the skating should keep him in trim.

Ambrose popped open two cans of beer in the kitchen and handed one to Wayne. 'Sit down and get your breath,' he said, 'before we go into attack.'

He enjoyed Wayne a lot, found his quirky intelligence refreshing, and welcomed these interludes of playing and private chats.

Wayne was obsessed by computer games too and was always au fait with what was currently hot. He spent endless hours surfing the internet which was one of his uses to the team. It was amazing he got any work done. Wayne's Saturday night had been steamy in the extreme. He had, he confessed, only a vague recall of it at all. Drinking and snorting in a Finsbury Park dive until it was practically dawn.

'I really don't know how you manage it,' said Ambrose. He liked his ale with the rest of them but had given up drugs long ago. In fact, these days his life was almost depressingly clean. He sometimes wondered if he were getting middle-aged.

The board was set up on the kitchen table so they got down to it almost immediately. Ambrose, as host, allowed Wayne to choose a piece. Black, so he got to start the game. They played in deadly silence for a couple of strained hours until Wayne turned chalk white with lack of sleep and sustenance and Ambrose suggested that they break.

'Let's go to the pub,' he said, reaching for his jacket. 'I'd like to stretch my legs, if you don't mind.' Plus unclench his tensed-up mind, though he wasn't going to admit to that. He was damned if he'd let the younger man know that he'd got him on the run.

It was a clear, bright morning full of sunshine and spring flowers and the pub was just a couple of streets away.

'Where's the river?' asked Wayne, unfamiliar with this part of London, and Ambrose obligingly led him on a short detour.

'There,' he said as they leaned on the parapet and watched the oily waters flowing by. In the distance, to their right, bungee jumpers were hurtling down from a crane on Chelsea Bridge and they watched them for a while, enjoying the warm sun on their backs.

'I'd quite like to have a go at that,' remarked Ambrose surprisingly, causing Wayne, for a change, to be quite startled.

'You're joking!' he said. 'You'd never get me near it. Far too hairy for my liking.'

'But you're always taking risks.' Skating through traffic, shooting up in sordid dives. Changing his sexual partners with his socks.

'Not stupid ones like that. One slip and you're instantly dead. It's almost as bad as parachuting or sky-diving.' He shuddered despite the balmy air. 'Or playing Russian roulette.'

'Sky-diving rather appeals to me too,' admitted Ambrose. 'Think how it must feel floating up there alone in all that empty space. With nothing between you and the sky.'

'Or the ground.'

'Pessimist.' He laughed and suggested they go and eat. His stomach was starting to rumble, he imagined Wayne's must be too.

'Why this sudden fixation with dangerous sports?' asked Wayne, genuinely curious, once they were settled with their beers.

'Don't really know,' said Ambrose abstractedly. 'It's just something I've been thinking about for ages.'

'Well, you certainly surprise me.' Wayne drank his beer and began to unwind. They both ordered lasagne, the lunch dish of the day. He started to feel better with some solid food inside him. He would trounce his opponent when they got back to the game.

'I suppose it's because my life lacks genuine thrills.' Ambrose had always been a law-abiding man who had trod a solitary path for much of his life. Working first at Weinbergs and then for McLennan Graphics had been fun and exhilarating but not what he'd call full of kicks. Standing on the sidelines again, watching the world live its life. There was a great big hollow emptiness which he preferred not to have to confront.

'You should try getting married and having a bunch of kids. That should put a bit of pep into your life.' Wayne often wondered why Ambrose still lived alone. Though Melody was still his secret, he intended never to let her go. She'd become far too important a fixture in his life. He found, to his amazement, that he liked being half of a pair.

Ambrose gave a fake shudder and warded off the idea with both hands. 'That would be much too terrifying,' he said. 'I know I just couldn't cope.' He was serious, too. Fascinating. Wayne notched it up for further consideration.

As they strolled back along the riverside walk, they paused for another look at the scenery. To the left of where they were standing now, on the other side of the river, was the dramatically imposing tower of Chelsea Harbour topped by its distinctive coolie hat.

'That's where all the nobs live,' explained Ambrose, fairly sourly. With its private marina packed with expensive yachts. Battersea remained down-at-heel and unspoilt, but what the developers had done to the disused railway siding really got his puritanical goat. He disapproved of flamboyant excess, hated the flimsy workmanship and inflated property prices. He'd never actually been inside but had cased the place fairly thoroughly on his many nocturnal walks.

'You know who lives there?' he said as they started back. 'Julius Fucking Weinberg. Exactly what you might expect of that sort of social parasite. Too much money without enough taste. Why does he feel the need to live here at all?' They rarely ever saw him. Wayne was quite startled at the belligerent tone. Something about the Weinberg man seemed always to spark off this reaction. He knew they had history but wasn't quite sure what it was. And with Ambrose in his current tetchy mood it wouldn't be wise to ask.

'How do you know he lives there?' he said. 'I hadn't realised the two of you were so chummy.'

Ambrose just grunted disagreeably. There were all sorts of things to which he had secret access, much of which he didn't ever reveal. His knowledge of computing stood him in excellent stead. There was a lot a person could easily find out if only they knew where to look. He thought about Serafina and her fatuous, bird-brained questions. If she'd only told him what she was looking for, he could probably have helped her quite a lot. If she'd just stop nagging and wasting his time, these women were all the same. He hoped he hadn't made a mistake with Wayne, had assumed that, with his working-class roots, the lad would be on his side.

'Well, keep it to yourself,' he growled but couldn't really explain why.

By five even Wayne was beginning to wilt. By seven they called it a day. They shifted into the sitting-room and Ambrose produced whisky and two glasses. Wayne had not succeeded in giving him the trouncing he'd expected; they had ended up quite comfortably with a draw.

'I suppose I ought to be getting back,' said Wayne reluctantly. He was enjoying it here in this shabby, congenial pad, the sort he would like for himself when he had the money. The sofa and armchairs had seen better days but were covered efficiently with rugs. There was a small gasfire behind a painted screen and the walls were covered with books. Very much a bachelor establishment, remote and quiet and austere. Old Ambrose was a fairly complex devil. Wayne was learning more about him all the time.

'Toilet?' asked Wayne, finally getting to his feet. They had drunk quite a lot and he had a longish journey back.

'Down the passage, at the end,' said Ambrose, fiddling with his stereo and putting on some plaintive jazz.

The walls of the passage were hung with old engravings but it was too dimly lit for Wayne to see them properly. He liked the air of mustiness and age, like living in an antiquarian bookshop. He opened the door of the room on the left but was unable to locate the light switch.

'Where's the light?' he shouted then realised he was in the wrong room. The bathroom was Spartan but brightly lit and immaculately clean with a tidy row of washing drying primly over the bath.

'How many bedrooms do you have?' asked Wayne on his return.

'Why, are you thinking of moving in?'

'Wouldn't mind,' said Wayne, meaning it too. There was room and enough here for Melody and him. He could fancy setting up home with her on a much more permanent footing. Hackney was fine but rather too far away and a bit on the rough side for her. And since her traineeship was south of the river, this would really be most suitable. He would lure her over to Battersea one weekend for a proper look round without letting on his secret plan.

'Just the two,' replied Ambrose. 'The other I use as a study. I never have visitors, so it's just the right size.'

Another of the luxuries of the solitary life. Not for Wayne, not at this particular stage in his life, but he could well see the attractions for old Ambrose. On the long walk back to the railway station he thought about all he had learned that day. It was always fairly fascinating seeing someone else's lifestyle, gave you a better fix on everything else. He would not, for instance, have expected Ambrose to be quite so neat and orderly, though he was, of course, a perfectionist in his work. Dottie envisaged him living in sordid squalor but she, nurturer and carer that she was, was bound to think that of almost any bachelor. Well, it might be true of himself, thought Wayne, but he'd clean up his act when required. Putting together a home and amassing nice things was something you didn't do alone. Not unless you were Jinx, of course, but she was something else entirely.

35

When Ambrose let slip that he knew where Julius lived, Serafina felt her luck might finally be turning. There she'd been, assuming he had just the one home, in New York, and putting up at swanky hotels while he was in London. Now she discovered, like a gift from the gods, that he also maintained a flat in Chelsea Harbour. Smart address, high property prices, obviously unlisted telephone. Within easy walking distance of her own flat furthermore. She decided to pop over there to take a look at the setup. Though a proper bona fide excuse would be handier. She racked her brains.

Jinx, in the past few days, had been moody and taciturn, so unlike her customary cheery self that comments had been made all round.

'What's up with Jinx?' they had all inquired of Dottie, who truthfully hadn't a clue. She thought it might just be overwork, Jinx had not had a break for something like eighteen months and the pressures of that dratted deadline had to be weighing on her too. After all, it was Jinx who ultimately carried the can.

The money men were being reasonable right now but suppose their current sunny mood should change. Everyone knew how dangerous working for Julius could be. Jinx was hardly in an enviable position, always there in the firing-line.

Dottie tried sounding her out early one morning but she still continued to look desolate. It was almost two weeks since that disastrous dinner and she'd not heard a word from him since. Somehow she had managed to screw things up totally and this time didn't think they'd be correctable. There was no way she was going to crawl back and seek forgiveness. He'd behaved once too often like an arrogant male chauvinist, the onus was entirely on him. Maybe he'd even returned to the States, which seemed the most likely explanation. She was far more miserable than she ever let show, furious with both of them for allowing happiness to elude them once more. For the truth was, despite some fairly major flaws, Julius was all she'd ever dreamed of in a man. Witty, perceptive, with a matching sense of humour and a gritty intelligence she could genuinely respect. The idea of a future bereft of him entirely was actually almost unthinkable. But none of this could she share with Dottie, not yet.

'I think it's just that time of year,' she said. 'Spring always gets me this way, gives me itchy feet.' And that's not all.

'What are you doing over Easter?' asked Dottie but Jinx, as usual, had no particular plan.

'You could always come to Frinton with us. Hardly exciting but lovely bracing air.' And her mother would be thrilled to see her. The poor old dear went out so little these days.

Jinx laughed. Dottie was a darling, she felt guilty about being so down. She longed to have a real girls' heart-to-heart but didn't want to talk about it yet. Not till there was something, either good or bad, to tell. She was sick of parading her lovelife before all and sundry, an endless circus to keep everyone amused.

'I've still got to sort out the end of year accounts.' The start of the new tax year was the day after Easter Monday.

'All you ever seem to do these days is work,' said Dottie sympathetically. But it had to be done, could no longer be put off. And the four-day weekend did make the best sense.

'I guess that's the name of the game,' said Jinx rallying, trying her hardest to raise a smile. The show must go on, no matter how dispirited she felt. Like the fabled ballerina with a broken heart, she just had to keep on dancing. But Easter still wasn't for another week. If she got her act together and sorted things out, she still might make time for a break. Perhaps a trip to Bristol to catch up with the Phillipses or even to the Cotswolds to see Marjorie. There were enough nice places where she knew she was always welcome. It was just that right now all she wanted to do was hide.

She was out that afternoon when the call came through from IEP and Serafina hit the jackpot by happening to pick up the phone. Julius Weinberg's po-faced PA asking for Jinx McLennan. Contrary to her normal detached way, Serafina was out to help her with alacrity.

'I'm afraid she's out for the rest of the day. Is there anything I can do?'

She was put on hold. Then the girl came back and said that Mr Weinberg had been hoping to borrow a beta disc of DBI-2000 to show to some bigwigs at the weekend. The light of battle came into Serafina's eye as she wondered how to swing it without getting caught. Even talking about their top secret computer game could incur the full wrath of the marketing people, but Jinx wasn't here and need never find out. Not if she played her cards cleverly.

'I am not at all sure that will be possible,' she said. 'Would it help if I explained things to him direct?'

It was something of a longshot but miraculously it worked. The girl sounded grateful and instantly more human. He was a tough, demanding boss and she was sick of being screamed at all morning. Something just lately had been bugging him quite badly. The sooner he returned to his New York base, the better.

'Hold the line.'

Serafina glanced round to see if anyone was listening but Wayne, as chance would have it, was off at the post office while Dottie was making coffee in the kitchen. Serafina's palms were sweating profusely and she wiped them nervously on her skirt. Her prayers were being answered even sooner than she'd hoped for. Let nothing happen now to wreck her plan.

'Serafina,' said Julius's husky abrasive voice which always gave her the shivers. 'I hate to ask this at such short notice but I need to get hold of a beta disc fast. I've a couple of guys from Sega in town and now would be an ideal time to get them hooked. They fly back on Monday so it has to be quick. If I can get it to them for the weekend, I can hopefully firm up the deal.' He was, after all, the ultimate boss, as Ambrose was constantly reminding them.

Serafina thought fast then made her decision. It might well turn out to be a hanging offence but was definitely, to her mind, worth the risk. There was one uncut tape in the studio safe and she knew precisely where Dottie kept the key. She couldn't ask Jinx since she didn't know where she'd gone and was certain that Ambrose would forbid it. Weinberg might be the financier, he would say, but the bastard had no more right to a premature sneak preview than any of the other would-be purchasers. Ambrose, like Damien, was a bit of a fanatic. Hated anyone to see his work until all the testing had been done.

'Well,' she said silkily, doubt in her voice. 'It's possible I can swing it though I really ought to warn you . . .'

'Good girl. I'll send a messenger right away.'

'Hang on.' She was scared, he was rushing her too much. He might be the boss but it was Jinx who paid her salary and the job was still important until Plan B went into action. She was loath to let go of her vantage point too soon, not till she had succeeded in grasping the ring.

'I first have to locate the key to the safe and I can't say precisely how long that is likely to take. How's about I bring it over when I've got it? Save you the trouble of sending for it.' That way she'd get to see him again, he might even ask her for a drink. Would certainly give her points for efficiency.

Julius paused. She could hear him thinking.

'I'm having some folks in for drinks tonight and the Sega guys will be among them. Tell you what. Why not bring it to Chelsea around seven and come in and join the party.' She was sensationally good to look at and these men were travelling solo. It would do no harm to lay on some glamour while also annoying the hell out of Jinx. Which was rather what Serafina was thinking too. Now all she had to worry about was getting into the safe unobserved before streaking off home to prepare for this heaven-sent opportunity.

Her luck still held. Wayne was taking his time about the post and Dottie announced she was going upstairs to sort out the conference-room cupboard. She asked Serafina if she minded holding the fort and was mildly surprised when she happily agreed. The second she heard Dottie's feet clumping up the stairs, Serafina was over to her desk with lightning speed. Luckily Dottie kept a whole battery of things there – emery boards, sewing-kit, handcream, sticking plasters. All thoughtfully lined up for anyone to use. Dottie was the most generous of souls.

The key to the safe was in a ceramic flowerpot along with a clutter of pencils and pens. Jinx always thought that was fairly impractical, but Dottie's reasoning was simply that no burglar was likely to look there. Serafina scrabbled around and located it almost immediately. Now came the tricky part: gaining access to the safe. It was hidden discreetly in a storeroom adjacent to the studio, which was used for stowing stationery, old ledgers and stuff like that. It would mean shifting boxes and shoving things around, but Serafina was intrepid with a goal this important in view. She'd risk Wayne coming back and catching her, would think up some easy excuse to fob him off.

But everything went like clockwork and she soon had her hands on the disc. She rapidly replaced the cartons round the safe and carried it back to her desk. Still no sign of Dottie or Wayne. Today her luck was working overtime. She slipped the key back into Dottie's pot and the disc, in an envelope, into her bag.

'Mind if I leave a little early?' she called up the stairs. It was twenty past five, she was already cutting it fine.

'No problem,' Dottie shouted back. 'I'll keep an ear open for the phone.' Wayne should be back at any second now and things were usually quiet this late on a Friday.

'Have a good weekend,' she called as Serafina left. Serafina privately grinned and got a move on. She had every intention of doing exactly that. Once she had dolled herself up to the nines.

She arrived an elegant twenty minutes late and was helped from her cab by the doorman. She had dressed with much care for a smart drinks party in the sort of exclusive setting that had long been a part of her dreams. Play her cards right and she'd soon be on her way, with luck, to his offices in New York. What a piece of sheer good fortune that Jinx hadn't been around. She would milk it to the utmost while she could. Clutching the beta disc in its discreet brown envelope, she rode the lift to the penthouse floor where the guests were beginning to gather.

'Serafina,' said Julius smoothly, kissing her cheek. He looked at her approvingly, she certainly scrubbed up well. Her dress was black and severely understated and the Manolo Blahnik sandals added inches to her height. She was like a catwalk model with her expression of bored disdain. He could feel the other guests watching her as he ushered her into their presence.

They could not have been more Californian, Ed and Mal, with their even, round-the-year tans. Ed was intense with badly acne-scarred skin while Mal was a Barry Gibb lookalike. Bland

and smiling with cropped beard and perfect teeth, he kissed her effusively like a long-lost friend. Or perhaps even something a little closer. Julius, looking faintly disapproving, moved her on. The rest of the assembly was a mix of business and social, well-heeled, smartly dressed, above all intelligent. Julius was well known for his refusal to tolerate fools.

They were probably just about fifty in all, with white-jacketed waiters bringing drinks and Japanese snacks. For her own part Serafina was like a cow in clover, casting covetous eyes round this wonderful penthouse, a glutton for all she could see. This was more like it, the setting to which she aspired. She chatted demurely to whoever took her eye, dropping subtle mention of the Italian ancestry and playing down her business connection with her host. Since his wife appeared not to be present tonight, let them think whatever they liked. A soupçon of scandal harmed nobody's reputation, Lily Langtry and Mrs Parker Bowles could both bear witness to that.

Julius watched her mingling and was amused. She didn't fool him, not for a single second, but he admired an obvious gold-digger on the make. She certainly managed to look the part and would provide titillation for the men she was buttering up. She was flirting right now with a leading QC who was bursting his breeches with delight. His homely wife, in her dated frock, was glowering from the sidelines and would shortly be breaking them up. All part of the evening's entertainment, exactly what a party was for.

As she circulated relentlessly, Serafina's brain was working on overtime. Tonight could be exactly the break she was after provided she played her cards right. She was determined not to waste a single second. This was the one man in the world she really wanted and she wasn't intending to leave here empty-handed. She had heard a word dropped that some of them were going on to dinner, and rightaway a plan began to form in her devious mind. She must not be guilty of being the last to leave. It was somewhat naff to be seen lingering on in hope. Women of the class she aspired to be had diaries pre-packed with other social commitments. She doubted if Julius would include her in the dinner group; even she, in this hyped-up state, had few illusions about that. She studied the flow of the crowd with care and, as soon as it started to thin, put her plan smartly into action. She wandered off in search of a bathroom and chose one *en suite* to one of the guest bedrooms. There she would wait till the coast was clear and the penthouse finally deserted.

Julius wasn't enjoying himself particularly. He kept wishing Jinx was at his side. Parties like this he could take or leave. They were part of the drudgery of the affluent social scene. He had bought this apartment to further his wife's career but these days she rarely ever used it. Which is why it so much resembled an impersonal hotel suite, plush and expensive with no character at all. Pia had wanted a river view and he'd liked the idea of the extra security. With its round-the-clock guards and security barriers, Chelsea Harbour was a tight little enclave of privilege.

But the people he could do without and now he wished fervently that they'd leave. He was taking a core of them, just six closeish friends, on to dinner in Chelsea once the party was finally over. There were always stragglers but tonight he would be firm and leave the hired staff to cope with the hangers on. The sooner he got them out and to the restaurant, the earlier he could escape. He was tired and despondent and ready to go home. London without Jinx had lost its magic.

He still didn't quite understand what had gone wrong. One minute he'd had her with him, smiling and relaxed, the next she'd stormed out like a termagant. He was well aware that he occasionally lacked finesse but she must surely have learned when he was joking. His admiration for Jinx could not be higher, he had watched her career blossom and was impressed by all she'd achieved. Yes, she had an edge but that was all part of her charm.

He liked a woman with spirit, admired them when they kicked back. And Jinx was an all-time original, which was what had taken his fancy in the first place.

Not like the patently fake Serafina who was out only for what she could grab. He was aware of the way she ogled him, had watched her casing the joint. He glanced round the room to see what she was up to now but she had, for the moment, slid from view. Maybe she'd left without saying goodbye, struck lucky and latched herself onto one of his guests. She'd had that predatory look in her eye when she first came in, he'd been aware of it immediately. Well, that was OK with him, she'd served her purpose. He had needed that disc and she'd come up with the goods. She was free now to do what she liked.

If only Jinx had picked up that call. For a man of his years and sophistication, where she was concerned he was like a prepubescent. He was more or less certain she would not have allowed him access to the disc but he'd have tried to persuade her and at least got her talking again. He glanced at the silent phone like a lovelorn teenager. She was the only woman ever to affect him this way. He just couldn't rid her from his mind.

He moved round the party from group to group, smiling and shaking hands. At his request, the waiters had stopped circulating and were now in the kitchen clearing up. Mal and Ed, the Sega guys, were off with their booty to the Carlton Tower. If he could swing the deal they'd been discussing, they would all be millions richer soon and then surely even Jinx could not object.

Serafina waited till she heard the voices fade, then left the guest room to explore the rest of the flat. A couple of waiters were still active in the kitchen but she smiled at them authoritatively and they gave her scarcely a glance. It wasn't their business who lived in this fancy apartment. They were paid by the hour and the job was now at an end.

'Good night,' they called as they let themselves out and Serafina sank into a sofa to wait. She was in no hurry, it was Friday night. No one was expecting her which was all to the good. She had the whole weekend before her.

36

J inx couldn't remember ever being quite this miserable. She had suffered severely the first time Julius left her but that had been over twelve years ago. She was supposedly an adult now and therefore able to cope. Her mind flashed back to her fortieth birthday party and the jokes they'd made about life beginning now. Forty, someone had said, was this year's thirty which had made her feel a whole lot better about it. But now, just five months later, she was feeling jaded and spent, and the eyes that greeted her reproachfully in the mirror were sore and red from weeping hopeless tears.

It was Friday night and the weekend stretched before her devoid of anything to lighten it in any way. She was now convinced that he must have left London and returned to New York where his heart really lay. Where indeed it should do, it was where he belonged. He was married to a famous and beautiful woman, with a business and social life way beyond Jinx's league. All they'd ever had together was one brief night of passion years ago and a couple of flirty dinners since. Plus the rows.

Julius at his most withering was formidable in the extreme. Those basilisk eyes, with the power to make her quiver, could bore into a person with open contempt and reduce them to a pile of futile ashes. She thought back to the Weinbergs days and the way she had liked to mock him. All based on fear and a healthy though secret respect. She had recognised his brain power from the beginning and used what weapons she had to fend him off. Pulling a man was the easiest thing in the world but finding one worth the effort extremely rare. As Jinx had discovered to her own sad cost. Forty years old and still wearily footloose, vainly still seeking the one perfect love her romantic heart felt was her due. Though she would be the last to admit it, had always been quick to mock Dottie if ever the subject came up.

In some ways she almost envied Serafina, whose clearcut ambition was obvious to everyone, admirably palpable in its intensity. She, at least, knew exactly where she was headed, would kill to achieve her ultimate goal. Jinx had watched her tread a narrow line, fixated on whatever it was she desired. She had managed to reinvent herself many times. She was not aware of being watched, but Jinx had her measure pretty well even if some of the details needed filling in. She was a blatant opportunist, Serafina, though that wasn't necessarily bad. Her vision was blinkered and she lacked a first-class brain but more than made up for it by being streetwise.

Serafina's generation had things a lot easier now, even if they did still moan about men. Within the brief span of Jinx's own lifetime it was odd how far the pendulum had swung. She and her contemporaries had fought hard for their independence and evaded the shackles of marriage and commitment in favour of championing equality. Many women who had made it to the top remained single and childless as a penalty. Whereas Serafina, if she played her cards right, these days could really have it all. Career and babies were no longer in obvious conflict and today's smart thirty-something could more or less write her own script.

Yet Serafina was moody and spoilt and put herself out only when it suited her. She seemed to assume she had a right to a certain level of lifestyle, unaware of the effort and dedication that had made it all possible to those she most envied. In particular Jinx.

Jinx left the bathroom where she'd been studying her ravaged face, and moved around her house to look at her things. She loved this place with a fevered passion, it summed up all she had achieved. She might not have close family or a man she could depend on but she did have, in abundance, almost everything else. This mood of despair would soon work itself out, the Friday night blues she remembered from her youth. The cure was an early night with a soothing book, then to pick up the phone and call a friend. Or take herself off to the pictures on her own. That was the point of living here in Kensington, close to the pulse of the mighty city's heartbeat. There were clubs and bars and restaurants all around; what's more, she had the wherewithal to pay for whatever she wanted. Also the courage to go adventuring on her own. Lack of immediate company was no deterrent.

'So snap out of it,' she told herself briskly and went down to the kitchen to rustle up some food.

Julius, at La Tante Claire, was brooding too. He liked the group he had convened tonight and usually found them provocative and fun. A judge, a QC and a cancer specialist, along with their spirited wives. The great thing about them was they didn't talk shop, at least only amusingly with anecdotes all could share. They were hugely civilised, his London set, and he missed the ambience when he returned to New York. Which he was afraid would have to be soon.

They'd inquired after Pia and regretted her absence but he explained about the new movie and they'd all been enthralled and impressed. Robert de Niro, fancy; how fast she was rising. They were proud these days even to get to shake her hand. Julius laughed. His wife wasn't like that at all and well they knew it. They liked her lack of pretension and genuine sweetness of nature. If only they might be allowed to see her more. He told them he felt much the same. Since the marriage, eleven years before, their lives had grown relentlessly apart. It was nobody's fault, just what inevitably happened when two such high-flyers shared a life. Pia's increasing fame took her more and more over to the Coast whereas the burdens of Julius's own weighty career usually prevented him from accompanying her.

'You'll have to give up and just be her manager.' The judge's wife was serious though the others simply laughed. Men like Julius didn't take the supporting role, though neither was it suggested that the star should ever retire. She had tried doing theatre on Broadway but the real success lay in Hollywood. And Julius would never dream of blocking her upwards path, he cared about her far too much for that. A conundrum, pondered the QC, to which there appeared to be no answer. Just one of the tragedies of modern, affluent life.

'What if you ever have children?' asked his wife.

'Not a lot of chance of that,' Julius told her with a smile. They had both put the family thing on hold till life was less stressed and they felt like slowing down. It was a solid marriage, they liked each other a lot, but forces of circumstance seemed to conspire against them, at least in the immediate future. But it didn't stop him feeling dejected, though he valiantly tried not to show it in front of his guests. Something was miserably lacking from his life. Deep in his heart he knew it wasn't Pia.

The lights were still on but the place deserted when Julius eventually got home. The caterers had done their usual immaculate job and everything was cleared and put away. He sighed as he dealt with the elaborate safety locks. One thirty in the morning; another longstanding engagement out of the way. He pulled at the knot of his tie as he wandered wearily through the flat, checking that the windows were fastened and all was in order. He thought for a second of having one final snifter, then realised how tired he was, in need only of his bed. He sloughed off his clothes and made for the mirrored bathroom, noticing, in passing, that the coverlet had been turned down. The maid service here in Chelsea Harbour was excellent. They came and went invisibly with service as good as a hotel's. But that's what you got if you paid these massive charges, one definite perk of being this rich.

He couldn't be bothered to take a shower, just brushed his teeth and rolled right into bed. He usually read but tonight felt too tired even for that. He glanced at the bedside phone and renewed his fantasy. It was far too late to risk calling her now but her absence was weighing on his soul. If only he wasn't such a damned conceited fool and could learn not to blurt things out before he had properly thought them through.

He was just reaching over to the bedside lamp when he fancied he heard a movement inside the closet. He froze. Just the faintest rustle, as of clothes being gently disturbed, but there it was again, now distinctly audible. He was on the point of leaping out of bed when the door of the closet opened slowly and a figure wreathed solely in a filmy scarf emerged dramatically and advanced towards him. Serafina, wearing nothing else but a radiant smile, halted at the foot of the bed and struck a pose.

'Da-DA!'

She was certainly striking with her sinewy, lissom figure and her thick black hair swirled up high upon her head. He couldn't be certain through the opalescent veiling, but it seemed she had even rouged her nipples. For one long fraught second, time in that bedroom stood still.

Jinx couldn't sleep so she paced about, making herself milky coffee then regretting it; pouring instead a reckless glass of red wine. This was madness. She had taken enough knocks in her life to know better, to recognise futility when it stared her in the face. Let it go, she ordered herself sternly, enough. She still possessed too much dignity to succumb to the pain of a passing lost love. He was trash, he was history. She had been through it all before. She had nicer friends, more considerate; friends who positively cared. She thought warmly of Hamish who lately she'd rather neglected and resolved soon to give him a call. Not now though, not in the depths of the night when her memories were all spooking her and she had a powerful desire to cry.

Up and down she walked, thinking back to that night in New York, their endless lovemaking, his kisses and caresses, the tender things he had said. As clear today as if it were fixed in amber. She had believed him then because she had so much wanted to. She had found, she thought, after all those years of looking, the man with whom she could finally share her life. But he'd drastically let her down. So why waste time and energy now agonising over a treacherous love-rat who had even driven his own beloved uncle to the grave? It made no sense for a feisty free spirit like hers. First thing tomorrow, she vowed as she returned to her bed, she would phone round her friends and fan up some social life. Make a positive effort to start taking time off and not spend every waking second totally immersed in her work. There was a whole exciting world out there if only she'd bother to look for it. Time to throw off old memories and get back into the game.

'What in hell's name are *you* doing here?' asked Julius, once he had found his voice. Serafina stood posed like a Grecian statue, flaunting her nakedness with a small triumphant smile. Whatever she thought she looked like, she was ludicrous. His overwhelming emotion, apart from disgust, was fury at finding her still here. Pushy was one thing but this quite beyond the pale. She had obviously even been snooping through Pia's things. He recognised the scarf as one he had given her several years before. Serafina didn't answer but coquettishly fluttered her lashes. She tossed aside the scarf in a gesture of rapturous abandon and advanced with sinuous tread towards the bed. Any second now and she'd be leaping in beside him. Julius dived for his robe and covered up.

'Whatever you are up to, this is not the time,' he said sternly, dignity restored the minute he was back on his feet. Serafina froze in her tracks with incomprehension. She was presenting herself to him as bait; why wouldn't he bite?

'Oh, Julius,' she purred, 'don't be such an old prude. Come on, relax and I'll show you a good time.' She clasped both hands above her head to display her straining breasts and undulated slowly like an anorexic belly dancer. She was striking but ridiculous. She had to be out of her mind.

'Cover yourself up,' he ordered sharply, tossing her the discarded coverlet. 'Then put on your clothes and get out of here. I need my sleep.'

'I'll give you a lovely slow massage,' she said seductively, still apparently not getting the message. 'Then slip in beside you and show you some tricks. You'll like that.' It had never failed to work in the past; what was it with him now? Didn't he want her as much as she wanted him? She ran her hands lasciviously over her naked breasts and belly, closing her eyes in feigned rapture as she reached the significant spot. Julius was enraged, utterly turned off. Her presence there in his bedroom was a sacrilege.

'Go!' he roared. 'Before I throw you out. One more minute and I'll call the security guards.'

He stalked off into the living-room and poured himself a stiff drink while Serafina, beginning to feel a fool, searched for her clothes, abandoned in one of the bedrooms. What had seemed a workable plan just hours ago had gone horribly wrong now that she'd sobered up a bit. But she still didn't understand his resistance. The man was only human after all. And, wow, was he gorgeous when he started to get cross.

'Your wife's not here,' she pouted, joining him as she brushed her thick hair and restored it to a semblance of normality. She had heard them talking about Pia at the party, how these days they were almost always apart, which surely indicated cracks in the marriage. So why was he being so prudish all of a sudden? No one had ever rejected her advances before. Maybe it was the business connection but Serafina was a mistress of discretion.

'I'll not tell a soul,' she murmured softly as she slid up behind him and wound her arms around his neck. 'A girl can be very grateful, you'll find. You can trust me, I assure you.' Trust her to do his bidding and be his slave, to let him walk all over her if that was what it entailed. Until, of course, she had the ring on her finger and the reassuring certificate in her hand.

She'd restored her clothing, and even her stockings were in place, with the Manolo Blahnik heels bringing her close to his height. But as she rubbed her nose provocatively against his cheek, she dropped something wispy into his hand and purred as she nibbled his ear. Julius glanced down; her black satin thong. The girl was almost a joke if he weren't quite so cross.

'Go now,' he said less severely. 'And we'll forget all about it in the morning.' He shook her off.

'Aren't you even going to call me a cab?' She was petulant now and pouting. Her plan had misfired but he might have been more of a sport.

Julius's patience was finally worn through and he badly wanted to be shot of her.

'Pick one up yourself in the street,' he snapped crushingly. 'You shouldn't have any problem dressed like that.'

As soon as she'd gone and he'd heard the front door click, his irritation ebbed away and he actually found it quite funny. Foolish she might be but devious with it. He admired her spirit even though she'd blown it completely by getting him totally wrong. He was well accustomed to being pursued by women. She had just been overly crude in her attempt. And much of his anger had been fuelled by basic frustration. What he wouldn't give to have somebody here in his bed right now, just not her. The exhaustion he'd been feeling when he first got home had abated with the sudden adrenaline charge. He no longer felt very much like sleep. He lit a cigarette and recklessly topped up his glass. Tomorrow he'd have a mammoth hangover; at the moment he couldn't care less.

He slid back the doors and stepped out onto the terrace and gazed down at the slumbrous river below. His thoughts returned like a magnet to Jinx and again he glanced, by reflex, at the phone. It was almost three and the city still slept, though a distant lightening of the eastern sky reminded him that dawn was not far off. Not at this balmy time of year with the recent arrival of spring. He wondered what she was doing right now, hoped fervently that she was alone. Night thoughts were seldom a healthy thing and now the idea was planted he just grew more depressed. He had practically held her in his palm yet lost her again like the arrogant fool he'd always been. And this time, he knew, there'd be no easy reprieve. She'd forgiven him once, he could hardly expect that again. He wanted to be able to take her in his arms and tell her precisely how he felt. How the light had gone out of his life when she left, that the fairytale marriage had been mainly on the rebound. Which he'd never ever admitted before, not even to himself.

He glanced again at the silent phone. What more had he got to lose? He thought of Serafina with her wild, impetuous gamble, and a rueful smile softened the edges of his mouth. Once a fool, always a fool was how the saying went. And Julius Weinberg was one of life's great gamblers.

It was no good, she couldn't sleep and dawn was beginning to edge in. The sky was growing paler, already streaked with pink. Another insufferably lovely spring day. She tossed and turned and threw aside the duvet then snuggled down beneath it again to avoid the gathering light. She could always get up and try doing some work, those bloody accounts were still nagging at her conscience. But she needed her sleep, had been deprived too much lately. Must keep her wits about her and try to ignore the hurt.

She stared at the bedside phone as if she could make it ring, pitting her psychic energy against the relentless night. He had gone, she was resigned to it now, and it didn't make it any better to know it was all her fault. She had thrown away the best thing she'd ever had and all for the sake of her boring, pig-headed pride. She glared at the telephone, blaming all her problems on it.

And miraculously, bang on cue, it started to ring.

37

So here they now were at last, back together again, two benighted fools both crashingly in love, each unable to articulate properly exactly what they were feeling. Or had felt. When he rang the doorbell early that Saturday morning, while the milkman was still doing his rounds and the Daweses not even up, Jinx received him with a hammering heart, fresh from the shower with hair that was still damp. She had agonised greatly over what she should wear, the appropriate outfit for receiving an estranged lover with whom, until only minutes earlier, she had not been on speaking terms. In the end, because there was so little time, she settled for jeans and a fresh white shirt and stood there barefoot when she opened the door, without a scrap of jewellery on or makeup. She looked adorable, all the more so because she didn't realise it.

'Julius.'

'Jinx.'

Those were all the words they spoke, all that were needed at the time. He leaned forward to peck her politely on the cheek but ended up crushing her impulsively in his arms. As one, they moved backwards while she closed the door, then proceeded to devour one another. It had been so long. Weeks since those two rather spiky dinners, an eternity since they'd made love. Yet it still felt so right.

'We can't just stand here,' he said, finally breaking away. 'Is there somewhere more comfortable we can go?'

He glanced meaningfully at the staircase but she shook her head. This time she definitely meant to be more controlled. Despite the rapid surge of unmitigated lust, she remembered the last time and would not be so easily swayed. Let him wait a little till he'd served some sort of penance. He would not find her as easy as before.

'Jinx,' he said more softly as she led him through to the sofa. He cupped her solemn face in both his hands and gazed at her soulfully as if he were feasting his eyes. She was beautiful and flawless and he hoped she would soon be his. He hardly deserved her, how well he realised that now, but her apparent acquiescence gave him room to hope. She had not yet spoken a single snarling word and her body in his arms felt warm and compliant. Despite a whole night of broken sleep, her skin positively glowed with excitement and the eyes that met his were definitely starry. What price the sophisticated career girl now? Faced with true love, she was lost.

Despite the earliness of the hour, Julius looked immaculate but, then, she'd never known him not to be. It was all part of his customary façade. In deference to the weekend, he was wearing a blazer with grey pants and a crisp blue shirt. No jeans for Julius, absolutely not his style. He was expertly shaved and smelled divinely of cologne. Despite her attempt at staving off familiarity, she relaxed in his arms with content.

'You've no idea how much I've missed you,' he murmured into her hair then kissed her long and luxuriantly with a heartfelt passion she knew could not be feigned. Enough had been said on the telephone in the small hours for them each to be faintly confident, though wary, of how the other was likely to react. They had both come through fire and survived.

Feeling she should do something to forestall him, she pushed him away when she deemed they needed a breather and went off into the kitchen to make coffee. She had eaten nothing and felt quite light-headed after all those empty hours awaiting the dawn. He followed her through and leaned against the draining-board while she competently ground beans and boiled water. A nice kitchen, plain and serviceable, with scrubbed white tops and matching tiles on the floor. Idly he opened the fridge and laughed when he saw the extent of its contents. Designer water and coffee beans, a pot of caviar and several bottles of wine.

'I see you're not exactly a master cook,' he said.

'You'd be surprised what I can come up with when the occasion warrants it.'

Normally she ate out and usually not alone but she didn't bother explaining that to him. There was so much still they had to learn about each other. She looked forward to getting to know him better and falteringly hoped it would happen. This time round.

Halfway through their coffee break, passion took over again and soon they were rolling on the carpet, oblivious of any passers-by peering in.

'Jinx,' he moaned as his hands slid under her shirt, and though she tried initially to push him off, her attempt was only half-hearted. He was like a drug, she needed him so badly, the rain after an interminable drought. He tossed his blazer across the room then worked on the buttons of her shirt while she just lay there and shook with excitement, his for the taking which he knew. There was very little dignity in this situation but both of them were way beyond that stage. His skin was tanned and his stomach still flat as a board. All those years of good living had scarcely taken their toll. If anything, he was even better looking with the ravages of time adding character to his face. Certainly sexier and less constrained or maybe her memory was simply playing tricks. When he slid inside her she suddenly felt whole, restored to the blessed unity she'd been missing.

'My darling.'

'My love.' They were home at last.

'Tell me about your wife,' said Jinx over lunch. She had torn herself away from him just long enough to shoot across the street and pick up some basic provisions from the corner deli. Spicy Bloody Marys which he insisted on mixing, spiked with Worcester sauce and horse-radish, enough to make her scalp tingle. They sat at the dining-room table with the patio doors flung open, the filmy curtains moving gently in the breeze as a balmy breath of air disturbed them. She couldn't remember ever feeling this happy before. This togetherness was so right for them both, the fact he was married suddenly no deterrent. For this time round she trusted him absolutely and knew instinctively he was not going to hurt her again.

Julius sat in silence, caressing her hand. He had left his shoes and blazer in the front room, strewn across the floor in wild abandon. His shirt was unbuttoned and his hair in a bit of a mess. She leaned towards him and softly stroked his cheek.

'Pia,' he said at last, as if seeking to remember the name. 'A sweet girl, innocent and quite unspoiled. Warm and truly caring. Perhaps my best friend.' He paused again, they both did, then he raised her hand to his lips. 'We married after only six weeks. At the time it seemed the right thing.'

'Do you love her?' It was hard to ask the question but she needed urgently to know. This conversation was crucial to her future, might alter the course of her life. She cared for him distractedly but still had her pride. And would not play second fiddle to any other, no matter how painful another such parting would be.

'I do,' he said, after another significant pause. 'And doubtless always will.' He went into the kitchen and mixed them another drink and she watched him, as deft as any barman, too keyed up to break the long silence. She could feel her heart pounding and the tears rising close to her eyes. She had to be strong to live through this moment. He was being dead honest and that was how she wanted it, no more lies between them ever again.

'I'd go out of my way not to hurt her,' he said. 'Her happiness means a great deal to me.'

So where exactly did that leave them? He carried both glasses back into the room and set them down carefully on the table. There were taco chips and a dish of guacamole and he fed her as delicately as a child. Then pulled her gently back into his arms and covered her anxious face with hot kisses.

'I love her but am not in love with her. That's the truth. That place in my heart has always been reserved for you. I probably shouldn't have done it quite so hastily but I married her mainly to help ease the pain.' The loss, the deprivation, his anger at himself for having had the foolishness to lose her.

Jinx stared back at him dumbfounded. His expression was suddenly tortured and he turned away.

'You can't know how much I've missed you,' he said. 'I thought I had lost you for ever.'

She knew exactly, had been there too. Only she'd had the additional hurt all these years of seeing him photographed with another. And not just any old glamorous bimbo but a socialite filmstar with international acclaim. Up for an Oscar twice in recent years, adulated on Broadway before she even hit the big screen. No wonder he idolised a woman like that. Any man might have done the same.

'So,' said Jinx eventually, getting up. 'Why did you let me go?' Without so much as a plea to stay or attempt to make her understand. She walked across to the open French doors and stood looking out at her patio. At this time of year it was pretty drab and depressed with only the creeping honeysuckle from next door doing anything to mitigate its harshness. Here, again, she could use the skills of Dottie who would love to work wonders in this space. There just wasn't time to fit everything in, not even love it now appeared. He joined her and stood there pressing kisses on her neck and she leaned back involuntarily and accepted them.

'I don't really know,' he said at last, holding her so close she could feel his heart beat. 'Sounds silly now that I've found you again but then it seemed so final.' He had thought he had lost her because of his betrayal, had recognised the scorn in her eyes. But that was not something he cared to dwell on now. They'd have time enough in the future, all going well.

'One thing I swear and that's that this time we'll sort things out.' Then he twisted her round and kissed her long and hard before leading her masterfully up the stairs.

It was very nearly six by the time they re-emerged. Jinx wondered where the afternoon had gone. Hunger drove her to rouse herself from his arms and once more go foraging for food. Julius wanted to take her out but she wasn't yet ready for that. The last two spats in restaurants were still painful in her memory. She wouldn't allow that much space between them, not now she was back under his spell. She returned with a couple of steaks from the butcher over the road and he set about grilling them, man's work he said, while she prepared a salad and opened a bottle of claret.

'Look,' he said eventually, once they were seated. 'We will sort things out, that I promise.'

She looked at him inquiringly and he pressed her hand in answer. This was a man who would not go back on his word.

'I have to go back to New York,' he said. 'And I'll try to talk to Pia while I'm there.'

'But I thought she was shooting out on the Coast?' The story had been in all the papers.

'She is.' He nodded. 'But we're still a married couple. If necessary I will even go over there.'

'And say what?' She hated the thought of hurting another woman, of snatching someone's husband out of greed. She was perfectly well able to fend for herself – look how well she'd done it all these years. But Julius was determined, very much the man of honour. He had treated her prettily shabbily, now was the time to atone.

'The truth,' he said simply. 'That's the very least she deserves. She married me in absolute faith. I will not dishonour her now.'

Late on Sunday, after they had spent a turbulent afternoon in bed, snoozed a little then shared a long stimulating shower, they sank back on to the sofa downstairs to recover. They had taken one brief, idyllic walk in Holland Park, admired the peacocks and the immaculate Japanese garden then rushed back home for another urgent bout of lovemaking. Both were deliciously sated but the condition was only temporary. He couldn't get enough of her; she felt the same about him.

'Tell you what,' said Julius as she poured two glasses of chilled white wine. 'I have an idea. I need to be in New York by the end of the week for one important meeting. But after that I'm free for a while, at least for a few days.'

'It's Easter.'

'I know. But that's no big deal over there. And Pia's movie is already over budget so they're working all hours to catch up.'

He tasted the chardonnay, glanced at the label and laughed. 'Since when have you been buying South African wines? But it does show an educated palate.'

'Since only very recently when I heard that you were back. Silly I know, but they're good.'

'The best, as you'll discover when I take you to the Cape. But I digress. How would you feel about sneaking away and joining me in the sun for an extended dirty weekend? This country pretty much closes up so they won't even miss you at the office.'

He remembered Serafina and a smile quirked the corners of his mouth. Some day he'd tell it as the comic story it was but not quite yet. Wait till Serafina was out of both their lives. She was a pretty loose cannon at the best of times but he had no wish to embarrass her unduly. In fact he rather admired her spunk; in other circumstances she was bound to go far.

'You don't mean Cape Town?' That was far too far. Besides, she wasn't yet quite ready. He shook his head.

'Anguilla,' he said. 'I go there quite often. It's only four hours from New York.'

'What if someone sees us?' She was startled at the idea, still shaky at the thought of him telling his wife.

'Who cares?' he said with a wide, disarming smile. 'We'll go public just as soon as we can. Once Pia knows.'

'But what will she say? Won't she mind?'

It was then he told her of the charismatic French director, the new *enfant terrible* of Beverly Hills who'd been taking up so much of her time.

'She's having an affair?' What more was there to come out? Nothing appeared to be what it had seemed. The fabled love match was crumbling before her eyes. Jinx was profoundly shocked though she wasn't quite sure why.

'It was bound to happen,' he said in explanation. 'These long distances don't do any relationship much good. The affection is still there but, sadly, no longer the passion. We both have, if we're honest, been aware of it for some time. I suspect when she hears she'll even be relieved.' It would set her free to follow her heart just like him.

'And you have no children?'

'None. There was never time.'

Now she saw him for the brave, long-suffering man he really was and couldn't resist climbing on his knee. They paused for a romantic interlude, then he raised the subject again, shifting her alongside him while he tried to recover his breath.

'So what do you say? About Anguilla? I can fix things from here and meet up with you there?'

'Exactly when?' There was so much to do, those accounts still to be sorted. But Dottie would understand when Jinx explained. Emphatically Julius shook his head.

'No,' he said. 'It is vital you tell no one. Not till I've talked to Pia at least. It's only fair.'

Jinx had to agree. Dottie was a darling but she knew she'd be bound to tell Sam. They had few secrets, that happily married pair, and discussed almost everything at home. Particularly the state of Jinx's lovelife, that had long been a favourite topic with them both. Though she'd feel more comfortable the less Sam knew; she still had him slightly on her conscience. And once Sam was in the picture he'd be likely to tell Damien and then it would inevitably all get back to Ambrose. Those men were more gossipy than any vicarage tea party, she knew it from the past to her cost. And Ambrose, poor darling, would be bound to disapprove. And his disapprobation would be the hardest thing to bear.

'Penny for them.'

'I was thinking. Yes, you're right.' The fewer who knew now, the better till she was certain. She couldn't face going through all that palaver again. 'When are you leaving?'

'First thing Thursday morning. The meeting's on Friday, then I'm free.'

It was just what they needed, a whole week away from the world. And the team could cope without her, doubtless would be pleased. She told him, suddenly shy, that she'd really like to do it, and his answering kiss told all she needed to know.

They were eating again – all this sex made them ravenous – light pasta this time with a creamy smoked salmon sauce. It was late, very late and tomorrow they both had to work but he just couldn't find the strength to pull away. The night was so mild that they hadn't closed the French doors and the curtain was billowing slightly in the breeze. The heavy scent of honeysuckle floated in from outside. Spring in the heart of this city was more magical than he had known. Jinx started feeding him, dropping succulent pieces of fish into his mouth, until he grabbed her and wrestled her to the floor and they both lay there laughing till his kisses shut her up.

'Jinx, darling.' He lay on top of her and gazed into her eyes. All the rancour, the ongoing pain, had vanished as if it had never been. He rolled up her T-shirt in order to kiss her breasts but something suddenly alerted her and she gently pushed him away.

'I thought I heard something move on the patio. I'm sure there's somebody out there,' she said. The filmy white curtain was not quite opaque but in this light concealed what lay beyond. Julius, remembering Serafina with alarm, jumped rapidly to his feet but she tugged at his sleeve and detained him.

'Wait,' she whispered urgently. 'They'll be watching us. Close the curtains quickly and stay out of sight.' With his shirt half-off and his pants unzipped, he was certainly in no state for a citizen's arrest. He leapt at the door regardless and stuck his head outside but could see nothing at all in the dense darkness. Only the far lights from the pub next door, along with the muted babble of distant voices.

'It was probably just a cat,' he said. 'Or even an urban fox.' Completely undeterred, he did up his zip and tucked his shirt back into his pants. Then locked the French doors and shot home the bolt, turning to her with a triumphant smile.

'You're safe now,' he whispered with a wolfish grin. 'Except, of course, from me.' Then pounced and proceeded to devour her on the spot and they rolled once more on the rug in laughing ecstasy.

38

*S*he's been up to her old tricks again, the filthy disgusting whore, and this time I caught her at it in flagrante. They didn't see me but I saw them, behaving like depraved animals on the floor. I forced myself to witness every detail even though I was sickened to my stomach. How she can look me in the eye I just don't know, but the slattern appears to have no shame. The face of an angel but the morals of an alley cat, it is definitely long overdue that she was spayed.

I despise myself for loving her so much and also I now despise her. She deserves no more mercy for this aberrational behaviour for now she has really gone too far. She's corrupted, defiled, an untouchable. I have no other choice left to me now but to destroy her.

But first I will give her a chance to atone and prepare herself properly to meet her Maker. That's only fair and, besides.

I still love her.

39

'Susie, hi! C'est moi. Yes, I know it's been far too long but that's how it goes. I've been weighed down with work just lately and still have the bloody accounts to finalise before the finish of the tax year. And now Easter is looming and I've suddenly got the chance of a short break abroad. Lucky me. Just a few days in the Caribbean, you know how I love the sun. Here's why I'm ringing. I wondered if you'd care to do me a big favour . . .'

It wasn't that she really needed anyone there, the house was adequately protected with an alarm system and window-locks. It was just that Jinx preferred to play safe while also doing an old mate a good turn. She hadn't seen Susie Chandler in an age and this would be an excellent chance to catch up. She was feeling so wound up, could use the wise counsel of a trusted friend, preferably one not part of her regular everyday life. Also Susie was so non-competitive there was no chance of there being any sort of hidden agenda. They could have a girlie evening together and trade their most intimate secrets, then Susie could wallow in the London museums and galleries while Jinx jetted off to the sun. Not a word to the folks in the office, mind. She'd not hear the end of it otherwise. All her woebegone talk of impending tax dates while in reality she'd be skiving off. It made her feel deliciously wanton and devil-may-care. Quite like old times, in fact. All the old *joie de vivre* had returned in full strength since the knockout events of the past few days. She still didn't know if she was dreaming it all, was scared lest she suddenly awoke.

Susie, like most people where Jinx was concerned, was as docile and amenable as a lamb, glad of an excuse to take in some metropolitan culture, relieved at the prospect of escaping all those aunts. Besides, there was still the Monet she wanted to see if the holiday crowds were not too prohibitive. But probably at Easter the city would be deserted. She said she'd arrive early on Thursday evening which would give them both time for a good old gas while Jinx did her laundry and sorted out what to take.

The phone had been working overtime, the machine perpetually on the blink.

'Jinx, my darling, Hamish here. It's slightly short notice, I know, but I wondered what you are doing over Easter. Care to pop down for the long weekend and help an old codger get over his cabin fever? I'm just finishing correcting my latest set of galleys and feel like kicking up my heels a bit. All those lonely hours stuck at the computer make a chap feel quite out of touch, y'know. Well, you probably don't since you're always on the gad but a spot of country air might do you good. Give me a buzz, anyhow, if you find you have a minute. Otherwise, it'll have to be fishing with the boys. Hope to be hearing from you soon. Lots of love.'

Dear Hamish and she really had meant to call him. Just got carried away lately with everything else and not quite certain what to tell him anyhow. Of all her friends, Hamish had to be among the most stalwart. Only Ambrose had a closer acquaintance with what went on in her heart. They'd been a bit of an item on and off for ten years now and there'd occasionally been moments when she'd almost fancied she might be able to love him. But he was a little too easy-going for her taste, funny and attractive but not sufficiently focused. A laid-back writer who liked to fish; great for the occasional country weekend but not, to her mind at least, for life. Jinx scribbled down his message and promised herself that she really would call him back. Just not now.

'Jinx, where the hell are you when I need you? It's Veronica. Richard and I have been talking and thought we might have a drinks party here on Easter Day. Any chance of luring you along? Don't suppose so since you're always so busy but the invitation's there, just in case. The girls would love to see you anyhow. Your god-daughter's getting quite grownup. And if you could stay on a couple of days, we might fit in some tennis too. Anyhow, bring your racquet and we'll see how things pan out. Can't wait to see you. There's so much to tell. Bye now.'

Oh Lord, Veronica, traditionally her best friend. Loyal and caring, perpetually unchanging; the closest to unconditional love she'd ever found. Considering what a brick she'd always been, Jinx was aware how shabbily she treated her, using the comfortable house in Bristol if ever she needed a refuge from an over-assiduous admirer or simply to chill out. While ignoring her for months on end when life was too glamorous or too hectic to spare a thought for valued friends. Veronica was the sister she'd never had, raised from the same roots with identical references and values. Although their lifestyles differed so radically, Jinx relied upon her down-to-earth good sense to put her straight when she felt the need. To applaud her successes, too.

She would ring her straight back only she didn't really want to. There were things she'd only end up blurting out that, right now, no one should know. Best to leave Veronica until after she got back, just send her a tantalising postcard in the meantime. V would be mad with curiosity but she'd also be the first to hear the unbowdlerised version when Jinx was finally permitted to spill the beans. They had shared so much since their boarding-school days that she could hardly leave her long in the dark when her life had taken such a dizzying turn. 'V' she wrote under her scrawl about Hamish. Then, for emphasis, underlined it a couple of times.

'Hi, doll. Whaddya doin'? There's a Jinx-shaped hole right here in my heart and I aim at filling it pretty soon. Sooner rather than later, please. I miss your smile . . .'

She grinned and erased it. Joel the barman, bless his heart. What a pal he'd been on a couple of stressful occasions. Fun in the good times, too. She would never forget him or cease being grateful but now was most definitely not the time. Nor, she devoutly hoped, ever again. Life was changing fundamentally. She would look him up when things were properly sorted and hope he'd accept her explanation. Even be glad for her new happiness. He'd not hold it against her, of that she was certain, they had after all, only ever been pals. Both playing the field, independent and uncommitted. Two free spirits travelling solo.

'It's me!' That high-pitched warble could be one person only. Myrtle Hobday, as she lived and breathed, on the hunt like a truffle-hound for a free meal. *'I'm shopping in the high street and will be coming back your way. Thought I'd drop in for a chinwag. It's been ages since I saw you. Round about six?'*

Luckily she'd just missed her. Jinx wiped the message and moved on. Myrtle was all right for the occasional spot of gossip; meant no harm, she was certain of it, just never knew when to let go. And any genuine friendship they might once have shared had been over these past several years. None of her real friends could abide the sickening Myrtle, even saintly Dottie found her arch and insincere. Always on the lookout for what pickings she could scrounge, a pathetic scavenger of other people's lives though you'd not have guessed it from her attitude. The intriguing thing about Myrtle, with her prominent teeth and receding chin, was her blatant confidence in her own attractiveness. She positively strutted and bragged of the men she'd ensnared. Others might find this assumption grotesque. Jinx only thought her rather brave.

'Jinx. It's Norman. Pick up if you're there.' A pause while he waited, his usual imperative self, then a bah of impatience when he realised she wasn't going to. *'I've got to be in Liverpool over the Easter weekend. Granada want me to chair a discussion on crime and punishment, would you believe. Well, I wondered if you'd like some days away. There's a nice little country hotel that I know, off the beaten track and entirely discreet, where we could hole up for some R and R before the big debate. What say you? I'll call again in a day or two but can't leave it too long as I'll need to make arrangements.'*

With his wife, no doubt, the long-suffering Vera who must either be blind or preferred it that way. Jinx was beginning to realise that married to Norman it might be some relief if he *did* stray. She felt ashamed that she'd lowered her standards so far and promised herself never to speak to him again. She would drop him a line only that would be somewhat incriminatory. Never put anything in writing when you're playing away. She didn't add him to her list, simply erased the message. The less she thought of Norman right now, the better she'd enjoy the sunshine break. She was only glad no one else had access to her messages. It was bad enough that she'd done it at all, far worse if anyone were to know.

There were various other messages, one cold-calling about a dream kitchen, a couple of invitations to Easter drinks, and Damien sounding positively rattled. What now? Jinx heaved a sigh and her hand hovered over the phone while she made the truly adult decision not to return his call. Why should she perpetually be on duty night and day? Tomorrow was Maundy Thursday and tonight she had a date. Whatever was bothering the self-involved hysteric could almost certainly wait. And since he was safely in Jersey right now, he'd not come sniffing around the office and discover she wasn't there. Lately his paranoia had become so suffocating she thought twice about calling him at all. These days all he looked for were invisible slights. The person she least envied was poor Janey.

The rest of the messages were seven silent hangups. Goosebumps developed down Jinx's spine but she was feeling so euphoric she actually didn't care. She really had to change; Julius would shortly be here. He was taking her for dinner at the Ivy as a private celebration of the announcement they soon hoped to make. She whirled upstairs in a frenzy of excitement, leaving everything else on hold.

It had become an office tradition since the year they first set up shop to celebrate major holidays as a group. Sometimes they roped in a couple of outside guests but it was usually just the five of them alone. They tried out different local eateries and Jinx always footed the bill. They were an excellent team who worked hard all year. She felt it was the least she could do. This year Sam was included too and they'd chosen the Chinese restaurant in the high street. They would clear the decks for Easter before setting out, then close the office till the following Tuesday.

They sat round a huge round table and Jinx chose the menu for the lot of them. Chinese food was always a source of conflict; it was best when one person took control. The seaweed and bang bang chicken arrived, along with fizzy water and a couple of bottles of wine. Ambrose was late joining them since he'd been caught up on the phone, and when he did arrive he had Damien in tow. A nervy, dissatisfied Damien, wild-eyed, in one of his new smart suits. Inwardly groaning, they made room for him and he pulled up a chair next to Jinx.

'I called you last night to say I was in town,' he said accusingly. 'Did you not get my message?' She thought very fast then looked him straight in the eye and unblinkingly told a blatant lie.

324

'Sorry, I didn't get round to checking the machine. How wonderful to see you. I thought you were home in Jersey.'

Only slightly mollified, he ordered himself a whisky then told her that he'd had to come because there were things on his mind. *Thanks, Ambrose,* she signalled across the table but he, for once, had his attention fixed elsewhere and failed to acknowledge the sign. So now they were stuck with this dreary, ungrateful man and all scurrilous conversation would have to cease. It wasn't fair. While the crispy duck was being served Jinx decided it was time to grasp the nettle. Else it would just hang over them like Damien's mood and ruin their celebration.

'What's on your mind?'

'I can't help worrying about security,' said Damien twitchily. 'I'm scared it will all get out before it is finally wrapped. Before we have even come up with a suitable title.' *Doom* had been brilliant and *Final Fantasy VIII*. They needed something even better. Sometimes the hardest details were the final touches like that. The disc was now into its Beta III phase. He was right, they hadn't a lot of time. But his uninvited presence at their feast was still an unwarranted imposition. They were supposed to be relaxing together and having some end-of-term fun.

'That's just not possible,' Jinx reassured him quietly. 'Nobody outside our office has access to it.' She was suddenly aware of Serafina's beady attention and lowered her voice accordingly in order to shut her out.

'But what about this guy from New York? Julius Fucking Weinberg? Ambrose has just reminded me what a jerk he is.'

Thanks again, Ambrose, said Jinx grimly to herself. *Now smart talk your way out of this one.* Patiently and with supreme tact, she set about comforting her agitated client who seemed, if it were possible, even nuttier than before. The solitary life he lived in Jersey was clearly having an adverse effect. What she would advise him, if just for sanity's sake, would be to ignore the taxman's demands and return to the city for a more normal existence. Only then they would have him constantly underfoot and that would almost certainly be worse. Slowly, slowly Damien began to relax and even joined grudgingly in the laughter. She had always possessed the right soothing touch but the whisky was helping as well.

'How's Janey?' she asked brightly when she sensed the crisis was over, but Damien just stared glassily at her and grunted something unintelligible. Poor Janey, it couldn't be much of a life. Was all that fame and money really worth it?

'Where are you going for your holiday this year? Somewhere exotic like last time?' She felt a bit guilty, aware of her own deception, but Damien had forfeited the honesty of real friendship the day he started assuming all these airs. He muttered inaudibly and lit a cigarette, then crossed and re-crossed his legs. Something was still bothering him but he appeared not to want to share it. Well, that was entirely up to him. Now perhaps she could begin to enjoy her meal. She grinned across at Sam who was watching her closely and reminded herself, with a shiver of delight, what joys awaited her next week.

She banged on the table for silence. She had ordered champagne which was now being served, and raised her glass gaily in a toast.

'Here's to the lot of you for being such excellent troopers and making this already a memorable year.' She turned to Damien and lightly kissed his cheek. He flushed with sheer pleasure and gauchely rubbed the spot. Once a nerd, always one was Wayne's contemptuous verdict as he sat discussing chess moves with his mentor.

'With a special thanks to you,' she said, hating herself for her insincerity. 'Without your brilliant concept we'd be nowhere.' It hurt a bit to have to say that but she knew it was expected so bit the bullet. And anything that mollified Damien should help keep him off their necks. Compromise, Jinx had discovered years ago, was very much the name of this game. She winked at

Ambrose as she clinked her glass but he was busy with Wayne and didn't see.

Susie would be arriving shortly and Jinx still had a mass of things to do. It was hard keeping silent throughout this festive meal, she was bursting to tell someone about her new-found happiness. But she'd tell them everything as soon as it could be revealed and meanwhile had good old Susie to confide in. Jinx smiled fondly as she pictured her friend's rural home, sepia and samey in that sleepy Somerset village. What a sadly restricted life for such a wonderful person. At least she would have London to spice things up for a while. She was heartily glad now that she'd rung her and suggested it. While Jinx was off on a bender of her own, this might very well mark a turning-point in Susie's life too.

Serafina was seriously rattled as she listened to Damien's complaint and scared by the reason for his sudden outburst. Could it be that word had reached him of the security leak to Sega? She had trusted Julius when she'd spied for him but now was fast losing confidence. She had managed to slip the disc back into the safe when the messenger had returned it on Monday morning. But why should Julius have any loyalty to her after the devastating way he had rebuffed her? Seriously smarting from her damaged pride, she was scarlet inside from shame and fury. Mikey Rossetti, for all his bumbling faults, had always been there for her at all times. She was used to getting her way in all things and felt furious at Julius's rejection. She glared round the table with her big translucent eyes in search of a suitable target for retribution.

Part Four

40

H al Burton stood morosely at his office window, watching the sluggish traffic in the Earl's Court Road. Behind him on the desk were a couple of open files, the total evidence of his fruitless hunt for Susie Chandler's killer. It seemed inconceivable after such hard work that he was still no closer to the truth. But today Susie occupied only a corner of his brain. He was tired of running the suspects through his head, a meaningless exercise that threw up no new clues. He dwelt for a second on the crazy Serafina and her startling suggestion that the murderer might be Jinx. He'd dismissed it out of hand and not properly checked it out, which meant he was allowing exhaustion to cloud his judgement. But suppose there had been some secret between the two of them, a long-running feud perhaps from their office-sharing days. With a slow-burning fuse that had culminated in the killing. After all the years he had been in the force, he knew that nothing should ever be ruled out. And despite the obvious malice underlying the suggestion, Serafina could not be simply disregarded as a fool.

Anything was possible, he'd seen many and stranger things. It was his job to uncover the truth and quickly.

'I'm going out,' he said to Trudy, poking his nose round her door. She, too, was engulfed in a morass of meaningless paper, desperately trying to create some order from it all. She glanced at him sharply and noticed the furrowed brow. He was taking it all too seriously. She was beginning to fear for his health.

'Do you want me to join you?' She could do with a chance to stretch her legs, all this paperwork was giving her a headache. Hal shook his head. Lately he had become withdrawn and despondent, she seemed not to be able to get through to him any more. Which was bad. As a team they had always worked brilliantly, bouncing ideas off each other. This sudden lack of communication was starting to get her down.

'When will you be back?' He shrugged. It was already almost the end of the afternoon. Who knew where his peregrinations might take him?

'And what will I tell the Superintendent, should he ask?'

'Just that I'm out doing my job.'

Jinx, alone on her patio, was attempting to relax with a book, all the while straining like some lovelorn teenager to hear if the telephone should ring. It was pathetic. He'd only been gone just a couple of days yet the deprivation of even his voice was tearing her viscerally apart. She was growing to rely on him to a terrifying extent. She had never imagined that love could be like this, a churning, tumultuous, seasick sort of feeling that kept all her nerve-endings jangling. Talk about the hurly-burly of the chaise-longue. While things remained unsettled she'd continue to feel this way, but there was also an underlying contentment deep within her, confidence in his power to make it all come right in the end. It made her feel warm and comfortable inside.

He had gone to California to talk to his wife and there'd been ominous silence ever since. His attempt to catch up with Pia in

New York had failed because of her impossible schedule. And it wasn't something, as Jinx understood, to be broached in a telephone call.

'As soon as there's news, I will call you,' he had promised and she knew it was unreasonable to expect to hear from him yet. An eleven-year marriage could not be dissolved overnight, especially when the partners remained fond of each other. There would be explanations and things to discuss, regrets to be stated, apologies to be made. She would just have to curb her natural impatience and try to stay calm till he called. But supposing Pia were to prevail after all and refuse to allow him to leave her? Didn't want to end the marriage, suggested they give it another try? That was only reasonable and there'd be nothing Jinx could do. And Pia was so beautiful, sweet-natured as well as good. Not even Julius had a word to say against her, so how could he even think of letting her go? She was gradually growing maudlin and that wouldn't do at all, not when everything else in her life was suddenly looking so good. She must learn to trust him and allow him to fix things his way. That was what love was really about, respect and good faith on both sides. If they cared enough it was worth the wait. They had the rest of eternity together.

It was certainly peaceful out here in the privacy of the patio with only the murmur of Peggy and Arthur to disturb the early evening lull. They were gardening next door, as they did most nights, and had already popped their heads over the trellis to ask if she'd care to join them for a sherry. Jinx had declined with the excuse that she was waiting for a call, but felt calm and safe knowing they were just the other side of the wall. As neighbours went, they were as harmonious as any and on the whole kept themselves to themselves. Now that the police inquiry had apparently gone away, life in the quiet cul-de-sac had returned to its customary order, and the soothing aroma of Arthur's pipe-smoke simply added to her feeling of well-being.

She stretched and went inside for a glass of wine while starting to have thoughts about her supper.

Hal's frustrated wanderings had brought him eventually to The Devonshire Arms where he was dejectedly downing a beer with a whisky chaser. The night was fine and the atmosphere so mild that he carried both glasses out into the garden. Here flocks of bright young things were gathered together like starlings, the twittering of their massed voices a counterpoint to the hum of the Cromwell Road. He perched on the wall and stared down Stratford Road where, a few yards up, the cul-de-sac opened and curved round to Jinx's front door. He wondered if she were at home tonight and, if so, if anyone was with her. And then he remembered Serafina's insinuation that there might be someone new in her life. He gulped his beer.

He thought of going round there but was reluctant to be caught snooping beyond the call of duty. He really ought to be thinking of heading home. And catching up on some of the sleep he had lost in the weeks since this nightmare began. Yet still he lingered, reluctant to tear himself away. The wall that divided the houses from the pub was low enough to afford easy access to any person even halfway fit. And that open door was like a beckoning finger to a bold intruder with burglary, or worse, on his mind. Hal shook his head to break the grim train of his thoughts and went inside to the bar for that extra drink. He had done what he could to protect her, now it was time to let go and hope Jinx would stay alert and remember his warning. She was, after all, a mature and intelligent woman who had run a successful business all these years. If someone was still out there stalking her, she would have to learn how to cope alone. His part was almost finished; he would soon be moving on to another case.

Having watched the news and her favourite soap over a bowl of pasta with broccoli and parmesan, Jinx cleared the dishes then returned to her book, no longer on edge for the phone. One thing she was learning about Julius these days was that he loved her enough to be trusted. And however he might have behaved in the past, he was a man she knew now would keep his word. She softened as she thought of his flight to the Coast, to the woman he had married in good faith. What stronger proof of his love could she ask than this willingness to end a workable marriage? She hoped it might also bring renewed happiness for Pia, that they'd manage to remain friends, which was what Julius really wanted. Jinx was a woman who had never experienced jealousy and now her heart went out to the wronged wife whom she truthfully didn't wish to hurt. If only things could be that simple they could all live happily ever after with clear consciences.

It was getting too dark to go on reading outside so she shifted into the dining-room but left the doors ajar. It looked like being another hot, dry summer. On nights like this she was glad that she had the patio. Though not a gardener, she was an ardent sun-worshipper and her idea of heaven was a deckchair and a book. It was good to have somewhere secluded to laze. She stretched out on the sofa near the window, deep in the latest Anne Tyler. The filmy white curtains stirred restlessly in the breeze and she could see the lights from the nearby pub whenever she raised her eyes. Summer in the city was something she'd always loved. The noise, the bustle, the pulsating excitement, better by far than any country retreat. Her thoughts flicked back to poor Susie who had loved to escape up here. What a horrible and undeserved end to her orderly life. Jinx still blamed herself for having invited her in the first place and hoped she hadn't suffered too much. Which was pretty ridiculous considering her terrible injuries. She shuddered and felt those goose-pimples again. Whoever was making those endless silent phone-calls had to be relentlessly driven. Serafina had been plagued with them too, only her caller had actually spoken. Well, the behaviour pattern fitted nobody she knew. She was totally confident of that. If only Julius would ring and end this tension. The Daweses were making going to bed noises next door. It was already getting quite late. But the book was engrossing and she was too strung up to feel tired. She would read for maybe another hour.

The later it got, the quieter it grew and the noise from the pub became less intrusive. Car doors slammed and voices called goodnight. The buzz of the street began to fade. Soon they'd be closing and peace would be restored. She wondered what Julius was doing right now and how things were going with his quest. If it was eleven o'clock in London, it was still only three in California. He'd be out to lunch most probably, possibly even with Pia. Her heart beat faster as she imagined what might be going on. He was staying at the Bel Air Hotel and had left her the number just in case. She thought about calling him, just to hear his voice, then decided to leave things alone. She was still slightly cautious about initiating calls to him, and it was none of her business what went on between them as long as the outcome came out right. Her stomach churned with excitement and dread. She loved him so intensely that it hurt.

She returned her attention to the elegance of Anne Tyler, a writer whose books she had always admired. She flicked through to the end to see how far she still had to go and decided to finish it in one sitting. Only then would she think about bed, there was no rush. She might even call Julius after all, to find out if anything had happened. But she'd leave it awhile; there was absolutely no hurry, the time difference being in her favour.

Suddenly she stopped her reading and sat up straight, alerted to faint movements on the patio. She could be imagining it, there was a slight breeze, but she thought she could just detect the soft pad of stealthy footsteps. The doors were still wide open so she put down her book and stepped outside where the sky was radiant with stars. Everything was still, no sign of any intruder, not even a cat or hedgehog on the prowl. Her imagination must be working overtime. After all Hal's warnings and the details of Susie's murder, his anxiety was obviously beginning to sink in.

She returned to her book after closing the French doors and bolting them securely as directed. She let the curtains fall back into place to shield her from the scrutiny of any intrusive eyes. She must get a grip and not get spooked about the house. She had recovered, just, from the original trauma but could never continue to live here alone if she started imagining she heard things. This was a safe and affluent area. She had neighbours sleeping just through the wall. Poor Susie's murder had been a one in a million occurrence; the law of averages surely prevented it happening again. She returned to her book with a resolute spirit, telling herself firmly not to be a fool.

But now that her antennae had been alerted, she couldn't help listening for more sounds. She found it hard to settle so decided instead to make that call. With any luck, he'd be back at the hotel by now with time on his hands for a leisurely chat. For once in his life he had a completely clear diary so would doubtless be pleased at the diversion. And she had the right, after all that had been said, to call whenever she felt the need. She used the phone in the living-room where light slotted in from the streetlamp. At the front of the house, the cul-de-sac was deserted with no sign of life from the neighbouring houses. They were a clean-living bunch, reserved and unobtrusive, who went to bed early and kept their noses clean. For which she had always been thankful.

The Bel Air receptionist had a pleasant, efficient voice and put Jinx briefly on hold. Then she came back and told her that Julius had checked out. Early the night before as it so happened.

'Did he say where he was going?' Jinx's voice was sharp with alarm. Where was he just when she needed him most, and why hadn't he let her know?

'No, ma'am,' said the operator blandly before disconnecting abruptly.

Jinx paced the floor, feeling sudden huge anxiety, wondering what he was doing now and why he hadn't called. If the news had been good he would surely want to tell her. She hoped he wasn't having problems with Pia, or perhaps they'd gone off somewhere together. That was the worst scenario she could think of; she tried to block it from her mind. He had let her down badly a couple of times, she prayed he wasn't doing it again. But this was no way to have faith in her lover. She pulled herself together and returned to her book. It was losing its magical hold but there were only twenty pages still to go. So she poured herself a fortifying glass of wine and settled back determinedly to finish it.

Something suddenly moved at the periphery of her vision and a looming shadow fell across the page. She screamed in terror and sprang agitatedly from the sofa, kicking her glass of wine all over the carpet. Through the obscuring curtain she could just make out a shape. Someone was definitely out there, peering in. It wasn't just the work of her fevered imagination. She could even hear his breathing as he moved furtively about and hoped that he couldn't see her through the curtain. She leaned across and snapped off the lamp then backed against the wall in protective darkness. Lit by the night she could see his shape now quite clearly as he groped along as though seeking to find a way in. The outside door-handle was cautiously tested and Jinx suppressed another scream of terror as she frantically tried to remember if she had locked it.

When it didn't give, her breathing subsided a little and she realised she'd feel a whole lot safer close to a phone. Cautiously in the darkness, she edged her way across the room, hoping her careful movements would not be detected. But he must now know she was in there, had heard her scream and seen the light switched off, so why hadn't obvious occupancy scared him away? The answer was too terrifying even to contemplate and she made a sudden dash for the darkened front room. And then she remembered Hal's card with his direct line. She fished it out of her wallet and dialled it carefully in the light from the streetlamp, praying that he would answer and come over as fast as he could. She had been a fool to ignore his warning, she saw that quite clearly now. Susie's murderer had returned to finish the job just as Hal had always predicted.

But Hal's private number just rang and rang. It was way after hours, he had doubtless long gone home. She considered trying the main police switchboard but hated to be seen as a silly, hysterical woman. By the time they arrived, the intruder would be gone and she'd end up simply looking like a fool. She was safe here inside, for the doors were locked and bolted and the movements on the patio had been furtive. It was probably nothing worse than some stray fuddled drunk who'd wandered in accidentally from the pub. With all the noise she'd made perhaps she'd scared him off. She fervently wished she could believe that.

Softly and now shoeless Jinx tiptoed through her home, listening intently for any further sounds. But all was still. So she ventured back into the dining-room and even dared move the curtain to see if she could spot anyone outside. The patio was deserted; whoever it was appeared to be gone. She was on the verge of unbolting the door in order to take a proper look when the doorbell rang shrilly and urgently and she almost dropped dead from a coronary. Painfully aware of her hammering heart, she returned to the hall and stood there trembling, uncertain now what to do. The bell rang again and the letterbox moved. Whoever it was was insistent. She dropped to her knees and inched along the floor until she could get a glimpse through the letter flap.

The person outside was standing too close for her to be able to make out any details. But then the figure moved back a little to survey the upstairs windows and the face came suddenly into her line of vision. Jinx cried out again but this time with relief. What a stupid, neurotic fool she'd been, losing her cool in that way. Just as well she hadn't bothered the police. It was all so absurd, it was laughable. It showed how much she'd been living on her nerves, how the horrible murder had unhinged her.

'Coming!' she called out gaily as she fumbled with the locks, desperate now that her visitor shouldn't leave.

'I can't believe it's actually you!' she cried as she flung her arms about him. 'You gave me such a horrible fright, I was practically wetting myself! How lovely to see you. Please, come in. Have I got a story for you!'

41

They travelled together on the night bus back to Battersea, sitting up at the front on top like kids. Ambrose explained that he'd been working very late and had dropped by on the off chance that she'd be there.

'And aren't I glad you did,' said Jinx wholeheartedly, snuggling close to him. 'I can't remember ever having been that frightened.' She smiled up at him trustingly, secure in the warm approval of his eyes. Ambrose was one in a million, probably the best buddy she'd ever had.

'I didn't want to disturb you if you were sleeping but thought I saw the light go off and did a bit of snooping.' He'd been feeling lonely after all that solitary work, had looked her up on the off chance she might feel like playing. They'd had a couple of drinks which had helped to calm her and then he'd suggested, awkwardly, that she spend the night at his flat.

'Or as long as you care to make it,' he'd added. 'There's no point being here alone, scared out of your wits. Certainly not till they've caught that bloody murderer.'

Good old Ambrose, in there like the cavalry. She had always known she could rely on him, that he truly cared about her well-being.

'Are you certain you don't mind?' She also respected his fussy little ways and didn't want to crowd him, but the sight of his dear concerned face had been such a relief. Ambrose smiled benevolently and patted her arm.

'Jinx,' he said solemnly. 'Don't talk rot.'

So she'd thrown a few things in a bag and here they were, giggling together like teenagers out on a lark. She'd be back to normal in the morning, she assured him, once her nerves had had time to recover. Didn't know what had got into her, just something the policeman had said. And the minute Julius made contact and she knew for certain how things were, she'd be right as rain again as well as fully functional. Though she wasn't risking telling Ambrose that. For the time being it had to remain her cherished secret but she hoped he'd share her joy once allowed to know. After all the years of solid friendship they had shared he must surely have only her best interests at heart. And if that meant ending his ridiculous feud with Julius, it would surely be to everyone's benefit. Or so Jinx, fondly deluded by love, optimistically hoped.

Ambrose suggested a final drink before they turned in so she followed him into the kitchen while he opened a bottle. Champagne on ice, that was thoughtful and extravagant. Unusual for a bachelor like Ambrose to be so well prepared. It was years since Jinx had last been to this flat and she looked around with mild interest to see what alterations he had made. Nothing appeared to have changed at all except for more books and general clutter, but clean – she could see that at a single glance – with the surfaces scrubbed and his dishcloth soaking in bleach. There was a smaller, fancier computer on the table alongside a chess-board all set up. One of his interminable games with Wayne. She went over to study the pieces but couldn't work out the moves.

'Still playing phone chess? It must be as addictive as sex.'

Ambrose smiled slightly and handed her a glass. He studied the board thoughtfully then tentatively moved his bishop. He'd have to remember to tell Wayne in the morning. It was a devious move but he thought it might just work. Fool the lad into daring to shift his queen.

Jinx was beginning to flag. It was getting very late and she'd been through a lot of strain. And tomorrow was another working day so she'd like to be at her best. She looked around for the guest room and Ambrose directed her down the hall.

'Last door on the left,' he said. 'Bathroom's right beside it. I'll go and get you some towels.'

The room was immaculate, with clean linen sheets, carefully tucked in with hospital corners and covered by a faded patchwork quilt. It was sparsely furnished with an old-fashioned dressing-table topped by a hand-embroidered cloth. The window was firmly shut, the curtains closed, with a pervading scent of mixed lavender and dust. Jinx felt she'd taken a step back in time, that no one had disturbed this room in ages. She had always understood that Ambrose used it as a study, yet there was no sign at all of books or papers. He couldn't have tidied it specially for her since he'd had no idea that she'd be coming. Three of the walls were bare, apart from one ornate picture, hanging over the dressing-table with a string of black beads looped over the frame.

The fourth wall was covered by an aggregation of photos pinned haphazardly on cork, so densely packed that they overlapped like a collage of massed humanity. Curious, Jinx stepped over to take a look, then stopped in her tracks in surprise. There were pictures here going back twenty years to their first days at LCP. Group shots of hundreds of students she'd known and later of colleagues at Weinbergs. She recalled Ambrose once had an interest in photography but hadn't been aware he'd kept it up.

343

She looked even closer with a sudden sharp intake of breath. The pictures all had one thing in common. Every single one of them featured her.

'Ambrose,' she said as he entered the room. 'What on earth are you doing with all this?'

'I like keeping pictures of my friends,' he replied, handing her towels and a folded nightgown. He stood beside her and studied the display, then pointed out one of her old kitchen. 'That was in Islington, decorating your attic. The day we kicked over the paint.' Jinx had luminous red hair at the time and was wearing dungarees and a striped matelot sweater with a splodge of yellow paint on her nose. She looked like a clown, really cute. He studied it fondly.

'I asked you to marry me that night,' he said softly, 'but you never ever gave me an answer.'

She was shocked. She had no recollection of the occasion at all, probably high on grass or booze at the time. It certainly would appear that way from the hilarity of the posers. There were four of them with paint-brushes, all falling about with mirth. That was ages ago, at least a couple of decades. She couldn't believe he remembered it all so well.

'Did you?' she said with a sudden premonition. 'I'm afraid I don't remember that at all.'

She turned to the bed and shook out the folded nightgown, then gasped as she recognised it, one of her own long lost.

'How on earth did you get hold of this?' she asked incredulously. She had certainly never been here before, not to stay overnight. Ambrose didn't answer, just looked a little abashed. He was frowning closely at the collage of pictures, his mind right back there in the past.

'You mislaid it in France,' he told her eventually. 'So I brought it back here for safe-keeping.'

Jinx spun round to stare at him, quite baffled by what he was saying. This wasn't at all like the Ambrose she knew, her close and trusted buddy suddenly playing silly games.

'You still haven't given me an answer,' he muttered, refusing to look her in the eye. Jinx opened her mouth to speak but nothing came out. He couldn't be serious, had got to be having her on. But when he did finally turn to face her, his eyes were fearful and his features strained. He was totally serious without a hint of humour. There was yearning agony etched upon his face.

'I love you,' he said, 'and I think you love me too. Look how well we fit together, what fun we have always had. I've known from the start we'd grow old together, that it was only a question of time.'

Jinx, appalled, trod as tactfully as she could, fearing to damage his feelings if he really meant it. Though it was certainly a bolt out of the blue, she'd had no idea. 'Ambrose, love,' she said, reaching out to hug him. 'Of course I adore you and always will.'

'Then marry me.'

'No. That's out of the question.' She spoke too quickly but knew what she was doing. Damage limitation was what was called for now despite her solemn promise not to tell. 'The thing is, there's somebody else in my life. With whom I am hoping to have a future.' There, it was out but she'd not revealed the name and had no intention of doing so, not yet. But an ugly look crossed Ambrose's face and he stared at her with sudden cold hostility.

'It's that bloody Weinberg, I've always known it. I knew what you were up to right from the start. Well, if I can't have you, he certainly won't.' And without any warning, he slapped her hard across the face, screaming blue obscenities as if possessed.

'Fucking cunt! Filthy whore!' he shouted as he backed from the room and violently slammed the door. She heard a key turning in the lock.

'Hang on a minute! I need to use the bathroom.' She couldn't believe he was acting up in this way. She had never ever seen him in such a state. It couldn't be just the drink.

'There's a pisspot under the bed,' he bellowed. 'You can bloody well stay there till you've come to your senses. Or else you can rot in hell.'

When she heard the key turn and his footsteps moving away, Jinx was so mad she beat furiously on the door. Whatever had happened to Ambrose; he seemed to have finally flipped. Gone was the good-natured St Bernard puppy she had always played with, in its place a demented tiger with a grudge.

'Ambrose!' she commanded him. 'Come back here and let me out.' It couldn't be just an elaborate joke, she had never seen such hatred in his eyes. But the flat remained silent and the door resolutely closed. She realised he must have gone to bed. Bloody hell! She was dying for a pee and would now have to use the pot.

Once she'd sorted herself out and rubbed her hands with a tissue, she went on investigating the room. She was far too agitated and disturbed to think of sleep and damned if she was changing into that faded old nightgown. A nasty nagging suspicion was beginning to formulate in her brain. Ambrose appeared to know all about her and Julius. She wondered how that could be and then she remembered. That Sunday they'd made love with such abandon on the dining-room floor in broad daylight. And they'd both thought they heard a possible prowler on the patio, which Julius, half-dressed, had gone to investigate. So there had been someone out there after all. That would explain Ambrose's suddenly changed mood and what he was so angry about now. He'd always been a softie where she was concerned. She had never ever mentioned it but, if she was honest, had suspected the truth in her heart all these years. She had always believed that their friendship was platonic. Now it would appear she had been wrong.

The picture over the dressing-table was a touched-up portrait of a woman, sweet-faced and cherry-lipped, eyes cast devoutly up to the skies. It had all the primitive mawkishness of an amateur studio sitting and, although undated, must be several decades old. Beneath it, carefully centred, was a gaudy plaster Madonna, and Jinx now realised, with a jolt of surprise, that the beads were in fact a rosary. A miniature altar, complete with a posy of dusty dried flowers. There was something so tacky and saccharin about it, it gave her a powerful feeling of distaste. But then she had never been raised to go to church. Its sentiment was something she abhorred.

Right in the centre of this makeshift altar gleamed a knife with a honed and terrible blade. And propped against it a stiff white envelope which she saw, somewhat startled, was addressed to the DCI. Ever more curious, Jinx fingered both these items, careful to avoid the cruel cutting edge. Something macabre and horrible was unfolding slowly in her brain, a truth so dreadful she feared to confront it at all. There was a strong silent message quite clearly directed at her, a shocking inevitability she ought to have worked out sooner. She swung back to the collage of massed photos and took a more detailed look. And there it was, tucked away in one corner, the snapshot he must have removed from her house. Of herself in sunshine, in a quiet French street, grinning at the camera as she licked an ice-cream. He had always liked that snap, she remembered now. Had studied it smilingly when her film was developed and picked it out when they'd bought the *art nouveau* frame. She had always been touched by the warmth of his enthusiasm and had stuck it among her collection in order to humour him. He was a funny old thing, Ambrose, loyal and sentimental and she'd thought very little about it at the time.

There was nothing further she could do right now except sit back and wait. The night stretched ahead interminably and she greatly feared Ambrose's return. She tried hard to will herself to stay awake by remembering Susie's fate. She had brought a book but reading was definitely out. Until she looked at the envelope again and things continued clicking into place.

*   *   *

'I wonder what can have happened to Jinx,' said Dottie casually, sorting the mail. It wasn't at all like her to be in so late, especially not mid week. Ambrose either.

'Maybe they've run off together,' said Wayne flippantly as he figured out his next chess move, determined to conquer this time round. If Ambrose moved his bishop then he'd really be in trouble. He could only hope that it hadn't occurred; it wasn't an obvious move.

'Why on earth do you say that?' asked Dottie, intrigued.

'Well, it's no secret he's got a huge crush on her. Plain as the nose on his face.'

Out of the mouths of babes, thought Dottie, quietly satisfied. So she wasn't the only one to have observed they went well together. Wayne had grown close to Ambrose lately and not much escaped his eagle eye. Wait till she got home and told Sam. It was a minor victory but very possibly what had been making Jinx so bright and chirpy just recently. After all the turmoil they had just been through, a happy ending might be nice and well deserved. And if anything good were to come from poor Susie's death, it might be this unexpected bringing together of two friends. Though it still wasn't at all like Jinx not to be in touch. She was always first in in the mornings.

'Perhaps I'll just give her a ring,' she said. 'Check that nothing's wrong.' Since the recent trauma, you couldn't be too careful. They still hadn't caught the murderer.

'No point,' said Serafina snappishly, who'd been out of sorts for some days though they didn't know why. *Now* what was bugging her, with a face like vinegar? She went up and down like a yo-yo. Wayne caught Dottie's eye with a grin of delighted glee and for once she found herself reciprocating though she tried so hard not to take sides.

'Why's that?'

'If she were there, she'd call in. That's obvious. So as she hasn't, she isn't.'

'Unless she's dead,' said Wayne callously, moving a pawn.

'Then she wouldn't be able to answer. It would just be a wasted call.'

Dottie hated it when they started getting ghoulish but it was a routine they played out most days. All of it in the very worst taste or was she simply getting old?

'Maybe I'll leave it, then,' she decided doubtfully. 'At least until later in the day.' She couldn't have Jinx thinking she was always on to her case, snooping into her private life uninvited. And since that unscheduled bolt to the sun, she clearly had secrets she didn't want divulged. Well, good for her, thought Dottie valiantly. It was certainly more than overdue.

The phone rang again but this time Wayne got there first. 'It's for you, Serafina,' he said with a grin, giving Dottie a triumphant secret wink. The voice was young and uncertain and there was static on the line. And from the transformation on Serafina's face, it was clear that the news must be good.

'Silly boy,' she was muttering as she concluded the call, but a spot of colour had returned to each cheek. He might not come top of her current wish list but would do for the time being till she was ready to move on. And the title would certainly come in handy one day. She could do useful things with that once Mummy and Daddy finally bit the dust.

The letter directed to Hal Burton in Ambrose's elegant script was rambling but also to the point. He wanted to confess to two murders, he said, as well as explain his own suicide. He was sorry about Susie, which had been a mistake. He hadn't known she was staying there or that Jinx had gone away. And the room had been dark and he'd caught her unawares. He had only learned the truth with the rest of the world.

Please convey my deep sympathy to her family. She'd been a good kid when she worked at Weinbergs, he just hadn't known her all that well. But some things had to be done whatever the cost and Susie had got in the way. Which brought him to the second murder, that he knew in his heart was ordained. The whole of his life, he saw now very clearly, had been leading inevitably to this act. He had loved Jinx McLennan sincerely and single-mindedly from the very first moment their paths first crossed at college. One look had been all it took, that simple. She had simply given him that mischievous grin and his path had been set from then on.

There were at least ten careful handwritten pages, which Jinx read transfixed, leading to the main thrust of the message. Rather than be separated, he would see that they died together and so spend the whole of eternity as one. *I have no regrets*, he ended up. *What was meant shall now be fulfilled. I only wish that my mother could have known her, but we'll soon be reunited in heaven as a trinity.*

She sat there quite motionless, aware of her heart's rapid beating, and reviewed her whole relationship with Ambrose over the years. She was shocked she could have been so unobservant. Maybe she had allowed him to get a little too close but she'd only ever viewed him as just a friend. A big, reliable, brotherly best mate, the sort that every girl ideally should have. They had been through so much together, right from the start, that she couldn't now imagine life without him. Until she'd found romantic love with a man she hoped to marry and Ambrose appeared to have got it all horribly wrong. There was not and never had been anything even remotely sexual between them, certainly never on her side. He had managed to get his wires badly crossed and now even had her blaming herself. What she had always viewed as purely platonic, for him had become a festering sore, leading at last to this terrible crescendo of revenge. His thinking was suddenly terrifyingly clear. How could she have been so blind?

The window was firmly fixed with a burglar lock and, in any case, the drop was a sheer five floors. She couldn't see the ground from where she was standing but it was into an alley with spiked railings underneath. Not to be risked by even the most intrepid cat burglar but there was no other way she could see that she might escape. By the time she'd paced the room a bit and managed to get control of her frenzied breathing, the morning light was palely seeping in. Soon her deranged jailer was likely to reappear and she'd need all her wits about her for he was clearly now out of his mind.

It was hard to believe that a man so docile could transform himself into an animal just like that. He had always resented Julius, had never made any secret of that, and had apparently also been harbouring these feelings for her all this time. *If I can't have you, he certainly won't.* Those were the words that struck the most horror into her heart. She had heard the agonised threat in his cry and knew he was in deadly earnest. Right then she heard movement and the click of the bathroom door and looked round wildly for some possible means of protection. As the cistern flushed, Jinx selected her weapon and took up her position behind the door.

By late afternoon, Dottie made her decision; it was finally time to act. They had tried the numbers of both Jinx and Ambrose but her machine was constantly on while his just kept ringing.

'We could go round there,' said Dottie but what was the point? If she wasn't picking up then she probably wasn't there and it wasn't their business to interfere. Yet two normally rational people had disappeared and her conscience couldn't leave it like that. Not when it was Jinx and in view of the recent murder. Fear was beginning to make her feel quite breathless.

'I think,' she said, 'I'll just call the police.' Echoing, albeit unknowingly, Jinx's neighbour, Peggy Dawes at the sorry start of the whole wretched business.

42

'Think!' barked Hal, on the verge of losing control. 'You must have some idea where he might have taken her?' Trudy looked on in consternation. She'd not seen him so close to losing it before. He was totally antagonised by Wayne's impassive stare, hated the faggy bright yellow hair, the earring and the tattoo. He should try joining the police, he thought grimly. That way he'd find out what real life was like. Not that they'd ever accept him in the force.

Entirely unperturbed, Wayne sat silently considering, unmoved by all the noise and macho bluster. The cop was a bonehead to believe there was danger from Ambrose. He idolised Jinx, always had. They had been round to her house and found everything in order, doors locked, windows firmly closed, no sign at all of any reason for alarm. Lights turned off and the answering-machine on, the dishwasher neatly stacked. They had even rung the bell of number 9 and Peggy popped out, eyes like saucers. No, she told them when she understood their concern, she'd not seen a sign of Jinx all day.

'Mind you,' she said, 'she was certainly there last night. Sat reading out on the patio till it was dark.'

'You're sure of that?'

'Absolutely. We chatted a bit and asked her in for a drink.' Suddenly alarmed, she said she hoped there was nothing wrong, and Trudy quickly reassured her by explaining this was purely routine.

'Can't be too careful,' she said at her most mollifying. Especially till the murderer is caught.

'The knight,' said Wayne thoughtfully, slowly coming to life. 'One step forward and a jump to the side. Protecting his queen against all peril.'

Hal just stared at him in irritation but Trudy instantly grasped his point. She knew about the chess-games, Dottie had filled her in. And also that this young man was far smarter than he looked and would doubtless come up with the lead that they were after. If only Hal would not be so aggressively impatient.

'You tried his flat?' asked Wayne, which seemed obvious, and Hal just nodded and gave a dismissive shrug. Of course they had been round there the second they'd had the call and found that his phone just went on ringing. But there'd been no response to the outside bell nor anyone about, the building a grim and silent fortress. And now Hal was growing seriously worried.

'And she's never done this before?' he asked Dottie. 'Gone awol without any warning?'

Just the one time, but she wasn't going to raise that now. Too much muddy water to be disturbed. 'Not with Ambrose,' she said.

'There is just one thing,' said Wayne eventually and told them about the conversation he'd had with Ambrose about sky-diving. Quite out of character and really surprising for a sedentary scholarly fortyish chap who took no regular exercise. Apart from his ceaseless night-prowling.

'What exactly are you suggesting?' demanded Hal.

'Simply that I think he regrets a lifetime of lost opportunities and might be embarking on a slightly more colourful course.'

'Active rather than passive, you mean?' Wayne nodded. There were certainly few flies on this young man. Hal started to take him more seriously.

'Which leads us precisely where?' It hardly explained their disappearance.

'I'm not quite sure.' Perhaps to the root of the problem. He was starting, reluctantly, to hope they would get there in time.

Just then the phone rang and Dottie butted in and asked Hal quietly if he'd be willing to take the call.

'Who is it?' he inquired impatiently as she handed him the receiver.

'Julius Weinberg. From the airport,' she replied.

The downstairs doorbell rang a couple of times but it was clear that Ambrose had no intention of answering it. Nor did he show any signs of entering the room. Jinx, relaxing her guard, had carefully laid down her weapon but kept it at hand for immediate use should things change.

'You know we belong together,' he said, back to his reasonable voice and Jinx, wised up and quite desperate to please, said she did. She was dying for some coffee and the chance to brush her teeth. Perhaps if she kept on sweet-talking he'd let her out.

'Same sense of humour, same way of looking at things. The shopping, the antiques, the weekends away. We have had some really good times.' He was beginning to sound almost sentimental now. She slowly began to breathe more easily.

'And can do again.' If you'll only let me out. 'You know you have always been very dear to me.'

'So marry me.'

'I can't.'

'Then you're a fucking devious cow. Always giving me the come on, a regular little prick-tease.' It wasn't like Ambrose to use language so coarse unless he was really riled up. Jinx fell silent and waited for his next move but instead heard him shuffling away.

'I'd love some coffee,' she said in a wheedling voice.

'Starve, bitch!' was his only reply.

Julius arrived in a whirr of scorching rubber. 'I can't believe you allowed this to happen,' he said.

Hal stood his ground and regarded him belligerently. Now who was this joker poking in his nose, he wanted to know. Julius imperiously produced his business card then proceeded to cross-examine him like a criminal. They had wasted valuable time, he declared. The man ought to be locked up. And the key thrown away, if he got the final say.

'We don't know that anything's wrong yet, *sir*,' said Hal. 'The last time she disappeared, I believe, she'd just popped off abroad for a break.'

Julius, ignoring the insinuation, said there was no doubt Jinx was in danger since she'd vanished without a word. And Ambrose Rafferty was missing too which served rather to prove his point. Perfect teeth, notched up Trudy, impressed. With a signet ring on his pinkie. And the accent.

'Maybe they planned it that way,' suggested Dottie.

'No chance,' declared Julius with a snort. Trudy duly made a note. All sorts of elusive pieces were finally clicking into place.

'So where to now?' demanded Julius, taking the lead. 'We must draw up a plan and stick to it.'

'Back to the Battersea flat,' conceded Hal. They would even force the door, should that prove necessary, though they still hadn't any real proof that a crime had been committed. Or even that Ambrose was there at all. If only Jinx would ring in.

From time to time the phone kept ringing but Ambrose continued to ignore it. They were, she now realised, in a state of siege and her hopes for quick rescue receded. But there had to be some way; she refused to be defeated. This was, after all, dear old Ambrose she was dealing with, not some faceless assassin. He had always been the softest of touches especially where she was concerned. He surely couldn't keep all this up for long. Nothing had actually altered between them but his rage, and she hoped to be able to charm him out of that. It had always worked perfectly in the past. If she tickled his tummy, he'd roll over.

'Please let me out,' she pleaded, her voice at its most seductive, implying all sorts of unthinkable things if he would only open the door. Ambrose remained silent but she knew he was still there listening. She could hear his quick breathing just outside.

'Who is this lady?' she asked, trying another tack. 'She looks like a veritable saint.'

'My mother,' he growled, 'and she's too good for the likes of you. Don't even look at her, you cunt.'

'Tell me about her,' coaxed Jinx in as soothing a voice as she could muster. If only she could calm him down and make him love her again she might be able to persuade him to spare her life. But Ambrose wasn't about to be drawn this time.

'Whore!' he hissed. 'You're trying your tricks again. Always flirting and flaunting your body. You don't belong in the same room as an angel like her.'

'If you really want me, you'll have to come in and get me. I am lying here on the bed just waiting for you.' It was a disgusting image after all he had done to Susie but Jinx hadn't the time left for niceties. Unless she persuaded him in, she'd never escape. And the longer she left it, the tireder and weaker she'd become. She dared not envisage what might happen to her then.

There was a long and agonising silence, then she heard him moving again and was back in position behind the door, her weapon grasped firmly in her hand. It seemed an age while he fiddled with the key, but as he entered she raised the plaster Madonna in both hands and cracked it down hard on his head.

The knife would have been more effective but she knew she could never have used it. Certainly not on Ambrose, up till now most beloved of friends. Despite his erratic behaviour, she at least was still sane and humanitarian. And the thought of killing or even wielding a knife disgusted her even when fighting for her life.

Her ploy failed miserably. She had hoped at least to stun him long enough to bolt for the front door but he caught her wrist as he stumbled and fell and dragged her down, struggling, beside him.

'You bitch!' he hissed as he rubbed his head, but his grip on her arm never slackened. And now she realised that the knife was within his reach; there was nothing she could do to prevent him getting it.

Suddenly in the distance she heard the scream of sirens, growing louder as they headed this way. Ambrose was still groaning, groggy from the blow, and soon she was listening to the miraculous sound of the screech of tyres and doors slamming. This was her one and only chance or else she would probably be dead. She jerked her wrist suddenly out of his grasp and hurled the Madonna at the window, praying it wouldn't fall short. There was the shattering of glass and raised voices from below then Ambrose was upon her with the knife.

'There's definitely someone up there!' shouted Hal, leaping into the road and pointing frantically at the single lit window, from which something had just hurtled like a bomb. Julius, who had followed in his chauffeured limousine, was already attacking the main door. He tried every bell till he got someone to answer, then screaming 'police' begged admittance.

'Wait!' ordered Hal, sprinting up behind him. 'You can't go barging in like that without a warrant.'

'Bullshit!' growled Julius, taking the stairs at a run. Luckily he kept himself in shape though sheer adrenaline would have driven him on. Hal, though irritated, was also rather admiring. He had not put this foppish business tycoon down as a man of action. Despite his annoying supercilious manner, he certainly knew how to get things done.

'Let me go first,' he said, grabbing at Julius's arm. 'It could turn very nasty and you are an unarmed civilian.'

'Leave it!' roared Julius, frantic with alarm as he pulled away and streaked on up, using his longer legs to advantage. All he was aware of in his frenzy of maddened passion was that the woman he loved so dramatically was trapped at the mercy of a killer. He shouldn't have left her, not even for so short a time, while the murderer was still at large and likely to strike again. Though he was amazed that a man as meek as Ambrose should suddenly be displaying so much spunk. No wonder the police hadn't picked him up before. He'd seemed far too wet to be dangerous.

'Jinx,' he shouted with all the power of his lungs. 'I'm coming to get you, my darling!'

So that's the way things were, Hal thought sourly. He'd suspected all along that there was someone else in the equation.

Ambrose drove the point of the knife into the palm of Jinx's hand, and they both watched a fountain of blood arc upwards towards the portrait.

'Down on your knees, bitch, and beg for her forgiveness! For sullying her presence and behaving like a slut.' He forced her bodily down on to the floor and held the gleaming blade across her throat. Jinx looked upwards through a mist of red pain at the foolish, prissy face of the dead woman. Whatever sort of craziness was invading Ambrose's brain, it must have lain dormant all these years. She knew a bit about the orphaned childhood, the long cold years in an institution. The rejection by his father who had married again. But he'd said very little and had always been so self-contained, a model of calm forbearance, that was Ambrose. And then, like a miracle, she heard her name distantly called and knew that blessed help was on its way. If she could only manage to hold him at bay. His face was distorted with snarling hatred as he raised the knife again and plunged it in.

'If I can't have you, he certainly won't.'

Dimly she remembered the written confession and knew they were both going to die. He wasn't mad, he was as sane as she was, but frustrated love had tipped him over the edge. And he was too far gone to listen to her pleas, to turn back the clock to pure friendship. He stood towering over her, still holding the knife, his face drawn and ghastly like a skull. She was still bleeding profusely from her butchered hand and now had a chest wound as well. She could feel the cold steel slicing into her throat just with the movement of her breathing. They'd arrived too late, he'd not let her go now. They were doomed to die together the way he'd described. She would never get to see Julius again even to say goodbye.

She attempted to speak but the knife cut into her windpipe; the slightest move and she'd be dead.

'Jinx!' cried the voice, growing nearer all the time, and Ambrose gave a great grunt of rage then threw the knife down on the floor. That bastard always managed to get the last word. He was bloody well doing it again. He moved so quickly she didn't see it happen, just heard the mighty crash as he flung himself at the shattered window and hurtled precipitately to the ground below.

'Jinx, oh my love! What's he done to you, darling?' said Julius as he crashed through the door.

'It's amazing, really,' said Trudy. 'He always seemed so comfortable and safe.'

'Like someone's big brother, I believe you said.'

'Well, yes.'

They were driving back in a convoy of police cars while Jinx travelled separately in the limo. Once her wounds had been examined and found not life-threatening, her imperious protector had refused to allow her from his side.

359

'You've fucked up till now,' he told Hal rudely. 'Now I am taking control.'

Hal was too drained and dispirited to resist. The crime appeared at last to be solved so let the bully prevail. He had taken possession of Jinx, that was clear to them all, so there wasn't a lot left to do. Just the winding up and inevitable grilling by his superiors. And of course his reputation shredded throughout the press.

'It wasn't our fault,' said Trudy, reading his thoughts. 'Though he does fit the pattern of the stalker.'

'Eighty per cent of whom are usually known to the victim. That's where we might have been more on our toes.'

'We did our best.' It wasn't always a rewarding job, this endlessly gruelling grind. But they'd identified the murderer, whatever the means, so the case could be ruled a success.

Hal glanced across at her and gave her a weary smile. As WPCs went she was not at all bad. Once they'd handed over the corpse and filed the necessary papers he reckoned the least he could do was buy her a drink.